P9-BUI-974

A TENDER REUNION IN A SAVAGE LAND

As soon as his fingers touched hers, all the passion that simmered between them flared to stunning life. They came together with fierce inevitability, mouth to mouth and body to body, with none of the hesitance of new lovers.

It had been mad to speak of forgetting the past, for recognition of Ross's touch was imprinted on every fiber of Juliet's being.

They were tearing at each other's clothing when Ross abruptly went still, then pressed his face against Juliet's neck while he inhaled in ragged gulps. When his breathing had slowed a little, he pulled away and stood. "I've waited a dozen years for this. We're going to do it right. . . ."

PRAISE FOR MARY JO PUTNEY'S
SILK AND SECRETS

"A terrific romance . . . a page-turning plot . . . Mary Jo Putney is a gifted writer with an intuitive understanding of what makes romance work."

Jayne Krentz, a.k.a. Amanda Quick

"A wonderful story . . . twisted with passion, violence, and redemption. Ms. Putney just gets better and better."—Nora Roberts

"A romantic, exciting book—I read it straight through!"—Roberta Gellis

MARY JO PUTNEY

SILK AND SECRETS

AN ONYX BOOK

ONYX
Published by the Penguin Group
Penguin Books USA Inc., 375 Hudson Street,
New York, New York 10014, U.S.A.
Penguin Books Ltd, 27 Wrights Lane,
London W8 5TZ, England
Penguin Books Australia Ltd, Ringwood,
Victoria, Australia
Penguin Books Canada Ltd, 10 Alcorn Avenue,
Toronto, Ontario, Canada M4V 3B2
Penguin Books (N.Z.) Ltd, 182–190 Wairau Road,
Auckland 10, New Zealand

Penguin Books Ltd, Registered Offices:
Harmondsworth, Middlesex, England

First published by Onyx, an imprint of New American Library,
a division of Penguin Books USA Inc.

First Printing, July, 1992
10 9 8 7 6 5 4 3 2 1

Copyright © Mary Jo Putney, 1992
All rights reserved

  REGISTERED TRADEMARK—MARCA REGISTRADA

To the memory of my father, Laverne Putney. A reader and lover of history, he would have adored the fact that I have become a writer and would have wanted me to write a book about the Civil War. Maybe someday, Pop.

ACKNOWLEDGMENTS

Principal sources for this book include *Narrative of a Mission to Bokhara* by Dr. Joseph Wolff and *Travels into Bokhara* by Sir Alexander Burnes. Other important references included *A Person from England* by Sir Fitz-Roy MacLean and the book which gave me the idea, *Eccentric Travellers* by John Keay.

On a less literary level, I must give special thanks to Susan and Qadir Khalje, who did their best to save me from the error of my ways. Any mistakes are, of course, my own.

O Western wind, when wilt thou blow,
That the small rain down can rain?
Christ, that my love were in my arms,
  And I in my bed again!
—Anonymous, c.1530

AUTHOR'S NOTE

As a child, I was always fascinated by the blank areas of the map that are the mysterious heart of Asia. For two thousand years these remote, dangerous lands were traversed by caravans following the Silk Road, the trade routes that stretched from China to ancient Rome. The names of oasis cities like Samarkand, Bokhara, and Kashgar breathe romance.

Central Asia is sometimes called Turkestan, for many of the diverse peoples speak Turkic languages such as Uzbek and Turkoman. It was the home of the nomadic barbarian hordes that for centuries swept eastward into China and westward into Asia Minor and Europe, destroying and conquering more peaceful agrarian civilizations. Eastern Turkestan is now the Chinese province called Singkiang, while western Turkestan includes the Soviet Central Asian republics of Uzbekistan, Turkmenistan, Tadzhikistan, Kirghizia, and Kazakhstan.

South of the belt of Turkic languages lies a broad area where Iranian languages are spoken. These include Persian (the language now called Farsi in modern Iran and Afghanistan), Kurdish, and Pashto, which is a major language of Afghanistan and western Pakistan. Persian was the *lingua franca* of Central Asia, and was also used as a court and literary language, rather like French was in Europe. In addition, classical Arabic was, and is, the language of the Koran throughout the Muslim world.

While Turkestan had great ethnic and linguistic diversity, most of the inhabitants were bound together by Islam, though that did not prevent some of the wilder tribes from making slaves of brother Muslims. There were also communities of Jews, Christians, and Hindus. Muslims were usually respectful of Jews and Christians, whom they called "people of the book" because of the scriptural writings that are sacred to all three religions.

During the nineteenth century the expanding empires of Britain and Russia confronted each other across the broad wastelands of Central Asia, constantly skirmishing and scheming for advantage in a conflict that came to be called the Great Game. The British spread northwest from India while the Russians moved south, eventually annexing the independent Central Asian khanates of Khiva, Bokhara, and Kokand into what came to be called Soviet Central Asia.

The Great Game produced many true stories of high adventure, and *Silk and Secrets* was inspired by a real rescue mission that took place in 1844, after the Amir of Bokhara had imprisoned two British army officers, Colonel Charles Stoddart and Lieutenant Arthur Conolly. The British government believed that both men had been executed, but reports were confused and contradictory and a group of army officers decided that something more should be done for their fellows.

An eccentric Anglican clergyman, Dr. Joseph Wolff, volunteered to go to Turkestan to ask for the release of Stoddart and Conolly. As a former missionary to the Middle East and Central Asia, Wolff was uniquely qualified for the journey, so the concerned officers raised money to pay his expenses. Wolff successfully reached Bokhara, only to learn that the two officers had already been executed. The clergyman very nearly lost his own life as well; however, with the aid of the Persian ambassador, Wolff escaped and made his way safely back to England.

Though *Silk and Secrets* is fictional, I have tried to capture the flavor of Turkestan, and several events in the book are based on real-life incidents. Since the novel takes place three years earlier than Dr. Wolff's actual journey, I took some liberties with the timing of background events, but the Amir Nasrullah, the Nayeb Abdul Samut Khan, and the Khalifa of Merv were all real people and their characters are portrayed accurately in the book. References to British adventurers such as Lady

Hester Stanhope and Sir Alexander Burnes are also accurate.

Today British India has become India, Pakistan, and Bangladesh, while the Russian empire is undergoing massive changes as long-repressed ethnic groups reclaim their identity.

And the heart of Central Asia retains its mysteries.

BLACK SEA

Constantinople
(Istanbul)

OTTOMAN EMPIRE
(TURKEY)

MEDITERRANEAN SEA

ARABIA

Prologue

🌶

Autumn 1840

Night was falling rapidly and a slim crescent moon hung low in the cloudless indigo sky. In the village the muezzin called the faithful to prayers and the haunting notes twined with the tantalizing aroma of baking bread and the more acrid scent of smoke. It was a homey, peaceful scene such as the woman had observed countless times before, yet as she paused by the window, she experienced a curious moment of dislocation, an inability to accept the strange fate that had led her to this alien land.

Usually she kept herself so busy that there was no time to think of the past, but now a wave of piercing sorrow swept through her. She missed the wild green hills of her childhood, and though she had made new friends and would soon dine with a surrogate family that she loved, she missed her own blood kin and the friends who were now forever lost to her.

Most of all, she missed the man who had been more than a friend. She wondered if he ever thought of her, and if he did, whether it was with hatred, anger, or cool indifference. For his sake, she hoped it was indifference.

It would be easier if she felt nothing, yet she could not regret the pain that was still, even after so many years, a silent undercurrent to her daily life. Pain was the last vestige of love and she was not yet willing to forget love; she doubted that she would ever be.

Her life could, and should, have been so different. She had had so much, more than most women ever dreamed of. If only she had been wiser, or at least less impulsive. If only she had not succumbed to despair. If only . . .

1

Realizing that her mind was sliding into a familiar, futile litany of regrets, she took a deep breath and forced herself to think of the responsibilities that gave her life meaning. The first lesson of survival that she had learned was that nothing could change the past.

For just a moment she touched the pendant that hung suspended around her neck, under her robe. Then she turned her back on the empty window and the darkening sky. She had made her bed and now she must lie in it. Alone.

1

London
October 1840

Lord Ross Carlisle sipped his brandy, thinking with amusement that watching two lovebirds bill and coo was enough to drive a man to the far corners of the earth, which was exactly where Ross was about to go. It did not make it easier that the happy lovers were his best friends. Perhaps that made it harder.

His gaze drifted over the comfortable lamplit drawing room where they were enjoying an after-dinner drink; brandy for the two men, lemonade for Lady Sara, who was in the early stages of pregnancy and had lost her taste for alcohol. The three of them had spent many similar evenings together, and Ross would greatly miss the conversation and companionship.

Finally remembering his obligations, Ross's host broke away from the silent communion he had been sharing with his wife and lifted the decanter. "Care for some more brandy, Ross?"

"A little, please. Not too much, or I'll have no head for traveling in the morning."

Mikahl Connery poured a small measure of amber spirits into both of their crystal goblets. Lifting his goblet, he said, "May you have an exciting and productive journey."

His wife, Lady Sara Connery, raised her glass and added, "And after all the excitement, may you have a safe return home."

"I will cheerfully drink to both of those goals." Ross gave Sara a fond glance, thinking how well marriage

3

suited her. She was his cousin and the two of them shared
the unusual combination of brown eyes and burnished
gold hair, but Sara had a quiet inner serenity that Ross
had never known. For many years the only peace he had
found had been in travel, in challenging himself in ways
that engaged all his mind and strength. "Don't fret while
I'm gone, Sara. The Levant is less hazardous than many
of the other places I've been. Certainly it's safer than the
wild mountains where I met your alarming husband."

Mikahl drank the toast, then set his glass down. "Perhaps it's time to give up your restless wandering and
settle down, Ross," he said, lazy humor in his intensely
green eyes. He laid a large hand over Sara's. "A wife is
far more exciting than a desert or a ruined city."

Ross smiled. "There is no zealot greater than a convert. When you came to England a year and a half ago,
you would have laughed at the idea of marriage."

"But I am so much wiser now." Mikahl put an arm
around his wife's shoulders and drew her closer. "Of
course, there is only one Sara, but somewhere in England
you should be able to find a satisfactory bride."

Perhaps it was the brandy, or perhaps it was pure mischief on Ross's part. "Doubtless you're right," he replied, "but such a paragon would be of no value to me.
Didn't I ever mention that I already have a wife?" With
immense satisfaction Ross saw that for once he had managed to surprise his friend.

"You know damned well that you never told me any
such thing," Mikahl said, his black brows drawing together. Not quite believing, he looked questioningly at
his wife.

Sara nodded confirmation. "It's quite true, my dear.
In fact, I was maid of honor at the wedding." Transfer-
ring her grave regard to her cousin, she added, " A
dozen years ago."

"Fascinating." Mikahl's gaze became unfocused for a
moment, as if reviewing the past from a different perspective. Then, since he was totally lacking in polite
British restraint, he said with vivid interest, "You've
certainly done a good job of hiding the woman. What is
the story, or shouldn't I ask?"

"You shouldn't ask," Sara said, aiming a stern wifely glance at her husband.

Ross smiled faintly. "You needn't scowl at Mikahl like that, Sara. It's not a secret, merely very old news." Feeling the need for more brandy, he poured himself another glass. "I was just down from Cambridge when I met Juliet Cameron. She was a schoolfriend of Sara's, a tall red-headed vixen quite unlike any other female I'd ever met. As the daughter of a Scottish diplomat, Juliet had spent much of her youth in exotic places like Persia and Tripoli, and since I was a budding orientalist, I found her quite irresistible. We married in a blinding haze of mutual lust. Everyone said that it would never work, and for once, everyone was right."

Ross's casual tone must have been unconvincing, for Mikahl narrowed his eyes with an uncomfortable degree of perception. However, he asked only, "Where is your Juliet now?"

"She is no longer my Juliet, and I haven't the remotest idea where she is." Ross downed his brandy in one swallow. "After six months of marriage, she ran away, leaving a note saying that she had no desire to see either me or England again. According to her lawyer, she is prospering, but I have no idea where or how. Knowing Juliet, she probably set up as a pasha in the Sahara and has the world's only male harem." He stood. "It's getting late. Time for me to go home if I want to be off before dawn tomorrow."

Sara rose and crossed the room to enfold him in a heartfelt embrace. "I'll miss you, Ross," she said softly. "Be careful."

"I'm always careful." Ross kissed her forehead, then turned to his friend.

He had intended to shake hands, but Mikahl, once more un-English, gave him a quick, powerful hug. "And if being careful isn't enough, be dangerous. You're rather good at that, for an English gentleman."

Ross smiled and clapped the other man on the shoulder. "I've had good teachers."

They were all laughing as Ross left. He always preferred leaving with laughter rather than tears.

Constantinople
January 1841

The British ambassador to the Sublime Porte lived a
dozen miles from Constantinople, in a large village on
the Strait of Bosphorous. As Ross entered the embassy
to pay a courtesy call, he was amused to find an interior
that would not have looked out of place in Mayfair. As
a bastion of Englishness, the ambassador's residence
could not be faulted, even though on the outside it
looked like the home of any wealthy Turk.

A servant had taken Ross's card in, and only a few
moments passed before the ambassador himself, Sir
Stratford Canning, came out to greet the distinguished
visitor.

"Lord Ross Carlisle!" The ambassador offered his
hand. "It's a great pleasure to finally meet you. I've read
both of your books. Can't say that I always agree with
your conclusions, but they were most interesting and
informative."

Ross smiled and shook Canning's hand. "To a writer,
it is enough to be read, Sir Stratford. Being agreed with
would be too much to hope for. I recently finished another book, so soon you will have more things to disagree
with."

The ambassador laughed. "Will you be in Constantinople for long, Lord Ross?"

"Just a fortnight or so, until I've made arrangements
to go south into the Lebanon. After that, I intend to visit
northern Arabia. I'd like to travel with the Bedouins."

Canning gave an elaborate shudder. "Better you than
me. My fondest wish is to spend all of my time in England, but the Foreign Office persists in sending me
abroad. This is my third posting in Constantinople. Flat-
tery, you know; they keep telling me that no one else
can fill the position as well."

Knowing Canning's formidable reputation, Ross smiled.
"Very likely the Foreign Office is right."

"I was about to have some tea in my study. Would
you care to join me?" After Ross nodded, Canning led
the way down a hall and into a neat office with book-

lined walls. "There have been letters waiting here for you for several weeks."

"Originally I had planned to reach Constantinople at the beginning of December," Ross explained as he took a seat. "But I decided to stay for a few weeks in Athens. That is the advantage of traveling purely for my own pleasure."

Canning rang for tea, then crossed the room and opened a drawer in a cabinet. After a moment of rummaging, he brought out a packet of letters tied with ribbon and brought it to Ross. His face suddenly sober, he said, "I'm afraid that one of the letters may contain bad news, for it is black-bordered."

The ambassador's words dispelled Ross's light sociable mood. Taking the packet, he said, "Will you forgive me if I read it immediately?"

"Of course." Canning handed his guest a letter opener, then sat down behind his desk and made a polite show of busyness.

Ross flipped through the letters quickly, noting the handwriting of Sara, Mikahl, and his mother, among others. The black-bordered letter was near the bottom of the pile. He was relieved to see that the address was written in his mother's bold hand, which meant that she at least was well.

He steeled himself before breaking the seal. His father, the Duke of Windermere, was nearly eighty, and though his health was good for a man of his years, it would not be surprising if death had called for him. If so, Ross hoped the end had been quick.

Having prepared himself to accept the death of his father, it took Ross a moment to comprehend that the letter did not say what he had expected. When the contents registered, he exhaled softly and closed his eyes, rubbing his temple with one hand while he thought of the ways this news would change his life.

Quietly Canning said, "Is there anything I can get for you, Lord Ross? Some brandy, perhaps?"

Ross opened his eyes. "No, thank you. I'm all right."

"Is it your father?" the ambassador asked hesitantly. "I met the duke some years ago. A most distinguished man."

"Not my father." Ross sighed. "My brother—half-brother, actually—the Marquess of Kilburn, died unexpectedly last month."

"I'm sorry. I didn't know Lord Kilburn, but I'm sure that it must be a great loss to you."

"Not a personal loss." Ross stared down at the letter, feeling a distant regret that his only brother had lived and died a virtual stranger. "Kilburn was considerably older than I and we were not close." In fact, they had barely been on speaking terms, and now there was no chance that they would ever be able to close the breach that pride and anger had put between them. Kilburn had not approved of his father's second marriage, nor of the child of that marriage. It had been a great sadness to the Duke of Windermere that the marriage that had brought him such happiness had also alienated him from his older son and heir.

A speculative look came into the ambassador's eyes. "I am not acquainted with your family's circumstances. Did your brother leave a son?"

Therein lay the crux of the problem. "Kilburn had a daughter by his first marriage," Ross said. "After his first wife died a couple of years ago, he remarried, and his new wife was with child when I left England. The baby was born a few days after Kilburn's death, but unfortunately, it was another girl."

"So you are now the Marquess of Kilburn." Canning's gaze studied his guest narrowly. "You think that is unfortunate? Forgive me, Lord Kilburn, but most men would not be sorry to become the heir to a dukedom. It is hardly your fault that your brother did not breed sons to succeed him."

"It was never my ambition to be the Duke of Windermere." Face set, Ross tried to adjust to the fact that he now carried the title of the brother who had spurned him. "Becoming the heir means that my traveling days are done. My parents want me to return to England immediately, for my father cannot afford to lose his last son. Besides, there is a great deal of family business that must be attended to."

Canning nodded slowly. "I see. I'm sorry. I hope you

will find some comfort in the fact that you have already been to many places most men only dream of."

"I know." Ross made an effort to master his disordered emotions. "I have had a great deal of freedom and privilege in my life. Now the bill has come due and I must take up the responsibilities that go with privilege."

The tea tray arrived then, and for the next half-hour they spoke of more impersonal topics.

When Ross rose and took his leave, the ambassador said, "I hope you will dine with us before you leave Constantinople. Lady Canning most particularly desires to meet you." He stood to escort his visitor out. "Perhaps tomorrow night?"

"It will be my pleasure to join you."

The two men left the office and had almost reached the reception hall when another visitor was announced. Canning muttered a mild oath under his breath when he saw the new arrival, then smoothed his features to diplomatic impassivity. "Excuse me, Lord Kilburn. This will take only a moment."

Ross stayed back in the shadowed hall, momentarily struck dumb at the sight of the tall auburn-haired European woman who had just arrived. His instinctive reaction was over almost before it began, for the auburn hair was shot with silver and the strong, attractive face was lined by half a century of living. But he knew the woman, and her presence here was almost as much of a surprise as her daughter's would have been.

Canning stepped forward and greeted the newcomer. "Good afternoon, Lady Cameron. I'm sorry, I have heard nothing new since your last visit."

"But *I* have learned something, from a Persian merchant who just arrived in Constantinople. He was in Bokhara for months, and he swears that no Englishman was executed there." Lady Cameron fixed her intense gaze on the ambassador's face. "My son is alive, Sir Stratford. Isn't the British government going to do anything to rescue a man who was imprisoned while on the queen's business?"

Patiently Canning said, "Lady Cameron, there have been a hundred rumors concerning your son's fate, but almost all of them agree that he has been put to death.

McNeill, the British ambassador in Teheran, has no
doubt about what happened, and he is closest to Bokhara." His voice softened. "I'm sorry. I know that you
don't want to believe it, but your son is beyond mortal
aid, even that of her majesty's government."

Ross stepped forward and joined the other two. "Lady
Cameron, I could not help but hear. What has happened?"

At the sound of his voice, the woman turned toward
him. "Ross!" She stepped forward, hands outstretched
and her face brightening. "You are the answer to a
prayer."

"You know each other?" Canning asked, surprised.

"Rather." Ross caught the woman's hands, then bent
to kiss her on the cheek. "Lady Cameron is my mother-
in-law."

Canning grimaced. "Then this is a doubly unlucky day
for you. I gather that news of Major Cameron's tragic
fate had not reached England before you left."

"I have heard nothing." It had been several years since
Ross had seen Jean Cameron, but he had always been
fond of her, and had been grateful that she hadn't
blamed him for Juliet's defection. He frowned as he studied her drawn face, seeing that her usual vagueness had
been replaced by the steely determination that was more
characteristic of her formidable daughter. "Something
has happened to Ian?"

"I'm afraid so. He has always had the greatest talent
for getting into trouble, except for Juliet. Letting her run
wild with her brothers was the worst mistake of my life."
She tried to smile, but her hands clenched on her son-
in-law's. "As you know, Ian has been stationed in India.
Early last year he was sent on a mission to Bokhara, to
ask for the release of all the Russian slaves being held
there. The idea was to remove any provocation that
would give Russia an excuse to invade the khanate, since
Britain prefers Bokhara to remain independent. The
amir not only refused the request but took Ian prisoner
as well." She gave the ambassador a scathing glance.
"Now the government that sent my son there has abandoned him."

Canning regarded her sorrowfully. "If anything could
be done, we would do it. But, Lady Cameron, you must

accept that it is too late. The Amir of Bokhara is dangerous and unpredictable and he dislikes Europeans. Your son was a brave man. He knew the risks when he went there." The words were an epitaph.

Lady Cameron had opened her mouth to speak, when a new group of visitors was admitted, this time richly dressed Ottoman officials. After a quick glance at the newcomers, Canning said to Ross, "I must leave now, but if you and Lady Cameron would like to speak further, you may use that room across the hall."

She said earnestly, "Yes, Ross, we must talk."

As Ross followed his mother-in-law to the small reception room Canning had indicated, the faint but reliable voice at the back of his mind told him that trouble was brewing.

As soon as the door closed, Jean Cameron began pacing back and forth restlessly. "It is such a relief to see a friendly face." She smiled without humor. "Canning and his people are polite, but they all dismiss me as a foolish, unbalanced woman who won't face facts. They shudder whenever I come around."

"They are uncomfortable knowing that they are helpless," Ross said quietly. "Canning seems to think that the evidence of Ian's death is very strong."

"But he isn't dead! I would feel it if he were gone." She gave Ross an oblique glance. "It is maternal instinct, you know. Even though I miss Juliet dreadfully, I do not worry about her, for I know that she is well, at least physically. Ian is not well, but he is not dead—I am absolutely certain of that."

He hesitated for a moment before saying carefully, "Considering how prisoners are treated in that part of the world, Ian would have been lucky to be killed quickly."

She glared at her son-in-law. "That is easy for you to say. Do you even care whether Ian is dead or alive?"

"Today I learned that my own brother is dead." Briefly Ross closed his eyes, thinking of his wild red-haired brother-in-law. Ian was just a year older than Juliet, as exuberant and full of life as his sister. Opening his eyes, Ross said bleakly, "I do not regret his loss half as much as I do Ian's."

His quiet statement shocked Lady Cameron out of her anger. Drawing a weary hand across her forehead, she said, "That's right, Sir Stratford said that you were doubly unfortunate today. I'm sorry, Ross, I should not have lashed out at you." Being knowledgeable about the Carlisle family, she went on, "Did Kilburn manage to father a son on his new wife?"

When Ross shook his head, her eyes narrowed thoughtfully. "So you are going to become a duke. I suppose I should start calling you Kilburn."

"You've known me too long to become formal now." His mouth twisted, "Being a future duke is a dashed dull business. I'll be sailing for London in a few days."

"I envy your mother. A pity my own children haven't the sense to stay safe at home in Scotland, but they're scattered to the four winds. That's why I'm here alone." Lady Cameron sat on the sofa, spreading her full skirts with unconscious grace. Returning to the subject closest to her heart, she said, "Sir Stratford spoke as if there is clear proof that Ian is dead, but that is not the case. You know what this part of the world is like—it is over two thousand miles from Constantinople to Bokhara, and there is no reliable method of learning what happens there. The closest British consul is Sir John McNeill in Teheran, which is still a thousand miles away."

"What reports have McNeill and Canning heard?"

She gave an eloquent shrug. "That there have been no English visitors to Bokhara for years, that there is an Englishman there who converted to Islam and is now chief of the amir's artillery, that an Englishman arrived last year and was shot, or beheaded, or imprisoned in the amir's Black Well. It is also said that the amir has a dozen European prisoners, but they are all Russians. So many rumors—and they add up to nothing. The Persian merchant I spoke with this morning was in Bokhara recently and he swears that he heard nothing to indicate that a European has been executed. However, the embassy prefers to believe that Ian is dead because that is easier for them."

"I think you do the embassy an injustice. Even if there has been no public execution, that doesn't prove Ian is alive."

She scowled, half-humorous and half-serious. "The one thing I have always deplored about you, Ross, is your fair-mindedness. It is enough to drive a hotheaded Scot wild."

He turned away and strolled across the small room, stopping in front of an undistinguished painting of an English landscape. "Quite right. It had that effect on Juliet."

He heard a small intake of breath behind him and knew that Lady Cameron was regretting her remark. In spite of their mutual affection, it was easier not to see each other, for conversations between them were always fraught with tension as they tried, usually unsuccessfully, to avoid painful topics.

Speaking quickly to fill the silence, she said, "I've given up trying to get any help from the embassy here. I've thought of going to London and raising interest among the British people, but time is precious and it would take months to get results. I just don't know what to do."

Turning to face her, he said, "I know you don't want to hear this, but the best course of action is to accept that there is nothing you *can* do. As Canning said, Ian had to have known the risks of going to Bokhara. The odds are about even whether a European who visits there will be welcomed or killed, and I don't think an officer bearing a request from the British government would have been welcomed, no matter how diplomatic he was."

She opened her mouth to speak, then closed it again. After a long speculative pause she said, "Do you know, I have been so distracted that I forgot that you went to Bokhara with Lieutenant Burnes several years ago. I've wondered why you haven't published an account, as you have with your other journeys."

"Alex Burnes was the leader of the expedition, and his own book said everything that needed to be said. Besides, at the time I was more interested in traveling through the Sahara than going home and writing." Ross caught her gaze with his, then said slowly, every word emphasized, "It is precisely because I have been to Bokhara that I think the situation is hopeless. The amir is a whimsical man who believes that the desert will pro-

tect him from all reprisals. He would not have hesitated
to order the execution of an inconvenient or irritating
European prisoner."

He saw the exact moment when Jean Cameron's weary
frustration turned to excitement. "Ross, you are one of
the few Englishmen who has actually been to Bokhara,"
she said eagerly. "Will you go there now to learn what
has happened to Ian? If he is alive, you can ask for his
release. And if not . . ." She gave a shuddering sigh. "It
is better to know for sure than to spend the rest of my
life wondering."

So Jean was not as confident that Ian was alive as she
pretended. Ross felt deeply sad for her, but that did not
alter the facts. He had seen sudden death in too many
places to believe in miracles. "I'm sorry, but I can't go.
With my brother's death, I am needed back in England.
Having just canceled my plans to go to Arabia, I can
hardly jaunt off to Bokhara. It would be one thing if
such a journey would serve any useful purpose, but it
wouldn't. One way or another, Ian's fate has surely been
decided long since."

"But going there *will* serve a useful purpose," she ar-
gued. "And not just for me. Ian is betrothed to an English girl in India, the daughter of his colonel. How do
you think she feels, not knowing if he is dead or alive?"

Until now Ross had kept his equilibrium, but Jean's
words struck deep. "I'm sure that she feels as if she is
in hell," he said harshly. "No one would know that better
than I. But my obligation to my family must come first."

Her face colored, but she did not give up. "Please,
Ross," she said softly. "I am begging you to do this. I
could not survive the loss of another of my children."

In her intensity, for a moment she reminded him un-
bearably of Juliet. Ross spun away and stalked angrily
across the room. Over the years he had felt many things
about his failed marriage: grief, fury, and endless despairing questions about why Juliet had left him. And
inevitably there had also been guilt as he wondered what
nameless crime he had committed that had sent his young
wife flying away to bury herself in a distant land. If they
had not married, she would never have felt the need to
declare her independence in such catastrophic fashion.

He and his mother-in-law had never discussed the subject, but he was sure that she knew how much he blamed himself for what had happened. And now Jean was using that knowledge to coerce him into undertaking a dangerous, futile mission.

He stopped and stared out the window, where the slanting rays of the late-afternoon sun illuminated an exotic un-English scene of domes and minarets. Deliberately he studied the window construction as he fought to regain control of his emotions. Unlike Turkish houses, there were glass panes to keep out the winter air. Several inches beyond the glass, a gracefully shaped iron grille served as both decoration and protection in case a local mob ever decided to direct its anger at the infidels.

The fragile foreign glass was a fitting symbol of the British presence in Asia. A foreigner could die a thousand ways here: of disease, from fierce heat or cold or thirst, at the hands of robbers or an angry mob. Ross had risked all those things many times before, but now he owed it to his parents to have more care for his life.

As his anger faded, he released the breath he had been holding. In truth, having just left England, he had little desire to return so soon. And no matter how hard he worked to fulfill his obligations to his family, ultimately he would fail because of the foolish, headstrong marriage he had made when only twenty-one years old. As long as Juliet lived, he would be unable to produce an heir to carry on the Carlisle name. Yet in spite of everything, he could not wish her dead merely so he could take a second wife and perform his joyless duty. A pity that his older brother had fathered only girls.

Ross had failed his wife and failed his family; perhaps, he thought wearily, he might find some absolution by doing what Jean Cameron was asking of him. There were only two real drawbacks to his going to Bokhara. If he died, it would be very hard on his parents; and if his father died during the extra months he was away from England, it would be very hard on Ross. But by now he was an expert at living with guilt.

He turned and leaned back against the window frame, arms crossed on his chest. "You're a ruthless woman,

Jean," he said with rueful resignation. "You know that
I can't refuse when you ask like that."

For a moment she shut her eyes to disguise sudden
tears of relief. "I do know that, and it is no credit to my
sense of honor that I'm willing to take whatever advantage I can," she said in a shaky voice. "But I would not
ask this of you if I thought it would cost you your life."

"I wish I shared your optimism," he said dryly. "I was
fortunate to visit Bokhara once and live to tell the tale.
Going a second time is definitely pushing my luck."

"You will come back safely," she said, refusing to let
his words tarnish her hope. "Not only that, I have a
strong feeling that this mission will benefit not just Ian,
but you as well."

He raised his brows sardonically. "If you recall, it was
just such a feeling that led you to believe that Juliet and
I were made for each other, though everyone else was
doubtful. If you had not given permission, we could not
have married and a great deal of grief would have been
avoided. I'm not blaming you for doing what Juliet and
I both wanted, but forgive me if I am not convinced of
the reliability of maternal intuition."

Her gaze slid away from his. "I still don't understand
what went wrong," she said in a small voice. "You and
Juliet seemed so right for each other. Even now, in my
heart I cannot feel that it was wrong for you to marry."

"God preserve us from the ghosties, ghoulies, long-
legged things that go thump in the night, and unscrupu-
lous Scotswomen with imperfect intuition," Ross said,
misquoting the old Scottish prayer, but his tone was affectionate. If he had a child, he would doubtless be as
ruthless as Jean in trying to protect it. He crossed the
room and put one hand on her shoulder. "I swear that
I'll do my best to learn what happened to Ian, and if
possible, bring him home."

He did not say aloud that the greatest success he could
imagine would be returning with Ian's bones.

2

Northeastern Persia
April 1841

R oss lifted the waterskin from behind his saddle and sipped a small mouthful, just enough to cut the dust in his mouth, then slung it back in place. The high plateau of northeastern Persia was cold, dry, and desolate, though it was paradise compared to the Kara Kum desert, which they should reach in another day.

In spite of Ross's best efforts at speed, over three months had passed since Jean Cameron had persuaded him to go to Bokhara. There had been a maddening fortnight in Constantinople while he prepared for the journey. He had already been well-supplied with everything he might need, from compasses and a spyglass to gift items like Arabic translations of *Robinson Crusoe*, and routine travel documents like passports had been no problem. The delays had lain in getting letters of introduction from influential Ottoman officials. Ambassador Canning had been very helpful with that, even though he thoroughly disapproved of Ross's mission.

The fruits of their labors were now sewn into Ross's coat. He had letters from the sultan of the Ottoman Empire and the reis effendi, who was the minister of state for foreign affairs. Probably even more valuable were the introductions from the Sheik Islam, who was the highest Muslim mullah, or priest, in Constantinople. The letters were directed to a variety of influential men, including the amir and mullahs of Bokhara. Ross had enough experience of this part of the world to realize that such letters could save his life, but he had still been impatient during the length of time it had taken to acquire them.

17

Finally he had been able to leave, taking a steamer along the Black Sea to Trebizond. From there he had set off overland, then been immobilized by blizzards for almost three weeks high in the Turkish mountains at Erzurum. The only bright spot was that a party of Uzbek merchants was among the other stranded travelers. Ross had used the delay to polish his knowledge of Uzbeki, for that was the principal language of Bokhara. Since his Persian was already fluent, Ross was now linguistically as well prepared as possible.

After the snow had melted enough to resume traveling, it had taken another three weeks to reach Teheran, where he stayed at the British embassy and discussed the situation with Sir John McNeill, the ambassador. McNeill had heard enough rumors to be convinced that Ian Cameron was dead, but he also recounted a story about a high Bokharan official who had supposedly been executed, only to reappear after five years in the amir's prison. The only conclusion Ross could draw was that he would never learn the truth without going to Bokhara himself.

After collecting more letters from the shah and his prime minister, Ross had hired two Persians, Murad and Allahdad, to act as guides and servants. The nearly six hundred miles between Teheran and Meshed had been covered without major incident. As a ferengi Ross always attracted considerable attention, but he was used to that. The word "ferengi" dated back to the Crusades. Originally just the Arabic pronunciation of Frank, in time the term had come to mean all Europeans, and over the years Ross had been called "ferengi" with every nuance from curiosity to insult.

Now only five hundred miles remained until he reached his destination. The rest of the journey should take about a month, but it was the most dangerous part of the route, for they must cross the Kara Kum, the Black Sands, a desert with far too little water and far too many marauding Turkoman nomads.

As Ross kept a wary eye on the tawny, broken hills around them, Allahdad slowed his mount so they were riding side by side. "We should have waited in Meshed for another caravan, Khilburn," he said with gloomy rel-

ish. "It is not safe for three men to ride alone. The Allamans, the Turkoman bandits, shall capture us." He spat
on the ground. "They are mansellers, a disgrace to the
faith. They shall sell Murad and I as slaves in Bokhara.
You, perhaps, they will kill, for you are a ferengi."

Ross suppressed a sigh; they had had this conversation
a dozen times since leaving Meshed. "We shall overtake
the caravan at Sarakhs, if not before then," he said
firmly. "If raiders pursue us, we shall outrun them. Did
I not buy us the finest horses in Teheran?"

Allahdad examined the three mounts, plus the packhorse Ross was leading. "They are fine beasts," he admitted with a gusty sigh. "But the Turkomans are born
to the saddle. Unlike honest folk, they live only to plunder. We shall never escape them."

As usual, Ross ended the discussion by saying, "They
may not come. If they do, we shall fly. And if it is written
that we shall be taken as slaves, so be it."

"So be it," Allahdad echoed mournfully.

The chief of the fortress of Serevan was pacing the
walls, watching the plains below with keen eyes, when
the young shepherd arrived with news that he thought
might be of interest.

After bowing deeply, the youth said, "Gul-i Sarahi,
this morning I saw three travelers going east on the Bir
Bala road. They are alone, not part of a caravan."

"They are fools to travel this land with so little
strength," was the dispassionate answer. "And doubly
fools to do it so close to the frontier."

"You speak truly, Gul-i Sarahi," the shepherd agreed.
"But there is a ferengi, a European, with them. Doubtless it is his foolishness that leads them."

"Do you know exactly where they are?"

"By now they must be nearing the small salt lake,"
the shepherd said. "This morning I heard from a friend
of my cousin that his uncle saw a band of Turkomans
yesterday."

The chief frowned, then dismissed the shepherd with
the silver coin the youth had been hoping for. For several
minutes Gul-i Sarahi regarded the horizon thoughtfully.

So there was a ferengi, and a stupid one, on the Bir Bala road. Something must be done about that.

As the terrain became rougher, Ross increased his alertness, for it would be easy for raiders to approach dangerously close. If, indeed, there were any Turkomans in the vicinity; given the poverty of this frontier country, it hardly seemed worth a bandit's time. He glanced at the barren hills, thinking that there should be more signs of human habitation, then studied the track, which did not look as if it was used often. "Murad, how far is it to the next village?"

"Perhaps two hours, Khilburn," the young Persian said uneasily. "If this is the true road. The winter has been hard and the hills do not look the same."

Correctly interpreting the remark to mean that they were lost again, Ross almost groaned aloud. So much for Murad's assurances in Teheran that he knew every rock and shrub in eastern Persia. If Ross himself hadn't kept a sharp eye on his map and his compass, they would have been in Baghdad by now. Dryly he suggested, "Perhaps we should retrace our path until the hills begin to look familiar."

Murad glanced back over his shoulder, offended at his master's lack of faith, then stared past Ross, his expression changing to one of genuine fear. "Allamans!" he shouted. "We must flee for our lives!"

Both Ross and Allahdad turned in their saddles and saw that half a dozen riders in characteristic Turkoman garb had rounded a bend about a quarter of a mile behind them. As soon as the Turkomans saw that they were observed, they shouted and spurred their horses forward, one of them firing a wild shot.

"Damnation!" Ross swore. "Ride!"

The three men took off at full speed, Ross offering a fervent prayer that the track they were on wouldn't come to a dead end. If they had room, they should be able to outrun their pursuers, for he had chosen mounts that were large, fast, and well-fed. Turkoman horses were tough and had great stamina, but they were smaller, and at the end of the winter they should be feeling the effects of months of poor forage. And if speed didn't work, Ross

had his rifle, though he would prefer not to shoot anyone, for both practical and humanitarian reasons.

At first it seemed as if his strategy would save them,
for the gap between the two groups of riders slowly
began to widen. Then Ross's mount put one foot into an
unseen animal burrow. The horse lurched, then pitched
violently to the ground with a shriek of equine agony,
pulling the pack horse with it. With the lightning responses developed during thirty years of riding, Ross
kicked free of the saddle, flinging himself sideways so
that he wouldn't be trapped under the falling horses.

For a fraction of a second, too many things were happening at once. As Ross automatically tucked his body
so that he would hit the ground rolling, Murad shouted
and reined back for an instant, his expression stricken as
he briefly considered coming to his employer's aid. Self-
preservation won and Murad spurred his horse forward in
renewed flight. Then Ross slammed into the rocky ground
and all thought disappeared into bruised blackness.

He recovered consciousness a few moments later to
find himself lying on his back, all of the breath knocked
out of him and pain stabbing through his left side, which
had taken the brunt of the fall. The vibration of thundering hooves shook the ground and he looked up to see an
appalling worm's-eye view of six horses stampeding down
on him.

His hat had fallen off, and at the sight of his bright
gold hair a voice shouted, "Ferengi!"

At the last possible instant before trampling Ross, the
horses veered off, their dancing hooves throwing up a
cloud of grit and dust as the riders formed a milling circle
around him. The Turkomans' foot-high black sheepskin
hats gave them a military appearance, rather like a squad
of royal hussars. They had Mongolian blood in their an-
cestry, and the dark slitted eyes that stared down at their
captive showed emotions ranging from curiosity to greed
to flat-out malevolence.

Ross forced his dazed mind to think and analyze, for
they were all young men, and the young hold life more
cheaply than the old. They might kill on impulse, without
stopping for second thoughts. His rifle was still holstered
on his horse, which lay twenty feet away, whimpering

with pain, its right foreleg bent at an unnatural angle. The packhorse had scrambled to its feet and appeared to be unhurt. In a few moments the Turkomans would start plundering both horses, but for the moment Ross was the center of attention.

As he pushed himself upright, one of the Turkomans snarled, "Russian swine!" and lashed out with his riding whip.

Reflexively Ross raised his arm and managed to protect his face from the blow, though the force of it rocked him back and stung viciously through his heavy coat. As his assailant's mount pranced away, Ross scrambled to his feet. Fortunately the Turkoman language was similar enough to Uzbeki that he could both understand and reply. "Not Russian. British," he croaked through the dust in his throat.

The whip-wielding rider spat. "Pah! The British are as bad as the Russians."

"Worse, Dil Assa," another agreed. "Let us kill this ferengi spy now and send his ears to the British generals in Kabul."

A third rider said, "Why kill him when we can sell him in Bokhara for a pretty price?"

Dil Assa snarled, "Money is soon spent, but to kill an unbeliever will assure us of paradise."

"But there are many of us," another objected. "Can we all go to paradise for killing only one infidel spy?"

Before a full-scale theological debate could develop, Ross interjected, "I am not a spy. I am traveling to Bokhara to learn news of my brother. I have a letter from the Sheik Islam, commending all of the faithful to aid me on an errand of mercy."

"The Sheik Islam is nothing to us," Dil Assa sneered. "We care only for the blessing of our khalifa."

Having known that the Sheik Islam was a long shot, Ross was ready with a direct appeal to cupidity. "I am a lord among the ferengis. If you help me, you will be richly rewarded."

"You are a British dog, and like a dog you shall die." As Dil Assa unslung his old matchlock rifle and pointed it at Ross, his companions burst into a babble of comments that was too quick for Ross to follow. Several appeared to favor preserving his life for possible gain, while others were vying for the privilege of killing the infidel. Ignoring the opinions of his fellows, Dil Assa cocked the hammer of his rifle and aimed the weapon at Ross, his eyes black and deadly.

The hole in the end of the barrel loomed as large and lethal as the mouth of a cannon, and momentarily Ross was immobilized by the sight. After escaping random death in a dozen other lands, finally his luck had run out. There was no time for fear; instead, all he could think was that Jean Cameron's blithe optimism had been misplaced once more.

Preferring to go down fighting rather than being shot like a pig in a pen, Ross made a futile dive toward Dil Assa. Once more the world exploded into the messy chaos of violence. The gun went off at deafeningly close range and simultaneously a whole volley of shots sounded, the ragged echoes booming back and forth between the stony hills. As the Turkoman horses began whinnying and rearing in a wild melee, Ross was struck in the shoulder. The impact spun him about, then knocked him down. As he fell, he was uncertain whether he had been shot or merely clipped by the flailing hoof of one of the horses.

One of the Turkomans called out a warning and pointed at a nearby hill, where a group of a dozen horsemen were thundering down toward the track, firing rifles as they came. Ross managed to get to his feet again and darted over to his injured horse to retrieve his rifle and ammunition. After that, he intended to get on the packhorse and move as fast and far as possible, before he became trapped in the middle of a skirmish between the two bands of locals.

Seeing the ferengi run, Dil Assa bellowed and reversed the discharged rifle so that he held the barrel in his hands. Then he rode straight at Ross, swinging the gun like a club. Once more Ross dodged, barely escaping a skull-cracking blow.

Then suddenly the Turkomans were in retreat, fleeing before the newcomers. As the horses galloped by Ross, one sideswiped him and knocked him to the ground again.

This time he did not quite black out, though his vision

darkened around the edges. Dizzily he decided that he had not had quite such a bad day since the memorable occasion when he had met Mikahl in the Hindu Kush. He felt numb all over from the punishment he had taken, and was unable to decide whether he was mortally wounded or merely bruised and breathless.

From where he lay he had a clear view of what was happening, and he saw the group of newcomers split, half going off in pursuit of the Turkomans, the others riding directly toward Ross. By their clothing, they were Persians, and with luck they would be less bloodthirsty than the Turkomans.

Then, as the riders drew closer, Ross blinked in surprise, not believing the evidence of his eyes. What the bloody hell was a Tuareg warrior doing in Central Asia, three thousand miles from the Sahara?

Tall, fierce, and proud, the Tuareg were legendary nomads of the deep desert; they were also the only Muslim tribe whose men veiled their faces and women did not. Ross knew the Tuareg well, for he had lived among them for months when he was traveling in North Africa, and it was incredible to see a Targui, as an individual was called, so far from his native land.

As the horsemen galloped up, Ross wearily hauled himself to his feet. He was bruised all over, and bloody abrasions showed through rips in his clothing, but there appeared to be no major wounds or broken bones. He had gotten off rather lightly. At least, so far.

The riders pulled up a short distance from Ross and they all stared at the foreigner. Ross stared back, his scrutiny confirming that the rider in the center wore the flowing black robes and veil characteristic of the Tuareg. The long blue-black veil, called a tagelmoust, was wound closely around the man's head and neck, leaving only a narrow slit over the eyes. The effect was ominous, to say the least.

Besides the Targui, the group contained three Persians and two Uzbeks. It was an unusual mixture of tribes; perhaps they came from one of the Persian frontier forts and served the shah. Ross didn't sense the hostility he had felt from the Turkomans; on the other hand, they didn't look especially friendly either, particularly not the

Targui, who radiated intensity even through the enveloping folds of his veil.

Subtle signs of deference within the band implied that the Targui was the leader, so Ross said in Tamahak, the Tuareg language, "For saving a humble traveler from the Turkomans, you have the deepest gratitude of my heart."

The Targui's sudden stillness implied that he was startled to hear his own language, but with face covered and eyes shadowed, it was impossible to read his expression. After a moment he replied in fluent French, "Your Tamahak is good, monsieur, but I prefer to converse in French, if you know it."

The veiled man spoke scarcely above a whisper, and it was impossible to tell from the light, husky sound if he was young or old. With cool deliberation he reloaded his rifle, a very modern British breechloader, then rested it casually across his saddlebow. Though the weapon was not pointing at Ross, there was a distinct sense that it could be aimed and fired quickly if necessary. "There were two other men with you. Where are they?"

Unable to think of any purpose that would be served by silence, Ross replied, "They continued on when my horse fell."

The Targui made a quick gesture and two of his men turned and cantered off in the direction of Ross's vanished servants. With noticeable dryness he said, "You should choose your men more carefully, monsieur. Their loyalty leaves much to be desired."

"A horse carrying a double load could not have outrun the Turkomans. There is no wisdom in a meaningless sacrifice."

"You are rational to a fault, monsieur." Losing interest in the subject, the Targui dismounted and crossed to Ross's injured horse, which was sprawled on its side, chest heaving and eyes glazed with pain. After a moment's study of the beast's fractured foreleg, he calmly raised his rifle, set it against the horse's skull, and pulled the trigger. As the gun boomed, the horse jerked spasmodically, then lay still.

It took all of Ross's control not to recoil. It was necessary to destroy the injured animal, and Ross would have done so himself if he had had the opportunity, but there was something profoundly chilling about the Targui's dispassionate efficiency.

Swiftly the veiled man reloaded once more, then swung around to face Ross. He was about five-foot-nine, an average height for his people, which made him tall for an Arab, though several inches shorter than Ross. His slight built and lithe movements implied that he was young, but his air of menace was ageless and timeless. "You are bleeding. Are you injured?"

Ross realized that he had been rubbing his aching shoulder and immediately dropped his hand. "Nothing to signify."

"You will come with us to Serevan." It was not a request.

Dryly Ross said, "As your guest or your captive?"

The way the Targui ignored the comment was answer enough. In Persian he gave an order to the smallest of his companions, a boy in his teens.

The boy replied, "Aye, Gul-i Sarahi." After dismounting, he offered the reins of his horse to the ferengi.

Ross nodded thanks, then glanced at the Targui. "Please allow me a moment to collect my saddle and bridle."

After the veiled man gave an impatient nod, Ross stripped the harness from his dead horse. The saddle would probably be useful in the future; more to the point, a substantial amount of gold was concealed inside, which was why Ross preferred to lift it himself. He fastened the saddle to his pack animal, then mounted the loan horse while the boy climbed behind Gul-i Sarahi.

Briefly Ross wondered at his captor's name, which did not seem Tuareg. Then he shrugged; there were so many better things to worry about. It appeared that he was not going to be killed out of hand, but he suspected that regaining his freedom would be expensive. Worse, arranging a ransom would take time, which was a far more precious commodity.

As they rode east toward the frontier, the Persians surrounded Ross, eliminating any possibility of escape. He considered starting a conversation with the nearest men, but decided against it, for there might be some advantage in concealing his knowledge of the Persian language. Besides, when in doubt, he had always found it best to keep his mouth shut.

The journey took about an hour, the track growing narrower and steeper until they were winding single file up a mountain. Near the top, the track swung around a tight turn, and suddenly a sprawling walled fortress loomed above them. Someone behind him announced, "Serevan."

Ross drew his breath in, impressed, for this was no shabby village but an enormous compound reminiscent of a feudal castle. Sophisticated irrigation created lush fields and orchards in every bit of arable soil on the hillside and the valley below, and the laborers working in the spring-green fields looked strong and prosperous, unlike most of the villagers who lived in this hazardous, much-plundered border country.

Like most construction in Central Asia, the massive walls and buildings of the fortress were made of plaster-coated mud bricks, and they glowed pale gold in the afternoon sun. As the party rode through the gate into the compound, Ross noted that the buildings seemed quite old, but they had been repaired within the last few years. There were many abandoned ancient strongholds in this part of the world, and probably Serevan had been one until recently.

Gul-i Sarahi raised a hand and the troop pulled to a halt in front of the palace that was the heart of the compound. As the Targui dismounted, boys skipped over from the stables to collect the horses, and a gray-bearded man came out of the palace. For a moment Gul-i Sarahi conferred with the newcomer, who appeared to be an Uzbek. Then the Targui turned and ordered, "Come."

Ross obeyed, the rest of the riders trailing inside after him. The palace had a feeling of great age but was well-kept, with whitewashed walls and handsome tile floors. Gul-i Sarahi led the group into a large reception room furnished with traditional Eastern simplicity. Cushioned divans lined the white walls, and rich bright carpets lay on the floor.

As the men formed a loose circle around the stranger, the Targui studied Ross. He had brought his riding whip in, and he drew the leather thong through narrow, long-fingered hands. In his husky, whispering voice he said, "The Turkomans are mansellers. Did they wish to make a slave of you?"

"They were divided between that and killing me out of hand. A wasteful lot," Ross drawled in his best cool English style. There was a volatile atmosphere in the room, and being unsure what he was up against, Ross followed the basic rule of not showing fear, much as if his captors were a pack of dogs that would turn vicious if they sensed terror. "I carry letters of introduction from the shah and several honored mullahs, and am worth more alive than dead."

"I should think you would be worth a great deal, monsieur." Gul-i Sarahi began pacing around Ross with cat-like grace. Abruptly he said, "Take off your coat and shirt."

There could be several possible reasons for such a request, and all of them made Ross uneasy. He considered refusing, but decided that would be foolish; though he was the largest man in the room, he was outnumbered six to one and his captors would probably be very rough about enforcing their leader's orders.

Feeling like a slave being forced to strip in front of a potential buyer, he peeled off his battered garments and dropped them on the floor. There was a murmur of interest from the watchers as Ross bared his torso. He was unsure whether they were impressed by the pallor of his English skin, the flamboyant bruises and lacerations he had acquired earlier, or the vicious scars left by a bullet that had almost killed him a year and a half earlier. Probably all three.

Gul-i Sarahi stopped in front of Ross, posture intent. Once again Ross cursed the tagelmoust, which made it impossible to interpret his captor's expression.

With delicate precision the Targui used the handle of his riding whip to trace around the ugly, puckered scar left where the bullet exited. That mark and the entrance wound on Ross's back had faded over time, but they were still dramatic. Then Gul-i Sarahi skimmed the handle over the bruised and abraded areas on his captive's chest and arms. There was an odd gentleness about the gesture that Ross found more disquieting than brutality would have been.

Softly the veiled man circled behind Ross and touched the other scar. As the swinging leather thong brushed Ross's ribs, he felt his skin crawl with distaste. Given the strange undercurrents of the situation, he did not know whether to expect a caress or a sudden slash of the whip; either seemed equally possible, and equally distasteful.

Lightly he said, "Sorry about the scars—they might lower my value a bit if you decide to sell me."

Sharply Gul-i Sarahi said, "To the right buyer you would still be worth a pretty penny, ferengi."

Ross went rigid with shock. In his irritation, the Targui had abandoned whispering for a normal speaking level, and the husky voice was hauntingly familiar. Familiar, and more stunning that anything else that had happened today.

Telling himself that what he imagined was impossible, Ross spun around and stared at his captor. The height was about right, as were the light build and supple, gliding movements. He tried to see the shadowed eyes through the slit in the tagelmoust. Were they black, like the eyes of most Tuareg, or a changeable gray that could shift from clear quartz to smoke?

Mockingly Gul-i Sarahi said, "What is wrong, ferengi—have you seen a ghost?"

This time the voice was unmistakable. With a surge of the greatest fury he had known in a dozen years, Ross recklessly stepped forward and seized the edge of the veil, just below the eyes, then ripped downward, exposing Gul-i Sarahi's face.

The impossible was true. His captor was no Targui, but his long-lost betraying wife, Juliet.

3

❧

Juliet did not flinch, merely regarded him with cool, guarded eyes. Her blazing red hair had been pulled casually into a heavy knot at the nape of her neck and she looked as sleek and lovely as a finely tempered blade. Raising her brows, she said in English, "Since you are in my fortress, surrounded by my men, don't you think that showing a little more caution might be the better part of wisdom, Ross?"

He was too furious to care what happened to him. Dropping his hand from the tagelmoust, he snapped, "Go ahead and do your damnedest, Juliet. You always did."

Her brows drew together. Then, raising her gaze to her men, she made a quick gesture and they left the room. The older Uzbek went with obvious reluctance, until Juliet said in Persian, "Do not concern yourself, Saleh. The ferengi and I are well-acquainted. Please send in warm water, bandages, and ointment, and perhaps tea as well."

Still seething, Ross said, "Your friend Saleh is quite right to fear that I might wring your neck."

Juliet brought her gaze back to him as she unwound the veil, which was easily six yards long. "Nonsense," she said calmly as she tossed the length of dark fabric on the divan. "You might be tempted to commit mayhem, but you are too much of a gentleman to do so, no matter how richly I might deserve such treatment."

It did not improve Ross's temper to acknowledge that she was right. Even on that devastating night a dozen years ago, he hadn't laid a hand on her, and his anger now was a pale shadow of what he had felt then. "What was the purpose of that little charade?" Yanking his shirt on again, he glowered at his wife. "Are you intending to hold me to ransom? That would be redundant, considering the size of the allowance I've been giving you for the last twelve years."

Sharply Juliet said, "I never asked for money—you were the one that insisted on giving it."

"As my wife, you are my financial responsibility." Ross's gaze traveled over her. It was impossible to tell that the body beneath the layered robes was female; if she had continued to disguise her voice and wear the tagelmoust, he would never have guessed her identity. "Besides, I was worried about just how you might choose to earn a living if I did not support you."

She caught his insulting implication and colored. "Ross, I apologize for indulging my warped sense of humor."

"Is that what that little scene was—a joke?" he said, unmollified. "Your sense of humor is more than warped. It has become downright malicious."

"Were you frightened?" she asked, a note of surprise in her voice. "You did not appear to be."

"Only a fool would not be frightened when surrounded by men who are armed and probably hostile," he said dryly, "but I didn't think that groveling would improve my situation."

She bit her lip. "I'm sorry. I behaved very badly."

"I seem to bring that out in you,"

Juliet looked as if she wanted to snap an angry reply, but the entry of a small servant girl caused her to hold her tongue. The girl carried a tray with medical supplies and tea, which she set on a low circular table before bowing and leaving the room.

The interruption gave Juliet time to regain her temper. "It is true that you bring out the worst in me," she said with regret as she poured a cup of steaming tea, then stirred in a spoonful of sugar. Handing Ross the cup, she continued, straight-faced, "I was a model of demure, maidenly propriety before I met you."

That was such a blatant falsehood that Ross choked on his first sip of tea, torn between fury and reluctant amusement. "Your memory is deficient, Juliet," he said when he could speak again. "You were the devil's daughter even then, you just lacked the experience to fully express your natural outrageousness."

"You are less of an English gentleman than I thought, or you wouldn't mention that." She offered a fleeting, hesitant smile.

The smile made Ross's heart lurch oddly. How typical of Juliet to be simultaneously infuriating and disarming. After treating him like a slave being graded for value, she had turned around and remembered exactly how he liked his tea.

His anger began to fade, which was fortunate, for he would need all his wits about him to deal with the impossible female. Suddenly weary, he sat down on the divan.

Juliet brought over the tray of medications, then perched next to him. "Take your shirt off again," she said, her voice matter-of-fact.

Ross flinched when she made a move to help him. Her touch had disturbed him earlier, when he had not known who she was, and now it would disturb him even more. Showing his skin to a doctor would have been one thing; doing the same with his estranged wife, with whom he had had a passionate, obsessive relationship, was quite another. But his injuries did need tending, and under the cirumstances, modesty would be ridiculous. Mastering his disquiet, he pulled off the shirt. "You arrived in the proverbial nick of time today. How did that happen?"

"I learned that a European with only two servants was in the area, and that a band of Turkomans had also been sighted," she explained. Moistening a pad of fabric, she started gently cleaning grit and dried blood from his lacerated left wrist, which had sustained the worst damage. "I decided to intervene before the idiots ended up in the Bokhara slave market."

The warmth and sweetness of the tea having steadied Ross's nerves, he leaned back against the velvet cushions and willed himself to relax. This was possibly the strangest day of his life. To be sitting here next to Juliet after so many years, with her patching him up like a coat that needed darning—it was too unreal to believe. Yet her presence was also too vivid to deny. He was intensely, physically aware of the warmth of her fingers, her faint spicy scent. She, on the other hand, seemed quite unaffected by their closeness.

Needing to break the silence, he said, "Do you often play guardian angel for foolish travelers?"

"If I hear of potential trouble, I do what I can."

Juliet began spreading ointment over his abraded upper arm, but though her fingers were deft and gentle, the effect was not soothing. Ross felt edgy, ready to jump out of his skin.

She went to sit on his right side and began working on the cuts and grazes there. "Needless to say, it was a considerable shock to find that you were the ferengi in question."

"I don't doubt that, but why didn't you identify yourself right away? I found your little games unamusing."

She hesitated. "I wasn't going to identify myself. I intended to send you on your way without revealing who I was."

"Then you shouldn't have succumbed to the urge to humiliate me in front of your men." His voice was edged. "Up until then, I had no suspicion."

Color rose in her face again and she became very busy with cleaning a deep, still-oozing scrape on the side of his hand. "I wasn't trying to humiliate you. Believe it or not, the main reason I asked you to take your shirt off was that I was concerned. When we arrived on the scene, it appeared that you had been seriously injured. In fact, at first I thought you were dead, for I saw that Turkoman shoot you at point-blank range."

"It isn't easy to hit a moving target from horseback." He chuckled. "Still, I hope that Dil Assa is now berating himself for his bad aim."

"He's probably too busy fleeing my men to have time for that." Juliet's tone was light, but her first horrified recognition of the man lying on the ground still burned in her mind. She had never thought to see her husband again; certainly she had not expected to see him killed before her very eyes. "While it was quickly obvious that you weren't dead, you had been roughed up rather thoroughly and you moved as if you were in pain. When we arrived back here, I wasn't sure whether you were being stoic or were injured worse than you knew. So I decided to see for myself."

"Perhaps concern was your main reason, but that implies other reasons. What were they?"

Juliet felt herself flushing again and cursed the clear, pale redhead's complexion that too often signaled her emotions. "You were so . . . so damned imperturbable, in spite of the circumstances. I succumbed to the unworthy desire to see if I could make you show some reaction." Finished with her task, she set her medical materials back on the tray.

"If a reaction is what you wanted, you were certainly successful." Drawing on his shirt again, Ross said reflectively, "Interesting that you thought my calmness was so irritating. The same thing almost got me killed once before. Does that mean the British stiff upper lip is dangerous?"

"So it would seem." Certainly Juliet had found his stoic detachment infuriating. When they were married, she had seen him withdraw behind that barrier of remoteness with others, but never with her. "Was the bullet through your chest a result of excessive calmness?"

"No, that came when someone tried to kill a friend of mine and I stupidly got in the way."

Juliet considered questioning him further, but decided against it. Ross, the understated aristocrat, would never admit to anything as embarrassing as bravery. Besides, there was no reason why she needed to know what had happened to him.

As he fastened his cuffs, he said, "While it would have been simpler if you had managed to keep your identity secret, you didn't, and I find that I have rather a lot of questions to ask. You may have one or two yourself. Shall we begin?"

Now that the cat was out of the bag, Juliet could not, in fairness, deny him the chance to ask how she had come to be here on the edge of the world. But at the moment she was in no state to begin what would be a profoundly difficult discussion.

"Not now." She stood, her black robes swinging. "There are some things I must do this afternoon. Will you dine with me this evening? We can talk until we're both hoarse and furious."

"As we surely will be," he said, a glint of amusement in his brown eyes.

Ignoring the comment, she continued, "Between now and then, you should rest, perhaps visit the bathhouse. Hot water will help some of those bruises." She gave him the small jar of ointment so that he could reapply it as needed.

"Very well." Ross rose and pulled on his battered coat. "By the way, am I a prisoner?"

Juliet gave him a startled look. "Of course not." Then she bit her lip, knowing there was no "of course" about it, not after the way she had treated him earlier. "I'll take you to your room. Your things should be there already."

Silently Ross followed her through the sprawling building to the suite of rooms assigned to him. Inside were his saddle and the luggage from the packhorse.

After giving directions to the men's hammam, or bathhouse, Juliet said, "Until an hour after sunset. I shall send someone for you."

It flashed through her mind that every other time they had stood at the entrance of a bedroom, they had been going in together, not separating. Perhaps, from the enigmatic way he regarded her, Ross was thinking along the same lines.

Abruptly Juliet turned on her heel and strode off without looking back, forcing herself to move at walking speed rather than running for her life. She turned the corner into another passage, walked the length, then turned again. The palace had many fewer inhabitants now than in its heyday, and this section was usually empty. Finally she was alone, for the first time since she had discovered Ross.

The resolve that had carried her through the last several hours crumbled away and she leaned against the wall, her knees so weak they would barely support her. Dear God, Ross had been right, it would have been infinitely easier if he had never learned who she was . . . and Juliet had no one to blame but herself for giving away her identity.

She clung to the wall, shaking, her cheek pressed to the rough plaster and her breath coming in shallow gasps. If only she hadn't decided to goad him! True, she had been concerned about his injuries, as well as frustrated by his cool detachment, but the underlying reason for her appalling behavior had been anger. Once more her damnable redhead's temper had gotten away from her, and her action had backfired, as anger so often did.

Her rage had not been for Ross himself, but rather for his presence. Juliet had spent years striving to rebuild her life, to find contentment, and in an instant her husband had shattered both. He had a whole world to wander; why the devil did he have to turn up in her own front yard?

Ross would have died if it hadn't been for the timely appearance of Juliet and her men, so she could not truly regret this particular twist of fate. But she had still been angry, and her misdirected rage at life's unfairness had caused her to treat him like merchandise at a slave mart. Ironically, her shocked reaction to the ugly scars of the old bullet wound had prolonged the moment and made it seem more threatening than she had intended. As a result, she had infuriated a man who was known for his easy disposition and condemned herself to what would be a deeply painful confrontation. And worst of all, by seeing and touching Ross's beautiful, familiar body, she had reawakened feelings that she had tried to bury a dozen years before. . . .

Juliet had hated making her debut in London society. She was too tall and gawky, her red hair was a flaming, inglorious beacon, and her background too unconventional for her to be a social success. The fact that she hadn't wanted that kind of success did not make her humiliating failure any less painful.

Without Sara St. James, the Season would have driven Juliet mad. Lady Sara would have been popular even if she had not been a great heiress, for she was everything Juliet was not: petite, lovely in a graceful, feminine way, and possessed of a quiet charm that made everyone she met feel important and honored.

Their schoolgirl friendship could easily have foundered on the shoals of society. Instead, Sara had done everything she could to ease Juliet's way, insisting that her friend be included in invitations and coaxing her own numerous admirers to dance with Miss Cameron. Juliet had not liked being an object of charity, but the alternative would have been far worse, and she knew that Sara was acting from genuine kindness.

Juliet had heard often about Sara's favorite cousin, Lord Ross Carlisle, but had never met him. Then she had gone to a noisy, crowded ball at a house whose name she no longer remembered. Sara had been swept off by the attractive youth she was falling in love with. Juliet had found a quiet corner and was trying not to look as awkward and uncomfortable as she felt.

Then a young man was brought over by Juliet's Aunt Louise, who was her sponsor and chaperone for the Season. The stranger was very tall and sinfully handsome, with butter-blond hair and an air of quiet confidence. From Aunt Louise's fawning deference, he was also rich and wellborn.

The ballroom was so noisy that Juliet had not caught the young man's name when he was introduced. While she did not particularly want to dance with the fellow, standing alone was worse, so she had ungraciously accepted his invitation.

He waltzed very well, but that hadn't mollified Juliet. Doubtless he was another of Sara's suitors and had been coerced into asking the wallflower to dance. The thought made it impossible to enjoy what would have otherwise been very pleasant.

She had answered all of his conversational attempts with a terseness just sort of incivility, until he had said, "I understand that you speak Arabic."

That had caught her attention, and she had looked up into his face for the first time. Deciding to play a small private joke, she had replied, "Yes. Shall I say something in Arabic?"

He had indicated that he would be delighted to hear an example, so Juliet thought a moment, her long dark lashes hooding her eyes. Then she said sweetly, in classical Arabic, *"Thou art a frail, useless fellow, a chattering monkey with no spark of life's wisdom."*

His deep brown eyes had widened. Then, with a

wicked gleam, he had said in slow but fluent Arabic, *"Thou hast the tongue of an asp, daughter of the desert, but being only a frail, useless fellow, I have been vanquished by thy flaming beauty."*

Juliet had been so shocked that she had stopped stock-still in the middle of the dance floor, staring up at her partner. The distinctive contrast of blond hair and brown eyes, the knowledge of Arabic . . . It took only an instant for her to realize what she should have known from the beginning. "You must be Sara's cousin Ross," she had gasped.

He had grinned, the unexpected warmth of his eyes drawing her close rather than mocking her for her rudeness. "None other. I gather that you missed my name because of all the racket."

"I'm afraid so. I thought you were just another fashionable popinjay," Juliet had blurted out.

He had laughed at her unflattering frankness, so hastily she continued, "Sara told me that you have been studying oriental languages at Cambridge and that you want to travel in the Middle East and Asia."

"Correct." He had drawn her back into his arms so they could resume waltzing. "I have been longing to meet you, Miss Cameron, for Sara has told me of your fascinating past. Please, tell me what it was like to live in Tripoli."

Like Sara, he had the ability to make a person feel special. As they danced, Juliet had responded like a flower unfurling in the sun, chattering about Tripoli and Teheran and the frustrations of returning to England. They had danced three dances in a row, until Aunt Louise had hauled Juliet away and given her a lecture about forward, immodest behavior.

Juliet had not cared. For the first time in her life, she was in love—wholly, miraculously, ecstatically in love—and to her wondering amazement, Lord Ross Carlisle was also attracted to her. Her hostility toward England dissolved and she realized that her dislike had been a product of loneliness and feeling like a misfit. Now that she was happy, there was nowhere she would rather be. She had loved Ross's confident strength, his kindness, the way he laughed at her jokes and made her feel beautiful and witty.

For the rest of the Season she and Ross had made tongues wag by spending far too much time together at social functions and taking frequent rides and drives. It was a relationship of teasing and laughter and playfulness, as natural as being with her brothers, but with the addition of sizzling physical attraction. Occasionally they found the privacy for a swift kiss, and the sweet fire of that had left Juliet trembling with confused yearning. Then had come the house party in Norfolk.

At the thought, Juliet's fingers curled into the plaster, digging until whitewash flaked away under her nails.

A gentle touch on her elbow brought her back to the present. "Gul-i Sarahi, what troubles you?"

It was Saleh. With effort Juliet composed herself, then turned to face the man who had made her life at Serevan possible. "Nothing troubles me, Uncle. I was just thinking for a moment."

The Uzbek would never have dreamed of calling her a liar, but the tilt of his grizzled brows was eloquent with disbelief. "Has the ferengi offended you?"

"No!" she said quickly. After a moment's thought she sighed, realizing that she must tell Saleh the truth. "The ferengi, Ross Carlisle, is a great English lord. He is also, as it happens, my husband."

"You have a husband!" Saleh sucked his breath in between his teeth as he considered her startling statement. "Has he come to steal you away from us? Though it is written that a wife should be obedient to her husband, your humble servants shall not let him take you against your will."

"My lord has not come to take me away. It was purely the winds of chance that brought him here. He was as surprised as I, and as displeased." Juliet gave a quick, brittle smile. "Nor would he wish to take me to his home. We have not seen each other in a dozen years. There is naught between us but a contract sworn when we were young. Too young."

Saleh stroked his thick gray beard thoughtfully, his deep eyes penetrating. "The winds of chance are often the winds of fate, child."

"Not this time," she said firmly. "Come, let us go to the stables. I wish to choose a mount for my husband so he may depart on the morrow."

For the sake of her peace of mind, he couldn't go soon enough.

Dealing with the routine tasks of Serevan restored Juliet's balance. She and Saleh and the village headman discussed the rebuilding of a long-ruined section of irrigation channels; she selected a horse that would be up to Ross's weight; she talked to the kitchen about cooking a special dinner for two.

She also spoke with her men as they returned from the earlier foray. The group that had chased the Turkomans had had no success; the raiders had reached the open desert, where their horses were without peer, so her men had given up the pursuit. The search for Ross's servants had been more successful. On being overtaken, the two had been glad to hear that their employer had survived the accident, and happy to come to a secure Persian fortress rather than risk meeting more Turkomans.

The afternoon sped by, and all too soon Juliet had to begin preparing for dinner. First she went to the women's hammam to bathe and wash her hair. Then one maid brushed her hair while another fanned it dry.

Back in her rooms, she decided that washing her hair had been a mistake, for it had turned into a fiery, ungovernable mass with a mind of its own. Determined to subdue it, Juliet ruthlessly twisted her locks into her usual knot. Then she caught sight of herself in the long mirror. Wearing a dark Tuareg robe and with her hair skinned back, she was an androgynous figure, stark and unappealing, her eyes too large, the bones of her face too prominent.

Heaven knew that she did not want to attract Ross; not only would that be dangerous, but judging by the way he had looked at her earlier today, quite impossible. Nonetheless, she was woman enough not to want to look like a complete hag. Releasing her hair, she stared sightlessly at a wall hanging as she thought about what she might do to improve her appearance. Certainly she could dress her hair in a softer style around her face, which would draw attention away from her too-strong features. After all, she thought acidly, her flaming tresses could draw attention from almost anything.

What to wear? As Gul-i Sarahi, she always wore men's clothing and owned no rich oriental women's robes. However . . .

With considerable hesitation Juliet went to the small room behind her bedchamber. There she kept a battered chest that contained the relics of her European life, including two gowns. She had not opened the chest for years, but had been unable to bring herself to throw the contents away.

Even when the garments were new, they had not been fashionable. Shortly after her marriage, Juliet had delivered an impassioned diatribe on the subject of how wretched and painful corsets were, and why didn't Europeans like women's real shapes? Ross had assured her that he loved her real shape; then, with breathtaking simplicity, he had suggested that she have her dresses made to fit her uncorseted figure, since her waist was quite slim enough without lacing.

It had not occurred to Juliet to flout convention to such an extent, but she had seized her husband's suggestion with enthusiasm. Though the dressmaker had been appalled, she had not wanted to lose the custom of Lady Ross Carlisle, so two gowns had been designed and made up, one for day and one for evening. Ross claimed to have liked the results, and Juliet had worn the garments when the two of them were private. She would have had more made if she had not run away. Now they were the only English dresses she owned.

Hesitantly Juliet knelt and unlatched the chest, then lifted the lid. A wave of lavender scent was released into the air and she drew her breath in sharply. She had forgotten that she had packed the clothing in lavender to protect it, and now the sweet tanginess struck her fragile emotions like a blow.

Hands trembling, Juliet folded the tissue back from the blue silk evening gown. The delicate material shimmered with subtle highlights and flowed sensuously under her hands as she lifted it from the chest. The fragrance released as the gown opened triggered a flood of memories and Juliet buried her face in the fabric, her breathing ragged. Dear God, Norfolk lavender . . .

The Season had just ended, and Juliet, her aunt, and her mother, newly returned to England, had gone to a house party at the estate of the Duke and Duchess of Windermere. Although marriage had not yet been mentioned, it was the sort of visit during which potential relatives appraised each other. Aunt Louise was jubilant that her unpromising protégée had attached a duke's son, while Lady Cameron adored Ross and thought he would make a perfect son-in-law. The Windermeres were less encouraging, for even though they were kind to Juliet, they made it clear that they thought she and Ross were too young to marry.

For Ross and Juliet the visit to Norfolk had meant the opportunity to spend more time together, since the country was traditionally less formal than London. Even so, for the first three or four days there was no chance to be alone. Finally, however, the opportunity came to go riding, just the two of them.

The day had been flawless English summer, with warm sun, soft breezes, and fluffy clouds drifting across an intensely blue sky. After an hour's ride they had dismounted in a beech wood surrounded by vast fields of Norfolk lavender. Spring had come early that year and the crop was well-advanced, the fields hazy with violet and blue, the air heavy with rich herbal fragrances.

Ross had brought a blanket to sit on and a picnic of fresh bread, local cheese, ale, and fruit tarts. Though the atmosphere between them vibrated with tension, they had behaved with perfect propriety while they talked and ate, not touching, only exchanging yearning gazes. When she finished eating, Juliet had started to brush the crumbs away, but Ross caught her hand and brought it to his lips, kissing her palm reverently.

She had gone into his arms eagerly. What followed was a fevered delirium of kisses, magical and innocent as only first love can be. When Ross's hand came to rest on her breast, Juliet had trembled with delight, wanting more, though she had only the vaguest idea of what that meant.

As their kisses intensified, they sprawled full-length on the blanket, frantic bodies intertwined. All vestiges of sense and control dissolved and Juliet had arched convulsively against Ross. In response, he had given a suffocated groan and thrust back, his hips grinding into hers. She had cried out as liquid fire, splendid and terrifying, blazed through her.

With an effort so intense that she could sense it crackling around them like heat lightning, Ross had become utterly still, his cheek pressed against hers, his arms gripping her with rib-bruising force. Eyes closed, Juliet had been vividly aware of their pounding hearts, his raw, anguished breathing, and the lingering warmth of his skin against her lips.

She had been shaken and a little frightened. Finally she understood why young girls were chaperoned, for passion was a raging beast, the most compelling power she had ever known, and to be alone with a man was to court ruination. Yet even in this strange new country, she had trusted Ross utterly.

For a long, long interval there was silence, except for the drone of bees, the fluting songs of birds, and the soft rasp of leaves rustling in the lavender-scented wind. Slowly Ross's breathing had eased and his embrace had loosened, becoming tender rather than crushing. At length he had murmured, "Juliet?"

After she had opened her eyes, he touched her cheek with an unsteady hand. His hair clung to his forehead in damp gilt strands. "I think we should get married," he said, his voice husky and intimate. "The sooner the better."

"Yes, Ross," she answered meekly.

And that had been that. There was no formal marriage proposal or acceptance, just an absolute conviction on both their parts that they belonged together.

A storm had broken over their heads when they announced their intention to marry, but Ross was about to turn twenty-one and did not need his parents' permission. He would also come into a legacy on his twenty-first birthday and could support a wife in modest comfort even if his father cut off his allowance.

Since Juliet's father was dead, only Lady Cameron's

permission was needed, and she had given it without hesitation, though the duke had tried to persuade her to withhold it. At length resigning themselves to the inevitable, Ross's parents had surrendered and accepted the marriage with good grace.

And ever since, no matter what her circumstances, the fragrance of lavender would instantly transport Juliet back to her first discovery of passion and a time when she had known perfect certainty.

Disoriented, she raised her face from the silk gown and returned to the present. She was not basking in an English summer but shivering in the sunset chill of a Persian spring. And in a few minutes she must face the only man she had ever loved, a man who had every reason to despise her.

Wearily she rose to her feet and shook out the blue silk gown, which was surprisingly unwrinkled. Though the fabric was luxurious and the color rich, the style itself was simple and unprovocative. The chest also contained a chemise and petticoat, so she pulled them out and dressed hastily, for she had wasted too much time on her memories. Then she pulled her hair softly back over her ears and pinned it at the crown, letting the rest fall in waves down her back.

Juliet removed the simple gold chain and pendant which she could not wear tonight, then studied her image doubtfully. After years of wearing only loose, high-necked robes, the form-fitting gown made her feel badly overexposed, particularly since it was rather tight across the bust. That was one area in which she had grown, though the rest of her seemed much the same as when she was seventeen. Because of the close cut, a neckline that was modest by English standards seemed quite daring, which was not the effect that she wanted.

After a moment's thought she remembered a richly patterned Kashmir shawl that a visitor had once given her as a return for hospitality. After draping it around her shoulders, she inspected herself again. The dusky blues and grays of the shawl went well with her gown, as well as rendering it more modest. Unfortunately, she now looked respectable to the point of dowdiness, which wasn't quite right either. She was not an English governess, but the eccentric warlord of a Persian manor; she did not want to face her husband looking like a timid wren, as if she craved his approval.

What the outfit needed was gorgeous, barbaric Turkoman jewelry, and Juliet just happened to have some. Like the shawl, various ornaments had been given to her over the years by grateful travelers, though she had never had a reason to wear them. After careful consideration, she decided on flamboyant multistrand earrings that dangled almost to her shoulders and a matching necklace which filled in some of the bare expanse of skin above her décolletage. Both necklace and earrings were made of gold-chased silver, brightened with swinging, irregularly shaped beads of carnelian and turquoise.

Braving the lavender again, she found a small pot of pink salve, which enhanced her lips. Rouge she did not need, for her cheeks had enough natural color.

The final touch was purely local. In all the desert lands of Africa and Asia, men and women, especially women, blackened their eyelids with a cosmetic made of antimony and oil. Called variously kohl or surma, the preparation had been in use since at least the days of ancient Egypt, both to soothe the eyes and to provide some protection against the sun's glare. It also looked very dramatic and would be the perfect accent for her costume. Juliet took out a small embroidered pouch of surma and deftly applied it, blinking down on the spreading stick as she drew the cosmetic along her lids.

Finally she regarded her image with satisfaction. She looked like a blend of East and West, certainly not provocative, but also neither masculine nor hopelessly plain.

Then, as ready as she would ever be, Juliet sallied forth to meet her husband.

4

~

An hour after sunset, a polite soft-footed young man escorted Ross to the chamber where he was to dine with Juliet. The lamp-lit room appeared to be a study that had been converted to temporary use as a Western dining room. The Eastern custom was to eat sitting on the floor or on cushions around a low table, but this room contained a wooden table that had been covered with a linen cloth and set with plates and silverware in European style.

The servant bowed and left Ross alone. He didn't mind, for he found it interesting to examine his surroundings, which bore a distinct resemblance to his own untidy office back in England.

Besides unusual bits of pottery and statuary, there were books and scrolls in half a dozen languages, both European and Eastern. Several of the Asiatic texts were so unusual that they filled his heart with scholarly lust. Briefly he wondered if there was any chance that Juliet would let him borrow them, or stay long enough to make his own translations. Then he recalled his mission and reined back his enthusiasm. He would have to return alive from Bokhara before he could borrow any books.

Even more interesting were Juliet's own maps and notebooks, where she had recorded her observations of the land and its peoples. There were more than a dozen notebooks, and he thumbed quickly through several. Perceptive and ironic, the journals would be a great success if published in London under some title such as *Persian Travels of an English Gentlewoman*. They were also an interesting insight into the woman his wife had become.

Lifting the last notebook, he opened it at random and glanced down to see, written in Juliet's distinctive angular handwriting, the words "I wish to God that I had never met Ross Carlisle."

His heart jerked as if a sliver of ice had stabbed into it, and he slammed the book shut and returned it to the shelf. Then he stood very still, breathing deeply to counteract his incipient nausea. So she kept a private diary as well as a record of external observations, and within its pages she was characteristically frank.

Bleakly Ross regarded the tooled leather binding of the journal. The answers to all his questions about what had gone wrong in his marriage were probably in that book—and he did not have the courage to look inside.

At the sound of approaching footsteps, he turned and tried to look as casual as if he were taking his ease in his own library. Then Juliet pushed aside the door hanging, and he stiffened. She had always had a genius for the unexpected, and now the damned female was doing it again. This afternoon in her Tuareg robes she had looked like a warrior queen. Now, dressed as a cross between a governess and a Turkish dancer, she was every inch a woman.

She paused in the doorway, her expression wary. "Good evening, Ross. I'm sorry that I'm late."

"No matter," he said easily. "I assumed that either you were delayed by the unexpected or you've developed an Eastern sense of time."

"A little of both, perhaps."

As she entered the room, he studied her face, comparing it with the past. The rounded features of youth had slimmed and hardened as the strong underlying bone structure became more prominent. Juliet would never be pretty in the soft, helpless, feminine way that many men liked. Instead, she was quite shatteringly beautiful.

Gesturing at the table, she said, "I thought you might like to eat Western-style, and the table here in my study was best suited for that."

"It will be a pleasant change, assuming that I haven't forgotten how to use a fork in the last three months."

As she gave a slight smile, a man and two boys entered with trays of food, which they set on a worktable along one side of the study. The man said, "Do you wish anything else, Gul-i Sarahi?"

'No, Ruhollah. We shall serve ourselves. You may retire for the evening."

The three bowed, then departed.

Juliet explained, "I thought it would be best if we had no interruptions."

"I agree. I also just realized what your name means. I had thought it was a Tuareg word that I didn't recognize, but it must be the Persian phrase *gul-i sara-i*: flower of the desert."

"It's because of my coloring." She lifted a self-conscious hand to her bright head. "The first time we met, Saleh called me Desert Flower and the name stuck."

"Why did you prefer to speak French rather than Tamahak this afternoon?" he asked curiously. "I thought you had learned the Tuareg language when you lived in Tripoli."

"I did, but you spoke Tamahak so well that I was afraid you would notice if I made a mistake. I haven't spoken Tamahak in years, so French seemed safer." She lifted a bottle. "Would you like some wine?"

Ross raised his brows. "That must be hard to come by in this part of the world."

"It is, but I like to keep a little wine and brandy on hand for those guests who want it." She opened the bottle and poured two glasses of red wine, keeping her fingers away from his as she handed him one of the glasses. "Since alcohol is forbidden to Muslims, there is no problem with the servants drinking up the wine cellar, as there often is in England."

For the next several minutes she was busy ladling soup into bowls and setting platters of bread and other food on the table.

Ross watched in silence, taking an occasional sip of the wine. He remembered her blue silk gown very clearly, and she looked better than ever in it, for her lithe body had added a few more curves. In fact, she looked so provocative that he wondered if she had deliberately set out to tease or seduce him, and if so, which of those two things would be harder to endure.

She glanced up at him, her fiery hair swirling and dancing around her shoulders as she turned her head. The sight was enough to make a man forget every wise resolution he had ever made, yet as her gaze met his, uncertainty was briefly visible in the clear gray depths of her eyes. At seventeen Juliet had not understood how intensely alluring she was, and, to Ross's surprise, she still had that same quality of innocence.

Which had to be false, considering the swath she had cut through Mediterranean manhood before disappearing into Asia Minor. The rumors about her behavior had been so lurid that he would not have believed them, had he not had irrefutable proof. Nonetheless, he acquitted her of any desire to tempt him tonight; if that had been her aim, she would be doing a better job of it. Instead, her wariness seemed as great as his own.

Oblivious of his speculations, Juliet said, "By the way, your two servants are here, none the worse for wear. They are staying in the men's quarters."

"I'm glad to hear that." Trained to be polite under any circumstances, Ross pulled out a chair for her. After a moment's hesitation Juliet sat down. Her silky hair brushed the back of his hand as she did, and Ross jerked back as if scalded. His mother's training in manners had not extended to how a man should behave when dining with an estranged wife who wished that she had never met him.

Taking his own seat, Ross asked, "How long have you lived here, Juliet?"

"Over nine years now. After I . . ."—she hesitated, then chose a neutral term—"left England, I traveled through the Mediterranean, then into the Ottoman Empire. As you know, I lived in Teheran as a girl, when my father was posted there. I wanted to see Persia again, so I spent quite some time journeying through the country. I was about to return to Constantinople when I discovered Serevan."

Ross tasted his soup. It contained yoghurt, rice, and mint and was delicious. "Was the fortress a ruin then?"

"Yes. This eastern frontier of Persia is terribly poor from the constant Turkoman raids. Many of the villagers were taken to Bokhara as slaves, and others left for safer places."

He tore off a piece of flat bread and used it to scoop up a mouthful of hummus, a blend of chickpeas and various flavorings. "Serevan looks capable of withstanding attacks."

"It is now, but when I came here the walls were crumbling and the main well had been poisoned, so only a few people were left in the village." Juliet sipped at her wine, her expression distant. "I fell in love with the place, though. There is something very pure and elemental about the mountains and the desert. Saleh was living in the village. He is an Uzbek, from Bokhara originally."

That caught Ross's attention; he would have to talk to Saleh before he went on, to see if the Bokharan might have some useful suggestions. He also wondered if the Uzbek was Juliet's lover; the man might be old enough to be her father, but that meant nothing. His mind veered away from the thought. "And since you admired Lady Hester Stanhope, you decided to emulate her and set up a little kingdom of your own here?"

"I suppose one could put it that way." Juliet stood and cleared the empty bowls away. Then she placed on the table a platter of roast lamb surrounded by rice mixed with nuts and dried fruit. "I was tired of continually traveling and wanted to settle somewhere. Money is power, and my fifteen hundred pounds a year has been enough to finance new wells, rebuild the fortress, and buy livestock and seeds. Once they knew they would be safe, people began trickling back. Now there is quite a sizable community. Mostly Persians, but there are Uzbeks and Afghans, even a few Turkomans. All are welcome, as long as they will live in peace with their neighbors. It is a rather feudal arrangement, with me as lord of the manor."

Reluctantly Ross admitted to himself that she had made good use of his money. It would have been easy to lavish it on herself in the fleshpots of Europe; instead, she had created an island of peace and prosperity in a troubled land. And it took more than money to rule here; the men of Serevan would not obey her orders if she had not earned their respect. "Speaking of Lady Hester Stanhope, did you hear that she died? About a year and a half ago."

"No, I hadn't heard. I shouldn't be surprised, I suppose—she was well along in years. But she was a legend for so long that it's hard to believe that she's gone." Juliet looked wistful. "When I was in Cyprus, I thought of going to Syria to meet her, but decided to wait until after my trip to Persia. Since I stayed here, now I'll never meet her."

"Perhaps that's just as well," Ross said. "She was a fascinating person, but she liked men much more than women and would probably have been very uncivil to a young female who so much resembled her. This way, you can retain your illusions."

Juliet's eyes rounded. "You actually met Lady Hester Stanhope?" When Ross nodded, she exclaimed, "Please, tell me everything about her!"

"Not tonight." Ross divided the last of the bottle of wine between his glass and hers. "Why the Tuareg costume?"

She smiled. "It lends an aura of mystery, which is no bad thing in a land where myth is as powerful as reality— perhaps more so. Also, the veil protects my face from the sun and disguises the fact that I'm a woman. Everyone at Serevan knows, of course."

"It sounds like you have created a unique niche for yourself here." Ross paused, then found himself adding in a soft voice, "Have you been happy, Juliet?"

Her face closed and she looked down at her plate. "I am content. It is important to do something worthwhile." Then, with an obvious desire to change the subject, she asked, "How is Sara?"

"Very well. She's expecting a child early in the summer."

"Does she have other children? I suppose she could have half a dozen by now."

"Not considering that she's been married less than two years," Ross replied. "This is her first."

"Didn't she marry that young man she met when she came out?" Juliet asked with surprise. "They certainly seemed on the way to the altar. I forget his name, but his father was a viscount and his uncle was a cabinet minister."

Ross had not forgotten the name, but he never used

it. "No, he decided that he didn't want to marry a woman who might be crippled for life. Since there was no official engagement, it was easy for him to withdraw after Sara's accident. Not very honorable, but easy."

Juliet had been about to sip her wine, but at Ross's words she set her goblet down on the table, hard. "What accident?"

"Don't you know? I assumed that your lawyer communicated news to you, along with the bank drafts."

"He is under orders to restrict himself to things like deaths in my immediate family. He never said anything about Sara." That had been a deliberate choice on Juliet's part, because she did not want to be weakened by longing for her friends and family. Now, shaken, she realized how much she had missed.

"Just a few weeks after you left England, Sara had a riding accident. She nearly died, and would never have walked again if she was not so indomitable. Her horse had to be destroyed. It was that pretty gray mare, Gossamer." Ross's face hardened. "I've sometimes wondered if the accident happened because she was distracted with worry about you and me. I know that she was very upset about what had happened, and it wasn't like Sara to be careless, particularly when she was riding."

Juliet gasped at the implied accusation, wanting to refute it, but she could not, for Ross was right: it was not like Sara to be careless. Juliet swallowed hard. All of the years she had been thinking Sara happy, her friend had been suffering pain, probably despair and loneliness at the loss of the man she loved—and quite likely some of the blame could be laid at Juliet's door. Every action produced ripples of reaction, and Juliet would never know all of the consequences of her mad flight from England. Her voice tight, she asked, "How is Sara now?"

Ross's face eased. "She couldn't be better. She married a friend of mine and they are quite besotted with each other. Mikahl suits her much better than the vapid young fool who abandoned her."

So perhaps the ripples of consequence from Juliet's actions were not all bad. Or perhaps, she thought with the fatalism she had developed in her years in the East, she had just been a very small link in Sara's chain of fate. At least Sara was happy now.

Lost in thought, Juliet did not react quickly enough when she caught a familiar flicker of movement out of the corner of her eye. In one graceful bound a sleek black cat leapt onto the table. The tablecloth skidded under the intruder's weight so that the cat slid across the surface, ending with both forepaws in the lamb platter and looking as surprised as Ross did.

Embarrassed, Juliet exclaimed, "Scheherazade!" and scooped the cat up in her arms. "I'm sorry, Ross. When I'm writing, she usually sleeps sprawled here on the table. I suppose she thought I was working and wanted to join me. I don't think she intended to end up in the platter, for she never interferes when I'm eating Eastern-style."

He smiled as he observed Scheherazade's avid interest in what was on the table. "That may not have been her intention, but she's willing to be flexible." Taking a small piece of lamb, he leaned over the table to offer the tidbit to the cat, who accepted eagerly.

"You're corrupting her," Juliet said ruefully as Scheherazade struggled in her arms. "If she starts expecting to be rewarded for disrupting a meal, she'll become impossible."

The humor that had briefly illuminated Ross's face died and he leaned back in his chair. "Sorry."

Juliet bit her lip, wishing she had said nothing. Throughout the evening, Ross had maintained his distance, polite, contained, and thoroughly formidable. The back of her neck had been prickling as she waited for some kind of explosion from him. Then, when he finally relaxed a little, with a few careless, teasing words she had broken the mood.

Fortunately an interruption arrived in the form of Fatima, Juliet's favorite six-year-old. "I'm sorry, Gul-i Sarahi," the girl said as she pelted into the room. "Scheherazade ran away from me." Then the child stopped and stared, her dark eyes widening. "Gul-i Sarahi?" she said questioningly, not at all sure about this strangely dressed female.

"It is really I, Fatima," Juliet assured her. "I am wearing the costume of my people in honor of the visit of this gentleman, Lord Ross Carlisle. He is . . . an old friend from my native 1and."

The girl's gaze went to Ross. Suddenly she blushed and pulled her veil across the lower part of her face so that only her bright, fascinated eyes were visible. Rather dryly Juliet observed to herself that her husband frequently had that effect on females. In this part of the world his height and golden hair made him seem more than mortal.

Untangling the feline from her Kashmir shawl, Juliet said, "Here, my dear, take Scheherazade and go back to bed."

When Fatima had collected the cat, Juliet gave her an affectionate hug and a pastry from the dessert plate. The girl paused by the door hanging and gave a polite bow, her gaze going to Ross again. Then she skipped away.

When the child was gone, Ross asked, "Is she your daughter?"

"Good heavens, no," Juliet replied, startled. "She is Saleh's youngest." Though Juliet should not have been surprised at the question, since Ross did not know what she had been doing over the last dozen years. Or not doing, in this case.

Unnerved by her train of thought, she rose from the table and removed the empty plates and remaining food. "Would you like some coffee? It is French-style rather than Turkish or Arabian."

When he nodded, she poured two cups from the pot, which had been keeping warm over a candle, then set them on the table. She glanced up at Ross, who in the lamplight was the epitome of casual English elegance. It was like the evenings at Chapelgate, where they had spent hours talking over after-dinner coffee, the conversations covering every topic imaginable.

Though Juliet knew it would be wiser not to reminisce, she found herself saying quietly, "It's strange. Dressed this way, with you across the table, I feel like Lady Ross Carlisle again."

"But you aren't Lady Ross Carlisle," he said expressionlessly. "Not anymore."

Juliet froze, all of her muscles temporarily numb. In

its way, this was an even greater shock than seeing Ross lying apparently lifeless on the road. Though her final note to her husband had urged him to divorce her, she had been selfishly glad that he had not done so. Through all the years and miles of separation, she had found secret comfort in the knowledge that they were still husband and wife, that an invisible thread of connection joined her to Ross. Losing that bond hurt more than she would have dreamed possible.

Forcing her voice to be level, she said, "So you finally got a divorce, as I suggested all of those years ago. I'm surprised that my lawyer did not inform me, but likely the letter was lost." She set the plate of pastries on the table, then sat down again, hiding her hands so that he would not see them trembling. "Have you remarried?"

"I have not divorced you. English law hasn't changed, and the only ground is still adultery." He stirred sugar into his coffee. Quite without inflection he continued, "Your progress through the Mediterranean generated a number of rumors, and if even a quarter of them were true, you were providing a positive embarrassment of riches in the way of evidence of adultery. However, obtaining a bill of divorcement is a very sordid, very public process. I did not want to subject myself or my family to that. There had been quite enough scandal about our marriage, and I was already quite enough of a laughing-stock." Though Ross's voice did not lose its softness, pain and anger pulsed just below his surface composure.

For one of the very few times in her life, Juliet found herself literally speechless as an unholy mixture of shock and guilt surged through her. Taking a deep breath, she focused on what he had said earlier. "If you didn't divorce me, why did you say that I am no longer Lady Ross Carlisle? Surely it was not possible to annul the marriage."

"No, it was not. We are still legally husband and wife." His gaze was ironic, as if he could read the maelstrom of emotions that he had set off. Perhaps he could. "My brother died last autumn and left no sons, so you are now the Marchioness of Kilburn. Congratulations. If we both live long enough, you will be the Duchess of Windermere."

Curiously, her first reaction was neither relief that they were still married nor anger that he had deliberately baited her. Instead, what she felt was sympathy. "Ross, I'm so sorry." Impulsively she laid her hand over his, where it rested on the table. "I know that you never wanted to be the heir."

Though his hand did not move, the tendons went rigid under her touch. Very carefully, as if Ross were a fused bomb, Juliet withdrew her own hand. "Or have you changed your mind about that? What seemed like a prison when you were twenty-one might look like a prize now that you are older. Certainly most men would not be sorry to inherit a dukedom."

"No, I haven't changed my mind." He sighed, then gave her a wry half-smile. "You were the only person who ever understood. When other people hear that I'm now Lord Kilburn, they react to the news with congratulations, as if surviving my brother is some great achievement on my part."

"It's ironic that now everything will come to you, even though you don't want it. Still, you will use the Windermere wealth and influence better than your brother would have. He had a small soul." After a fractional pause Juliet continued, "Of course, now it is much more important that you have an heir. I don't blame you for wanting to avoid the notoriety of divorce. Still, if you want to take another wife, I swear that I will never come to England or cause trouble in any way."

"You've been in the East too long, Juliet." Ross's brows arched. "While Muslims may have several wives, in England such behavior is called bigamy and it's quite illegal."

"I didn't mean that!" she said with exasperation. "You can have me declared dead. It wouldn't be hard to produce some kind of proof for the English authorities. Then you would officially be a widower and could marry again without scandal."

He regarded her thoughtfully. "My father always said that the female of the species is ruthlessly practical, and he was right. Frankly, even if I were free to remarry, I would not do so, for I have neither the stamina nor the optimism to take another wife. The ancient Windermere title and extravagant Windermere fortune can go to one of my second cousins when the time comes." He chuckled suddenly. "Still, thank you for making the offer. While wrong-headed, it was generous of you."

Juliet felt foolish when she realized all the implications of her impulsive suggestion, such as her own family thinking her dead. But at least Ross was amused again. Getting the coffee pot, she poured more for both of them. "What are your plans now? Are you going back to Teheran? Not Herat, I hope. Afghanistan is even more than usually dangerous just now."

"Neither." He chose a flaky cardamom-flavored pastry from the plate and took a bite. "Delicious. You really have a fine kitchen here." He finished the pastry with a second bite. "In fact, my destination is Bokhara."

She stared at him. "I hope you're joking. That is the most dangerous place in Asia for Europeans. If you absolutely must travel farther into Central Asia, go to Kokand or Khiva, where you have a reasonably good chance of leaving again."

"Unfortunately, only Bokhara will do." He wiped his fingers on the napkin. "This is not a pleasure trip, Juliet. Have you heard that the amir is holding a British army officer prisoner?"

"I've heard rumors to that effect, but I've also heard that the officer was executed."

"Perhaps. Perhaps not. At any rate, I intend to learn the truth of the situation, then see if I can do something about it."

Juliet bit her lip with concern. "It is the British government's place to act, not yours. You don't have any official status, do you?"

"None whatsoever—I am going as a private citizen."

"You're mad," she said flatly. "If you just march into the amir's palace and ask him to let the officer go, you'll end up imprisoned or dead yourself."

"You're undoubtedly right," Ross agreed. "However, I am still going to try. The officer's mother asked me to, and I found I could not refuse."

"Well, you should have," she snapped, appalled at how blithely he brushed aside the dangers. "This afternoon you said there was no point in your servants sacri-

ficing their lives in a futile attempt to save you from the
Turkomans. This is the same thing, only worse. At least
the Turkomans would have only made slaves of the Persians—if you go to Bokhara, you're a dead man. The
only question is whether you will be killed quickly or
spend years rotting in the Black Well first. There is no
point in taking that risk on behalf of a man who is already dead."

"The situations are not comparable," he said mildly.
"For one thing, it isn't clear if the British officer has
been executed. And if he is dead, perhaps I will be able
to persuade the amir to release the major's body so I can
return it to his family for burial."

"No doubt his family would appreciate that, but it isn't
worth you risking your life."

His level gaze met hers. "Not even though the officer
in question is your brother Ian?"

Juliet caught her breath, feeling as if she had been
struck a physical blow. "Dear God, not Ian," she whispered. It was too much. Shaking, she buried her face in
her hands. Perhaps this whole day was just a nightmare
and she would wake in the morning to find her life at
Serevan unchanged. Or better yet, the last dozen years
had been a fever dream and she was still at Chapelgate,
sleeping safe and warm in her husband's embrace.

"Oh, damnation," Ross said helplessly.

She heard him get up from his chair and come around
the table. Gently he touched her hair, saying, "I'm sorry,
Juliet, I should not have told you like that."

Instinctively she turned toward him and he put his
arms around her as she buried her face against his side.
For a few moments, as she battled tears, she allowed
herself to accept the dangerous comfort of his embrace.
For so long she had hungered for a man's touch. For
Ross's touch.

Finally she pulled away, though not so quickly that he
would interpret her movement as rejection. "You needn't
apologize," she said, her voice unsteady. "There is no
way to break such news gently." She drew the back of
her hand across her eyes. "It seems impossible to believe
that Ian is gone. He was always so alive. I used to think

that if anyone was going to turn out to be immortal, it would be Ian."

Ross retreated to his own chair. "While I don't want to give you false hope, there is a chance that he is still alive."

"Do you honestly think so?"

He shrugged. "As I said, there is a chance. All the way from Constantinople, I've talked to anyone who claimed to have information. The results were inconclusive, mostly third- and fourth-hand reports. In Teheran I did meet a man who claimed to have witnessed the execution of a ferengi several months ago, but the description could have fitted almost any European."

"Even if that wasn't Ian, it doesn't mean that my brother is still alive," she said bleakly. "He could have died in prison, or been executed since then. And if, by some remote chance, you reach Bokhara and find Ian alive, there is no reason to suppose that the amir will release him—or you."

"Nonetheless, I promised to try my best, and I will."

Remembering what else he had said, Juliet said with an edge in her voice, "This is all my mother's doing, isn't it?"

He nodded. "I met her at the British embassy in Constantinople. She had been trying unsuccessfully to persuade Sir Stratford Canning to do something through official channels."

"If Canning refused, the government is convinced Ian is dead." Juliet's mouth tightened. "Blast it, my mother had no right to ask you to risk your life on a futile mission."

"She had a feeling that Ian was alive and that we would both return safely," he explained, faint amusement in his eyes. "So who am I to argue with female intuition?"

"I sincerely hope you did not place any faith in my mother's dubious intuition," Juliet snapped. "For God's sake, Ross, give up this mad scheme! There is no virtue in noble suicide."

"Be that as it may, the subject is not open to discussion," he said with finality. "I've been to Bokhara once and survived. Perhaps I'll be lucky again. If not"—he shrugged with a fatalism worthy of an Asiatic—"so be it."

"You've been to Bokhara already? But . . ."

When her voice trailed off, he said dryly, "Surprised that someone so scholarly and unadventurous would dare such a journey?"

Juliet colored, knowing that she could start a whole new argument by pursuing his remark; perhaps that was why he had made it. Refusing to let herself be distracted, she considered the possibilities. She would never be able to change his mind, not when he had that damned "word-of-a-gentleman" expression on his face. And though she was tempted, she really could not lock Ross up for his own good.

She muttered a Persian curse of whisker-singeing intensity. There was only one thing she could do that might increase his chances of surviving the journey. "Very well," she said with a calm implacability that was the equal of his. "If you insist on going to Bokhara, then I'm going with you."

5

❦

Damn and blast and damn again. Ross stared at his wife, thinking that he should have seen this coming. "Absolutely not."

She raised her brows. "I wasn't asking for your permission, Ross. I'm going and there is no way you can stop me. You may have traveled through Central Asia, but I've lived here for nine years. I know the customs and people better than you do, and have more resources at my command."

"Don't be absurd," he said forcefully. "You know that women have no status in this part of the world. On your own, you would be able to do nothing, and as my companion, your presence would make the situation worse. My task will be much harder if I must worry about your safety as well as my own."

"Save your worry for yourself," Juliet retorted. "You will be in much more jeopardy than I, for I am not going as a woman."

Ross opened his mouth, then closed it again. "With your height, wearing Tuareg robes and veil, I suppose you can pass for a Targui if you don't make any major errors in behavior," he admitted reluctantly. "Though the costume is somewhat conspicuous in Central Asia, you would still be safer than if you traveled as a ferengi woman. But that is beside the point. I see no advantage in your presence, and considerable disadvantage. To use an argument that we have both overworked today, you would be going into danger for no good reason."

"They say that Bokhara is a snake den of spies and informers. If I go there as a Muslim man, I will have much more freedom of movement than you, and will be able to learn things a ferengi never could." She nibbled her lower lip as she thought. "I suppose I should go as your servant, so that I can get information to you without arousing further suspicions."

He almost choked on the last of his coffee. "You, a servant?" he said incredulously. "It is easier to believe that you can pass as a man than that you will ever do what anyone tells you to do."

Juliet gave an unexpected grin. "Touché. I'll admit that taking orders is not my strong point, but I am not a fool. With our lives in the balance, I will be a model of obedience."

Why did she have to have such flashes of unexpected, irresistible charm? It would be so much easier if Juliet was a bitch. But Ross never would have married her if she were; instead, she was merely impossible. "I don't care if you can follow orders like a trained gun dog. Under no circumstances will I take you to Bokhara as my servant."

"You are being unreasonable," she said patiently. "The men you hired in Teheran may be saints and heroes, but they have known you for only a few weeks and there is no way you can be sure of their loyalty. Certainly they did not distinguish themselves today when they abandoned you to the Turkomans. At least you can trust me not to betray you if danger threatens."

With deliberate cruelty he said, "Trust you not to betray me? Based on your past record, I would be mad to do that."

Juliet's skin went bone white against her red hair as blood drained from her face, revealing a pale ghost of freckles across her cheekbones. "Obviously it was a mistake to entrust me with your honor," she said, her voice almost inaudible, "but you can trust me with your life, and you know it."

In spite of what he had said, Ross believed Juliet's statement. She might have betrayed her marriage vows, but she would never be cowardly or treacherous, especially not if her brother's life was at stake. And, for honor's sake if not affection, she would do nothing that might endanger her husband.

Nonetheless, to accept her proposal was unthinkable. Ross had never thought much about the afterlife, but he knew that spending several months in close proximity to his wife would be a fair approximation of hell. "I can't stop you from coming," he said wearily, "but neither can you force me to take you as my servant."

"Then I'll go instead of you," she said, undeterred by his attitude. "In fact, that is the way it should be. Ian is my brother, not yours, and you have suffered quite enough because of the Camerons."

As her challenging gaze met his, the atmosphere changed, the center shifting from the mission to Bokhara to Ross and Juliet. The anger and tension that pulsed between them tonight stemmed from one raw, unresolved wound: their failed marriage. It was time to address it directly.

"If we are both determined to go to Bokhara, there is probably a better chance of survival if we work together," Ross said, his voice harsh. "But we can't do that unless we stop trying to provoke each other. Ever since we met, we've been dueling, looking for changes and weaknesses."

"You're right." She sighed. "I'm not particularly proud of my behavior, and you haven't been at your best either. It's time to declare a truce."

But before that could happen, Ross must find an answer to the question that had tormented him for a dozen years. "Why did you leave me, Juliet?" he asked quietly. "Were you in love with another man?"

She looked away. "No," she said, her voice equally low. "There was no one else."

He waited for her to say more. When she did not, he said reflectively, "Since we were together constantly, I suppose that you would scarcely have had time to fall in love with someone else. Very well, if you did not run away to be with a lover, was it because you could not bear to confine yourself to one man and one bed forever and were too honest to stay and become an adulteress?" Given Juliet's passionate nature and subsequent activities, he had thought that was the likeliest explanation.

"I don't know whether to feel complimented by your opinion of my honesty or insulted by your appraisal of

my morals," she said in a tight voice. "No, Ross, there
are other reasons for ending a marriage besides sex. I
did not leave you to follow the siren call of promiscuity."

"Then why *did* you leave?" Trying to sound detached,
as if the subject had nothing to do with him, he continued, "I was happy, and you seemed to be also. We had
only a few disagreements, and to me, at least, they did
not seem serious. What did I do that was so unforgivable?"

Her eyes met his, stark and miserable. "You did nothing wrong, Ross. The problem was me. I should never
have married, not you, not anyone else." She pushed her
chair away from the table and stood, drifting across the
room away from the circle of lamplight. "That's what I
was trying to explain in the letter I left. I must not have
done a very good job, or you would not still be wondering why."

Unable to keep the bitterness from his voice, he said,
"I gave you credit for trying to spare my feelings, but in
spite of your explanation, it was hard not to take it personally when you left. In fact, impossible—particularly
since you were so quick to ask for a divorce. England is
full of miserable marriages, but Parliament grants scarcely
a divorce a year. It seemed like you could barely wait to
get rid of me."

She turned toward him, her face unreadable in the
shadows. "I'm sorry that you took it that way. I swear
that there has never been anyone else that I cared for as
I did you. I suggested that you seek a divorce so that
you would be free to start again with someone else. A
better woman, one who would make you happy."

But he had never wanted anyone else. Taking a deep
breath, he asked once more, "Then if you didn't leave
for love, or lust, or because you despised me, why did
you go? Please give me a straight answer, Juliet. I need
to know."

There was a long silence before she replied, a catch in
her throat, "The simple, unvarnished truth was that I
feared that if I stayed in England, I would lose whatever
it is that makes me what I am. I don't think it's possible
to explain more clearly than that."

Slowly Ross expelled the breath he had been holding.
There was probably some truth in Juliet's words, though

he doubted that it was either simple or unvarnished. At any rate, it was clear that she had said as much as she was going to.

While her evasiveness had given him an answer of sorts, there was another issue that must be addressed before he could undertake a difficult, dangerous journey with her. Ross moved across the room until he was standing only an arm's length away from her, so close that he felt the warmth of Juliet's body radiating through the cool evening air. She was a tall, graceful shape in the dim light, an image from a dream. From ten thousand dreams. He murmured, "There is one more thing I must know before declaring a truce."

Her shawl had slipped down, revealing the Celtic paleness of her skin. As the faint erotic scent of lavender twined around them, he placed his hands on her shoulders and drew her to him, his thumbs sliding under the intricate Turkoman necklace to caress the smooth bare hollows below her collarbones.

Juliet did not try to avoid the kiss. With a long, shuddering sigh, her mouth welcomed his. She was so tall that he had to incline his head only a little, and her supple body molded effortlessly to him as his arms went around her.

A dozen years dissolved in the space of a heartbeat, and what had been a tentative, questioning kiss became a whole universe of sensation. The taste and feel of Juliet were as familiar as his own body, more desirable than life eternal. His hands glided over the well-remembered curves of her back and hips, and through the silk gown he felt the flex of her taut muscles as she pressed against him. For she did more than merely accept the embrace passively; she responded with fierce longing, her hands and mouth reckless and demanding, as if this was the only moment they would ever have.

And all too soon the moment was over. Abruptly she pulled away from him, body trembling and eyes dazed as she whispered, "No, Ross. Not this. Never again."

"Why not? Our marriage was not all bad." Ross lifted his hand to her cheek, his fingertips tracing the subtle planes and curves. "Don't you remember?"

"I remember," she said, her voice breaking. "I wish that I didn't."

His hand dropped away. For an instant Juliet stood statue-still. Then, freed of the spell that had briefly bound them together, she turned and lifted one of the lamps. Movements taut, she left the room without looking back.

For a moment Ross closed his eyes, telling himself that he would not die of sexual frustration, even if he might briefly wish to. And he had learned over the last dozen years that rejection wasn't lethal either. Deliberately he focused on the scrapes and bruises he had suffered earlier, knowing that physical pain would be an improvement over what he was feeling now. Yet though every muscle, bone, and tendon hurt, he still looked on the encounter with the Turkomans as pure pleasure compared to dining with his long-lost wife. It seemed impossible that only a few hours had passed since he had met her again, for he felt as if he had aged half a century in half a day.

With immense effort he began the process of detachment that would enable him to function again. He was very skilled at mentally separating himself from his emotions, and soon he had distanced himself far enough to feel a wry admiration for Juliet's thoroughness; in a mere handful of words she had not only rejected him in the present but also denied the past they had shared. An efficient woman, Juliet.

Mechanically he extinguished all but one of the lamps, then took the last light and left the study. Though he had watched closely when being escorted to dinner, it was easy to take a wrong turn, and it took time to find the way back. As he made his way through the long blank corridors of the old palace, the scholarly, organized part of his mind busily analyzed what had happened.

While his passion for distant places was quite genuine, Ross had always known that one reason for his restless traveling was a vague hope that someday, somewhere, he would find Juliet again. Not precisely for love, and certainly not for hate, but because of the aching sense of incompleteness that she had left behind.

Today, by pure chance, he had found her, and as a result, the door to the past had irrevocably closed. On some dim level he had thought that Juliet might have run away on a rash impulse, then not known how to come home again. And if they met once more, there might be a chance to start over.

Now that faint, never wholly admitted possibility had died. By the time he reached his room, Ross was wrestling with an agonizing suspicion that he would like to deny but couldn't: that he lacked the ability to inspire or hold a woman's romantic love. He could love and be loved by family and friends, but whatever it took to build and preserve a deep man-woman relationship was beyond him.

Given his birth and fortune, it would not have been hard for Ross to find and keep a wife who was a boring social sparrow, but he had wanted more than that; he had wanted a wife who was his equal, a companion in all things. His parents had had such a partnership, and he had considered that as usual until he began to see more of the world and realized how many kinds of marriage there were, and that most of them did not appeal to him.

There were only two women he had ever been able to imagine marrying. One was his cousin Sara. When they were young, she had seemed like the other half of himself, yet she had never seen him as anything other than a brother. At the time, he had thought that was because they had grown up together, and he had accepted that she would never have romantic feelings for him.

At first Juliet had been different from Sara. Believing that she loved him, she had given herself with absolute, unquestioning trust. For Ross, their closeness had been intoxicating and deeply rewarding, exactly what he had hoped for. But after several months, everything changed. Her naturally joyous nature had dimmed and she began watching him with bleak, tragic eyes.

He had known something was wrong, but did not recognize that her love for him was dying. Or perhaps Juliet had never truly loved him: once he had been certain that she did, but after she left, he had never been wholly certain of anything again.

They had begun to have arguments, usually over the journey to the Mideast they were planning. Juliet had

been anxious to leave, but Ross had delayed because
his much-loved godfather was ill. She had made sharp-
tongued comments about the postponement, perhaps
fearing that they would never go. Then he had made the
mistake of going away to visit his godfather, leaving Juliet behind because she claimed to feel unwell. When he
returned, she was gone.

From the vantage of his present advanced years, it was
easy to see that Juliet's youth and inexperience had led
her to confuse her discovery of passion with love. He
had rushed her into marriage before she had time for
doubts, but it had not taken her long to realize her mistake. Any other woman would have been content to stay
with him for the sake of wealth and propriety, but not
Juliet. Though tonight, with quixotic gallantry, she had
denied that the failure of their marriage was his fault, he
knew better. As true as a blade, and with the same ruthless honesty, she had left her husband rather than live a
lie.

Over the years since, there had occasionally been
women, when Ross was so hungry for physical intimacy
that he could no longer deny the need. But none of the
pleasant, easygoing females he had visited had ever fallen
in love with him. Though he had been grateful at the
time, now that fact was confirmation that there was a
fundamental flaw in his nature.

He became aware that he had arrived back in his room
and was now standing motionless in the middle. Setting
down the lamp, he stripped off his clothes, tossing them
heedlessly on the divan, then doused the light. In a curious state of numbness, he lay down on the thick cotton-
filled mattress and pulled the covers over him.

It had been . . . interesting to discover that the desire
Juliet inspired was as powerful as he remembered. More
powerful, in fact; time had blurred the line between
memory and dream, until tonight's embrace had resur-
rected his memories with jarring vividness.

Even more interesting was the undeniable fact that she
had also felt desire, though not enough to overcome her
objections to him. Clearly the sentence that Juliet had
written in her journal, wishing that she had never met
him, had not been a momentary aberration. Yes, it

would have been better for both of them if they had
never met. In spite of passion, in spite of the laughter
and talk and understanding that they had briefly shared
so many years before, at heart they had always been
strangers—and now they always would be.

A bottle of claret divided between two people would
not have been excessive in England, but as Juliet un-
twisted the sheets from her damp body, she realized that
here it had been a disastrous mistake. Not that either of
them had been drunk, but, living deep in Islam, she virtually never drank, and Ross, always a light drinker, had
probably not touched alcohol during his months of travel.
As a result, two glasses had been enough to loosen constraints to the point where he had wanted to kiss her—
and she had been fool enough to let him.

Let him. With a mirthless laugh she rolled over and
buried her face in the pillows. She had not just acqui-
esced, she had all but pulled him down onto the Khora-
san carpet. Half a glass of wine more and she would have
done so. And, dear God, she wished that she had. In
the morning she would be grateful that she had retained
a particle of sense, but now desire raged through her.

All of her dormant memories of lovemaking—of taste
and touch, sight and scent and sound—had come to anguished life in Ross's embrace. If she tried, she was sure
that she could have counted and described every single
time they had made love. And the tally would have been
substantial; though they had lived together only six
months, they had been young and passionately in love
with each other.

One of her most vivid and sensual memories was of
their wedding night. The wedding had not been a large
one, for they had not wanted to wait while an elaborate
ceremony was arranged. In fact, during the period of
their betrothal, Juliet had once laughingly suggested that
they follow the old Scottish marriage custom of leaping
over a sword together so they would not have to wait
any longer. But wait they did, less for morality than because of the difficulty of finding privacy to make love
properly.

The ceremony had taken place in Scotland, at the vil-

lage kirk on the estate of Juliet's uncle. Then the young
couple had driven to a nearby hunting box owned by a
friend of the Duke of Windermere. There, finally, they
were alone, for the servants knew better than to intrude
on a couple that had just wed.

After they had eaten a light supper, Ross had given
Juliet time alone to wash and change and ready herself.
To her intense embarrassment, she developed a last-
minute case of nerves even though she had longed for
this night for weeks. When her new husband came into
the bedroom, she was not waiting in the massive four-
poster bed. Instead, she was huddled on the window seat,
arms wrapped tightly around her drawn-up knees, shivering a little in her sheer white nightgown.

Ross had come to her side at the window. Looking out
at the crescent moon floating in a black velvet sky, he
had circled her shoulders with his arm and asked,
"Cold?"

She shook her head.

He caressed the back of her neck, his warm hand loosening the tight muscles. "Nervous?"

She had swallowed hard and turned to look up at him.
"Everyone said we were too young. Perhaps they were
right."

"No," he had said simply.

Then he had bent and scooped her into his arms. Startled, she clutched at him for balance as he turned and
settled down on the window seat, then arranged her
across his lap.

Ross continued, "They—whoever *they* may be—are
wrong. I love you, and you love me. Age has nothing to
do with it." He thought a moment. "Except, perhaps,
that the young are more willing to take risks."

In the face of his calm certainty, her own doubts had
vanished. She might be young and volatile, but Ross was
not. He was strong and steady and wise, everything she
was not.

She had relaxed against him like a cat, her face pressed
against his neck. He had just bathed, and smelled fresh
and clean, with a subtle masculine scent that belonged
to him alone. In his soft, low voice he talked idly of the
things they would do together, the places they would go,

the discoveries they would make. And all the time he caressed her, his touch light and tender and infinitely kind.

Though they had waited for this night with fierce impatience, there was no hurry now that it had finally arrived. She had felt like an instrument played by a virtuoso musician as Ross had explored her body and gently encouraged her to do the same with his. Starting shyly, she had slipped her hand inside his robe and discovered that his warm chest was covered by the delicious texture of hair. She felt his heart beat under her palm and was moved and awed as the rate increased at her touch.

By the time he carried her to the wide bed, all her nervousness had melted away. Her mother had told her that it would hurt the first time, and Juliet was braced for that, but when they finally joined, there was no pain. Instead, there was only a moment of discomfort and a fleeting sense of strangeness at the new sensations, and that had been followed immediately by joy.

She would never have believed the power of intimacy without experiencing it. His warmth and scent and pulse had been indistinguishable from her own, and she had truly understood why the marriage service spoke of one spirit, one flesh.

It had been a magical night, and she had thought that nothing could ever be lovelier. But the nights that followed had been better yet, for as the months passed, they had become more and more attuned to each other's desires and responses. It had been like that right up until the time when she realized what was happening to her. Then her world had crumbled in terror.

She had no one to blame but herself. If she had been a stronger woman, she would have stayed in England. Instead, from fear, she had destroyed her own life. Far worse, she had hurt her husband terribly; she had not realized just how much until tonight. Though she had known he would be upset at her leaving, Ross had a quality of calm, confident strength that had led her to believe he would put her from his mind and recover fairly quickly.

But he had not fully recovered, or he would never have said tonight that he had not the stamina or optimism to take another wife. When they had married, he had had the strength and optimism for anything. Perhaps, instead of running away, she should have arranged a fatal accident. If she had died, Ross could have mourned her properly, then gotten on with his life.

But instead she had run, and almost immediately realized that she had jumped from the frying pan into the fire. Terrified and more alone than she had ever been in her life, she would have gone with Ross gladly if he had come after her and been willing to take her back. But he did not come, and it wasn't long before she committed the ruinous mistake that destroyed any chance that he might ever forgive her.

She wondered what lurid tales had reached England; probably rumors that she had engaged in mad orgies or some such. Not the truth, of course, but enough to convince Ross that it wasn't worth soiling his hands by coming after her.

Another thing that she had not fully realized until tonight was just how much it must have hurt his pride to have been abandoned by his wife. A private person like Ross would have hated being the subject of gossip. It had been easier for her, for she had left respectable society behind. She had not had to face the stares and whispers of people she knew.

She wondered what he felt about her. Tonight, had he wanted to bed her, or had he kissed her merely from curiosity? She suspected that the matter could have gone either way. Even now, if she went to his room and slid in beside him, he might be willing to tumble her, for it seemed that he still found her attractive. It would not be the same as the passion they had shared when he had loved and trusted her, but it would be profoundly satisfying on a physical level.

A pity that it wasn't possible to disconnect her body from her emotions, but physical intimacy would come at a price of emotional devastation. If she and Ross became lovers again, she would never survive the ending of the affair, and end it surely would, for the underlying problems would not go away.

Juliet realized that she was lying curled up on her side, clutching a pillow to her chest as if it were a life preserver. The corner was damp with tears. Taking a deep breath, she rolled onto her back and forced herself to relax, one muscle at a time, starting with her toes and working her way up her body.

She must take control of herself or this expedition to Bokhara would be catastrophic. To endure the journey, she and Ross would have to work together efficiently, without doubts and recriminations. Certainly she could not moon over him like a lovestruck milkmaid. She must do whatever was necessary to help Ross, and, if he still lived, Ian. And when they returned safely to Serevan, she must have the wisdom and dignity to let her husband go once more.

6

The next morning Ross awoke from a restless sleep feeling like the survivor of a shipwreck. But he had survived, and confronting the Amir of Bokhara should be easy compared to facing and accepting his own failings.

He had just finished dressing when a servant summoned him to break his fast. Ross followed with some reluctance, wondering if he was being taken to Juliet. To his relief, the only person sitting at the low table in the small sunny dining room was the elderly Uzbek who seemed to be an overseer for Serevan.

The Uzbek wore a white turban and a brilliantly patterned robe of the woven silk material called ikat. When Ross entered the room, he inclined his head politely. "Salaam Aleikum, my lord," he said, offering the traditional greeting that was a wish for peace. "I am Saleh, the most humble servant of Gul-i Sarahi. Pray forgive me for not rising to greet you, but my knees are old and feeble and they protest when they are used too often."

Ross folded down onto a cushion by the table with the ease of long practice. "Aleikum Salaam," he said, returning the wish for peace. "I am greatly honored that you have asked an inconsequential traveler to share bread and salt with you. I would be desolate if your knees were to suffer as a result."

Saleh laughed, his eyes bright and curious above his gray beard. Clearly he had something to discuss, but first he plied his guest with tea, white cheese, and fresh hot bread.

When Ross had finished eating and was sipping an-

74

other cup of tea, Saleh said, "You speak Persian with great skill, my lord."

"The beauty of the language rewards its study." And, like most Eastern tongues, it encouraged flowery expression. Switching to Uzbek, Ross said, "But if you prefer, we can use another language."

Saleh's expression lit up. "Ah, you speak the tongue of my homeland. That will be most useful in Bokhara."

Ross gave him a sharp glance. "Juliet, or rather Gul-i Sarahi, told you of that?"

"Aye. This morning she told me that her brother was taken prisoner by the amir, and that you will go together to learn his fate." Saleh picked up a peach and used his thin-bladed knife to begin peeling off the skin in a continuous strip. "I have considered the matter and believe that I should accompany you."

Ross raised his brows, wondering if everyone at Serevan was going to decide to come along. Still, a native Bokharan could be useful. "The road is long and hard, and danger lies on all sides. Are you sure you wish to go?"

"In truth, no." The Uzbek finished peeling the peach, then sliced it into pieces. "I am an old man and fond of my comforts. But I owe a considerable debt to Gul-i Sarahi, and going with her to Bokhara may be a small repayment."

Interested, Ross said encouragingly, "Indeed?"

"I came of a good Bokharan family and was considered a promising young scholar," Saleh explained. "But the amir took a dislike to me. Not the present amir, Nasrullah, but his father, whom Nasrullah killed. In fact, Nasrullah murdered his brothers as well, just in case one might have wished to displace him. A difficult man, the amir, but such is the way of royalty.

"Would you like some peach? It is the first of the season and very fine." He pierced a slice of fruit with the tip of his knife, then gracefully offered the tidbit to Ross. "For the benefit of my health, I decided to leave my native land. I made the pilgrimage to Mecca, visited Constantinople and Teheran, and saw much of the world. Eventually I took a wife and settled here in Serevan, which was a thriving community then. Then Allah the merciful, who works in mysterious ways, withdrew his blessings. There were plagues and drought and Turkoman raids. The village was dying, until Gul-i Sarahi came. It was she who put the heart and health and strength back in Serevan."

Ross accepted the peach slice. "She is a remarkable woman."

"Aye, she is." Saleh's hands stilled, his eyes becoming distant. "And it was not only the village that was dying. When Guli-i Sarahi first came, my only son, Ramin, lay near death from fever. She gave him English medicine and nursed him with her own hands until the fever passed. She said it was the grace of Allah that healed the lad, not her, but my wife and I knew that it was Allah who sent her." Returning to the present, he offered Ross another piece of peach. "And so I will go with her to Bokhara."

Ross gracefully refused the fruit, thinking that the story meant that Saleh would be loyal to Juliet, if not necessarily her husband. "You know the city and its ways. What do you think of our chances for success?"

The Uzbek shrugged. "It will be difficult. Crossing the Kara Kum desert is very dangerous now, for the Turkomans recently killed the governor that the Amir of Khiva had put over them. The Turkoman tribes have split, some for Khiva, some for Bokhara, many only for themselves. If we survive the crossing of the desert, we shall likely find that your British officer is dead. Even if he lives, the amir will not release him. But with Allah's mercy, it should be possible to learn the officer's fate and return here safely." He sighed. "And then, I fear, you shall take our desert flower away from us."

Instantly wary, Ross said, "Why would I do that?"

"Are you not her husband?"

Surprised that Juliet had told Saleh, Ross replied, "Under English law only. There is no true marriage between us. Serevan is the home she has chosen, and here, I am sure, she will stay."

Saleh regarded the other man shrewdly but said nothing. He had wondered what response his statement would elicit, and the way the English lord had blanked his face and voice was interesting, most interesting. Gul-i Sarahi and her handsome husband might deny that there was anything between them, but their reactions said otherwise.

The English lord continued, 'Though I think that I need not say this, I will anyhow. The woman I knew as Juliet Cameron was headstrong and brave to the point of madness. I trust that you will watch over her, and use your influence to prevent her from throwing her life away unnecessarily?"

More and more interesting, Saleh thought. "You are correct that you need not ask. I will do whatever I can to protect her. And after her, you." With a secret smile he poured more tea. He had always thought that Gul-i Sarahi should have a man, and it appeared that she did, one that was well worth keeping.

After taking care of the day's most pressing tasks, Juliet decided to use the discipline of target shooting to calm her tightly strung nerves. A brisk walk brought her to the deep ravine she and her men used for rifle practice. It was an excellent natural range, for the configuration of the hills muffled sound to the point where the shots could hardly be heard in the nearby fortress and village.

She pinned palm-size green leaves to the earthen embankment for targets, then began shooting. For the next half-hour Juliet used ammunition extravagantly, rationalizing that the dangerous journey ahead required her marksmanship to be at its best.

Yet in spite of her concentration and the distorted echoes of rifle fire, she was instantly aware when someone began a soft-footed descent of the steep path behind her. Just as quickly, she identified who it was, both from the gait and the subtly different sound of European-made boots on stone and gravel.

Knowing that Ross was coming made the back of her neck prickle with self-consciousness. Since she had no idea what to say to him today, she continued firing until she had discharged the handful of cartridges she had been holding. By the time she finished, half of her leaf target had been ripped away.

As a cloud of dust rose from the point of impact, Ross said from behind her, "Impressive. I don't believe I've ever seen anyone shoot so quickly without losing accuracy."

"This breechloader makes speed easy." Juliet gratefully accepted the neutral topic. As she turned and handed Ross the rifle, she remembered that one of the things she had always liked about her husband was his calm acceptance of her expertise at traditionally "male" skills. Most men acted as if her riding and shooting were a personal attack on their cherished masculinity.

He expertly broke the rifle down and inspected it. "Lovely. Custom-made by a British gunsmith, I think?"

"Yes, it's a refinement of the Ferguson design, and it shoots very true. In this part of the world a good gun is essential. Care to try it?"

When he nodded, Juliet scooped half a dozen cartridges from her ammunition pouch and handed them to him. Wordlessly they managed the transfer without their fingers touching each other. It was ironic what perfect teamwork they could exhibit in avoiding contact. Even more ironically, offering him her rifle was a kind of intimacy that she had not allowed any other man.

Ross spent a moment more familiarizing himself with the weapon, then aimed at one of the remaining leaf targets. When he began shooting, Juliet started mentally counting the time. He fired all six shots in a little under a minute, which was not quite as fast as she had done—but the whole of the leaf had been obliterated, ripped to infinitesimal green fragments.

"I may be a bit faster," she said judiciously, "but you have the edge in accuracy."

"Perhaps." He returned the weapon. "The real trick is to be able to shoot that well when it counts. My rifle didn't do me any good yesterday when it was on my horse and I was not."

In some subtle way, Ross had changed overnight. As Juliet studied his face, she realized that the day before, there had been a questioning, tentative air about him, an openness to possibilities. Now that openness had vanished. He had made up his mind about his errant wife, and whatever he felt about her was locked behind a barrier of control as impervious as volcanic glass. His brown eyes showed neither warmth nor anger, just the impersonal politeness he would give any chance acquaintance.

Mentally Juliet resolved to try to match his detachment, because that would be easier for both of them. Unfortunately, she was doubtful how successful she would be, for controlling her emotions was not one of her strengths.

Ross leaned casually back against a boulder and folded his arms across his chest. "Do I look that strange? Or are you hoping that if you glare long enough, I'll vanish?"

"Sorry, I didn't mean to stare." Juliet felt her face coloring; she had blushed more in the last day than the whole previous year. She was tempted to retreat into generalities, but stopped herself. Control might not be one of her strong points, but directness was, so she should exercise some now. "I don't know how to act with you, Ross. You are both familiar and a stranger at the same time. Do you have any suggestions?"

Though he did not move, she had the impression that he stiffened before he replied. "Familiarity is an illusion. We knew each other very briefly a dozen years ago, in a relationship that was intense but basically superficial. We've lived most of our adult lives apart, doing different things in vastly different cultures. We are strangers, Juliet, though for the next couple of months we will share a common goal. I suppose we should act like distant relatives who have nothing in common but who are amiably disposed to each other."

Her lips twisted with painful amusement. For better and for worse, her love for Ross had shaped and defined her life, yet he could dismiss their marriage as "basically superficial." However, having asked him what he felt, she deserved whatever answer he gave. "Very well," she said, making her tone light. "I'll think of you as a second cousin."

"A second cousin, long since removed," he said with dry humor. "Then, once we begin our journey, it would be appropriate if you show a groveling desire to please your employer."

Juliet raised her eyebrows loftily. "I was planning on being the sort of servant who is erratic and unreliable, but who won't let you be cheated by anyone other than myself."

"That does sound more your style than groveling," he said with a hint of a smile. "Speaking of servants, I've decided to dismiss the two I hired in Teheran. Having spent the night in your fortress, they will have heard about the mysterious Gul-i Sarahi by now, and once they know that a tall ferengi woman is the chief of Serevan, there's a good chance they'll guess who my new veiled servant is. That could be dangerous."

"I hadn't thought of that." Juliet frowned. "My people are unlikely to have said much about me to strangers, but you're right, it is wiser to dismiss your servants. Though I usually dress as a man, I've never tried to masquerade as one for a long period of time, and it might prove difficult to conceal my identity from people I am with constantly. Better to pay your servants off now." Mentally she reviewed other issues that needed to be discussed. "Did Saleh speak with you?"

"Yes. He will be an asset in Bokhara, and I assume that he can be trusted not to betray your identity. Can you and Saleh be ready to leave for Sarakhs by noon? We can be there by nightfall, and with luck we'll catch the caravan I missed in Meshed."

Juliet was momentarily startled by his haste, but managed to conceal it. Ross was right; if there was any chance that Ian was still alive, speed was vital. Glancing at the sun, she estimated that it was two hours until noon. "We'll be ready."

"Good. We'll need camels for crossing the Kara Kum desert. I assume we can get some in Sarakhs?"

She nodded. "I know a man there who will sell us decent camels for an only mildly extortionate price. Some of my men can ride with us to Sarakhs, then bring our horses back here."

That settled, Juliet scanned her husband's well-tailored European coat and trousers, her brow furrowed. After years of seeing only loose, multilayered Eastern clothing, it was strange to see a man in garments that followed the form. Finding herself disturbingly aware of the contours of his lean, muscular body, she took a deep, slow breath. There were other, less personal reasons to be concerned about his mode of dress. "I think it is a mistake for you to wear Western clothes."

"Dressing like this is a calculated risk on my part," he explained. "Whatever status I might have in Bokhara is as a ferengi who has traveled a great distance to plead on behalf of my countryman, so I thought I should look the part. Also, I was afraid that wearing Asiatic clothing would leave me open to charges of being a spy, since it's unlikely that I can convincingly pass as a native."

"Those are valid points," she agreed, "but I think we will all be safer if you wear local dress until within a day's ride of Bokhara. Admittedly it would have been hard to conceal your foreignness when traveling with just your servants, but it is much easier to be inconspicuous in a caravan. All you have to do is dress like everyone else and cover your hair with a turban. I can get you local clothing if you're willing to wear it."

"Very well. English dress worked well enough at first, but since it almost got me killed yesterday, I suppose it's time to change my strategy." His glance fell on Juliet's dark blue veil. To take advantage of the spring sunshine, she had loosened it to lie in coils around her neck. "Since we're on the subject of clothing, I'm curious about your tagelmoust. How do you prevent the indigo dye from staining your skin?"

She smiled; how like Ross to think of such a thing. "You've found me out: this is not a genuine Tuareg tagelmoust. To avoid stains, I use a European fabric of the same color and texture."

"I'm glad to hear that vanity is not entirely dead."

"One needn't be very vain to dislike having blue skin," Juliet retorted, glad to hear a teasing note in his voice. "Speaking of skin, it helps that yours is sun-browned. Allow it to get dirty, and no one will guess that you are a ferengi."

"You're in no position to throw stones," he pointed out. "I never saw a Targui who was remotely as clean as you."

"That doesn't matter, since I probably won't meet anyone in Turkestan who has ever seen one of the Tuareg." She looked down at her black robe. "Still, in the interests of accuracy . . ." She handed him the rifle, then lay full-length on the ground and began rolling in the earth.

To her delight, Ross began to laugh. "You're absurd."

When Juliet had rolled over several times, she stood and began brushing off the surface dust. The result of her labors was a robe with a nicely mellow amount of ground-in dirt.

There was a gleam of amusement in her husband's eyes, and he had lost some of his coolness. "It's fortunate that no one will know what the Tuareg look like, since every one I ever met had brown eyes. However, gray eyes are not unknown in Central Asia, so yours shouldn't attract too much unwelcome attention. I think you'll need a new name, though. Since Gul-i Sarahi is Persian, someone might think it an odd choice for a North African male."

She wrinkled her nose. "I already have too many names, but I suppose you're right. Do you have any suggestions?"

He considered. "How about Jalal? It sounds a bit like Juliet and Gul-i Sarahi, so it should be easy to respond to."

"Fine. But you'll need another name too."

"My servants pronounce my title as Khilburn, which sounds suitably Central Asian, so I'll use that." He regarded her thoughtfully. "It will probably be best if you pretend to know little Persian and speak as little as possible."

"Are you telling me that if I keep my mouth shut, I'm less likely to get into trouble?"

"Exactly."

Juliet chuckled. "Much as it pains me to admit it, you're right. Very well, I'll be silent and eccentric with everyone but you and Saleh. But there is also something you must be careful about, Ross. Or rather, Khilburn. Forget those beautiful manners the duchess taught you. Don't help me with heavy loads, allow me through a door first, or show me any of the courtesy you usually show a woman. In fact, forget that I'm a woman."

"When you are swathed head to foot in black draperies, that won't be difficult," he said dryly as he stood and returned her rifle. "We'll have to stop wasting time if we're going to leave in two hours, Jalal. Packing won't be hard for me, but I imagine that you and Saleh will have a great deal to do."

"To say the least." Juliet slung the rifle across her back, then drew the veil around her head again. As they walked back to Serevan in a not unfriendly silence, she decided that they had gone from being second cousins, once removed, to first cousins. That was about the right distance; any closer would be dangerous.

Ross's reasonable plan went awry when he tried to discharge his servants. Allahdad accepted dismissal and a severance payment with an unflattering amount of pleasure, but Murad balked. After Allahdad left the room, the young Persian said, "I know you wish to punish me for my cravenness in abandoning you to the Turkomans, but please, Khilburn, do not dismiss me."

"I am not punishing you—there would have been no purpose in your sacrificing yourself," Ross said, a little surprised at the young man's vehemence. "But thinking you were gone, yesterday I hired two new servants. Since they are more knowledgeable about the Kara Kum and Bokhara, it makes sense to keep them on and release you and Allahdad. It should be easy for you to find more work in Meshed, and because of the severance payment, doing that will be more profitable for you than staying with me would be."

"I do not want another job!" Murad said. "I wish to go with you to Bokhara."

Ross studied the young man. About twenty, Murad was a handsome, likable youth even if he had proved to be an erratic guide. Still, the reasons Ross had given Juliet for dismissing his servants were still valid. "I'm sorry, but I will not need you for the rest of my journey."

His dark eyes tragic, Murad said, "You do not trust me, Khilburn, and justly so, but I swear I will not fail you again."

Ross thought about it. He judged that Murad was sincere, but unfortunately, he was also young and rather volatile. "It is not just a matter of being loyal to me, Murad, but to the other members of my party. I have decided to make the rest of the journey dressed in Asiatic clothing in the hope that I will not attract unwanted attention, but there is a danger that I might be thought a spy. Also, one of the men I hired here is a Targui from the western desert of Africa. I met him many years ago and know that he will be valuable on the journey, but the ways of the Tuareg are unusual. If you casually tell someone else in the caravan that I am a ferengi, or say how odd the Targui is, you might jeopardize the whole party. I cannot risk that."

"You are a good man, Khilburn, even though you are a ferengi. I swear I will say nothing that might bring trouble on you. As for the Targui . . ." Murad shrugged. "The tribes of Asia are many and varied. I have known Uigars, Kafirs, Baluchis, Kirghiz—I doubt that a Targui is so much more unusual."

"The men of the Tuareg always go veiled. With their faces covered, they seem uncanny, for it is impossible to know what they think. Even in their own desert lands, they are a legend."

"If the Targui is a believer and a reasonable man, I shall not quarrel with him." The young Persian leaned forward earnestly. "Yesterday I disgraced myself, and only by serving you well can I redeem my honor. I beg you to give me the chance."

Ross made a sudden decision. Besides the fact that he liked Murad, he felt that the young man would prove useful, and Ross had learned to trust his feelings. "Very well, you may come. Call me Khilburn and try not to think of me as a ferengi. If we return safely to Serevan and you have done your job well, I will give you a bonus beyond the fee we agreed on in Teheran."

Murad bowed. "I will serve you well, not for the bonus but for honor's sake." He flashed a charming smile. "Though I shall not refuse the bonus. You will not regret keeping me, Khilburn."

Ross certainly hoped that would prove to be true.

After sending Murad off to pack his belongings, Ross had a servant take a message to Juliet that the young man would be accompanying them and she would have to be in her role of Tuareg man from the very beginning. From Ross's perspective, the sooner she obliterated herself in folds of fabric, the better; if he couldn't see any of her lovely face or body, it should be easier to control his inconvenient desire. Down at the shooting range, with her fair complexion set off by her black robes and a thick braid of fiery hair falling over her shoulder, he had had to back away and cross his arms to ensure that he would not involuntarily reach out and touch her. Having Juliet break his arm for impertinence would be a poor start to their journey.

On returning to his room, Ross found his new wardrobe laid out on the bed. Inspecting the garments, he decided that the quality was just right, neither lavish nor impoverished. But then, he would never expect Juliet to be anything less than efficient, even on such short notice.

Loose, multilayered clothing was worn throughout the Islamic world. However, although there were endless variations, the rule of thumb was that North African clothing was generally simpler, most often consisting of robes that pulled over the head like a nightgown and mantles that wrapped around the body in various ways. That shapelessness was why Juliet could successfully disguise herself in Tuareg apparel. In contrast, Asiatic clothing tended to be more structured and usually involved one or more long, loose, sleeved coats worn over a tunic or shirt and trousers.

After stripping off his English clothes, Ross donned his new garments. Fortunately Juliet had managed to find a white cotton tunic wide enough in the shoulders to fit him. The baggy gray trousers could have been a bit longer, but were not so short as to arouse comment. A green-and-black-striped coat called a chapan went over tunic and trousers and fell to his knees. He belted that in place with a long white sash, then topped the outfit with a quilted coat that reached almost to his ankles. He was glad the garments were comfortable, because he would probably be wearing them day and night for the next month.

Not surprisingly, there was no footwear, for his feet were definitely not a standard size in this part of the world. However, his own dark brown leather boots were of unremarkable appearance and should not attract attention, particularly in their present scuffed condition.

Under the pile of clothing was a beautiful curving dagger. Sliding the blade from its sheath, he saw that it was not just decorative, but a lethally edged weapon that meant business. He thrust the dagger in his sash; with that, his rifle, a pistol, and the knife in his boot, he was armed like a hill bandit. But with luck, none of the weapons would be needed; he had long since decided that the only good fight was one that never happened.

Finally Ross turned his attention to the yards of white muslin intended for his turban. Turbans were vastly practical garments, protecting the head from both sun and cold, absorbing sweat, capable of being drawn over the mouth against dust or sand. And, with grim practicality, there was enough material in one to cover a man's body completely so that it could be used as his shroud if necessary.

But a turban was a great deal more than practical: it was a statement of tribe and class, of fashion and personality. After careful consideration, Ross decided that an Afghan style would be best. Afghans were often tall, so his height would be less conspicuous. Also, like most Central Asians, Afghans were Sunnis, members of the largest, most orthodox branch of Islam, while most Persians were of the Shiite sect. Outside of their own country, Shiites were often harassed, sometimes even killed, so it would be best not to look like a Persian, for safety lay in being as unobtrusive as possible.

He put on the felt skullcap that Juliet had sent, then folded the length of muslin into rough pleats. It had been several years since he had worn a turban, and then it had been a Hindu style, but his hands remembered the general technique, and after only a couple of false starts he managed to wind and tuck the fabric into a very respectable Afghan turban, complete with a tail hanging down the side of his neck.

Juliet had even supplied a small pouch of surma. Though his lashes and brows were several shades darker than his hair, they were still light by Asian standards, so after applying the surma to his eyelids, Ross carefully rubbed a little into his eyebrows.

Then he surveyed himself as best he could in the small mirror. Not bad, he decided; it was a pity that he didn't have a full dark beard, but it was now unlikely that anyone would immediately single him out as a ferengi.

As important as altering his appearance, and rather more difficult, was changing his thinking to that of an Oriental rather than an Englishman so that he would not betray himself in subtle ways. He had done that successfully before, in less critical circumstances, so he would be able to do it again.

Next he cut the letters of introduction from the lining of his English coat. Sealed in oiled cloth packets, they were easily sewed into the padded chapan. Then he turned his attention to his European wardrobe, packing some garments to take to Bokhara while leaving more at Serevan.

Finally he was ready to go. Looking at his baggage, he smiled humorlessly. The journey across the Kara Kum would be hazardous, his reception in Bokhara much more so. Yet more difficult by far would be living cheek by jowl with the only woman who had ever had real power over him. Because, God help him, she still did.

7

🙢

The camel lowered its head and brayed malevolently at Ross. Guessing that it was about to spit at him, he sidestepped neatly and muttered under his breath, "I think you're pretty ugly too."

A soft chuckle came from behind him. Then, in a voice too low for anyone else to hear, Juliet said, "Actually, as camels go, this one is rather pretty."

Ross repressed a smile. "And as camels go, this one will." He handed the reins to Juliet so that she could lead it over to join the others they wanted to buy. In fact, Juliet was quite correct: the camel was rather attractive, if you had a taste for beasts that looked as if they were designed by God on an off day.

The camels of Mongolia and Turkestan were of the two-humped Bactrian variety, and they were shorter, stockier, and shaggier than the single-humped dromedaries found in North Africa and western Asia. Bactrians were perfectly suited to the Central Asian climate, which had wide extremes of both heat and cold, so apparently God at least knew what he was doing when he set the camels in their respective territories.

Having placed the latest selection in Murad's charge, Juliet returned to help Ross choose the final camel they would need for the journey. The next one they examined was a cranky bull. Juliet expertly kneaded the humps with her hands, then shook her head. "Not enough fat. This one needs to be put out to pasture for several months. Probably wouldn't survive the trip to Bokhara."

Ross accepted her judgment. He had had a fair amount of experience with camels, but Juliet had more. In spite of the beasts' phenomenal endurance, they were in some ways curiously fragile and needed long spells of recovery after hard use. Only the fittest camels could survive the demanding journey across the Kara Kum, and Juliet had already rejected a number of the merchant's available stock.

The next possibility was a female with a sleek coat and thick, curling black hair along the underside of her throat. She batted her eyes flirtatiously, then swung her head around and belched in his face. For a camel, that counted as good nature.

Cautiously Ross inspected the animal's broad padded feet while Juliet gauged the camel's fitness. After a thorough examination of the humps, she said, "This one will do."

"I like her." Ross gave the camel a friendly slap on its flank. "I'll ride her myself and call her Julietta."

His wife's eyes flashed evilly through the narrow opening in her veil, but she refrained from comment because the owner of the camels, Mustafa Khan, was approaching.

They had set out from Serevan only about half an hour later than the time Ross had aimed for. Saleh had put aside his brilliantly colored silks for the sober dress of a merchant, and Juliet, in her veil and flowing dark robes, had been thoroughly convincing as a proud, prickly male servant. Murad had been openly curious about his Tuareg companion, but had not dared to venture any comments after his first tentative greeting was met by a cold stare and a single gruff syllable.

Escorted by half a dozen men from Serevan, they had descended from the mountain plateau to the arid plains that rolled endlessly into the distance, and hard riding brought them to Sarakhs before sunset. The unimpressive mud-brick community sat by a shallow, silty river on the edge of the desert. Nominally under Persian control, it consisted of perhaps two thousand families of non-nomadic Turkomans.

Wanting to choose the camels in daylight, Ross had had Juliet take them to the stock dealer as soon as they reached the town. Now, as darkness gathered, Ross sat down with the dealer to drink tea and bargain for the selected beasts. Bargaining was both art and entertainment in the East, and Mustafa Khan started the process with relish, demanding an outrageous amount.

Ross could have afforded what was asked, but spending too much might attract dangerous attention, and would certainly have proved that he was not Oriental. He countered with an offer a fifth of the asking price, then watched with deep appreciation while Mustafa Khan moaned, his eyes screwing shut with misery and his black mustaches drooping.

The Turkoman merchant pointed out that honored Khilburn had selected the finest beasts on the lot. Then, after speaking eloquently of his love for the camels, of how they were like his own beloved children and he offered them for sale only as a service for travelers like his noble visitor, Mustafa Khan lowered his price by ten percent.

Years of experience in the bazaars of Asia and Africa had given Ross a very respectable skill at bargaining, so he countered with a lengthy diatribe on the camels' flaws: the weakness of their muscles, the poorness of their condition, the probability that they would drop dead before they reached the middle of the Kara Kum. While it would surely be in his best interest to purchase his camels elsewhere, the affection and esteem that had instantly sprung to life on meeting Mustafa Khan led him to offer much more than the mangy beasts were worth.

When Ross named a new figure, the merchant clutched his heart and murmured that honored Khilburn wanted to orphan and beggar Mustafa Khan's children, then lowered his price again. And so it went, most pleasurably, through two hours and six tiny cups each of tea, while the other members of Ross's party took their ease with Eastern patience. Except for Juliet, who paced restlessly about the yard, looking dark and dangerous.

Twice Ross got up and started to leave, Saleh, Murad, and Juliet right behind him. The second time they actually reached the street before Mustafa Khan overtook them with a new offer.

Finally a deal was struck that included five camels, two pack saddles, and several other pieces of equipment that they would need. After mournfully announcing that the final price had ruined him, the merchant gave Ross cheerful directions to the caravansary where the rest of the caravan was spending the night.

In her guise of Jalal, Juliet had the job of chief camel driver, so she took charge of saddling and loading the two animals that would carry their supplies. After the first camel was saddled, she tightened the girth twice, then couched it—that is, made the beast kneel so that it could be loaded. Couching was invariably a strenuous procedure. First Juliet twisted her fingers in the long hair under the camel's throat. Then she pulled on throat hair and nose rope, at the same time kicking the beast on the shin. It bawled a complaint but sank to its knees as Ross watched with amusement. With a horse, such treatment would be considered abuse; with a camel, rough handling was necessary just to get the animal's attention.

When Ross brought over an armful of baggage to be loaded, he asked under his breath, "How did I do with the bargaining?"

"You paid a few dinars more than I would have," Juliet said, dodging back as the camel swung its head around and bared an impressive set of molars, "but it was a creditable showing against an old bandit like Mustafa Khan."

Ross grinned and went to saddle and couch the other pack camel. He and Juliet really should be more careful about these *sub rosa* exchanges; neither of them seemed able to resist the temptation to exchange thoughts and irreverent comments. It was unlikely that anyone else would understand, for they spoke in Tamahak with English words filling in when no Tuareg term existed, but it was still unwise to behave with such familiarity.

Their departure from Mustafa Khan's yard was delayed when the second pack camel managed to shed its load while lurching to its feet. Unsurprised, Ross sighed and started over on the tedious business of couching and packing. Since almost the only intelligence camels showed was for throwing their cargo, loading them required skill, and Ross had not done it in several years. In a few days he would have the knack again.

With Juliet's wordless help they successfully repacked and set off for the caravansary, leading their camels since the distance was short and the streets became progressively busier as they approached their destination. Having a caravan in town meant that all the peddlers and bazaar stalls were active, hoping to do more business before the travelers moved on.

Boisterous talk and laughter echoed through the narrow alleys, and here and there a fluttering torch illuminated faces in the teeming crowd. It was a society of men, for the few women present were veiled so thoroughly as to be almost invisible. Merchants and potential customers bargained, storytellers spoke to rapt audiences, scribes wrote letters for the illiterate, odors of food, unwashed bodies, spices, and dung filled the air, and twisting around all the rest was the acrid bite of smoke as peddlers roasted kebabs over tiny fires. Even with his eyes closed, Ross would have known instantly that he was in Central Asia.

Though Ross's height and beardlessness attracted a few glances, he was glad to see that no one was unduly interested in him. With her veil and sweeping dark robes, Juliet drew more attention, but it was simple curiosity rather than suspicion or hostility. Men traveled thousands of miles from their native lands along the great caravan routes of Asia and Africa, so "Jalal" was just another exotic visitor. Taller than most of the men around her and walking with perfect masculine swagger, she seemed entirely at home in her surroundings. If Ross had seen her in a Tuareg camp in the Sahara, he would never have guessed her identity.

Once they set out on the trail, the rations would be Spartan, so Ross decided that they would eat well tonight. As they worked their way through the crowd, he purchased skewers of sizzling roast mutton from a kebab seller, then added fresh bread from a baker and pastries from a confectioner. Murad carried the food, along with a small bag of charcoal for a fire.

Caravansaries were hotels for both men and beasts and were found along all the caravan routes from the Atlantic to China. When Ross and his party entered the caravansary through the high gates, they found that this one was laid out in typical fashion, with small rooms for visitors and stables for the beasts all opening onto the large central courtyard.

Because the caravansary was full, animals were bedded down in the open and numerous small fires burned in the courtyard, both for cooking and for warmth against the chilly night. With human voices and animal complaints bouncing from the mud-brick walls, the caravansary was a noisy place. Travelers sipped tea and exchanged news around the fires while peddlers wandered through the yard, seeking customers for their wares. At least a dozen languages and races could be discerned, including turbaned Hindus, a group of Chinese with long black queues dangling down their backs, and Arabs with white head-scarves tied in place with black camel-hair cords.

A lantern hung above the door to the innkeeper's office, and Saleh went in to book their lodging for the night. Fortunately there was space available and they were assigned a cubicle in the farthest corner of the building. After they had moved their baggage into the small room, Murad started building a fire, Juliet began bedding down the camels, and Ross and Saleh set off to find the kafila-bashi, the leader of the caravan.

As they worked their way through the crowded court, Ross admitted to himself that Juliet had been right to warn him to restrain his chivalrous instincts. It was difficult for him to stand by and watch her do heavy physical labor. Rationally, he knew his reaction was nonsense; if he had not known Juliet was a woman, he never would have questioned her competence at wrestling with camels and their loads. She was taller than either Murad or Saleh and, though lighter in build, was probably as strong as either of the men. Nonetheless, old habits die hard, and it was an effort for Ross to treat her the same as he would a man.

The basic problem, of course, was that it was impossible for him to forget that she was a woman. Quite impossible.

The kafila-bashi was holding court in a larger cubicle near the entrance to the caravansary. As Ross and Saleh entered, the leader was dealing with the chief of a group of Afghan merchants who had just arrived from Herat and wanted to join the larger caravan. After discussing terms and marching order, the kafila-bashi dismissed the Afghanis and turned to Ross and Saleh.

"Salaam Aleikum." He waved his hand for them to be seated. "I am Abdul Wahab. How may I serve you?"

As Ross returned the greeting and settled down onto the packed earth floor, he studied the kafila-bashi, whose dress and features indicated that he was an Uzbek. He was a broad-shouldered man of middle years, with shrewd dark eyes and the air of authority of a natural leader.

Ross introduced himself as Khilburn, then presented Saleh and made arrangements for their party to join the caravan, which would depart before dawn the next morning. Then, making a decision based on his favorable judgment of the kafila-bashi, he continued, "I think you should know that I am a ferengi, an Englishman."

Abdul Wahab's eyebrows rose. "You speak Persian well for a ferengi. A trace of accent only—I thought you might be a Baluchi from southern Afghanistan." His gaze went to Saleh. "Surely you are not also a ferengi?"

Saleh shook his white-turbaned head. "Nay, I am an Uzbek, the same as you. The other members of our party are a Persian and a Targui from the Sahara. Only Khilburn is a ferengi."

The kafila-bashi's thoughtful glance returned to Ross. "Why have you told me this?"

"The welfare of the caravan is your responsibility. I did not want to conceal a fact that might cause trouble for you."

"An honorable motive." Frowning, Abdul Wahab stroked his black beard. "Do not go to Bokhara, Khilburn. If you do, you will be a son of death, for the amir despises all Europeans. If you wait in Sarakhs for a few more days, there will be a caravan that will take you to Khiva, which is my own native city. It is a safer destination for a ferengi."

Opinions on the wisdom of his going to Bokhara were nothing if not unanimous, Ross thought wryly. "I have no choice. I wish to learn the fate of my brother, a British officer who went to Bokhara on an official mission and was imprisoned by the amir."

The caravan leader's bushy brows drew together. "Is he a tall, fair man like you?"

Ian's hair was auburn rather than blond, but he was Ross's height, with very fair skin. Ross nodded. "He is."

"With my own eyes, I saw a ferengi of that description beheaded several months ago, behind the amir's palace in Bokhara. In the crowd, it was said that he was a soldier." Abdul Wahab's expression was compassionate. "I am sorry to be the one to tell you this, but surely the man executed was your brother. Very few ferengis ever reach Bokhara—and fewer leave alive. Do not continue your journey, for there is now no reason for it."

At the kafila-bashi's words, Ross felt a constriction deep in his chest. In spite of all the rumors and hearsay evidence, this was the first time he had found someone who had personally witnessed the execution of a foreigner who could be Ian. The faint hope that he had carried from Constantinople flickered and died. For a moment he considered following everyone's good advice and ending his journey here. Not only would that be wiser, it would save him weeks of painful proximity to Juliet.

As the thought of stopping formed in his mind, it was immediately followed by a vivid mental image of Jean Cameron's pleading face. *Please, Ross, I am begging you.* Even now he could not be completely certain of Ian's fate, and Jean would still be left with a faint, destructive thread of hope.

And beyond that, Ross realized with painful clarity, he did not entirely want to be saved from the bittersweet pleasure of Juliet's company. "Your counsel is wise, Abdul Wahab, but I cannot go back without positive proof. If my brother is dead, perhaps the amir will allow me to take his body back to England."

The leader looked pessimistic, but nodded. "So be it."

Wanting to know more about the ferengi, Ross said, "The man who was executed—what was his condition?"

"Very grave. He was scarcely more than bones, with terrible sores all over his body. He looked like an old man, though I think he was not." Abdul Wahab grimaced. "Did you know that the amir breeds special vermin in the Black Well, solely to make the prisoners suffer

more? I do not think that the ferengi would have survived much longer as a prisoner. At least the sword
spared him further suffering."

"My brother would have died bravely," Ross said, his
voice not quite a question.

"Aye, he did. Though he was weak, he stood tall and
with his right hand he made the sign of the cross over
his breast as he spoke in his own language. I cannot
know for certain, but I believe that he commended his
soul to the Christian God." The kafila-bashi inclined his
head respectfully. "It would have been more fitting for
a warrior to die in battle, but I assure you that he did
not disgrace himself or his family."

Ross was briefly surprised, for his brother-in-law had
never been religious, and the sign of the cross was hardly
standard practice among Scots Presbyterians. But after a
moment's thought, he understood the gesture. Quite apart
from the fact that months of imprisonment could change
anyone's spiritual beliefs, crossing himself sounded like
Ian's last gesture of defiance, a public proclamation of
his nationality and religion. Even at the end, he had been
unbroken. Perhaps that would be some comfort to his
family.

"Thank you for your information, Abdul Wahab."
Ross got to his feet. "As compensation for the fact that
my presence might cause trouble, I and my servant Jalal
are well armed, and we will gladly use our weapons in
the defense of the caravan."

"God willing, your arms will not be needed, but I am
glad to know that you have them." Two more men entered the cubicle, so the caravan leader gave a nod of
dismissal and turned to deal with the next problem.

Saleh beside him, Ross went out into the courtyard,
thinking that matters were going well. The kafila-bashi
seemed a capable and tolerant man, and with luck they
would make it across the Kara Kum without incident.
Ross looked forward to beginning the last leg of the
journey.

Unfortunately, before that would happen, he must tell
Juliet what he had learned about her brother, and *that*
he was not looking forward to at all.

8

Juliet hunkered against the wall of the caravansary, arms crossed on her raised knees as she idly watched Murad tend the fire and prepare the evening meal. During the course of the day, the Persian had given up trying to make conversation, for she responded to his efforts with either silence or a growled monosyllable. While she regretted the rudeness, she knew that it would be folly to become friendly with the young man; the less Murad knew about her, the better.

She shifted position to ease the chafing of the vestlike garment she wore under her robes to flatten her breasts. She had never bothered with such a thing before; though she habitually wore male dress, it had always been a matter of convenience rather than a serious attempt to disguise her gender. However, this journey was different, so she had taken precautions to reduce the chance that anyone might realize that she was female. Knowing that she would have to wear it continuously, she had deliberately fashioned the vest to be as loose as possible, but it was still a nuisance. At least the weather was temperate now; the garment would be far more uncomfortable in the summer heat.

Glancing across the courtyard, she saw Ross and Saleh weaving their way between the fires and dozing camels. Ross wore his Asiatic garments as if he had been born to them; it was hard to believe that he was an English aristocrat. Her expression safely hidden behind her veil, Juliet smiled a little, thinking that now he looked like an oriental aristocrat. There was nothing her husband could do to make his appearance undistinguished.

Now that everyone was together, it was time to eat. After Ross, Saleh, and Juliet had seated themselves around a low circular table, Murad set a large platter in their midst, then took his own place. The chunks of roast mutton purchased in the bazaar were served on a bed of cooked rice obtained from the caravansary cookshop, and there was fresh flat bread as well.

Throughout the Islamic world, it was customary to eat with the fingers of the right hand only, since the left hand was ritually unclean and could never be used in a communal platter. Juliet had been eating Muslim-style for so long that it was second nature. She was skilled at rolling rice into a ball with her right hand, then deftly popping it into her mouth with a flick of her thumb, since it was bad manners to put the fingers in the mouth. However, she had never attempted to eat while keeping her face covered, and doing so proved unexpectedly difficult. Even among the Tuareg, only the strictest men stayed veiled while eating, and during Juliet's exasperating struggle to master the technique, she learned why.

She had loosened the tagelmoust so that she could bring her hand up under it, but found that constant care was needed to avoid displacing the veil. Twice she fumbled while raising her hand to her mouth, and scattered rice down the front of her dark robe. The second time that happened, she caught Ross's amused glance on her. She glared back, silently daring him to laugh.

Fortunately custom divided the communal platter into invisible zones, and it was discourteous to take food from another person's area, or she would not have gotten her share of the meal. By the time she finished, the rest of the platter had long since been emptied and the men were drinking tea.

Juliet accepted a small teacup herself and promptly learned that drinking while veiled was even harder than eating. Furthermore, it would be impossible to drink from a waterskin without lowering the tagelmoust. She would have to be careful to drink only when no one but Ross or Saleh could see her. With luck, anyone catching a fleeting glimpse of her face would assume she was a beardless boy, but she would rather not rely on luck.

After they were all done, Ross said to Murad, "We

will be leaving before dawn." Then he glanced at Juliet. Speaking in Tamahak, as if he were repeating the same message, he said, "Meet me behind the caravansary in about a quarter of an hour."

She gave a noncommittal murmur of assent, curious about why her husband wanted to talk to her privately. Well, there was only one way to find out, so she got to her feet and stalked into the courtyard without explanation. Pretending to be a brusque Targui was giving her the opportunity to behave like a rude schoolboy, and she had to admit that it was rather fun.

The hour was getting late and the noise level was dropping as people began to retire for the night. Taking her time, as if she had no particular destination in mind, Juliet checked the bedded-down camels, then ambled across the courtyard and through the entry arch into the bazaar-lined street. There she turned left and followed the caravansary walls around to the back.

In stark contrast to the front of the building, she found empty desert stretching to the east as far as the eye could see, and a good deal farther. Beneath a thin crescent moon, a fitful wind blew from the north, rustling the thorny shrubs that clung tenaciously to the gravelly soil.

Juliet took a deep breath of the dry, desert-scented air, then exhaled. As she did, she felt tension flowing out of her; apparently her masquerade was more of a strain than she had realized until now, when she could lower her guard. It was one thing to wear male garb when riding with her own men, who knew her for what she was, and quite another to be committed to weeks and months in disguise. But she had gotten through one day successfully, and tomorrow would be easier.

She stood unmoving in the shadow of a gnarled, scrubby tree, letting her eyes adjust to the starlight. There was no one else about, for men who traveled through the vast emptiness of the desert usually preferred to enjoy the companionship of their own kind when it was available.

About ten minutes later, Ross came around the corner of the caravansary, his stride unhurried. Even in the darkness, she had no trouble recognizing him by his height and the controlled power of his movements. Juliet held still, wondering if he would be able to find her. About a hundred feet away, he hesitated for a long moment, then came straight to her.

Impressed, Juliet wondered how he had located her so quickly; he had been upwind, so it could not have been scent, she had not made a sound, and her dark robes must have been invisible in the shadows. However, she refused to give him the satisfaction of asking how he had done it. When he was half a dozen feet away, she said in English, "Is something wrong, Ross?"

"I'm afraid so." In flat, uninflected sentences, he told her that the kafila-bashi had seen a ferengi executed, then went on to recount the conversation in detail.

Juliet accepted the news stoically, for it was not really a surprise. Yet when Ross described the physical condition of the man who had been executed, and how he had faced death, she drew an anguished, involuntary breath.

"I'm sorry, Juliet," Ross said, his voice almost inaudible.

"This makes Ian's death seem real," she said, struggling to keep her tone even. "In my mind, he was still twenty, with endless energy and exuberance. To think of him emaciated, tortured, perhaps, so weak he could barely stand . . . it seems so wrong." She drew a shuddering breath. "When we were young, we both wanted to see the whole world, to dare everything there was to dare. And now Ian's adventuring days are over, ended in blood in front of a crowd of curious strangers."

Her voice broke. A vision of her brother suffering had replaced her mental image of him in strength and health, and it was impossible to dislodge. Dully she wondered if that was how adventures usually ended—in pain and senseless tragedy, thousands of miles from home.

For a moment Ross touched her shoulder in silent commiseration. His sympathy almost broke what remained of her control. Juliet bent her head and buried her face in her hands, wanting to weep for all her losses: for the murder of her brother, for the weary erosion of youth and hope, for the death of love. Most of all, for the death of love.

Angrily she drew the back of her hand across her stinging eyes, wiping away the tears. Then, feeling the need to breathe more deeply, she pulled her veil down, letting the wind touch her face for the first time in many hours.

"Do you want to abandon the journey?" she asked when her voice steadied. "If we are going to turn back, now is the time."

"I've considered it," Ross said slowly, "but while Abdul Wahab witnessed the execution, we still don't know why Ian was killed. Such knowledge could be valuable for the government as well as your family, and the only way to learn the whole story is to go to Bokhara. Plus, it would mean a great deal to your mother if Ian's body could be returned to Scotland for burial."

"It would also mean a great deal to me." Juliet wanted to say more, but her throat closed and she could not.

"Come. Let's walk before we go back." Putting a light hand on the back of her waist, he guided her toward the open desert.

As she began walking, she wondered if Ross was even aware that he was touching her. Probably not; the contact had the casual familiarity of an old friend, with nothing erotic about it. She could tell the difference from the night before, when there had been lucent passion between them.

For her, passion still burned, and all day she had been constantly, painfully aware of her husband's nearness. But she sensed that he had turned off desire as thoroughly as if he had extinguished a lamp. That he could do so did not surprise her; it had been far more surprising that he had ever wanted her in the first place. She had not understood his interest when she was seventeen, and now she understood it even less. Yet because he was the only man who had ever made her feel truly desirable, the withdrawal of his regard left her bereft.

Thank God there was still some sympathy between them, even if it was only a pale shadow of what had bound them together in the past. For tonight, as she struggled with the vision of her brother's death, she needed his kindness.

After several silent minutes, when the only sound was the faint crunch of gravel beneath their feet and the whisper of the wind, Ross said, "Do you ever miss Great Britain, Juliet?"

"Sometimes," she admitted. "I miss the greenness. Strange to think that the British see rain not just as normal, but frequently as a nuisance. Here, water is a gift from God."

He chuckled. "Here, sunshine and heat are considered normal and sometimes a nuisance. During a bad summer in England, those same things are considered a gift from God."

She smiled a little. "That's true, isn't it? It is human nature to yearn for what is rare." Then she fell silent again, wondering how much she could say without admitting more than she wanted to. "Much as I love Serevan, I will always be an alien in Persia. I did not fully realize the extent to which I was formed by European values until I began living in the middle of a foreign society. Oddly enough, I have less trouble dealing with the men than the women."

"I assume that is because the way that you live—riding, carrying weapons, giving orders—is exclusively male behavior here. You have never lived a life as circumscribed as that of Eastern women, so you have less in common with them."

"I never thought in those terms, but that is exactly the case." Juliet gave a self-mocking smile. "At first I tried to change things. I wanted to liberate the women of Serevan, persuade them to go unveiled, to demand more respect."

"From your tone, I gather that you met with little success."

"None at all." She sighed. "The women of Serevan were happier with their veils, their women's quarters, their separate lives. Finally I gave up. Even Saleh's wife, who is intelligent and wise, just listened, then tut-tutted and said that it sounded like an Englishwoman's life is an uncomfortable one."

"Culture is stronger than ideology," Ross observed, "and most people are happier following the customs they were raised with. Born rebels like you are rare."

"So it seems. But I regret having so little in common with the women here, because it limits friendship. I miss having female friends—in particular, I miss Sara." Juliet stopped, realizing that she was getting too close to the dangerous ground of their mutual past.

Perhaps feeling the same, Ross changed the subject. "The fact that you can enjoy the company of women makes you very different from Lady Hester Stanhope. She despised her own sex and would have much preferred to be born male. As a man, she would have made a splendid general or politician."

Juliet seized the new topic with enthusiasm. "That's right, you visited Lady Hester. When did you go? What was she like?"

Ross hesitated. Apparently the years had not dimmed his wife's innocent admiration for the self-styled "Queen of the Arabs," and he did not want to disillusion her. "I visited Lady Hester six or seven years ago. She was witty and opinionated. Capricious. Admirable, but also rather pathetic."

Taken aback, Juliet said, "How could such an incredible woman ever be pathetic? There has never been anyone like her."

"That is certainly true." Ross realized that he must be very careful of what he said; his wife had had enough bad news tonight, and she did not need more. "But when I visited, Lady Hester's health was failing and she no longer left her fortress for any reason. For a woman who had been a splendid rider and a great traveler, that must have been difficult."

A little shyly Juliet said, "When I decided to live at Serevan, I promised myself that I would try to live as Lady Hester did: to welcome all refugees, no matter what their tribe or creed—to protect those within my walls, never to send anyone away hungry." Her voice became dreamy. "It still amazes me that a woman who was the niece of William Pitt, who had lived at the very center of British politics, could turn her back on society and create a kingdom of her own in Syria."

"In a way, it makes perfect sense," he said thoughtfully. "Lady Hester was born to rule, but what influence she had came from being the niece and hostess of the prime minister. After Pitt died, there was nothing left for her in England but obscurity, and she would have hated that. In the East, she could do exactly as she wished, and she had authority again."

Wistfully Juliet said, "She was incredibly brave. Did you ever hear the story of how she became the first European woman ever to visit the ruins of Palmyra? She had the courage to put herself entirely under the protection of Bedouin raiders—" Abruptly Juliet cut off her monologue. "Sorry . . . of course you know all that. Please, tell me what it was like to meet her."

"I had been in Cyprus, so I decided to go over to the Lebanon in the hopes that Lady Hester would see me. After all, it isn't often that one has a chance to meet a living legend."

They were some distance from the caravansary now, so by mutual consent they sat down in a patch of soft sand, with the lee of a hill protecting them from the wind. Ross continued, "While all visitors were offered hospitality, she often refused to see them personally. But I was fortunate—she remembered my father from her political days, so she decided to receive me." He chuckled. "It was quite an experience. Though Lady Hester was nearly sixty, she still had enough vanity that she would entertain only after dark, since lamplight was more flattering. After her servants gave me an excellent dinner, she sent for me."

"What did you talk about?" Juliet asked eagerly.

"I didn't talk," Ross said rather dryly. "My job was to listen. She spent the whole night describing her metaphysical theories. Though her overall health was not good, there was nothing wrong with her tongue. I wasn't dismissed until dawn."

"I had heard that Lady Hester was a great talker, and so intelligent that Pitt said she would never marry, for she would never find a man with more wit than she had," Juliet observed. "What did she look like?"

"She was an impressive figure, a couple of inches taller even than you. She wore the robes of a Turkish pasha, and had a manner to match." Casting his mind back, Ross described the more interesting aspects of Lady Hester and her fortress of Djoun, glad that he was able to distract Juliet from her grief over her brother. Juliet and Ian had been as close as Ross and Sara, and though they had not seen each other in years, Ian's death must leave a bleak hole in her world.

As Ross talked, he kept a carefully casual eye on his wife's listening profile. With the veil down, her face was a pale, pure cameo against the black velvet night. There was a bitter irony in the scene: here they were, alone together in a desert in a remote and exotic part of the world. It was exactly the kind of romantic episode they had once intended to share. Before Juliet had run away, they had been planning a lengthy journey into the Middle East. Illness in Ross's family had forced a postponement, and Juliet had been upset at the delay. In fact, that was when they had their first arguments.

Now here they were a dozen years later, doing exactly what they had intended—but only up to a point. When they had planned their journey, they had always assumed that a scene such as this would end in passionate lovemaking. Yet now that their long-ago dream had been realized, they were so thoroughly estranged that romance was unthinkable.

Yet he was thinking about it. Knowing that if he did not move, he would be unable to stop himself from touching her, Ross stood abruptly and brushed the sand from his robes. "That is enough of Lady Hester for tonight." His fingers balled into a fist as he restrained himself from offering his wife a hand. "It's time to get some sleep. Dawn will come all too quickly."

Lithely Juliet got to her feet. As they began walking back toward Sarakhs, she said, "What will you do when you return to England, Ross? Managing the family property may be necessary, but I imagine you'll find it rather dull, and it certainly won't be enough to absorb all your energy."

Rather hesitantly he replied, "For years I've had an idea in the back of my mind to establish an institute for oriental studies, a place where Eastern and Western scholars can meet and exchange knowledge. I had intended to do it when I could no longer travel. Now that time has come, a little sooner than I expected." He glanced sideways at his wife. With her long swinging stride, she kept up with him effortlessly. "Have you

heard about the new railways that are being built in
Europe?"

"I've read about them, but they sound like just a passing novelty. It's hard to believe that people can—or want
to—move so quickly. And surely the time and money
involved in laying railroad tracks must be prohibitive."

"It is expensive, but not prohibitive. Over the next few
decades, railroads will change the world," Ross predicted. "Someday soon, not only will there be railroads
connecting every part of Europe, but also crossing the
whole width of Asia and America. The world is getting
smaller, and in the future it will be increasingly important
for different peoples to learn to understand each other.
In a small way, perhaps my institute can contribute to
that." He stopped, abashed, thinking that it was foolish
of him to say so much about what was only a vague
dream.

"It's a wonderful idea," Juliet said warmly, "and no
one could do a better job of running such an institute.
You've always been so good at talking with people from
every walk of life, and at getting them to talk to each
other." She laughed softly. "Sometimes I used to find
your ability to see all sides of a question exasperating,
but that fair-mindedness is one of the best things about
you. I'm glad you will be putting your talents to good
use."

Ross felt absurdly pleased at her approval; if there was
one thing he remembered clearly about his wife, it was
that she would never perjure herself by praising something she considered a bad idea. He glanced at her again.
They were nearing the caravansary, and as he watched,
she raised the tagelmoust and pulled it tightly around her
lower face. By the gesture, she distanced herself from
him, becoming once more the servant Jalal. They com-
pleted the walk in silence.

An oil lamp hung in the entry arch of the caravansary,
but the courtyard was still, with only embers showing
where fires had burned. Here and there a camel snorted
or a man coughed, but no one else was still up; they had
talked much longer than Ross had realized. Carefully
they picked their way through the maze of sleeping bodies, both human and animal.

When they arrived back at their own cubicle, the door to the small room was open to the night air and the faint light was enough to show the interior. The back end of the cubicle was stacked with their supplies and baggage, leaving an area about seven feet deep and just wide enough to allow four men to roll out their mats side by side. Murad and Saleh were lying next to each other on the left side of the room, leaving the two places on the right for the absent members of the party. In fact, their sleeping rugs had been laid out in position for their return.

Taking it in at a glance, Ross muttered an oath under his breath. Why the devil couldn't Saleh have managed matters so that the older man would be sleeping between Ross and Juliet? Simultaneously Ross and Juliet turned to look at each other. It was impossible to read any expression behind the tagelmoust, but he had no doubt that she was as dismayed as he was. The ease that had been between them vanished, replaced by palpable discomfort.

Well, there was nothing that could be done about it now, not without calling undesirable attention to their sleeping arrangements. Wordlessly Ross pulled the sheathed knife from his sash and laid it on his mat. Though it was unlikely that a caravansary would be robbed, through long habit he liked to keep a weapon near to hand, just in case. Then he lay down in the middle spot, leaving the wall position for Juliet. After wrapping his heavy wool blanket around him, he rolled onto his side, turning his back to where she would be lying.

Moving as quietly as he, Juliet also lay down and wrapped herself in her blanket, settling as far away from him as possible. Yet even though Ross was turned away, he was acutely, painfully aware of her nearness.

It had been hard enough the night before, when he knew that she was sleeping under the same roof; having her lying eighteen inches away was well nigh unbearable. Every sound she made, from the rustle of fabric to her nearly inaudible breathing, grated across his raw nerves like a saw-toothed blade.

But Ross would bear it because he had to; he had always been excellent at doing his duty, and at accepting the inevitable.

Deliberately he set out to calm his unquiet mind, using techniques he had learned at a Buddhist monastary in India. Muscle by muscle, he relaxed, at the same time slowing his breathing. He forced himself to concentrate on the feel of air as it flowed into his lungs, then drifted out again. In, out. In, out. His ribs expanding, then contracting. This, too, shall pass. It was not his maddening, beautiful, infinitely desirable wife lying less than an arm's length away, but a rude young Targui named Jalal. . . .

It would have been easier to convince himself that fish could fly.

9

❧

Huddled in her blanket against the wall, it took Juliet a long time to fall asleep. She was a light sleeper at the best of times, and with Ross only an arm's length away, her nerves were strung as tightly as a drumhead. Finally her weary body succumbed to fatigue, but at first her dreams were troubling ones of panicky flight and wrenching loss.

Yet sometime in the night, her distress eased. As she drifted into the hazy early-morning state that lies between waking and sleeping, she was just conscious enough to know that she was at peace. It was such a warm, comfortable feeling that she was reluctant to make the transition to full wakefulness.

Though it was still dark, she knew that it must be almost time to rise. Still, she let herself savor her lazy contentment, knowing that the least sound or movement would jerk her out of her golden mist. A gentle, rhythmic pulsing filled her awareness, like the touch and sound of a heartbeat. . . .

Bloody hell! Abruptly she snapped awake, feeling such a profound sense of shock that it was all she could do not to fling her body backward. For she was twined in Ross's embrace. He lay on his side, his arms loosely linked around her, while her left arm circled his waist, her unveiled face pressed against his broad chest, and her left knee tucked between his legs.

The fact that they were both swathed in layers of heavy fabric made little difference, for the impact such closeness had on Juliet's disordered senses could not have been much greater if they had been naked. Every fiber in her body vibrated with a reaction that was part physical yearning, part something deeper and more disturbing.

Shaking, she exhaled carefully, terrified of waking Ross. Thank God he had always been a sound sleeper. His breathing was deep and steady and he was obviously unaware that during the night they had drawn together like the opposite poles of a magnet. They had always slept intertwined like this, unconsciously adjusting and moving in harmony so that they were in constant contact. Last night, when their minds submerged in sleep, their bodies had immediately reverted to what had been so natural a dozen years ago.

It would have been rather amusing if it weren't so profoundly upsetting. Exercising exquisite caution, Juliet backed out of Ross's embrace. Yet she paused before completing her withdrawal. For the first time since they had met at Serevan, she had the luxury of studying him at leisure.

In the faint predawn light his strongly sculpted features had a mesmerizing masculine beauty. He really was the handsomest man she had ever met, even unkempt and with a hint of beard shadowing his jaw. In some subtle, undefinable way the years had planed down his face so that he looked harder and more formidable than he had at twenty-one. Yet still visible was that basic quality of decency that she had always loved in him. She had had so much, and had thrown it all away.

On impulse she leaned forward and kissed the hollow where his jaw intersected his throat, so lightly that her touch could not possibly disturb him. A prickle of whiskers teased her lips, and a faint taste of salt lingered as she drew back.

The kiss was a mistake, for in spite of her care, Ross's breathing changed. Worse, she felt a stirring of arousal against her hip, which was still pressed against him. Making slow, languid love in the early morning had always been one of the very best times. . . .

Savagely she bit her lower lip to counter the sensual warmth unfurling deep inside of her. With more speed than caution, she finished the job of disentangling herself from her husband, then promptly rolled over so that she faced the wall. Behind her, Ross sighed and shifted position, still asleep. Thank God for small blessings.

Juliet wrapped the veil back over her face, then settled down to await the dawn call to prayers. Yet even pulling the blanket tightly around her, like armor, could not restore the loss of Ross's warmth.

Despairingly she wondered why the devil life had to be so complicated.

Traveling through endless, trackless desert induced a state of near-meditative blankness that the Arabs called kif. Ross recognized and welcomed it, for kif was the mind's way of dealing with the great void. Still, one could not stay mindless forever. It was late afternoon and they would stop soon, so he yawned, then slid from the saddle and began walking beside his placid camel. Trailing behind on a lead was one of the two pack beasts.

Four days into the desert crossing, the caravan had settled into a regular routine. During the summer, travelers would set out in late afternoon and continue through the night to avoid the killing heat, but since it was now springtime and temperatures were moderate, they rose before dawn and stopped around sunset. Most men performed their prayers as they rode, as the Koran allowed travelers to do, though some of the most devout stopped to pray, then caught up with the caravan later.

It was necessary to keep moving for twelve to fourteen hours every day, for camels ambled along at the leisurely pace of about two miles per hour. The beasts foraged continuously; although most Europeans thought of a caravan as a sinuous line snaking across the desert, in fact the camels spread out so they could snatch whatever scant mouthfuls of shrubbery were available.

Ross knew dispersion was necessary so the camels could find enough to eat, but the practice made his neck prickle. If Turkoman bandits struck, it would be almost impossible for the caravan to defend itself; the raiders would be able to pick and choose their victims. Apart from the modern rifles he and Juliet carried, the only other weapons in the caravan were knives, swords, and a handful of ancient matchlock muskets.

However, so far there had been no sign of trouble, at

least not from raiders. The weather was another story; the second day out from Sarakhs, they had awoken to a mixture of fog and dust so dense that it was impossible to find landmarks, so the caravan had wandered off the regular route and been lost for hours.

Eventually the sky had cleared and the guide had gotten them back on track again. Then the next morning they awoke to find the encampment covered with several inches of snow, which was unusual so late in the season and which delayed their departure.

Ross grinned. Lord, the camels had hated the snow, complaining with raucous bitterness when they were forced to rise and begin the day's trek. But then, camels complained about everything. Guiltily he gave Julietta a pat on her shaggy neck. She turned and gave him a benevolent glance; she really was sweet-natured, for a camel.

Ross glanced around in one of his periodic checks on his companions. He and Juliet each had two camels in charge, one for riding and one pack animal. Since the pace was so slow, they alternated riding and walking as the spirit moved them.

The fifth camel had been equipped with panniers, a pair of deep riding baskets that hung on each side of the animal. Saleh rode in one, balanced on the other side by Murad. Since neither of the men was an expert camel rider, it had seemed wiser to keep them together; if the beast bolted and one man was unable to control it, perhaps the other one would be more successful. But so far the docile female that carried them had caused no trouble.

Ross next looked at Juliet, who was about a hundred yards away and slightly ahead of him. She walked like a desert prince, long black robes swinging around her long strides and her face completely obscured by her tagelmoust. She was perfect in her role as Jalal; apart from a surly Uzbek camel driver who occasionally heckled her, no one had shown more than a mild interest in the uncommunicative Targui. Certainly no one suspected that she was female and a ferengi. Juliet had proved to be a surprisingly good servant; he suspected that there was a

hint of mocking humor in her deference, as if to show
that she could take orders when necessary.

His gaze lingered thoughtfully on his wife. There was
no question that the most interesting thing that had happened so far had been that night in the caravansary. He
had learned to sleep lightly when traveling in dangerous
lands, and the hesitant touch on his shoulder had shocked
him to instant wakefulness. But to his bemusement, he
found not danger but Juliet, who had inched over and
was sliding her arm around his neck. When he had turned
toward her, she settled her sleeping self against him with
a soft sigh of contentment that made him ache with
memories.

Relaxing, Ross had put his arms around her and allowed himself to pretend that the last dozen years were
a bad dream and that he and his wife were slumbering
peacefully in their own bed at Chapelgate. He had refused to go back to sleep, for her closeness was an unexpected gift and he intended to enjoy it for as long as
possible.

Through the lovely, drowsy night hours, he did his best
to suppress desire, though not with complete success. He
could not help wondering what would happen if he kissed
her . . . or caressed her breast . . . or touched her more
intimately. How would she respond, and how long would
it be before she awoke? But he had not tried to find out,
for he would be a fool to throw away what he had by
trying for more.

When Juliet did waken, she went rigid in his arms, and
her appalled reaction persuaded Ross that it would be
the better part of wisdom to pretend that he still slept.
Her gentle, almost affectionate kiss had nearly startled
him into betraying himself, but fortunately he had been
able to convince her that he was dead to the world. He
did not regret his dishonesty, for it would have been
vastly embarrassing for both of them to admit what had
happened, and the situation was difficult enough already.

Regrettably, there had been no recurrence of the episode; on each of the succeeding nights, Juliet had taken
care to sleep a little apart from the three men, and always
closest to Saleh. Ross wondered what, if anything, the
incident had meant. Perhaps she missed a lover left be-

hind in Serevan and had turned to Ross because he was a convenient warm male body, though he found the thought an unpalatable one. Or perhaps her behavior was just another sign that the bonds of marriage were not easily sundered. Strange how no amount of conscious will seemed capable of severing the subtle connections between them.

Or the not-so-subtle ones. Being so close to Juliet was keeping Ross in a constant, simmering state of sexual tension, even though they had not spoken privately since the night outside Sarakhs. He had thought that the fact that she was virtually invisible would make things easier, but no such luck; imagination easily overcame the barrier of her shapeless, enveloping clothing. In fact, there was something ragingly erotic about knowing precisely what was concealed under those dark robes. Whenever he looked at her, he had a vivid mental image of her slim, supple body, her glorious long legs, the fall of flaming hair over pale, silken skin. . . .

Sharply he turned away, for thinking along those lines would make him a mental and physical wreck in no time.

A few minutes later the caravan leader, Abdul Wahab, came trotting up to Ross. The kafila-bashi rode one of the tough, wiry little desert horses, and during the day he circulated steadily among his charges, checking to see that all was well and lending aid where necessary. As he approached Ross, he called out, "Salaam Aleikum, Khilburn."

Ross smiled and returned the greeting. "And peace be upon you. Will we make camp for the night soon?"

"Not for a while yet." The kafila-bashi frowned. "Wandering lost for most of a day was unfortunate, for now the water supply is dangerously low for many members of the caravan. I think it best to push on late tonight, for I will not be easy in my mind until we reach the well of Karagosh."

Ross gestured toward the northern horizon, where dark storm clouds were visible in the distance. "It might rain soon."

The other man contemplated the clouds, then shook his head. "It is raining there, but I think we will not be so lucky. Though perhaps God in his mercy will prove me wrong." Lifting a hand in farewell, he trotted off to check on the next knot of travelers.

Ross understood Abdul Wahab's concern, for the single most important duty of a caravan leader was assuring that there was enough water. However, Ross himself was not overworried; the water supply might be low, but the mild spring temperatures made the shortage less critical than it would have been during the summer. Even if they did not reach the well tonight, the situation was not yet grave.

Distant flashes of lightning and an occasional rumble of thunder came from the north, but as the kafila-bashi had predicted, the storm did not move in their direction. Since they would not stop for several hours more, Ross dug dried dates from the supply on his pack camel and gave a handful to each of his three companions. As he withdrew to a safe distance from Juliet, he noted how much better she had gotten at eating without removing her veil. Even another Targui would not suspect her identity now.

They were traveling through a region of low sandy hills that were home only to lizards and occasional scrubby tufts of grass. Once they passed an outcropping of rock, and a rude gerbil stuck its head out of its burrow and chattered at Ross. The scene was a peaceful one, with no hint of danger. The loudest sound was the faint tinkle of the bridle bells on the lead camel.

The hills became rougher, channeling the caravan into a more compact group as they followed a ravine that sloped downward. Eventually the track leveled out when it intersected one of the dry riverbeds called wadis. Ross saw that Abdul Wahab had stationed his horse on the far bank and that the kafila-bashi was frowning as he glanced first at the storm clouds in the distance, then at where the wadi curved out of sight a couple of hundred yards away. Turning to the caravan, Abdul Wahab raised his voice in an exhortation to hurry.

Ross's expression hardened as he guessed what the kafila-bashi was thinking: though no rain had fallen on the caravan, there was a chance that the wadi might flood with sudden lethal violence if the storm had dropped enough water farther up the river's course. It was typical

of the desert that one could go in an instant from being
endangered by the lack of water to being in danger from
too much.

Though the storm was distant enough that Ross
thought the chance of flooding remote, he tugged at Julietta's bridle to increase her speed. She gave him an
offended glance but began walking faster, the pack camel
an obedient echo behind her. With Ross's urging, it took
them only a few minutes to cross the wadi and clamber
up the steep embankment on the far side.

As a steady stream of men and beasts poured across
the sandy channel, Ross scanned the group to find his
companions. The camel carrying Saleh and Murad had
already made its way to higher ground. However, Juliet
was still in the middle of the wadi because her pack animal was having an attack of balkiness.

Both Abdul Wahab and Ross had thought flooding improbable, but in the next moments their judgment was
proved wrong. As Juliet struggled with the camels, a low
wave of silt-brown water came surging around the bend.
Within seconds a swift, ankle-deep current was slowing
the progress of everyone still in the wadi. From his horseback vantage point, the kafila-bashi shouted, "Hurry!
More water is coming!"

Realizing the danger, everyone who had already crossed
was lining up along the bank to watch the drama below.
Cold panic jolted through Ross when he saw Juliet's camels put their heads down to drink from the water swirling
around their hairy fetlocks. In another moment they
might lie down and start wallowing, as camels often did
in water holes.

He was on the verge of going to her assistance when
she got her beasts moving by ruthlessly lashing their
flanks with her whip. Even above the sounds of rushing
water and babbling voices, he could hear her cursing in
a colorful mixture of languages.

Bellowing angrily, the camels surrendered to her superior will and let themselves be chivied up the embankment to safety. By the time they escaped the wadi, the
water was knee-deep and rising rapidly. Another wave
flooded the channel to waist depth and pummeled the
handful of men and animals still in the wadi with floating

debris. A man on a donkey was nearly washed away, but was saved from disaster when his small mount was shoved against the solid bulk of a camel long enough to regain its feet.

One by one, men and beasts floundered through the churning water and were pulled up the embankment by other members of the caravan. Soon the only one left was an elderly Uzbek tea merchant who had fallen behind. Ross had once talked casually with Muhammad Kasem and had found him to be a combination of quiet dignity and elfin charm.

When the old man was almost within arm's length of safety, Ross exhaled the breath he had been holding. Then, just beyond the reach of helping hands, Muhammad Kasem's donkey stumbled and went down, pitching its rider into the water. At the same time, another wave came raging down the channel, moving almost as fast as a man could run and deepening the river to drowning depth.

The merchant's high-pitched wail of anguish was barely audible above the roar of the flood. His turban had been torn off and his shaved head looked horribly vulnerable among the dark waves. As he submerged beneath the roiling water, a shuddering collective sigh rose from the onlookers.

"Father!" The horrified cry came from a man poised on the edge of the wadi. From his desperate expression, Ross guessed that, like most desert dwellers, the man could not swim. Even so, perhaps he would have dived in if two other men had not grabbed him. No one else attempted to assist Muhammad Kasem, not even by looking for a rope to throw.

A merchant near Ross said sorrowfully, "It is God's will."

"So be it," another agreed. "Blessed be the name of God."

Ross realized that this was one of those moments when Eastern fatalism parted company with Western action. Even as the thought flashed through his mind, he was sprinting along the embankment, shoving past other members of the caravan. He preferred not to draw undue attention to himself, but it was impossible to stand by and watch someone drown if he might be able to prevent it.

The donkey had thrashed its way to dry land and was now shaking its coat and braying, but the current had swept the merchant into the middle of the flooded channel. Briefly Ross wondered if his turban was long enough to unwind and use as a lifeline, but he decided that the old man was too far out for the length of fabric to reach.

By running at top speed, Ross managed to outpace the current and get ahead of Muhammad Kasem. Then he stopped and hastily stripped off his knife and outer clothing and dropped them on the ground. He also yanked off his boots, for under flood conditions he did not want to wear anything that might weigh him down.

Then he dived into the river, his body cleaving the torrent with a force that carried him far out into the channel. The water was cold and viciously rough, but he had grown up swimming in the North Sea, and his powerful strokes rapidly took him to where he had last seen the merchant's bare head.

Since the old man had submerged again, Ross dived below the surface to find him. The water was salty and thick with silt, with visibility only a few inches, so he searched by touch, swimming along with the current. Twice he came up for air, then went under again, before his reaching fingers found fabric. Grabbing a fistful of material, he kicked upward.

For a moment after emerging into the air, Muhammad Kasem floated as still as death, his face blue-white and waxy. Then his eyes opened and he began coughing.

Ross's relief was short-lived, for the reinvigorated merchant began flailing about with the strength of panic. A knee struck Ross in the stomach, knocking his breath out. Before he could recover, the old man locked his arms around his rescuer's neck, dragging both of them under.

Lungs burning, Ross struggled to break Muhammad Kasem's strangling grip. As he swallowed the salty water, there was a moment when he thought that this was the end, that he would die here in Central Asia, right in front of Juliet's eyes.

That would be a rotten memory to leave her with. The

thought gave him a burst of energy that enabled him to free himself from the merchant's lethal grasp. As he fought his way to the surface again, he turned the old man around, immobilizing and supporting him with an arm across the chest.

Breaking through into the air was bliss to equal anything Ross had ever experienced in his life. For a few moments he was content to drift with the current while he reveled in the luxury of breathing. Then Muhammad Kasem began stirring, his limbs thrashing feebly.

"Relax, Uncle, and lie still," Ross murmured soothingly. "You are safe."

Though his breathing was ragged with fear, the old man obeyed, and Ross struck out for the embankment, towing Muhammad Kasem behind him. His eyes were blurred with silt, but dimly he saw a knot of men calling encouragement to them.

Progress was slow, since he had only one arm for swimming and the water was as turbulent as a mountain stream. Debris battered them, including a twisted tree trunk that pushed both men under again. It took most of Ross's remaining strength to fight free of the entangling branches, but he went doggedly on.

When he was near the shore, someone skidded down the steep side of the wadi, grabbed his arm, and hauled Ross and his burden the last few feet to the embankment. Even without the English words in his ear, he would have known who it was.

"You stupid bastard," Juliet snarled as she lifted Muhammad Kasem away, then boosted the old man's frail body over the edge of the wadi into waiting hands. "You could have drowned."

"But I didn't," Ross gasped, too exhausted to think of a clever retort.

"Damned hero," she muttered. Since Ross could barely move, Juliet wrapped an arm around his waist and dragged him onto dry land by main force.

He promptly doubled over on his knees and began retching up the silty water he had swallowed. Juliet's arms supported him throughout, and they were much gentler than her voice had been. When he finally straightened up, throat raw, she lifted her waterskin and held it to his mouth so he could rinse away the salty taste of the floodwater.

Still shaky, Ross managed to stand with Juliet's help. He was shivering from the cold water, and the chilly breeze cut right through his clinging, saturated tunic and trousers. Juliet, who was eyeing him with apparent exasperation, was equally wet, but luckily the loose mantle she wore over her robe disguised any contours that might have been suspiciously female.

Then he lifted his head to find that everyone in the caravan had gathered to watch the drama, and most were staring at him. Water darkened hair, but not enough; his blond head and white feet didn't leave much doubt about his foreignness. Among the murmuring voices in the crowd could be heard the repeated word "ferengi."

Next to him, Juliet tensed, her hand dropping from his arm to the hilt of her knife. She said nothing, but as she scanned the onlookers, a cold flash of gray eyes was visible through the narrow opening in her tagelmoust. Ross was reminded of a furious mother cat defending her kittens; she might call him a stupid bastard, but he did not doubt that she was prepared to fight anyone who attacked him.

Fortunately, heroics should not be necessary, for the crowd seemed more surprised and curious than hostile. The only threatening expression was on the face of a surly Uzbek camel driver called Habib, who frequently taunted other menial members of the caravan, including "Jalal." Juliet had always ignored his gibes, but the man was a troublemaker, exactly the sort who might try to foment the crowd against a foreigner.

The fact that Ross was exposed as a European did not automatically mean trouble; he and Alexander Burnes had not had any serious problems on their earlier journey through Turkestan. But that had been years ago and Central Asia had been quieter and less dangerous. It might take only one malicious ferengi-hating man to cause trouble.

Habib spat on the ground. "Not just a ferengi, but an infidel and a spy."

Confused voices rose around the camel driver, then cut off abruptly when Abdul Wahab pushed his way through the crowd. "The wind is cold," he said, handing Ross a length of coarse toweling. "Dry yourself before you take a chill." Then he turned and called out, "Since there is water, we shall camp here tonight."

The caravan leader's acceptance of the ferengi quelled any potential hostility, and the order to make camp caused most of the onlookers to turn away and start looking for suitable sites to build fires and tether their animals.

Ross was mopping water from his hair when Murad arrived, having stopped to collect his master's discarded garments. Gratefully Ross pulled the warm quilted coat over his soaking tunic and trousers. He was pulling on his boots when Muhammed Kasem approached, supported by his son.

"I am an old man and my life is worth very little, but still I am grateful to you for preserving it." The merchant's steps were a little unsteady, but his voice had a note of wry humor. "You demonstrated the courage and strength of a lion. In return, I almost drowned you."

His son, a handsome, authoritative man of about thirty, added, "Truly it was God's mercy that you were here, Khilburn." He bowed deeply. "For saving the life of my father, I, Hussayn, and all my kin are forever in your debt."

"There is no debt, for I did only what any man will do for another if it is within his power." Ross slid the sheathed knife into his sash. "By God's grace, I was raised by the sea and learned to swim as a child. To have that skill and not use it in your father's service would have been a sin."

"Your modesty becomes you, Khilburn," Hussayn said. "Nonetheless, you risked your life for my father, and I shall not forget." Then he turned and helped the older man away.

Ross glanced at Abdul Wahab. "I'm sorry. I did not wish to draw attention to myself, but I felt there was no choice. Do you think there will be trouble?"

The kafila-bashi shook his head. "Not when you risked your life to save one of the faithful. I will let it be known why you are traveling to Bokhara, which will gain you even more respect." He gazed thoughtfully after the departing merchant. "Besides performing a selfless act of courage, you have made a powerful friend. Though they dress humbly when traveling, the Kasems are one of the wealthiest families in Bokhara. Perhaps their influence will be useful to your quest." With an inclination of his head, Abdul Wahab took his leave and returned to his duties.

Saleh now joined the rest of the party, leading all five of their camels, which he had tethered in a line. Four of the beasts were straining toward the water, but Julietta, who was in the lead, was more interested in her master. On seeing Ross, she quickened her step until she reached him. Then she lowered her head and butted his chest, more like a horse than a camel.

An affectionate gesture from a beast the size of a camel is not easily ignored, and Ross was almost knocked from his feet. "Easy, there." He laughed as she began mouthing his wet tunic. Stroking her nose, he said, "I suspect that you just like the fact that I'm soaked."

From behind him came the muttered comment, "It's your own fault. Brainless females love a hero."

Ross grinned. When they had lived together, his wife had occasionally accused him of being overprotective, but she was a worse nag than he ever had been. It appeared that concern for the other's welfare was another one of the indissoluble threads of their marriage.

Saleh said, "Khilburn, you and Jalal are both wet and need food and warmth. If you two will take care of watering the camels and filling our waterskins, Murad and I will gather fuel and build a fire."

Agreeing to the suggestion, Ross and Juliet led the camels along the bank of the wadi until they found a shallow side pool where the beasts could drink safely, without risking a fall into the still-dangerous torrent. Fortunately the camels were not extremely thirsty or they would have been uncontrollable. Even so, they crowded each other like rowdy schoolboys as they waded into the water.

While Ross managed the camels, Juliet unloaded the nearly empty waterskins and began refilling them. The water was silty, but most of the grit would settle out.

Besides, in the desert, thirst rendered such shortcomings unimportant.

There was no one near enough to overhear if they kept their voices low, and Juliet took advantage of that fact to say, "That was an appalling risk you took, Ross. I'm a good swimmer, but I would never have dared such a flood."

"This is one of those cases where sheer size and strength count," he said mildly. "I would not have made the attempt if I thought it suicidal."

"Perhaps not, but to me it looked as if you misjudged the risk, and very nearly died as a result." Realizing that she was railing like a fishwife, Juliet clamped her mouth shut, but she still trembled from the sheer terror she had felt when Ross had disappeared under the surface for so long. She had wanted to scream to the heavens that he could not die, that there was still unsettled business between them. Part of the horror lay in knowing that unfinished business would not make a damned bit of difference to whether he lived or died.

Using all of his weight, Ross reined back a camel that showed signs of wanting to savage one of its fellows. "Would you have had me leave Muhammad Kasem to die?"

She hesitated a moment, then said reluctantly, "I suppose not, particularly since the outcome in this case was fortunate. But I would not have you throw your life away, either. Especially not for a stranger."

His brows arched upward in amusement. "It's foolish for you to worry about me dying in a flood when there is an excellent chance that I will die much more unpleasantly in Bokhara."

Exasperated at his levity, she said, "I would rather you didn't die in either place."

"Look at the silver lining. If that happens, at least you'll be a free woman again."

"I'm already a free woman," she snapped. "I don't need your death to prove it. When I saw him drag you under the water . . ." She bit her lip, grateful that the veil hid her expression.

"I'm sorry—I suspect that that was harder to watch

than to experience. And worse lies ahead." His face sobered. "I wish to God that you had stayed at Serevan."

He was quite right; the risks would be greater in Bokhara, and Juliet would have to be more in control of herself than she was now. Strange; over the years her life had been in danger more than once, and she had always reacted with a calm that awed her men. She took a long, slow breath before saying, "You couldn't have stopped me from coming."

"I know. That's the only reason you're here." He lifted one of the heavy filled waterskins and heaved it onto a pack camel. "I want you to promise me something, Juliet."

She had been about to secure the waterskin, but she stopped and regarded Ross warily. He stood only a foot away, and his closeness sparked a swift, unnerving memory of how he had looked when he emerged from the flood, his wet tunic and trousers outlining every muscle in his hard body. She swallowed hard, trying to dismiss the distracting image. "Promise what?"

As he loaded another waterskin, he said with resignation, "I should have known you wouldn't agree to anything without first finding out what it is."

"Of course not. Knowing what you're signing is the first law of contracts." She began tying the waterskins in place.

"I'm not talking about a contract." He reached out and covered her hand, stilling her fingers on the packsaddle rope. "Juliet, look at me."

She did so reluctantly. Most of her face might be covered, but he could see her eyes, and she feared that they might show too much.

Deadly serious, he said, "If things go badly, I will never leave Bokhara alive, but as a Muslim servant there is a good chance that you will be able to escape my fate. Promise me that you will do what you must to survive. If it will save your life, I want you to abandon me, even denounce me to the amir's men if necessary. And for God's sake, don't try any wild, hopeless schemes in a vain attempt to rescue me. I don't want you to die because of stubbornness or bravado or guilt."

When she said nothing, his hand tightened on hers. "Promise me, Juliet. Please."

Hating the conversation, incapable of matching his ruthless practicality, she said, "Isn't it my life to lose as I choose?"

"Perhaps, but that isn't the point." He sighed and released her hand. "Will it make a difference if I say that I would die a little happier if I knew that you were safe?"

The lump in her throat was so large that she feared it would suffocate her, as the floodwaters had almost drowned Ross. "It makes a difference," she said brusquely. "Very well. I promise that if they condemn you and overlook me, I will accept the situation quietly and not do anything foolish."

His long tanned fingers touched the back of her hand very lightly. "Thank you."

Silently she turned and secured the waterskins. She had made the promise—but she was not sure that she would be able to keep it, any more than Ross had been able to restrain himself from daring the flood. It would be easier to risk her own life in a doomed attempt to help than it would be to stand by and do nothing when someone she cared for was in danger.

Say it, Juliet, admit it, if only to yourself. No matter what the dangers, it will be impossible to stand by and not try to prevent the death of the man you love.

10

During the flash flood, Juliet had had to endure watching her husband risk his life. Ross's turn to stand helplessly by and see Juliet's life in jeopardy came a week later.

The caravan was a day's travel from Merv, the largest town between Sarakhs and Bokhara. They had settled for the night by a small well of scant, bitter water, and the travelers were pitching tents and building fires when a band of Turkomans galloped into the camp.

Everyone stopped what he was doing and stared as the riders went by. Compared to the merchants, the Turkomans were wolf-lean and dangerous.

Murad was making desert bread, which was a flour-and-water dough placed in a sand hole, then covered with more sand and hot coals for cooking. Sitting back on his heels, he said uneasily, "Surely bandits would not ride openly into our camp."

"No," Saleh agreed. "Probably they are in the service of Khiva or Bokhara and are here to tax the caravan. A form of robbery, perhaps, but a mild one."

Being the most innocuous-looking of the party, Saleh went to the center of the camp to learn what was happening. After a half-hour or so he returned and reported his findings. "The leader is called Khosrow Khan and he is a yuz-bashi, the 'commander of a hundred.' He is an officer of the Amir of Khiva and is here to levy a tax of one in forty." Squatting on his heels, Saleh accepted a cup of tea from Murad. "Each group must make a list of goods. The yuz-bashi will visit each fire to check the records and collect the tax."

126

Ross nodded, unsurprised. "I imagine that some of the merchants are disappointed. With fighting going on between the khanates, the caravan might have been lucky enough to avoid Khivan taxation altogether."

Saleh smiled. "Aye, there is some disappointment. There will be another tax collected in Charjui, when we enter the kingdom of Bokhara, and still another will have to be paid at the customhouse of the city itself. Still, paying the taxes protects the caravan from most of the plunderers." He sipped the tea, his face becoming troubled. "Abdul Wahab told me that this Khosrow Khan is known to hate ferengis. It will be best if you do not attract his attention, Khilburn."

"I'll be unobtrusive," Ross promised.

During the next hour Abdul Wahab escorted the yuz-bashi and his men around the camp. The travelers carried on with the usual camp routines, though all were aware of the movements of the Khivans. Juliet and Ross tended the camels while Murad made an onion gravy to go with the bread and Saleh wrote out an inventory of their goods.

Though the Turkomans were not opening baggage, their threatening appearance encouraged rigorous honesty. Palpable tension gripped the camp. No one wanted to anger the yuz-bashi for fear that he would forget that he was a Khivan official and revert to the behavior of his wild Turkoman cousins, who would take not one part in forty, but everything.

Juliet kept a watchful eye on her husband, who seemed unconcerned by the presence of the Turkomans. If there was a book of instruction on how to achieve British coolness, he must have written it. No, not British coolness—English. As a Scot, she was also British, and not cool at all.

When the bread was done, Murad dug the flat loaf from the cookhole and knocked chunks of sand from the crust, then called the others to dine. Served hot with the onion gravy, the bread was delicious, although not the easiest food to eat when veiled.

They were just finishing the meal when Juliet glanced up and saw that Habib, the hostile camel driver, was taking one of the Khivans aside for a private word. Visibly surprised, the Turkoman glanced in their direction, then hastened forward and spoke to his officer. Juliet frowned, but before she could warn the others of what she had seen, the yuz-bashi and his entourage turned and came directly to their campfire.

The yuz-bashi was a squat, powerfully built man with the slitted eyes common among Turkomans. After scanning the members of the party, he said brusquely, "Give me your list of goods."

Silently Saleh complied. As the yuz-bashi studied it, Juliet saw Habib standing a short distance away, a gloating expression on his face. A number of other travelers were also gathering, as if expecting some kind of drama, but most looked concerned rather than eager.

The yuz-bashi glanced at Juliet and, apart from showing mild interest in her tagelmoust, obviously dismissed her as a poor servant of no interest. Sure that she would not be missed, she rose and drifted into the crowd, circling until she located Hussayn, the son of Muhammad Kasem.

In terse, heavily accented Persian she explained that she thought Habib was trying to make trouble for Khilburn, and perhaps Jalal and Hussayn should watch to see that no injustice was done. Eyes watchful, Hussayn followed Juliet, and together they took a position a little behind Habib.

While they were gone, the yuz-bashi had collected the tax from Saleh. Ross was still sitting quietly by the fire, sipping tea and looking composed, as if he had no reason to be concerned.

However, instead of moving on to the next campfire, the yuz-bashi walked over to Ross and stared down at him, suspicion in his narrow eyes. "They say you are a European. Is this so?"

Unhurriedly Ross looked up at the Khivan officer. Only someone who knew him as well as Juliet would recognize the rigorously concealed tension behind his mild expression.

Ross opened his mouth to reply, but before he could, Abdul Wahab said, "Khilburn is an Armenian and a *mirza*, a scribe."

Muhammad Kasem chimed in from where he stood

with the onlookers, "Aye, Khilburn is an Armenian. A Christian, of course, but a God-fearing man. Anyone who says otherwise is a lying mischief maker."

The yuz-bashi gave Ross an intimidating scowl. "Is it true you are Armenian?"

In a voice of limpid sincerity Ross said, "It is."

"Do you worship the one God?"

"Aye, in the ancient manner of my people."

"What say your people about the Prophet and his teachings?"

"We honor the Prophet, on whom be peace, for the law he gave the faithful is at its heart the same as the laws our prophet, Jesus, gave to us," Ross said, his voice steady. "And truly, it could be no other way, for God's laws are eternal and universal."

Apparently satisfied, the yuz-bashi nodded. "The tax on Christians is one in twenty, not one in forty, so you must double your payment. How much gold do you carry?"

"I have twenty gold tillahs. One moment and I shall give you the tax." Ross produced a small purse from inside his coat and handed over a coin. Juliet knew that he had more money concealed in his baggage, but the yuz-bashi accepted the payment without question, probably because of Ross's modest attire.

Glancing around the loose group of onlookers, the yuz-bashi said, "Who claimed this man was a ferengi? Anyone who wishes to bear witness against him should come forth and speak now."

Juliet held her breath as she scanned the faces of the other members of the caravan. Young and old, Uzbek and Kurd, Persian and Afghan—all regarded the yuz-bashi in silence, though every one of them knew Ross was European. With his nationality common knowledge, Ross had been more outgoing during the last week and had made many friends among his fellow travelers. No one wanted to betray him—except Habib, who smiled with vicious satisfaction and opened his mouth to speak.

Juliet darted forward to stop him, but Hussayn was closer and got there first. There was the brief flash of a knife, then the Uzbek merchant drove the tip of the blade through fabric to rest against the camel driver's spine. "The honorable Khilburn is Armenian," Hussayn murmured. "Do you not remember, dog's turd?"

Habib stopped dead in his tracks, a sheen of sweat appearing on his face. "Why do you lie for an unbeliever?" he hissed.

"Why do you persecute a man who has done you no wrong?" Hussayn countered. "Does not the Prophet counsel tolerance, especially to people of the book?"

Habib spat on the ground but dared not say more.

After another minute passed in silence, the yuz-bashi decided that the charge that Khilburn was a ferengi must have been no more than idle malice, so he continued to the next campfire. When the Turkomans were out of earshot, Hussayn sheathed his knife. "Come, Habib, and join me at our fire. I will not share bread and salt with one such as you, but I wish to keep you in sight until the Khivans are gone."

His expression furious, Habib obeyed, but before walking away, he gave Juliet a malevolent glance, rightly blaming her for Hussayn's intervention. She guessed that he would not dare retaliate against Hussayn, who was rich and powerful, but that he might well try to take out his fury on her later.

Shrugging, she returned to her fire. If he did, so be it.

Retribution arrived later that evening, when half the caravan had already retired for the night. The well they were camped around was feeble and had been rapidly depleted when they arrived. Since the past few hours had given the well time to replenish itself, Juliet went to draw water for use the next day.

She had just filled her waterskin when she heard a stealthy footstep behind her. Alert for trouble, she whirled around to find Habib half a dozen feet away.

In the darkness she could not see his expression, but there was no mistaking the malice in his voice when he spoke. "You take more than your share of water, Jalal. Is it because the Tuareg are thieves, or did you learn to rob the faithful from your ferengi master?"

"Thy tongue wags like an ass's tail," Juliet said in husky, crude Persian.

"At least I do not defile myself by serving a swine of a ferengi," Habib jeered, moving closer to her.

"My master may be an unbeliever," she said contemptuously, "but unlike you, he is an honorable man." Lifting the waterskin, she started to walk around the camel driver.

Habib stepped into her path. "Khilburn is a ferengi swine, and serving him makes you a flea on a swine's arse."

Juliet stopped and regarded him steadily while she weighed the situation. She was neither helpless nor terrified, but she would certainly rather avoid a fight with a dangerous lout who loved brawling and hated anyone who was different. Unfortunately, it appeared that avoidance might not be possible.

Provoked by her silence, the camel driver snarled, "What's the matter, little boy, frightened of me? Maybe you should call your ferengi to protect you." He spat on the ground. "You are gutless sons of plague dogs, both of you."

With a mental sigh, Juliet resigned herself to the inevitable, for if she did not deal with Habib now, she would undoubtedly have to do so later. And while he might outweigh her by forty pounds, he was stupid. "The Tuareg are warriors," she said with cool deliberation. "We do not soil our hands with talebearing camel drivers who smell of dung."

Her words were all the trigger Habib needed. With a roar, he launched himself at her. And as his hand swept through the darkness, a shaft of moonlight slid along the blade of his descending dagger.

Ross was preparing to roll up in his blanket, though he would not actually do so until Juliet returned from the well. As unobtrusively as possible, he kept a protective eye on her, and he suspected that she did the same for him. It was rather amusing; they were like a couple of maiden aunts with each other.

He was about to remove his boots when he heard a shout from the direction of the well. "Khilburn, come quickly!"

He froze. Was that Juliet's voice? No, it sounded like

Murad. Yet, for no rational reason, he was absolutely certain that Juliet was in danger. He leapt to his feet and pulled a burning brand from the fire to use as a torch.

Saleh had been drowsing in his blanket, but he snapped to wakefulness as other voices were raised. "Trouble, Khilburn?"

"Perhaps," Ross said tersely. "I'll find out."

Moving as quickly as possible over the broken ground, he made his way to the well, which was attracting a growing crowd of men, several holding crude torches like his own. He could not see what they were staring at, but he easily recognized the ugly, unmistakable sound of metal shrieking against metal. Knives.

His blood like ice, Ross pushed his way through the bystanders to find a torch-illuminated killing ground. Wind-tossed flames threw wild, erratic shadows across the clearing as two crouching figures circled each other, daggers ready in their hands. It was an eerie echo of the scene that had taken place earlier with the Khivan officer, but darker and more violent.

It was also Ross's worst fear come true. No, not the worst, for Juliet seemed unhurt. But even as Ross watched, Habib stabbed his long knife up toward her heart. With a movement quicker than the eye could follow, Juliet blocked his attack with her own blade, then disengaged, the tip of her dagger nicking the camel driver's wrist.

For a moment Ross was paralyzed with fear and horror so profound that his vision darkened around the edges, eliminating everything but the image of Juliet and the danger that threatened her. Instinctively he started to step forward with the intention of throwing himself between the combatants. Then a firm hand grasped his forearm, halting him in his tracks. Eyes dazed, he looked down to find Saleh beside him.

The old man said softly, "No, Khilburn. Interference will increase her danger."

Ross very nearly wrenched away, but he had just enough sense left to realize that Saleh was right: if he disturbed Juliet's concentration, he might sign her death warrant. But standing helplessly by was the most excruciating experience of his life.

Juliet was much faster than Habib, and deftly fended off all the camel driver's attacks while she waited with slit-eyed ferocity for the right opening. She had thrown off her mantle and in her dark robe and tagelmoust she was a shadow warrior, eerie, silent, and lethal. Habib was not silent, but snarled a string of insults and filthy oaths as he darted and slashed, his eyes shining with blood lust.

Watching her controlled, graceful movements reminded Ross of a fact he had almost forgotten: as a girl, Juliet had learned fencing with her brothers. When she discovered that Ross was also skilled at swordplay, she had suggested that they might fence with each other, but he had flatly refused; he could not imagine brandishing a weapon at his wife even in sport.

But she was good, damned good, at the related skill of knife fighting. Taller than Habib, she had a better reach and was consistently able to ward off his attacks. In some strange way, Ross felt as if he were linked into her awareness, sharing her fierce focus, anticipating her enemy's moves as she glided wary and light-footed over the broken ground.

Time and again Juliet could have killed Habib, for his wild lunges left him critically exposed, but she waited for an opening where she could cripple him without taking his life. But where, Ross wondered helplessly, would it end? This was no wrestling match; in a knife fight with a killer, any error could be lethal.

He glanced around the growing circle of onlookers, hoping to see Abdul Wahab, the only man with the authority to stop the fight, but the kafila-bashi had not yet appeared.

There was an ear-piercing shriek of metal against metal, followed by a collective gasp from the watchers. Ross snapped his gaze back to the fight. The long blades of the combatants were locked together hilt to hilt, a position in which Habib's superior strength gave him the advantage.

As vividly as if he were inside Juliet's skin, Ross felt her muscles strain as she tried to hold the camel driver's dagger away from her, but inexorably the joined blades were being driven back toward her throat. She could not even kick out at him without risking a disastrous loss of balance.

When Juliet's strength was forced to the very limit, the camel driver twisted his dagger with so much pressure that she had to drop her own weapon to save her wrist from being broken. As it tumbled, glittering in the torchlight, Habib gave a shout of triumph and lunged forward to administer a killing stroke.

Once more, only Saleh's iron grip kept Ross on the sidelines; the next day, he would find faint bruising where the older man's fingers had dug into his arm. But even if Saleh had allowed Ross to interfere, he could not have done any good. It was up to Juliet to save herself.

She reacted to being disarmed with a cat-swift retreat from Habib's attack. Since it was impossible to retrieve her knife with the camel driver standing over it, she bent and grabbed the full waterskin behind her. With one smooth motion she opened it and tossed it at him, growling, "Cleanse thyself, swine."

The onlookers roared with derisive laughter as Habib howled with rage and fell back, dragging his sleeve over his eyes to dry them. By the time his vision was clear again, his opponent had retrieved the fallen knife.

Furious at being an object of mockery, Habib lunged at Juliet like a maddened bull. She parried his knife thrust easily, but this time his strategy was different. Barreling into her like a battering ram, he knocked her to the ground, Habib landing on top.

Ross's nails stabbed his palms from the force of his clenching fists. In close combat, Habib's strength would overpower Juliet. Also, though at the moment it seemed of minor importance, he might yank off her veil or feel enough of her body to realize she was female. God only knew what would happen then, but Ross doubted that Habib would be overcome by sudden chivalry.

For a moment Juliet lay still, stunned by the force of her fall. Then she began struggling furiously to break free of her opponent. The combatants rolled across the ground in a cloud of dust as Habib tried to thrust his dagger past her guard. When he finally stabbed, she managed to deflect the blade from striking a vital area, but it slashed deeply into her upper arm. Juliet gave a sharp, quickly choked-off cry of pain that pierced Ross like another knife.

Then Habib made a mistake, though an understandable one. He lifted his weight a little above his opponent to get extra power, then smashed his knee between her legs in a blow that would have paralyzed a man.

The onlookers moaned with horrified sympathy, but Juliet was not incapacitated as much a man would have been. Taking advantage of Habib's momentary imbalance, she managed to hurl his body off hers. He landed sprawling on his back two feet away.

Making what all the watchers assumed was a superhuman recovery, Juliet leapt to her feet. Then, in a flurry of perfectly judged motions, she ended the fight. First she kicked Habib, her booted foot knocking aside his knife before smashing into the same ultravulnerable spot he had attacked on her. He screamed and doubled convulsively around his genitals.

With her opponent beyond all thought of self-defense, it was simple for Juliet to lean over and hamstring his right leg with one precise cold-blooded slash. Suddenly it was over, leaving Habib in no condition to pick another fight any time soon.

Juliet stood over the moaning figure of the man she had defeated, her dagger still ready in her hand as she breathed in great wrenching gasps. So intensely was Ross absorbed in her struggle that he felt every rasping breath as if it were his own, just as he shared the fierce exultation of her triumph.

Then Abdul Wahab appeared, finally drawn by the sounds of fighting. "What is going on here?" he barked, his gaze going from one of the combatants to the other. "Who started this?"

Since neither Juliet nor Habib seemed disposed to explain, Murad spoke up. "Sir, I was returning from visiting a friend at another fire and happened to be near the well when the fight began." He made an insulting gesture at Habib. "This son of a scorpion taunted Jalal. Ignoring him, Jalal tried to return peacefully to our fire, so Habib attacked without warning."

"Is this so, Jalal?"

"Aye." In her exhaustion, Juliet spoke in her normal

voice, several tones higher than the one she used as Jalal. Ross was surprised that no one noticed that it was a female voice, until he realized that her demonstration of fighting skill had made it literally unthinkable that she could be a woman.

A Kurdish merchant spoke up. "When they fought, Habib was trying to kill. The Targui showed great mercy in sparing him." A murmur of other voices confirmed the statement.

The kafila-bashi stared down at the camel driver. "You have gotten what you deserved," he said coldly. "You will be left in Merv, for I will have no troublemakers in my caravan." Judgment given, Abdul Wahab turned on his heel and stalked away.

Most of the onlookers began to drift back to their own campsites, voices buzzing in excitement as they discussed the fight. There was no question that Jalal had been the popular favorite. Even the two fellow camel drivers who lifted Habib to carry him back to their own fire did so with visible distaste.

Ross wanted to walk over to Juliet and wrap himself around her until his heart slowed its chaotic beat, but he did not. He doubted that she would find such behavior acceptable even if half the camp was not watching. Instead, he followed Saleh through the group that surrounded her. "You can congratulate Jalal tomorrow," Saleh said, his voice cutting through the babble of voices. "Now his wounds must be tended to."

By the light of his torch, Ross saw that blood was pouring from the slash in her upper left arm, soaking the sleeve of her robe, and dripping from her fingers onto the sand. Wordlessly he handed the torch to Saleh, then yanked off his turban and wrapped the length of fabric around her arm, using it as both tourniquet and bandage. Juliet was shaking and her skin had a clammy chill, and he guessed that she was suffering from shock.

Murad joined them, saying enthusiastically, "You were splendid, Jalal! As quick as a serpent, as deadly as a lion. Could you teach me how to use a knife like that?"

Before Juliet could reply, Ross said, "That's a question for another day, Murad. Will you fetch some water for us? I don't think Jalal is up to the task just now."

Reminded of practical reality, Murad went to retrieve the empty waterskin. Since Saleh did not suffer from all of the complicated constraints that bound Ross, he took Juliet's uninjured arm to steady her during the walk back to their fire.

As soon as they arrived there, Ross laid his sleeping rug by the fire so Juliet could sit near its warmth. Then he tossed on more fuel to brighten the flames. When she had settled down on crossed legs, Saleh knelt beside her and unwrapped the temporary bandage so he could assess the wound. Juliet drew her breath in sharply as he examined her, though he worked as gently as possible. The gash was about six inches long and ran diagonally along the outside of her upper arm. Even with the rough tourniquet placed higher up, it still bled.

When Saleh was done with his examination, he said in a troubled voice, "I think it should be cauterized."

Ross swore under his breath and glanced at Juliet. For a second their gazes met. Then she turned her head away. He knew that she understood what was being proposed and had accepted the necessity, but Ross could not bring himself to do the same. He said to Saleh, "Surely cauterization is not necessary."

"I would not recommend it if I did not think it needful. Habib was a filthy swine and his knife was likely tainted. There is a grave risk the wound will fester if it is not burned clean."

Before Ross could say any more, Juliet said, "If you think cauterization best, so be it." Her strained voice seemed on the edge of breaking. "Khilburn can do it."

Ross felt as if a cold hand had clenched around his heart. Was the damned woman deliberately trying to drive him crazy? He had performed cauterizations in the past and had also once endured the procedure himself; the thought of inflicting such pain on Juliet was unbearable. Good Lord, he had found it impossible to fence with his wife even if both carried blunted foils and wore protective padding.

He opened his mouth to say that Saleh should do the procedure, but the sight of Juliet made him hold his tongue. She sat cross-legged and immobile, her neck bent and her gaze on the rug beneath her. As usual, her expression was hidden by her veil.

Yet even though she was not looking at him, he knew, with the same uncanny sense of connection he had felt earlier, that under her stoic exterior she was shaken and in pain. Her request that he do the cauterization was not inspired by a desire to torment him, but was an oddly touching act of trust. He doubted if she realized that consciously, or she would not have asked. But since she had, he could not deny her.

"Very well," he said brusquely. "I'll use my dagger."

It seemed an appropriate choice, for it was the beautifully made weapon Juliet had given him at Serevan. The charcoal bed was the hottest part of the fire, so he laid the long steel blade across the glowing coals, back edge down. Taking a piece of heavy paper from his luggage, he rolled it into a tube, then blew on the coals to raise the temperature still further. The principle was the same as a blacksmith's bellows. However, he was not going to be shoeing a horse but branding his wife.

For the next few minutes no one spoke. Murad had brought water, and he quietly put some on to boil for tea. Saleh used more to clean Juliet's arm and rinse blood from her robe.

Finally the blade was as hot as it would get, and Ross could delay no longer. He wished they were in a Christian country so there was brandy to fortify Juliet for the coming ordeal. He could have used some brandy himself, for the thought of what he must do made his heart pound and his palms damp.

Juliet lay down on her right side, her body partially curled as she braced herself for the burning. Saleh placed his hands on her shoulder and waist to immobilize her in case she involuntarily tried to pull away.

Ross knelt beside her, careful not to let his shadow fall across her arm. Her bare skin was pale in the firelight, except for the scarlet gash of the knife wound. Face grim, he lifted the dagger from the coals. He had wrapped cloth around the handle to protect his hand, and even so the heat was uncomfortable.

He wavered a moment as he raised the blade in front of him. It glowed with ugly, sullen heat. At the thought of laying the metal against Juliet's raw, bleeding flesh, his muscles locked, refusing to do his bidding.

"Khilburn!" Saleh said sharply.

The man's voice pierced Ross's numbness. Delay was only making matters worse, so Ross grasped her elbow in his left hand to steady her arm, then swiftly laid the broad back edge of the blade along the entire length of the open wound.

As the red-hot steel seared her, Juliet jerked violently against the restraining grips of the two men. Her left hand had been lying by Ross's leg and her fingers spasmodically clutched his knee, the nails biting deeply.

The three seconds that Ross held the hot iron in place seemed eternal. To keep herself silent, Juliet had taken a fold of the tagelmoust between her teeth, but as the stench of burning flesh smoldered through the night air, she gave a suffocated cry that tore at Ross's heart.

With a shuddering sigh of relief he finally lifted the cooling blade away from her arm, but his relief was tempered by the bitter knowledge that for Juliet the pain was far from over. Wrapped in stoic, anguished silence, she seemed unaware that she still gripped his knee.

Saleh passed over a small jar of ointment. "This will take some of the pain away."

Hoping Saleh was right, Ross used his fintertips to gently spread the salve along the angry wound. He put a light bandage on for protection, but the bleeding had stopped. God willing, there would be no infection, though she would carry a scar for the rest of her life.

Murad, who had been watching sympathetically, helped Juliet sit up, then pressed a cup of heavily sugared tea into her hand. At first she simply stared down at it, as if drinking without removing her veil was too much effort. But after taking a deep breath, she managed to empty the cup in two long swallows.

Noticing how white her arm looked through the slashed sleeve, Ross decided that the tear should be repaired tonight. He always traveled with a basic sewing kit, so he dug it out, then closed up the torn fabric with crude but adequate stitches. Juliet sat cross-legged and uncommunicative throughout the procedure. Her mute suffering reminded him of an injured animal.

Saleh suggested, "Jalal, take some opium so you will sleep."

"No," she said brusquely. "I need only rest." She rose rather shakily to her feet, then crossed to her sleeping rug, which she had laid out earlier in the evening. Taking that as a signal that it was bedtime, Murad and Saleh went to their own rugs and settled themselves for the night.

Ross decided that this was one time that discretion could be damned, so after banking the fire he rolled out his own rug beside Juliet's. Since he doubted that he would be able to sleep, it should be safe to be near her, and he had a powerful, irrational need to stay as close as possible.

Juliet did not object to his presence. In fact, she had said scarcely a dozen words since the fight.

Most of the rest of the camp was already sleeping, and soon Saleh and Murad were also breathing with slow, deep regularity. Ross lay on his back and watched the night sky, acutely aware of Juliet's nearness. She was also lying on her back, since that position was the most comfortable for her injured arm.

After a half-hour or so had passed, he guessed that he and Juliet might be the only two people in the caravan who were not sleeping. Tuned to every one of her tense breaths and slight, restless movements, he knew that she was awake and in pain. In a voice so soft it could not have been heard more than a yard away, he said, "Clever of you to get into a fight with Habib. If you wanted revenge for what I put you through by diving into the flooded wadi, you've got it."

She responded with a breathy, scarcely audible chuckle. "I guess that makes it all worthwhile." More seriously she added, "I'm sorry I asked you to do the cauterization. I don't know what I was thinking of, but I don't imagine that you much enjoyed doing it."

"About as much as you enjoyed having it done," he said dryly. "But someone had to."

After another few minutes had gone by in silence, Juliet whispered, "You sew rather well, for a marquess."

Ross smiled into the darkness. "You fight rather well, for a marchioness."

She sighed. "None of my talents are the least bit ladylike."

Her words dissolved the control that Ross had been exercising for the last two hours, and he could no longer restrain himself from touching her. She was only eighteen inches away, so he reached out and took her restless hand in his.

Her cool fingers moved and he thought she was pulling away. Instead, she turned her hand palm upward and twined her fingers through his in a gesture that expressed the night's strain and pain more eloquently than words.

It was one of those odd moments between them when the past seemed more alive than the present, and Ross felt his tension begin to ease as her hand warmed under his.

In fact, to his drowsy surprise, it was even possible for both of them to sleep.

11

❦

Using a couple of rugs to make a comfortable nest in the sand, Juliet lounged back with her head supported by a saddlebag and watched Murad prepare their dinner.

It had been a lazy day. In order to rest for the last and most grueling leg of the journey, Abdul Wahab had decreed that the caravan would stay three nights at the oasis of Merv. Their group was too large for the small caravansary, so many of the travelers had to make camp outside under the palm trees. That was fine with Juliet; she preferred sleeping outdoors rather than in the crowded confines of a caravansary cell.

Even in the shade, the afternoon was very warm and she found herself yawning. One advantage of a tagelmoust was that it was not necessary to cover a yawn with a hand, so she didn't. If she got any lazier, she would turn into a rock.

Glancing across the campground, she saw Ross and Saleh approaching, carrying supplies they had bought in the town bazaar. She had been excused from that duty because of her arm, though it felt much better today than it had the day before. In a few days she would scarcely notice it.

After their purchases had been stored away, both men sat down on the opposite side of the fire, making idle conversation about the town. Ross's previous journey across the Kara Kum had not included Merv, so the community was new to him.

Juliet paid no real attention to their words, for it was more enjoyable simply to watch her husband. That was another virtue of the tagelmoust: if she was careful, no one could tell where she was looking. She took full advantage of that fact when she was around Ross. Since a blond beard would be conspicuous, he was clean-shaven and his handsome face, sun-browned skin, and Asiatic dress made him the very image of a dashing desert explorer. Rather sourly Juliet reflected that he must be a sensation in London drawing rooms when he was between journeys.

As she did with great regularity, Juliet found herself pondering the oddities of their relationship. For example, there was the way she and Ross had held hands after the knife fight. They had both slept soundly until wakened by the dawn call to prayers; then they had wordlessly disengaged their interlocked fingers. In the day and a half since, neither of them had made a single reference to the fact that they had spent the night handfast, as if silence meant that it hadn't happened. Not that Juliet was complaining, for she had been grateful for his gesture, but the incident had definitely been odd.

She gave herself credit for the fact that this time she had not ended up wrapped around him like ivy. She would have liked to think that was because she was becoming immune to his attractions, but knew that was not true. More likely, her injured arm had hurt so much that even her sleeping self had known better than to disturb it.

Juliet yawned again, wondering when dinner would be ready. For the first time since Sarakhs, they were having fresh meat, though the piece of lamb was a small one, in keeping with the humble way they were traveling. Murad was stewing the lamb with rice and vegetables, and it smelled delicious, but would not be ready for a while yet. That being the case, Juliet decided she might as well behave like a proper camel driver, so she pulled the end of her veil over her eyes and went to sleep.

Ross regarded his dozing wife with amusement. Her absolute lack of female fussiness had always been one of her most appealing traits, and she made such a convincing camel driver that even he had trouble remembering that she was a marchioness.

Saleh interrupted his thoughts by saying, "This morning I spoke with the kafila-bashi about Habib."

Ross turned toward his companion. "And?"

"Abdul Wahab said that when he dismissed Habib from the caravan last night, he gave the man a stern warning not to make more trouble for you and Jalal. Apparently Habib seemed very cowed when he left."

"I doubt that will last," Ross said dryly. "Still, we'll be here only another day. With luck, he'll be too busy recovering from his leg injury to do much harm before we leave."

Murad had brewed a pot of predinner tea, and the three men sipped in thoughtful silence. In spite of what Ross had just said to Saleh, he was not happy about the prospect of spending another day in Merv. Habib might be on crutches, but all he needed to cause trouble was his malicious tongue, and that was still in full working order.

Someone cleared his throat softly, and Ross looked up to see a small shabby Turkoman with a straggly beard. The fellow had been drifting around the campground, stopping here and there to exchange a few words, and had now reached their fire. He appeared to be a holy man, though his dress did not look like that of any of the orders of dervishes that Ross recognized.

The Turkoman bowed. "Salaam Aleikum."

"And peace be upon you," the three men murmured.

"I have heard that you are a ferengi, come all the way from England to learn your brother's fate in Bokhara," the man said, speaking directly to Ross. "My name is Abd. Never have I had the chance to speak to a man of your people. Will you tell me of the wonders of your great land?"

Ross's eyes narrowed. Apparently Habib had been talking about him; as a result, it appeared that Ross was going to be put to another theological test. Well, he had always done well with those, and this particular dervish seemed innocuous enough. "I am called Khilburn. You are welcome at our fire. I will be honored to speak with you of my country, and beg that you will in turn tell me more of your own people."

As Ross introduced his companions and Murad poured

more tea, the Turkoman knelt with the air of a man settling down for a lengthy discussion. "You are a Christian, my lord?" When Ross nodded, Abd said, "Tell me of your beliefs so that I may better know how our religions differ."

Thinking that that could be dangerous, Ross said, "I would prefer to discuss how our religions resemble each other."

The dervish's face lit up. "Truly thou art a man of wisdom. In your view, what are the similarities?"

"The desert is the home of three great religions—Judaism, Christianity, and Islam," Ross replied. "In these bleak and beautiful lands, there is little to stand between a man and the awareness of God's power. I think that is why the people of the book all believe so strongly in the One God."

Abd tilted his head to one side like a curious bird. "Being ignorant of the world that lies beyond the desert, I do not fully understand your meaning."

"In Britain, where I grew up, the land is moist and rich and teems with life. Everywhere there are trees and plants and animals. Perhaps that is why the ancient British people believed in many gods—surrounded by such overwhelming evidence of God's works, they saw a godling in every brook and every tree rather than the master hand behind it all," Ross said, warming to his theory. "It took the fierce anvil of the desert to forge a clear understanding of the One God."

"Ahh, what a new and intriguing thought you have given me," the dervish said, briefly closing his eyes with delight. "In the simplicity of the desert, one can truly be alone with God, as my nomad ancestors discovered. And the understanding born of that simplicity has been carried across the world."

"So it has, and that is what your faith and mine have in common. All the people of the book still carry the pure vision of the desert god in their hearts," Ross said. "Like most Englishmen, I feel a greater kinship with the sons of the Prophet than with Hindus, who have many gods, or Buddhists, whose God seems abstract and remote."

"That is good," Abd said, nodding thoughtfully. "Do you think the Hindus and Buddhists worship false gods?"

Ross shook his head. "I would not say that, for I do not know enough of their beliefs to judge them wisely, and I have known Hindus and Buddhists who were truly devout men. Perhaps in their different ways they also worship the One God. But the God of the Prophet I can understand immediately, with no need of interpretation, for he is also the god of my fathers."

It seemed that he had passed the test, for after nodding several times, Abd began an enthusiastic dissertation on the nature of fire and water, and whether God could have made them, since they were destructive and God was good. The dervish was still expounding when Murad checked to see if dinner was ready. Since it was, the young Persian gave Ross an inquiring glance.

Knowing exactly what was being asked, Ross said to the dervish, "We are about to partake of our evening meal. Will you honor us by sharing our humble fare?"

"The honor would be mine," Abd said happily.

The dervish looked so pleased that it occurred to Ross that the main purpose of this visit might not be theology but a simple desire to cadge a free dinner. Ross didn't mind; Abd was a pleasant old fellow and he obviously could use a solid meal.

Murad looked regretful at dividing the lamb one more way, but he made no protest as he piled the food onto the communal platter; Islam had a tradition of sharing that Ross thought the Christian world would do well to emulate.

With dinner imminent, Juliet came instantly awake and settled cross-legged by the platter. Ross introduced her as Jalal, adding that she spoke little Persian.

After murmuring a blessing, Abd remarked, "It is very rare to see a Targui in Turkestan."

"I am surprised that you have seen any," Ross replied.

"Aye, there have been one or two through Merv. The caravan routes are the lifeblood of Islam, and they carry the sons of the Prophet from one end of the earth to the other."

The dervish went on to expound on how caravans and pilgrimages promoted unity throughout the Muslim world, a topic which progressed into a general discussion of transportation. After Ross had described a railroad, the old man said, perplexed, "It sounds most unnatural. Of what value is such speed?"

"It shortens journeys and transports good more quickly so men might live better lives."

Abd shook his head firmly. "The pace of a camel or donkey gives a man time to see, to reflect, to understand—*those* are the things that create a better life. To a simple man like me, it seems that you ferengis are overconcerned with *doing* and *having*. In Islam, we are more interested in *being*."

Ross's opinion of the dervish rose still further. "As I gave you an intriguing new thought, now you have done the same for me. I thank you, good Uncle."

Altogether, it was quite an enjoyable meal. They were just finishing when a group of Turkomans galloped into the campground in a flurry of dust, shouting, and thundering hooves. In their tall black sheepskin hats, the riders looked like a light cavalry troop. Terrified goats and chickens scattering before them, they cut from one campfire to another while members of the caravan drew back and watched warily. Even though their dress indicated that they were of the local Tekke tribe, not raiders from a hostile Turkoman band, Ross felt a prickle of disquiet.

His disquiet deepened when he realized that the Turkomans seemed to be searching for something, or someone. Then the leader of the riders drew close enough to identify, and Ross swore under his breath. Aloud he said, "The man approaching is Dil Assa, the leader of the Turkomans I met near Serevan."

Remembering that Ross had almost been killed, Saleh and Juliet looked up sharply, while Murad, who might have been enslaved on that occasion, did his best to look unobtrusive. Only Abd was unalarmed. His back to the newcomers, he placidly mopped up the last of the lamb juices with a piece of bread.

A moment after Ross spoke, Dil Assa spotted his quarry and recognition became mutual. With a shout of triumph, the Turkoman spurred his horse toward their fire, reining his mount back just in time to avoid trampling the unconcerned dervish. "It is the British spy!"

Dil Assa roared, his gaze fixed on Ross. "Truly God is merciful, for he has given you into my hands again. This time I shall not fail to kill you, ferengi."

Juliet lunged for her rifle, which was only a yard from her hand, but Ross threw his hand up to stop her. "No! A gun battle here would endanger too many innocent people." Rising to his feet, he said, "I also remember you, Dil Assa. Why do you have this passion for killing Englishmen?"

"I need no reason. Prepare to die, dog!"

Dil Assa was raising his matchlock rifle when Abd stood and turned to face the Turkomans. Before Ross's fascinated gaze, the old holy man seemed to take on an extra six inches of height and an air of compelling authority. His voice cutting across the nervous camp like a lash, the dervish said, "If you wish to kill the ferengi, you will have to kill your khalifa first."

Ross sucked in his breath. Good Lord, their ragged visitor must be the Khalifa of Merv, the spiritual leader of the Turkomans and the only man with any influence on their wild behavior.

In the hush that fell over the camp after the old man spoke, Dil Assa's gasp was clearly audible. "Abd Urrahman!" He scrambled off his horse and bowed deeply, all of his men doing the same. "Majesty, I did not recognize you."

"No, for you were too intent on wickedness," the old man said sternly. "You shame me, Dil Assa. I have broken bread with the ferengi and find him to be an honorable man. If you slay him, my curse will be upon you and your tents."

Dil Assa blanched. "You have never protested when we take slaves among the Persians, majesty," he said feebly. "Indeed, you graciously accept a tenth of all our spoils."

"That is entirely a different matter," the khalifa said with dignity, "for a Turkoman raider does not take the lives of his captives, but treats them as tenderly as a father, for dead they are worthless. Besides, Persians are Shiites, and to fight them is a greater blessing than making a pilgrimage."

Murad, who as a Persian was a Shiite, flinched back

and drew closer to Saleh, who was a Sunni like the Turkomans. Ross found it ironic that Abd Urrahman was more tolerant of a Christian than of a fellow Muslim, but was too grateful for the khalifa's intervention to point out any inconsistencies of logic.

Abd Urrahman continued, "I want your word that you will never again try to harm this ferengi, his servants, or his friends." The old man's piercing gaze swept the other Turkomans. "I want the same promise from all of you here, and all the kinsmen in your tents."

Dil Assa swallowed hard. "You have my word, majesty, and I shall convey your wishes to the rest of the tribe."

"Very good." The khalifa's face softened. "It is well that you fear God, Dil Assa, for I know that you fear no man."

Taking the words as a compliment, Dil Assa brightened a little, though his expression was still ferocious when he turned to Ross again. The Turkoman glared like a tomcat; Ross was reminded of his early days at Eton, where boys felt compelled to prove themselves to each other.

Then a dangerous smile lit Dil Assa's dark eyes. His gaze swept around the gathered watchers, for as was usual in the East, everything happened with an audience. "As a gesture of friendship to the ferengi, I will invite him to share in one of the glories of Turkoman life." He paused for dramatic effect. "Tomorrow I shall hold a special *bozkashi* match in his honor. Not only that, the ferengi shall play with us."

After he said *bozkashi*, the crowd began murmuring with excitement, repeating the word over and over. Ross had heard the term and recognized it as a game played on horseback, but knew nothing more. Distrustfully he asked, "What is *bozkashi*?"

Dil Assa gave a wolfish smile. "It is the great game our ancestors have played since time immemorial. The name means 'goat catch,' for men on horseback contend for the headless body of a goat. The carcass must be carried around a distant post, then brought back and hurled into the circle of justice. Whoever throws the goat into the circle is proclaimed the winner. Of course, it is not to be expected that a ferengi might actually win, but still I will allow you to play with us."

It didn't take a genius to guess how much violence the brief description concealed. Unenthralled, Ross said, "You honor me, but I have no horse, nor any understanding of the game."

"No matter," Dil Assa said airily. "*Bozkashi* is so simple, even a ferengi can learn. I will lend you one of my own horses."

Ross glanced around at the expectant faces of the other caravan members. He had garnered a fair amount of goodwill among them, but refusing to play Dil Assa's barbaric game might dissipate much of that. There was no graceful way out; even the khalifa looked approving. "Then I shall be pleased to join you."

"Splendid!" Dil Assa swung onto his horse. "Come to our tents tomorrow when the sun has risen halfway to its zenith. And bring your friends so they can admire your riding prowess." With flamboyant showmanship he reared his horse, then wheeled and galloped away, followed by his men.

After mentally conceding that Dil Assa had won this round, Ross turned and bowed to the khalifa. "Many thanks for your intervention, majesty. I see God's hand in the chance that brought you to our fire."

Abd Urrahman's black eyes twinkled. "It was not entirely chance, though assuredly you were under God's hand. This morning a camel driver came to my house to tell me of the wickedness of you and your Tuareg servant. He wanted me to order that you both be stoned, but I thought it best to judge you for myself. I also guessed that Dil Assa might seek you out when he heard that a ferengi was in Merv, for his brother was killed by the British in Afghanistan. He is a good lad, Dil Assa, but impulsive." The old man inclined his head graciously. "I enjoyed our discussion, Khilburn. Your theology is novel, but the product of a reverent heart. Enjoy the *bozkashi* match tomorrow."

Even after the khalifa left, Ross's fire was the center of attention among the members of the caravan, who came over to enthusiastically describe *bozkashi* matches they had seen. The prospect of a game the next day put everyone in high spirits.

It was well after dark, and most people had drifted away to their beds when Juliet stood and murmured, "Join me for a walk."

A few minutes later, he also got to his feet and ambled away from the campground. As in Sarakhs, the caravansary was on the edge of town, and by the time he overtook Juliet, they were well into the desert. As they wound their way between moon-glazed sand dunes, he asked, "What have I gotten myself into?"

"Think of *bozkashi* as a cross between fox hunting and the battle of Waterloo," she said dryly.

He laughed. "That bad?"

"Worse. Since Dil Assa promised not to murder you, this is his best hope for putting you in the way of a fatal accident."

"I'm sure he wouldn't grieve if that happened," Ross agreed, "but I imagine that his main desire is to humiliate me as a salve for his wounded pride. Have you seen many *bozkashi* matches?"

"Only one. Everyone assumed I was a man, but I thought it wise not to press my luck by going to others. Turkoman women are not allowed to attend matches, so it might have been dangerous if I had been discovered." She stopped and plucked a pale flower that had blossomed after a brief shower the night before. "The men adore *bozkashi*. Even as we speak, the word is spreading across the desert. Hundreds, perhaps thousands, will come to watch tomorrow. It is a winter sport, and this will surely be the last match until autumn, for it is almost too hot to play."

"What are the rules?"

"There are none. There can be any number of players, from a dozen to hundreds, and it's every man for himself. My guess is that *bozkashi* began as war training for the conquering Mongol hordes. There is nothing the least bit subtle about the game—it's all brute strength and horsemanship." She gave him a doubtful glance. "You're an excellent rider, but you have seen what the Turkomans are like."

"All of them appear to have been born on horseback,

and I doubt that they are burdened by any gentlemanly nonsense about fair play." Ross shrugged. "I don't feel the need to outdo them at their own game. If I can stay on my horse until the end, I'll consider that I've done my bit for British honor."

"Will you remember that tomorrow in the heat of the game?"

He smiled and picked another white blossom, then tucked it into a fold of Juliet's tagelmoust over her ear. "I'll remember. I've never been mad for playing games."

Primly ignoring what he had done with the flower, she said, "I thought you were some sort of athletic hero at Eton."

"Yes," he admitted. "At Eton one doesn't have much choice whether to play or not, but my heart wasn't in it."

"My father would have been shocked speechless at such sentiments," she said, a hint of amusement in her voice. "He had no respect for men who were uninterested in sporting activities."

Curious, and not yet ready to end these precious moments of private conversation, Ross sat down in the lee of a hill where they had a distant view over the winding Merv river. Casually he took Juliet's hand and tugged her down beside him. When she came without protest, he briefly considered retaining her hand before deciding it would be wiser not to.

It was ironic; if he were a single man and had just met Juliet, he would be doing his best to court her, for she was in most ways the same woman he had fallen in love with. Instead, the fact that they were married and separated was an unbreachable barrier between them. At least, he did not know any way to overcome the past, nor was he sure that it would be wise to try, for the one crucial quality she lacked was interest in him. That first innocent courtship, when they had not feared to show their hearts, had been a lifetime ago.

Still casual, he said, "Do you know, I think that is the first time I ever heard you say a word about what your father was like. I know that he served in several exotic diplomatic posts and that he died when you were sixteen, but apart from that, I know nothing. In fact, I don't believe I ever heard any other member of your family mention him."

Juliet sighed. A breeze was blowing across the dunes, and she pulled her veil down so the soft air could cool her face. "He was a difficult man. Having children was something he owed his name—he had little interest in his sons, and even less in his daughter. While he was admirable in many ways, he was also something of a bully. I suppose that a dozen years ago the memory was too raw for anyone in the family to talk about him easily. Now enough time has passed to give me some perspective."

"How did you feel about him?"

She hesitated. "I desperately wanted him to be pleased with me, but because he was a bully, I fought with him constantly. All of us did, except poor Mother, who was caught between her husband and her children, as helpless as a new-fledged chick."

"Interesting," Ross murmured, his gaze fixed on the pale oval of her face. He wanted to reach out and touch her so much that he feared his hand would move of its own volition, so he deliberately scooped up a handful of coarse sand and let it trickle through his fingers. "Was his lack of interest in his daughter the reason you always ran with your brothers, learning the same things and getting into the same kind of trouble?"

There was a surprised pause. "Very likely, though I've never thought of it in those terms. At the time, it just seemed that boys got to do much more interesting things than girls. Also, it was my brothers or no one when we were living in Tripoli and Teheran. Since there were no European households with girls my age, I had no female playmates."

More than ever, Ross wanted to touch her, but he did not want to risk destroying the fragile mood between them. In the last few minutes she had told him more about the inner life of her childhood than she had revealed during their courtship and brief period of wedded bliss. Perhaps after he digested this new information he would be better able to understand the mystery who was his wife. "No wonder it was so difficult to be sent to an English girls' school after your father died."

"It was horrible," she said vehemently. "I wanted to

make friends, but didn't know how. At least, not until
Sara took me in hand. It added to my status enormously
that she befriended me, for she was the best-respected
girl in the school. More than that, she taught me how to
behave correctly. The English upper class is a positive
labyrinth of elaborate rituals, of right and wrong ways to
do things. If you make a mistake, you are branded forever as an outsider.''

"But you weren't an outsider," he pointed out. "Your
parents both came from what are called 'good families.'
You had as much right to take your place in society as
any other girl in your school."

Juliet gave a rueful chuckle. "Technically that might
have been true, but in practice it didn't work out that
way. Not only was I ignorant of the rules and the gossip
everyone else knew, but I was Scottish, the tallest girl in
the whole school, and had horridly unfashionable hair. I
didn't even know how to giggle properly! If it hadn't
been for Sara, I would have run away."

His heart aching for the unhappy girl she was allowing
him to see, he said, "The stories you told me about your
school were always amusing. I had no idea you had been
so miserable."

"Complaining is never very attractive, so I didn't. Besides, I was sure you wouldn't understand. You grew up
in the heart of society, with correct behavior so ingrained
that you always knew instinctively what to do, or what
the consequences would be if you disobeyed," she said
with wry humor. "In time I learned enough of the rules
to create the illusion that I belonged, but I still made
mistakes."

"I never noticed."

"Ah, but you did," she said gently. "When I was too
far out of line, you would mildly tell me where I had
gone wrong. That I had been too opinionated, or insuffi-
ciently deferential, or that I had broken one of those
damned little rules." It was Juliet's turn to scoop up
sand, then watch it flow from her taut fingers.

Though her tone had not been accusing, Ross felt as
if she had unexpectedly kicked him in the midriff, for
she was revealing one of the issues that had separated
them. And while he wanted to understand her better,

this cut painfully close to the bone. "Damnation," he swore. "I can't even remember criticizing you, yet I hurt you badly by doing so, didn't I?"

Swiftly she turned her head toward him. In the pale moonlight, her eyes were only dark shadows. "And now I've hurt you by mentioning it. I'm sorry, Ross, I shouldn't have said anything. Even then, I knew that the problem was not you, but my own uncertainty and sensitivity. When Sara corrected my behavior, I was grateful, but when you were critical, I felt . . . undermined. As if I were hopelessly awkward. I was sure you must regret having married me."

"If you were too sensitive, obviously I wasn't sensitive enough. I should have known I was upsetting you." Frustrated, he balled his hand into a fist and ground it into the yielding sand. It was better to know than to remain in ignorance, yet it was difficult to ask the next question, for he feared the answer she might give. "Did you leave because of my criticisms?"

"It was part of the reason, but only a very small part," she replied, choosing her words with care. "I became convinced that I could never be the kind of wife you wanted, and that trying to change was destroying me."

"I didn't want you to change," he said, his voice full of self-directed bitterness. "I liked you just fine the way you were. Yet in my youthful foolishness I drove you away."

For just a moment she touched the back of his hand. "Don't blame yourself—it was far more complicated than that. I was confused . . . so confused. No matter what you had done or not done, I don't think the result would have been any different."

No longer able to restrain himself, Ross raised his hand and very gently caressed her cheek with the back of his knuckles. Softly he said, "So our marriage was doomed from the start?"

For a moment he felt a touch of warm moisture on her petal-smooth cheek. Then with one lithe movement she got to her feet and moved out of his reach. "There is no point in talking about the distant past—it's upsetting and changes nothing," she said, her voice brittle. "The very young Juliet Cameron was wholly unsuited to be either a wife or an English lady. It's a great pity she didn't know that, for marrying an English lord distressed a number of people unnecessarily." She halted for a moment, then finished very quietly, "I learned my lesson. I just regret that I learned it too late to save you from suffering for my sins."

More slowly, Ross also stood. "So you buried yourself in a land where you are so much an outsider that no one will ever expect you to be like anyone else. Has that solved the underlying problem of feeling that you don't belong?"

In the silence that followed, she withdrew from their brief intimacy with a thoroughness that was almost tangible; Juliet had revealed as much as she was willing to, at least for tonight. She gave a light laugh, as cool and detached as any society woman in her own drawing room. "The worst thing about you, Ross, is that you are always right. Such a very maddening trait."

If she had had a fan, she might have tapped him with it. And if she had, he would have broken the damned thing in half.

His expression grim, he got to his feet. If he were always right, she never would have left him. "It's time to get some rest. I'm going to need all my strength if I want to avoid disgracing myself in Dil Assa's equine riot."

Juliet pulled the veil over her lower face again and removed the desert flower he had tucked over her ear. As she tossed it into the sand, she said, "Just remember your resolution not to try to beat him at his own game. We've had quite enough excitement on this journey."

Ross couldn't have agreed more.

12

With the exception of a few men left on guard duty, everyone in the caravan went out to Dil Assa's camp, which was a couple of miles up the river from the town. As the loose, good-natured group rode through the barren countryside, Ross glanced at Juliet, whose camel was ambling along by his. "You're right about how popular *bozkashi* is. Everyone's in a holiday mood."

Dryly she said, "In Turkestan it is considered great fun to watch animals rip each other to shreds—dogs fight dogs, cocks fight cocks, quail fight quail. Even bull camels are set to fighting each other when they're in rut. What does that tell you about *bozkashi?*"

He chuckled. "That I'll be glad when this is over and I am back at the caravansary, preferably with all limbs intact."

Their destination was a scattered collection of yurts, which were circular tents made of felt. The effect was rather like a collection of black-roofed beehives. Swarms of children, the next generation of plunderers, buzzed about. Most of the inhabitants wore bright clothing, red being the preferred color. To Ross's surprise, the nomad women were unveiled, a rarity in Islam. Instead, they wore high, elaborate headdresses with red or white scarves that fell behind to their waists.

Everyone stopped and stared at Ross when he rode into the encampment. Since it was common knowledge that he was a ferengi, he had decided to wear the European clothing he was most comfortable in, and his white shirt and plain buckskins were a stark contrast to the flowing, colorful robes of the Turkomans. His only Asiatic garment was his white turban, which he wore for protection against the sun.

As he dismounted from his camel, Dil Assa pushed through the gathering crowd. The Turkoman wore a cap edged with wolf fur, which was the mark of a *chopendoz*, an acknowledged *bozkashi* master. "Ah, my ferengi friend," he said with patent insincerity. "I am delighted to see that you have not had second thoughts. Here is a *bozkashi* whip. I will take you to your mount." After handing Ross a short lead-weighted whip, the Turkoman turned and led the way to the edge of the encampment.

Since the playing area was still some distance away, most of the other caravan members continued riding. However, Juliet dismounted and gave Murad the reins to both camels. Then, like a good servant, she trailed along behind Ross, watching his back. However, Ross did not feel as if he was in any immediate danger; if Dil Assa wanted to break the khalifa's injunction by killing the ferengi, he would surely not do so until after Ross had made a fool of himself in the game.

Dil Assa led Ross to where a dozen saddled horses were tethered along a picket line. "Here," the Turkoman said, indicating an elderly bay mare. "A fine, steady beast, perfect for a ferengi who has never played *bozkashi*."

Ross circled the horse with elaborate care, shaking his head all the while. "Have you no respect for the poor mare's years, Dil Assa? She would expire of exertion before the afternoon is over." He patted the angular rump. "I should profoundly regret being the cause of this venerable lady's demise."

Dil Assa scowled. "I chose the mare because I thought that even a ferengi who sits in the saddle like a sack of grain should be able to manage her. But if you think you can handle a real *bozkashi* steed, choose from among any of my other horses."

Thoughtfully Ross walked along the picket line, examining all of the beasts with an expert eye. They were similar to the legendary breed that the Chinese called the Heavenly Horses of Ferghana. Bred more for stamina than speed, they lacked the elegant conformation of Arabians, but the best of them could travel six hundred miles in under a week.

A number of other Turkomans crowded around, none of them showing Dil Assa's hostility, and all of them eager to offer comments on the horses. Ross didn't know the language well enough to understand all of the rapid talk, but he caught phrases such as, "A *bozkashi* horse must have the speed of a hawk, the agility of a goat, the heart of a lion . . . from full gallop to dead stop in an instant . . . needs patience, spirit, wit . . ."

Most of the horses looked capable of fulfilling the demanding requirements of the game, but Ross's choice settled on a tall white stallion, the most spirited of the lot. The horse's eyes glittered with fierce intelligence and its slight, impatient movements made the silver plates on its bridle flash in the sunlight. A challenging mount, Ross guessed, but one that would reward the effort of mastering him. "This one."

Behind him, Dil Assa gave a gasp of outrage. "Rabat is my finest horse. *I* am riding him today!"

"Ah, my apologies," Ross said, not entirely surprised, for the stallion's quality was obvious. "I would not dream of depriving you of the horse you need for victory."

The Turkoman gave Ross a smoldering glance, but pride compelled him to say, "I do not need Rabat to win, ferengi. You are welcome to ride him—if he will allow you to."

"You are most gracious," Ross said, suppressing a grin. "I imagine that Rabat has been trained to perform special *bozkashi* maneuvers. What need I know to ride him properly?"

Fortunately half a dozen men chimed in with answers, for Dil Assa seemed disinclined to reply. After listening for a few minutes, Ross thought he understood what he might expect of a Turkoman-trained horse.

To accustom Rabat to his voice, Ross spent a few moments stroking the wary animal's neck and talking softly in English. Then, after checking the tightness of the girth and lengthening the stirrups, he swung lightly into the saddle.

Outraged by the stranger's impertinence, Rabat immediately exploded into action, bunching his muscles and rearing up in a furious attempt to dislodge his unwelcome rider. The stallion had a really impressive repertoire of bucks, twists, and sideways hops, but Ross had noted the warning in Dil Assa's words and he was prepared for such behavior. As the audience prudently withdrew to a safe distance, there followed a brief, intense bout in which man and horse tested each other's mettle.

It required all of Ross's strength and concentration to stay on the animal's back and establish which of them was in charge, but as Rabat whipped sideways like a mongoose, Ross did catch one glimpse of Juliet. Even though she was veiled, he sensed her satisfaction with his performance. Score one for the British.

There was no real vice in the white horse, just high spirits and a mischievous refusal to tamely accept an unproved rider. After Rabat had burned off some of his excess energy, he settled down and began to respond to reins and knees.

Wanting to know just what his mount could do, Ross rode away from the tents into the open plain. Then he put the stallion through its paces, systematically learning how to make the beast stop, wheel, and jump. Rabat was amazingly quick, instantly sensing what his rider wanted. He could also turn on a farthing, and was one of the most powerful jumpers Ross had ever ridden. Testing the horse's capabilities was similar to testing a new rifle, only more challenging, because Rabat had a mind of his own.

The unfamiliar harness also required getting used to. There was only a single pair of reins, and the saddle was very high in front and back. In addition, a tall horn rose from the pommel. The configuration was unusual, but it would offer valuable support for a rider engaging in wild *bozkashi* maneuvers.

After a quarter-hour of increasingly strenuous activity, Ross felt that he and the stallion had developed a reasonable understanding of each other. As a final experiment, he put Rabat into a full blazing gallop, then grasped the saddle horn and slid down so that most of his body hung precariously over the stony soil. It was a dangerous trial, for a swerve or misstep by the horse would pitch Ross headfirst into the ground at high speed.

But in spite of his rider's unbalanced weight, the stallion held rock-steady as Ross plucked one of the fragile desert flowers. He pulled himself back into the saddle, then slowed to a canter and rode back to the watching Turkomans, laughing from sheer exhilaration. Most of the audience was smiling and calling out approving comments, but Dil Assa watched in dead silence.

Undeterred by his host's expression, Ross exclaimed, "Magnificent, Dil Assa! If you had the schooling of Rabat, he does you great honor."

With a blend of irritation and grudging respect, Dil Assa growled, "Aye, I trained him. When Rabat was born, I caught him with my own hands so he would not fall to the earth and break his wings. When he nursed, I fed his mother a dozen eggs a day so his coat would be sleek. For three years he ran completely free, unhampered by bridle or saddle. For six years more I have trained him in all the maneuvers of the game. There is no finer *bozkashi* mount anywhere. See that you use him well."

"I shall try to prove worthy," Ross said. "By the way, do you have another mount that my servant can use to ride with us to the site of the *bozkashi* match?"

Eyes narrowed with malice, Dil Assa scanned the remaining horses. After mounting a fiery-looking dark bay, he said, "Your Tuareg slave can ride that chestnut."

Speaking in Tamahak, as if translating, Ross told Juliet, "Careful, slave. I think our kind host wants to see someone's neck broken today."

Without deigning to reply, Juliet adjusted the chestnut's cinch and stirrups, then mounted. The nervous young gelding was not as hell-bent on having its own way as Rabat, but it was very skittish, so another battle for control took place. Juliet did not have Ross's strength, but she had an uncanny ability to sense what a horse would do next, and she brought the chestnut into order very quickly.

Dil Assa scowled. "Perhaps your slave should also play *bozkashi* today."

"No," Ross said flatly. "If Jalal is injured, who will care for my camels?"

Accepting the logic of that, Dil Assa ordered the rest

of his men to mount, and the group set off to the site of the *bozkashi* match. It was about two miles away, and as Juliet had predicted, hundreds of spectators had arrived and were spread out along the dunes, ready, willing, and eager to follow the action. Numerous peddlers were also present, busily offering food and drink to the crowd.

It was easy to pick out the *bozkashi* players, for they were idling about on their mounts. There were about three dozen, all of them lean and dangerous-looking. Most wore caps edged with karakul or fox fur, and all carried the short, ugly whips.

Juliet slid off the chestnut and handed the reins to one of the Turkomans, then went on foot to find Saleh and Murad. Dil Assa rode over and gave Ross a terse set of explanations. "There is the *boz*, the goat." The headless, sand-weighted carcass lay in the middle of a circle drawn with white quicklime.

He waved his hand toward the horizon. "There is the pole which the *boz* must be carried around. Since the sun is hot and this is only a small, friendly match, the pole was set near." In fact, it was just barely visible in the distance.

Finally he indicated the quicklime circle. "The *boz* must be returned to the *hallal*, the circle of justice. The man who throws it in the circle is the winner." With a wolfish flash of teeth, Dil Assa said, "Shall we begin, my ferengi friend?"

"Ready when you are," Ross said pleasantly.

At Dil Assa's signal, the *bozkashi* master, an older man with a whip-scarred face, gave a shrill whistle between his fingers. Immediately the players trotted over and gathered in a rough circle around the goat. Ross found a place opposite Dil Assa. The air vibrated with tension as the riders jockeyed for position, their faces avid with the desire to be first and fiercest.

The master raised his arm, then chopped it down. "Begin!"

Instantly the circle dissolved into a maelstrom of chaotic activity as the riders spurred their horses forward. Only Ross held back, preferring to observe until he better understood the game.

A slightly built man proved quickest, and he leaned over and jerked the goat from the ground. Immediately it was ripped away by two players who began pulling on different legs, both of them screaming like fishwives. A third man drove his horse between their mounts and reared his horse straight up, separating the other two so he could seize possession himself.

A whirlwind of activity followed as the goat changed hands over and over, passing high and low, over necks and saddles and under horses' bellies. Twice it fell to the ground, only to be instantly snatched up again. It was a scene of pure savagery, and soon the air was heavy with the pungent scents of horse, sweat, blood, and leather. Ross learned that the whips were less for horses than opponents. Hands and faces were slashed to the bone, but in the frenzy of competition, no one noticed. High-heeled boots kept riders in their stirrups when they lunged out to seize the prize, eyes wild and whips clamped between their teeth.

It was not just the players who fought, for their horses were equally aggressive, charging into the fracas with bared teeth, chopping hooves, and neighs of challenge. Riders and horses moved as one, like a race of centaurs in which a single will drove both man and mount. And at the very center of the storm was Dil Assa, the wildest of the wild.

Once the swirling mass of riders surged into the crowd. Howling spectators scattered in all directions, but some were not quick enough, and when the *bozkashi* action moved away, three bruised and complaining casualties were left behind.

Surrounded by an eye-stinging cloud of yellow dust, the struggling mass of riders slowly moved in the direction of the pole. To Ross it seemed that most of the players and their mounts would exhaust themselves long before the circle of justice was reached. By holding back and husbanding himself and his horse, a player would have a much better chance of becoming the ultimate winner. But strategy meant nothing to the men in front of him; they played for the sheer barbaric joy of it.

The tides of violence whirled around Ross and Rabat, kindling a fire in the blood that called them to surrender

to the madness and join that furious tumult. Trained and
honed for *bozkashi*, the white stallion fought to join the
fray, but Ross held him back, needing the full force of his
arms and knees to keep the raging horse under control.

Even more fiercely than he fought his horse, Ross battled the siren lure of violence. He had intended to participate in a moderate way once he had observed how the
game was played, but now he feared joining in. It would
be easy, so easy, to drown in that swirling chaos, to lose
all balance and restraint.

Though there had been a handful of times in his life
when his control had been on the edge of shattering,
Ross had never succumbed, for on some deep level he
feared what might happen if he did. If he once gave way
to madness, would he ever again be free of it? And so
he held back, keeping himself and Rabat on the edges
of the fray.

The match progressed slowly, every inch fought over
with grim determination until the *boz* was three-quarters
of the way to the pole. Then a single rider managed to
break clear, the goat slung across his saddlebow.

It was Dil Assa. In spite of hot pursuit, for a few
brief glorious minutes he ran free as the crowd shrieked
encouragement. He gave a bellow of triumph as he circled the pole, but in order to reach the goal, he had
to return the way he had come—and when he did, his
opponents were waiting for him. Once more the match
turned into a free-for-all.

Ross had been riding along at the edge of the main
group, watching but not taking part, more concerned
with his inner struggle for mastery than with who had
possession of the increasingly ragged goat. Then suddenly Dil Assa appeared before him, eyes wild and face
sheened with sweat and blood.

"Coward!" he snarled. "You waste the finest *bozkashi*
horse that ever lived. You are less than a man." Far
beyond remembering the promise he had made to the
khalifa, he raised his heavy lead-tipped whip and slashed
it at Ross's face. "I spit on you, ferengi!"

Reflexively Ross reared the stallion back, taking him
out of reach of the whip. Undeterred, Dil Assa drove

his mount forward and tried again, striking wildly in his fury.

The results were explosive. Usually Ross glided through life as a calm, detached observer, but proximity to Juliet had dangerously strained his control, and as the Turkoman's whip snapped viciously across his back and shoulder, rage shattered the remnants of his restraint.

When Dil Assa lashed out again, Ross reached out with cat quickness and grabbed the thong with his left hand. Ignoring the searing pain, he yanked back with all his strength, jerking the whip from his opponent's hand. "If you want to lose, Turkoman, so be it!" He hurled the whip to the ground. "Now I play to win!"

He wheeled Rabat sharply and set off in pursuit of the main body of players, which had passed by while Ross and Dil Assa were engaged in their private combat. There had been another breakaway where one man carried the goat halfway to the goal before being overtaken. Now all of the players were involved in a wild general melee.

The stallion trumpeted with joy at being given his head and charged over the barren plain like an avenging angel. Knowing that the *boz* would be in the center of the crowd of riders, Ross drove straight for it, intending to force his way straight in.

Then he realized that Rabat was gathering himself for a leap. In an instant of perfect communication between man and mount, Ross sensed that the stallion wanted to hurdle right on top of the brawling, seething mass of riders and horses.

It was madness, yet Ross didn't hesitate for an instant. In *bozkashi*, anything was allowed. *Anything*. His mind at one with his horse, Ross felt Rabat's sweeping strides and bunching muscles, the fierce equine aggression, as if they were his own. Together they rose into the air and for a moment soared like Pegasus.

Then man and beast smashed down on top of the roiling, cursing throng. It was pure chaos. Kicks, fists, and whip lashes rained down on Ross and the stallion, but the sheer weight of their descent forced a space to open beneath them, right next to where the goat was being fought over.

Oblivious to the buffeting of other riders, Ross clamped the whip between his teeth, then dived through the choking dust toward the *boz*, stretching perilously over empty air with only a boot heel and his grip on the saddle horn to anchor him to his mount. At the farthest limit of his reach, he managed to seize a back leg of the mangled carcass. The man who had possession fought viciously to retain it, but he lacked his assailant's fierce, fresh strength, and after a few seconds, Ross wrenched the prize away.

When the full weight of the carcass lurched into his grasp, Ross almost crashed down to the stony soil. It took all his strength to regain his seat, but he managed to do it without losing the goat to the clawing hands of other players.

Ross draped the battered *boz* in front of his saddle, then began the slow, violent process of fighting his way out of the melee. In his state of exhilarated fury, he felt none of the blows that fell on him, and he had no compunction about striking back in kind. Every hand and whip was raised against them, but he and Rabat were unstoppable as they barreled through the mob, knocking the other riders aside.

They emerged in the clear only a couple of hundred yards from the circle of justice. Dust stung Ross's eyes so that he could barely see the goal, but blindly he kicked Rabat into a gallop, relying on the stallion's training and instinct to take them to the circle at top speed. Needing to clear his vision, Ross lifted one hand from the goat and used the tail of his turban to wipe his eyes. And in the instant that his grasp on the carcass was less secure, another pair of hands seized it.

Once more it was Dil Assa, his black eyes wild with jubilant fury as he dragged the *boz* onto his own horse. Immediately he spurred the bay in an attempt to escape, but before he could succeed, Ross retaliated, stretching across the intervening space to grab one of the goat's hind legs. His muscles knotted with strain as he tried to wrench the carcass back, but Dil Assa held a front leg with equal stubbornness, refusing to let go.

The two horses thundered toward the goal side by side, for neither of the men would yield in their grisly tug-of-war. Other riders surrounded them, yelling and striking with their whips, but Ross was aware only of Dil Assa and the savage struggle for primacy between them.

To break the perilous stalemate, Ross locked one leg around the high cantle of the saddle, then slid down the far side of the horse, using his weight to get the extra force he needed. Something had to give, and with shocking suddenness, it did. The goat surged over to Ross, and he lost his precarious balance. He almost pitched off his mount under the hooves of the pursuing riders, but once again the saddle horn saved him.

As Ross heaved himself upright, he saw that the animal's front leg had torn away in Dil Assa's hands, leaving the main carcass in Ross's possession. Shrieking with rage, Dil Assa heaved the foreleg at his opponent and made another attempt to seize the *boz*, but it was too late. They had reached the goal.

As Ross flung the ragged carcass into the quicklime circle, shouts of *"Hallal, hallal!"* rose from the spectators. That quickly turned into a chant of, "Khilburn, Khilburn!"

When Ross raised one arm in acknowledgment, the crowd went wild. Fierce, primitive exultation surged through Ross's veins. Though he had played team sports in school with great success, no team victory had ever given him such pure, arrogant satisfaction in his own prowess. Rabat was equally exhilarated, and pranced and curvetted in a triumphant stallion strut.

Ross had noted earlier where Juliet watched with Saleh and Murad, and now he looked for her, instinctively wanting to share his elation. It was easy to pick her out, for she was a tall, slim raven among the colorful Turkomans.

For a moment their gazes met. He felt an odd jolt, but the distance was too great to read her expression. Then she turned her head sharply away. Perhaps she was upset that he had forgotten his intention to glide through the match without risk. Whatever the motive, her gesture served to bring Ross back to earth. As his mania ebbed, he was grateful to find that his sanity seemed intact, though he also became aware of just how hot, tired, and bruised he was. His chest heaved with exertion, and his ribs ached with every breath he drew.

The *bozkashi* master trotted over to Ross from his place on the sidelines, to perform one last ritual. While the clamor made it impossible to hear his words, the master's beaming face was easy to read when, with a flourish, he pressed a small object into Ross's hand.

Ross had not realized that the winner would receive a prize. He glanced down to find that he was holding an ancient gold coin that an Oxford professor of antiquities would kill to possess. From the looks of the Grecian profile on the face, the coin might date back to the days of Alexander the Great. His own scholarly instincts were aroused, but now was not the time to examine his prize, so he simply nodded graciously and shoved it into a pocket.

Now that the match was officially over, people began streaming onto the field to offer congratulations to the *bozkashi* players. Someone offered Ross a brass ewer of water, which he accepted gratefully. He tilted his head back and poured half the contents into his mouth, then splashed handfuls of water on his face and neck to rinse away the yellow dust.

It had been a hard-fought match and there was plenty of praise to go around, but Ross was the hero of the hour and everyone wanted to shake his hand and offer some comment.

Not quite everyone. As he shook still another hand, Ross realized that it wasn't just his sanity that had returned, but the British rules of sportsmanship that had been drilled into him when he was a child, rules that had found fertile ground in his natural temperament. He looked around for his primary opponent. Dil Assa was only a short distance away, surrounded by his own circle of admirers and commiserators. Moving Rabat slowly so that no one would be injured, Ross worked his way over to the Turkoman.

Dil Assa scowled at him with undiminished vigor. "You were lucky, ferengi."

"I was," Ross agreed promptly. "If it were not for this splendid horse"—he stroked Rabat's sweat-foamed neck—"or for the chance that made the front leg of the *boz* weaker than the rear, I would never have won."

"But still you have come to gloat."

"Not at all." Ross offered his hand. "In my country, it is traditional after a heated contest to shake hands with one's honored opponent."

Startled and uncertain, the Turkoman looked at the proffered hand. "Am I your honored opponent, ferengi?"

"Aye." His hand still extended, Ross added, "I have a name, you know. It's Khilburn. And you, Dil Assa, have the distinction of having made me lose my temper more completely than I have ever done in my life."

The Turkoman gave a sudden crack of laughter. "Then I have achieved a small victory today, though I would have been wiser to leave you to your lethargy." He took Ross's hand and shook it hard. "You ride well for a ferengi, Khilburn."

Ross laughed, feeling as buoyant, in a different way, as when he had thrown the goat into the circle. "To say that a Turkoman rides well is as unnecessary as to say that the summer sun burns or that water is God's gift to his children." He released his opponent's hand. "But I will say that it was by watching you that I learned how the game should be played—with fierceness and joy."

Dil Assa smiled and leaned over to pull off Ross's turban. Then he removed his own wolf-edged cap and plopped it down on his opponent's blond head. "If ever you return in the cool season, Khilburn, we will play again. And if, God willing, that happens, you will ride as a *chopendoz*, a *bozkashi* master."

As honors went, Ross decided as he returned the smile, the sweaty, bedraggled cap surpassed anything that Queen Victoria might bestow on him.

13

❦

For Juliet, watching the *bozkashi* match was a very mixed experience. Though she did not wholly share it, she was able to understand the enthusiasm of the other onlookers, for the game was intense and dramatic.

At the same time, she was glad that Ross did not throw himself wholeheartedly into the match. While *bozkashi* seemed more likely to produce injuries than fatalities, there was a very real chance that players might fall and break their necks or be trampled to death. There was also the possibility that Dil Assa would take advantage of the tumult to dispatch the hated ferengi.

Then Ross and Dil Assa clashed and her husband became a different man. She had always known that he was a superb horseman and had effortless physical mastery at everything he tried; even so, she had trouble believing what was happening before her very eyes. Ross was like an ancient Norse berserker, glittering with danger as he stopped at nothing to achieve victory. When he jumped his horse into the middle of the pack, she forgot to breathe until she saw that he had come through safely. Later, when he and Dil Assa engaged in that insane struggle over the goat while galloping at lethal speed, her heart pounded so loudly that it drowned out the roar of the crowd.

Then Ross threw the *boz* into the circle of justice and Juliet went wild herself, jumping and shouting as hysterically as any of the men around her. It was not only the excitement of the game that moved her, but a deep, primitive pride in her man, for in spite of all that separated them, he was still her husband, and she exulted in his accomplishment. If she had been close enough, she might have hurled herself into his arms in joyous celebration.

Then he looked across the crowd and their gazes met with an impact that coursed through her body like a physical blow. Ross seemed wild and menacing, not at all the civilized man she had loved and married. Certainly he was not the considerate, coolly detached companion of these last weeks of travel.

But it was not just the fact that he seemed a stranger that jarred Juliet. There was something intensely, dangerously sexual in Ross's eyes, and it aroused a matching response in her.

She bit her lower lip as she observed his lithe, sweat-saturated body. He was pure masculine animal, so powerfully male that she felt herself dissolving inside with involuntary female response. If they were alone, she would be ripping his clothing off, as wild as any jungle creature yearning for her mate.

Their gazes held for only an instant before Juliet turned away, but it was an instant that left her shaken. Throat dry, she made some inane comment to Saleh. A jubilant Murad was already pushing his way through the crowd to his master, but Juliet stayed with Saleh and the camels. The last thing she needed was to be closer to Ross.

Doggedly she tried to analyze the reasons for her reaction, in the hope that understanding would dissipate her unruly desire. Ever since their paths had crossed back in Persia, she had been continually aware of how attractive Ross was. But today was different, she realized, because the warrior wildness she had seen in his face was closely akin to the passion he had shown in the intimacy of their marriage bed. Seeing that intensity again, of course she had responded with matching desire.

Unfortunately, understanding her reaction did not dissipate the effect.

Juliet tensed when she saw Ross ride over to Dil Assa; she had no faith that the khalifa's command would keep the Turkoman in check, and Dil Assa had just suffered a very public defeat. Then the two men laughed and shook hands. She smiled behind the safety of her veil.

Leave it to Ross to make a friend out of an enemy. No doubt such behavior was good for the benefit of his soul; better yet, under these conditions such maturity was also very practical.

Soon the crowd began to thin as people headed for their homes, though they would be talking about this *bozkashi* match for years to come. Ross dismounted and handed the stallion's reins to Dil Assa. Then, after saying his farewells, he and Murad walked over to join Juliet and Saleh.

"Well played, Khilburn," Saleh said, rising to his feet. "You will become one of the legends of Turkestan: the ferengi who became a *bozkashi* master."

Ross laughed. "I must admit that I rather enjoyed the match. *Bozkashi* has the excitement of English fox hunting, with the advantage that the animal is already dead. I never quite saw the point of dozens of hounds and horses chasing one little fox."

The wildness had gone from Ross's expression, but he still looked like the romantic conception of a pirate. His damp white shirt was open halfway down his chest, exposing tawny curling hair, and the wolf-trimmed cap on his golden head was quite dashing, in a barbaric way. Though a dark bruise was forming on his left cheekbone, Juliet was glad to see that none of the whiplashes had seriously damaged his face. Scarring there would be like defacing a work of art.

As she studied him, she had the ridiculous thought that Ross had twice the shoulders and half the hips of the average man. Then she blushed. Thank heaven for the tagelmoust.

Having her husband within touching distance was making Juliet weak-kneed and soft-headed, so she turned away before she disgraced herself. He must be hungry after expending so much energy in the match. Silently she handed him a piece of flat bread and a chunk of goat cheese.

"Thank you." In a soft voice that Murad could not hear, Ross added, "Sorry I forgot my resolution to behave with proper British restraint. I hope you didn't find the match exciting to a fault."

When Juliet tried to reply, she found that her voice

did not want to work. After clearing her throat, she murmured, "I wouldn't have minded more boredom, but at
least you survived more or less intact." Then her gaze
fell to his hands. They were scraped and bruised, with
several bloody lacerations. "Perhaps not intact enough."

He flexed his fingers and grimaced. "Messy and uncomfortable, but nothing broken."

Juliet had brought clean scraps of cloth in case bandages were needed, so she dug out a square of cotton
and moistened it. Then she took his right hand in hers
and cleaned away the blood and dust. Falling into the
role of nurse steadied her and made it possible to touch
him dispassionately, though she was acutely aware of the
warmth of his fingers where they lay across hers.

When she finished with Ross's right hand and released
him, somehow his fingertips slowly stroked across her
palm with such sensual effect that she almost jumped
from her skin. So much for being dispassionate. She gave
her husband a suspicious glance, but he was conversing
with Saleh and Murad and paying no attention to her
ministrations. That erotic caress must have been an accident—but she took care that it didn't happen again when
she was cleaning his left hand.

Juliet frowned at what she found under the dust and
dried blood, for several of the deeper cuts were still
bleeding and needed further treatment. She glanced at
Murad, who was about to extinguish the small fire they
had used to make tea during the match. "Leave the fire."

Burnt hair was a classic and effective treatment for
small cuts. Juliet would have been happy to use her own,
but whipping her coppery tresses out from under the
tagelmoust would do her disguise no good, so she took
her knife and trimmed a handful of the long black hair
that curled beneath her camel's long neck. Then she laid
the hair on one of the fire rocks and placed a coal on
top so that the strands flared into brief, pungent flame.
After the burned hair had cooled into delicate ash, she
scooped it up, then went to Ross, who was watching her
curiously.

Juliet crumbled some of the ashes and sprinkled them
across the deepest laceration. Immediately the blood
coagulated.

"Interesting," he commented. "Is this a Persian remedy?"

"Afghan," she said as she treated the next gash. "Burned hair is suitable only for small cuts, but it stops the bleeding and reduces the chance of infection. Any sort of hair will do."

"So much more civilized than cauterization. Speaking of which, how is your arm?"

"Fine. I've almost forgotten about it," she said truthfully as she finished treating Ross's hands. Though now that she was reminded of the injury she had sustained just a few days before, she realized that her arm was throbbing. In the excitement of the *bozkashi* match, she hadn't noticed.

The ride back to Merv was much more relaxed than the journey out had been. Occasionally some locals would pass by and call out an admiring remark about the match, which seemed to have been witnessed by every man in this part of the Kara Kum. The process of Ross becoming a legend was well under way.

The road followed the river of Merv for the last stretch. Narrow and rush-lined, the channel wound through the desert in lazy curves, its banks incongruously green against the barren sandscape. They came to a place where the river pooled by some willow trees, and Ross reined in Julietta, regarding the water longingly. Then he gave a mischievous smile and turned his camel toward the river. "You can go on to the caravansary without me," he said to his companions. "I'll be back later."

After dismounting, he divested himself of boots, shirt, and *bozkashi* hat and dropped them in a mound on the sandy bank. Then, with a whoop of pleasure, he dived into the river.

The sight of Ross's half-naked body immediately unraveled all of the progress Juliet had made in controlling her inconvenient lust. The day was already blisteringly hot, but now a wave of heat swept over her so intensely that she felt faint.

Ignoring Ross's suggestion that the others continue without him, Murad said enthusiastically, "A splendid idea, Khilburn. We shall join you." He guided the camel he and Saleh shared over to the riverbank. Then he couched the beast, scrambled out of his pannier, and began peeling off his clothing.

Saleh also climbed out of his pannier, then removed his sandals. Glancing at Juliet, whose camel had followed the others to the river, he suggested, "If you do not swim, wade with me in the shallows."

More slowly than the others, Juliet dismounted. She was feverish, on the verge of burning up, and the water beckoned like paradise, but joining her husband in the river was unthinkable.

Ross glanced over and tossed a teasing handful of water in her direction. "Yes, Jalal. At least get your feet wet."

Wordlessly she shook her head. It would have been best to return to the caravansary alone, but at the moment the effort was beyond her. Spinning on her heel, Juliet strode along the riverbank until she was out of sight of her companions.

Her breathing harsh and irregular, she kept on until she found a small secluded pool veiled by willows and high rushes. No longer able to maintain even the faintest semblance of control, she folded down on her knees in the sandy soil at the edge of the water and dragged off her tagelmoust with trembling hands. Since leaving Serevan, she had been swathed in layers of fabric day and night, and in her present fevered state she felt as if she would suffocate if she wore the veil any longer.

She dropped the tagelmoust beside her, then used her cupped hands to splash water onto her face and throat. The blessed coolness was soothing to both mind and body.

She had thought that, over time, being around Ross would become easier. Instead, every day was harder than the one before. Today her sexual awareness of him had sizzled to a dangerous new level; if she continued like this much longer, she would incinerate.

No, she would not. She would do whatever was necessary, no matter how hard it was. It was Juliet who had insisted on accompanying her husband on this trip, and having done so, she must abide by the consequences. In another ten days they would reach the city of Bokhara

and she would not be constantly in Ross's company.
Surely matters would improve then.

Unfortunately that thought was of no help at the moment, so with deliberate brutality Juliet reminded herself
how hopeless the situation was. Yes, she desired Ross to
the point of distraction, but desire was only part of a
deeper yearning. Far more than passion, she craved the
love and acceptance she had found only in his arms, and
that she would never know again, for his love was long
gone, destroyed by Juliet's own actions. Even if Ross
was willing to bed her, which was by no means certain,
all she would find would be a fleeting sexual satisfaction
that would be paid for by utter emotional devastation.
The knowledge sobered her as nothing else could.

Juliet had fled to this private spot because she needed
to be alone, but when she regained her control, she realized that she would be a fool to waste this opportunity
to bathe. Swiftly she removed the clothing she had worn
day and night for the last two weeks. After releasing her
hair from its long braid, she stepped into the water. It
was pleasantly cool and felt wonderful, caressing her skin
like liquid silk. She waded out to shoulder depth and
ducked under the surface to wet her hair, then began
scrubbing her scalp with her fingertips.

She could have happily spent the rest of the day in the
river, but if she was gone too long, one of the men would
come looking for her, so she washed as quickly as possible. After climbing back onto the bank, she used her
mantle to roughly dry her skin and hair, then dressed
again. A pity she didn't have fresh garments to wear.

After donning her robe, she sat down on crossed legs
and began combing her fingers through her wet hair.
Working the snarls out was a time-consuming business.
It would have been more practical to cut her hair for this
trip, but she had been unable to bring herself to do that.
Ross had always liked her hair long, and leaving it uncut
was like a secret gift to him, one he would never know
or care about.

As Juliet began rebraiding her hair, she wondered
what her husband really thought about her. Though he
was always considerate, even kind in an impersonal way,
she suspected that he viewed her as a regrettable piece

of ancient history, a nuisance for whom he still felt a
reluctant sense of responsibility. Apart from that experi-
mental kiss at Serevan, he had shown no signs that he
still found her attractive. His disinterest was fortunate,
for she doubted that her willpower would last long if he
were to make a serious attempt to bed her, and that, as
she told herself—repeatedly—would be disastrous.

She was so absorbed in her thoughts that at first she
missed the sounds of footsteps behind her. At the last
moment she heard the soft rustling and steeled herself to
face Ross, though if she was lucky it would be Saleh.

It was neither Ross nor Saleh. Instead, Murad called
out, "Jalal, where are you? We are leaving now."

She whipped her head around just in time to see the
young Persian emerge from the tall rushes. Murad's
mouth dropped open as he stared at her face and copper-
bright hair. His gaze shifted to her familiar black robe,
then back to her face. Incredulously he said, "Jalal?"

Juliet scrambled to her feet, mentally cursing in every
language she knew. Her brief carelessness had negated
all their attempts to keep her identity from Murad; she
might not look like any woman he had ever met, but the
lad was not a fool.

Well, there was no help for it; she would have to tell
the truth and enlist him in the conspiracy, since the alternative was to drown him in the river. Murad was very
loyal to Ross, and she was reasonably sure that he could
be trusted.

Dropping her gruff tone and heavy accent, she said in
fluent Persian, "Is there any chance I can persuade you
that the Tuareg all have red hair and pale, feminine
faces?"

The evidence of his eyes confirmed, Murad exclaimed,
"No God but God! You are a woman—a ferengi
woman!"

"So I am," she agreed. "But on a journey such as this,
it seemed wiser to travel as a man."

His dark eyes narrowed. "Does Khilburn know?"

"He knows," she said dryly. "I happen to be his wife."

Murad thought about that for a time. "But you joined
us at Serevan. If you are his wife, how did you come to
be there?"

"I am the mistress of Serevan and have lived in Persia for many years, apart from my husband. Saleh is my seneschal there," she explained. "But the amir's prisoner is my brother, so I wished to accompany Khilburn to Bokhara."

"Ferengi men allow their women to behave in such a fashion?" he asked doubtfully.

Not wanting to undermine Ross's authority, she said only, "Khilburn is not like other men, nor am I like other women."

His gaze went to her bright hair again, this time with patent admiration. "Truly you are not."

Juliet tucked her braid inside the back of her robe, then lifted her tagelmoust and began wrapping it around her head and face. "It seemed safer that you not know about me, but since fate has decreed otherwise, it will simplify matters for us all."

Murad nodded absently. Then a new thought shocked him. "You defeated Habib!"

"Of course," she said coolly as she finished the complicated winding of the veil. "I am better with a knife than he, so I won. The fact that I am female was of no importance."

The young Persian did not look as if he accepted that, but his next question was, "What is your true name?"

"Juliet."

Murad blinked. "Like Khilburn's camel Julietta?"

"They are forms of the same name," she said shortly, thinking that Murad was regrettably quick-witted. Picking up her black mantle, she set off through the rushes. Murad followed, still shaking his head in astonishment.

When they rejoined the others, Juliet announced in English, "Murad caught me with my veil down, so I confessed all."

Ross made a rueful face. "I was afraid that might happen when I saw that he had gone off to look for you. Well, we'll just have to make the best of it."

"You didn't trust me," Murad said accusingly to his master.

Ross gave the young man his full attention. "It was not so much that I did not trust you, Murad, as that a man should be very careful where his wife's safety is concerned." Seeing that the comment had soothed the young man's sense of ill-usage, he continued, "Now that Juliet's identity is no longer a secret, we might as well take advantage of the four of us being private to discuss what to do in Bokhara."

At Ross's gesture, all four settled down in the shade of a willow. Saleh asked, "Do you have a plan?"

"Bokhara is a city of spies and suspicion. As a ferengi, I am going to be very conspicuous," Ross said. "It will be better if the three of you take separate lodgings from me. Besides being able to move about more freely, you will be less likely to attract the amir's wrath."

Saleh frowned. "There is some truth to that. I have family in Bokhara, and through them I might discover useful information. But someone must stay with you, for your rank requires that you have a servant. Also, if you are alone it will be more difficult and dangerous for me to communicate with you."

Ross considered. "That makes sense. Juliet will stay with you and Murad with me."

"No," Juliet said immediately. "Where you go, I go."

As the three men looked at her, she felt a moment of acute embarrassment. Her protest had been as irrational as it was powerful. Half an hour earlier she had been telling herself that she needed to be apart from Ross, yet the very thought of that now made her insides churn. Fortunately, Murad spoke up while she was still trying to think of a logical reason for her remark.

"I agree," the young Persian said slowly. "Madmen are considered holy fools in Islam and as such have great liberty." He gave a quick smile. "While 'Jalal the Targui' is not mad, the Lady Khilburn plays the role of half-wild desert man most excellently. Knowing that Jalal is unpredictable, our fellow travelers keep their distance and think no more about him. Her. In Bokhara she will be able to come and go scarcely noticed, like a nomad's dog." His smile broadened meaningfully. "Besides, should not husband and wife be together?"

Ross glanced at Juliet. His brown eyes had darkened to near black and in his face she saw the same ambivalence she felt herself. Both of them might wish the other at the opposite end of the earth, but until this mission was done, they were bound together. They were like two people sharing a bed that was too small for comfort, yet which could not be escaped. "Very well," he said at last. "If you want to play Ruth, so be it. Now, what can we expect at the Bokharan customhouse? I want to know if we'll be able to take our guns into the city."

"There should be no problem with the pistols," Murad said thoughtfully, "but if you try to take those two beautiful rifles into the city, they will be confiscated."

"Perhaps the rifles could be wrapped and left outside the city," Saleh suggested. "My brother still owns my family's estate, and it lies very near the caravan road. I think your weapons could be safely concealed in one of the outbuildings."

The men began discussing the possibility in more detail, but Juliet did not join in. She had a bone-deep conviction that staying with Ross was the right thing to do. She was equally sure that doing so would be miserably difficult for both of them.

14

The steep sand dune tilted Juliet's camels to such a treacherous angle that she dismounted and led her two animals down the sharply pitched surface. As their hindquarters lurched awkwardly, the camels bawled with irritation.

At the bottom of the dune Juliet remounted, then indulged herself in a very small drink of water. She used the fluid to moisten her dry lips, then held it in her mouth as long as possible before swallowing. Though warm and oily from the waterskin, it still felt ambrosial, for the heat was now more like summer than spring.

After Merv, they had spent three days crossing a stretch of desert with no oases. At Rafitak they were able to refill their waterskins, but only after digging out two wells that marauding Turkomans had filled with sand and stone.

Wearily Juliet rubbed at her forehead, thinking that it would be pleasant to feel the wind on her face; she was heartily sick of being swaddled from head to toe. However, quite apart from her need to stay disguised, high temperatures in the desert made it essential to wear multiple layers of clothing to prevent the body from losing too much moisture.

As they wound their way between the dunes, sand spurted into the air from the camels' padded feet, then whirled away on the wind. The Kara Kum would be impassable in summer if it were not for what the poetic residents of Turkestan called "the wind of a hundred days." It blew from the north, sometimes soft, more often fierce, but never ceasing. In the distance Juliet saw

a dust devil, a whirlwind that spun fine sand high into
the air. They were very common here; once she had
counted six different dust devils at the same time.

With a sigh, she put her waterskin away. Less than a
week to Bokhara. Then her troubles would really begin.

The caravan reached a water hole in midafternoon and
broke for the night, since the next well was two days
away. Because they had halted early, it was still full light
when Juliet and her companions finished their sparse
meal of bread, saffron-flavored rice, tea, and dates. Afterward Ross excused himself and went off somewhere,
probably to talk to one of the many friends he had made.
Saleh and Murad both settled down for a nap in the
shade of a blanket stretched between their panniers, and
the camels grazed contentedly on nearby camel thorn,
but Juliet, in spite of her fatigue, felt restless. Thinking
that it would be nice to be alone for a while, she decided
to go for a walk.

She chose to head east, into the area of towering two-
hundred-foot-high dunes that the caravan had been skirt-
ing. To her surprise, when she had walked her fill and
was about to return to the camp, she rounded a dune
and discovered Ross sitting in the sand, gazing absently
into the wilderness.

She was about to turn back when he heard the faint
sound of her steps and looked up warily. Recognizing
her, he relaxed. "I see that you weren't ready to rest
either. Come join me."

After a brief hesitation, Juliet did so. By her choice,
they had scarcely talked since leaving Merv. But over
the last few days her rampaging lust had subsided—heat,
fatigue, and thirst were amazingly antierotic—so it
should be safe to be in his company for a few minutes.

As she settled on the sand near him, she remarked, "I
thought you were visiting elsewhere in the caravan."

"Sometimes I like to be alone with the desert. Beautiful, isn't it?" He gestured toward the surrounding dunes.
In the late-afternoon sun they formed an elegant, other-
worldly scene of sensuously curving surfaces and dramatic shadows.

"Beautiful, yes, but bleak," she commented. "I can't

help thinking of how green Scotland is. All that lovely water."

He raised his brows. "Do you miss Scotland?"

"Sometimes. After all, I spent the first five years of my life there. I think that what one loves in childhood stays in the heart forever."

"True. England, the kingdom by the sea, will always be my home." His gaze went back to the scene before them. "But in spite of the dangers, I'm grateful to have another chance to travel on the Silk Road. It fascinates me to know that men have crossed this wilderness for thousands of years, carrying goods and ideas all the way from Rome to China and back again. We walk in the steps of Marco Polo and countless other merchants and adventurers."

"A romantic thought." Since he was looking away, she took the opportunity to admire his profile. Because of the shortage of water, he hadn't shaved in several days, and his cheeks and chin were dusted with dark-gold whiskers. Wrenching her gaze away, she said, "Is that why you've traveled so much—for the romance and adventure of it?"

"That's part of the reason." Before she could comment, he said thoughtfully, "I think that my next book, if I write another, will be about the Silk Road."

"Your next book? I didn't know that you had written any," she said, intrigued. "What were the others about?"

"Just commentary on my travels. One was about the central Sahara, another on the Northwest Frontier of India, the third about the Levant and northern Arabia."

"Impressive," she said admiringly. "Were they well-received?"

He shrugged. "Tolerably so. They've all had multiple printings, but part of the attraction is my title. My publisher says that having 'Lord' or 'Lady' on the cover always doubles sales."

Juliet suspected that he was being modest, but didn't dispute the point. "In that case, sales should quadruple when you can put 'the Duke of Windermere' on the cover."

"I suppose so," he said without enthusiasm. His gaze

drifted back to the horizon. Then his features suddenly tightened. "Damnation. A sandstorm is coming."

In the few minutes that they had been talking, the sky had darkened and the ever-present wind had stiffened considerably. Juliet looked in the same direction as Ross and saw that ominous blue-and-yellow clouds had formed above the dunes and a gray-tan wall of dust was sweeping down on them.

"It looks like a bad one." Ross scrambled to his feet. "Come on. We'd better warn the caravan to batten down."

Juliet stood also, but before setting off she spared a moment to study the storm, and what she saw chilled her to the bone. The dust cloud was racing toward them faster than a man could run, its leading edge a seething mass of spiraling columns. As it drew closer, an eerie, moaning sound filled the ears and rasped the nerves.

Shouting above the wind, she ran after her husband. "Ross, there isn't time! Get down and cover your head!"

A gust of wind struck with a power that almost knocked her from her feet and staggered even Ross. When he regained his balance, he turned and began moving back toward her, his figure blurred by the haze of blowing sand. He had pulled the tail of his turban across his nose and mouth, but Juliet knew that the light fabric was not enough protection for a storm like this one. Even her heavy, layered tagelmoust was not sifting out all the wind-blasted grit.

They were still fifty feet apart when the full force of the storm slammed into them. It was the worst sandstorm Juliet had ever seen, fierce enough to suffocate anyone who wasn't adequately covered. Visibility dropped to zero, and knife-edged grains of sand scoured her bare hands and stung the narrow wedge of face not covered by her veil. As she bent over to reduce the area she presented to the wind, she screamed, "Ross!"

She thought she heard him shouting back, but it was impossible to be sure over the banshee wail of the wind. Knowing that she was better equipped to weather the storm than Ross, Juliet tried to keep going in the direction she had last seen him, but she lost all sense of direction in the featureless, swirling sand. Though she called his name again and again as the wind pushed her forward, there was no response.

Near panic, she told herself that Ross was no fool; he knew enough to lie down and wrap his long coat around his head. But the garment he wore was secured by a sash and took more time to remove than her mantle did. If he spent too much time looking for her . . . if his mouth and lungs filled with sand . . .

When she had almost given up hope, she literally tripped over him. He was on his knees, trying to unwind more of his turban to protect his face, but he was coughing so hard that he was nearly helpless.

Juliet yanked off her long, densely woven mantle and folded it in half so they would have a double layer of protection. Then she dropped to the ground and pulled her husband down beside her. The wind dragged viciously at her mantle, threatening to whip it from her grasp, but she held on grimly and tucked the yards of fabric around their bodies from head to knees. In less than a minute she had created a snug cocoon that shielded them from the lacerating sand.

Ross was shuddering convulsively as he struggled for breath, so she lifted the small water bottle always slung at her waist when she was in the desert. It was difficult to maneuver it up to his mouth without loosening the mantle, but with care she managed to bring it to Ross's lips.

They were pressed together so closely that she could feel the movement of his muscles when he swallowed, then managed to draw in a lungful of air. He cleared his throat, then sipped a little more water before he could speak. "Thank you," he said hoarsely. "I'm glad you are better prepared than I. I've never seen a sandstorm this bad."

"Several years ago I was caught in one like this. Two men and several horses died." Juliet had to pitch her voice higher to make it heard above the roaring wind. After lowering her veil so that she could drink too, she recorked the bottle and replaced it at her waist. Then she wriggled back and forth, making herself a hollow in the yielding sand. "Since we will be here for anywhere from fifteen minutes to three hours," she explained, "we might as well make ourselves comfortable."

He laughed a little as he settled his arm around her shoulders. "Actually, this is quite cozy, though by the time the storm blows itself out, we will look like a minature dune. Quite a bit of sand has already drifted against my back. It's good protection against the wind."

Since they were lying face-to-face, Juliet found that the most convenient place for her arm was around Ross's chest. His back was to the storm, so she was shielded from the worst of the wind's buffeting. "As long as we stay still, our makeshift tent should remain secure," she said. "I just hope Saleh and Murad are equally well off."

"They're fine," he said reassuringly. "As perils go, this is nowhere near as dangerous as a flash flood, a dagger duel, or even a *bozkashi* match. All Saleh and Murad had to do was roll up in the blanket they were using for shade. Since most of the caravan was resting, the storm couldn't have hit at a better time."

"That's true," she admitted. "We were undoubtedly the only two people foolish enough to wander off to admire the scenery."

"Naturally. Everyone knows that the British are indefatigable tourists."

Juliet smiled. Then, since she was tired and there was nothing more to say, she decided to take a nap. Outside, nature might be at its most savage, but the two of them shared a secure oasis of touch and warmth and quiet breathing.

Nonetheless, she found it impossible to doze. Now that she knew they were safe, she found the fury of the storm exhilarating. Its vibrations throbbed through her, making her one with the wind and the earth—and with Ross, for, as always, their bodies fitted together as if designed as a matching set. She could not see him in the darkness, but his scent was in her nostrils and the drumming of his heart was under her cheek, blending with the primal sound and rhythm of the tempest.

Slowly but inexorably the passion Juliet had thought suppressed came to treacherous life. At first it was only a faint stirring deep inside her, but it grew, became a tingling that flowed through her veins until it animated every fiber of her body. If they were lovers, she would respond to that flowing desire without hesitation, skimming her hands over his muscular arms and chest. She would press her lips to his throat and taste the salt of his skin, teasing and inviting at the same time.

Instead, she lay stone-still, fighting the impulse to touch him. They had been this close in the caravansary at Sarakhs when Juliet had woken and found herself twined around him, but that time he had been asleep and she had been free to pull away. Now they were both awake and aware, and locked together for the duration of the storm. Sternly she told herself that she could not possibly be overcome by desire in the midst of a raging sandstorm that battered and bellowed a mere two layers of fabric away, but her body flatly refused to accept that conclusion.

Her yearning was as itchily uncomfortable as being tickled by feathers. Feeling that she would burst into flame if she didn't move, Juliet shifted her weight slightly, but though her intention was to ease herself away, instead she found herself settling more closely against her husband. Mentally she uttered an oath, displeased by the knowledge that she was not fully in control of her body. Then she concentrated on breathing evenly, praying that Ross would not become aware of what she was feeling.

Then, abruptly, she realized that she was not alone in her desire. Ross's groin was resting against the curve of her hip, and she felt growing, unmistakable evidence that he was also aroused by their closeness.

She bit her lip to suppress what would be hysterical laughter if she let it out. They were both mad. While a murderous storm pounded all around them, both of them were experiencing inappropriate passions. And maddest of all, each pretended complete ignorance of what was happening.

Juliet's mouth was so dry that she felt on the verge of suffocation, so she reached down for her water bottle. As she did, her mind flashed back a dozen years. The darkness and intimacy of their present situation were like the midnight privacy of their marriage bed, when she had had every right to touch her husband, and he had encouraged her to do so. There had been no barriers, no doubts, between them then. . . .

Wholly without conscious volition, her hand moved past the water bottle and came to rest on that warm, irresistible ridge of male flesh. He pulsed against her palm, hardening further at her touch. Her mind more in the past than the present, she drew an entranced hand along the familiar length.

Remembered delight lasted only an instant before his whole frame went rigid. "Jesus Christ, Juliet!" Ross exploded, knocking her hand away. "This is a hell of time for you to play idiotic games."

Shocked back to the present and horrified at what she had done, Juliet gave a strangled gasp. Mindlessly, wanting only to escape, she shoved herself away from him, tore the mantle from her face, and tried to clamber to her feet. Immediately, gritty, suffocating sand filled her mouth and nostrils.

As Juliet collapsed, choking, Ross wrapped his arm around her waist and hauled back so that her spine was pressed against the front of his body. Then, with precise angry movements, he drew the mantle over her again and recreated their safe haven.

Juliet was shaking violently, as much from humiliation as from her frantic need for air. Ever since this journey had begun, she had worked to conceal how much she was attracted to her husband, and now her weakness was revealed. She felt more exposed than if she had been stripped naked.

This time it was Ross who held the water bottle to her lips so that she could rinse away the stifling sand. Soon she could breathe again, but still she trembled. The barrier they had so carefully constructed between them, of words unsaid and deeds unadmitted, now lay shattered, a victim of the storm.

Despairingly she said, "I'm sorry, Ross, I didn't mean to do that. I wasn't playing games—it's just that . . . I couldn't help myself. I know it's wrong and shameless and *bloody* inconvenient, but even after all these years, I still desire you. Being together day and night has been driving me mad." Her throat closed again and she swallowed hard before finishing in a whisper. "I'm sorry, so sorry."

Even though her back was to him, they were folded so closely together that she could feel his reactions in his body. After a moment of surprise his tautness eased.

"One apology is enough, Juliet. My reaction was out of proportion to what you did, but you surprised the devil out of me at a time when I was trying my damnedest to control the effect you have on me." He wrapped a comforting arm around her waist. "As you noticed, I was having no success. You have also been driving me mad. Embarrassing and, as you said, bloody inconvenient, but there it is."

His calm words made Juliet feel less like a disgraceful idiot. More to herself than to him she said, "Why must it be this way? Why can't a marriage that is over be *completely* over?"

He sighed. "My mother, who as you may recall knows everything worth knowing about the mysterious ways men and women interact, once told me that the first two years or so of a passionate marriage are the most intense. After that, the raging, uncontrollable fire usually slows to a steadier and more manageable blaze. Unfortunately, you left before that happened. We weren't together long enough for the cycle to complete itself and the flames to subside. So, even though the rest of the marriage is ancient history, the physical attraction is still alive and well. Now that we're in each other's company again, all that unresolved desire has flared back to life."

"That makes sense." She gave an unsteady chuckle. "I keep thinking of the pillar of fire that guided the Israelites through the wilderness. On this journey, a pillar of fire has been hovering between us, but you dissembled so well that I thought I was the only one affected by it. There is some comfort in knowing that the madness is mutual."

"That it is." His arm tightened around her waist. "You realize that if we share lodgings in Bokhara, we may drive each other well and truly insane."

"The thought has occurred to me," she admitted, "but I feel responsible for you. If not for my brother and mother, you'd be safe in England now. Even though I know there will be nothing I can do to help if the amir condemns you, I still have this irrational need to stay close, to be available just in case."

"And, heaven help me, I feel the same way about you—as if I should keep you close, because no one else will take as good care of you as I would." His thumb began making slow circles on her midriff. As tantalizing warmth spiraled through her, he said softly, "We seem to be burdened with both mutual protectiveness and mutual lust. It might be easier for both of us if we do the logical and natural thing about the latter."

The very idea made her melt with longing. To be lovers once again, to give in to desire instead of fighting it—that would be heaven on earth.

Until he went back to England. Leaving Ross once had almost destroyed her; if they recovered their old closeness, she doubted that she would survive losing him again. "It would be easier only for the moment," she said in a brittle voice. "The effect on the future would be disastrous."

His hand stilled, then withdrew. "You're quite right," he said coolly. "Wise of you to remind me of that. Like most men, I find that lust totally disables my brain."

"The same thing happened to me," she said in a small voice. "Another of my hopelessly unladylike traits."

Once more she felt Ross's tension ease.

"That's one of the things I've always liked about you," he remarked. "Your directness is a double-edged sword, but I find that preferable to the sort of flirtatiousness with which some women enjoy baffling men."

She was glad to hear that there was something he liked about her besides her body. Not that she objected to his finding her attractive, in spite of the complications that passion was causing. After years of being the asexual, forceful Gul-i Sarahi, it was deeply rewarding to feel like a woman, and to know that she could still attract a man. Especially this man.

They lay in silence together, relaxed if not precisely comfortable. Though desire was unacceptable, Juliet savored his closeness. But, more's the pity, it would not last much longer, for the wind was dying down and soon they would have to return to their usual roles, their usual distance.

When the wail of the storm faded to the soft soughing sound of "the wind of a hundred days," Ross removed his arm from Juliet's waist preparatory to sitting up. Knowing that time had run out, she said hesitantly, "Even though I felt like a fool, it is fortunate that this happened. Now that the air has been cleared and we've openly acknowledged that there is a . . . a lingering attraction, it should be easy to deal with."

"I'm glad you think so," Ross said after a long silence. His voice was very dry. "The storm seems to have blown itself out. Shall we see what the outside world looks like?"

He pulled back the mantle, spilling rivulets of fine sand from every wrinkle and fold of the fabric. Darkness had fallen, but the sky was clear and a waxing moon cast ethereal light over the pale, voluptuously curving dunes. The temperature had dropped considerably and the fresh night air felt wonderful after the cramped confines of their makeshift tent.

Drawing a deep, deep breath, Juliet rolled onto her back and stretched her cramped limbs to their full length. "Desert stars are magnificent," she said as she gazed up into the velvet darkness. "I never tire of looking at them."

More concerned with the mundane than the celestial, Ross had pushed himself to a sitting position and was studying their surroundings. "A good thing that I have my compass, or we might be using these stars to find our way back to camp. The storm has changed the contours of the dunes so much that it would be easy to get lost."

"At least there's no rush. I'm sure that we'll get a late start tomorrow morning, because it will take hours to locate all of the objects that have been buried by the storm."

Juliet was about to sit up when Ross glanced down at her. The pale moonlight was just strong enough to sketch the classic perfection of his features.

"So convenient that we have both acknowledged that foolish lingering attraction," he murmured as he lifted one hand and traced the contours of her face. The faint roughness of his fingertips was delicately erotic as he skimmed the curve of her cheek and brushed lightly over her lips.

She caught her breath, wanting to tell him that this was not wise, but before she could speak, he leaned over and kissed her with deep, commanding sensuality. The desire Juliet had banked earlier flared like fresh-sparked tinder and she welcomed his mouth with a hunger that shocked her. It was an embrace such as she had forgotten, or perhaps not dared to remember.

Reaching up, she slid her arms around Ross's chest and drew him down on her, wanting contact with all of him. He came without breaking the kiss, enfolding her with his strength. Shamelessly she rolled her hips against him, and the pressure of his hard body gave her a fleeting satisfaction that was immediately consumed by rising need.

As she moved against him, he gave a long, shuddering gasp. Then he pulled the tagelmoust down, baring her throat. As he kissed the sensitive skin revealed, the masculine prickle of whiskers made a sweet, rasping contrast to the searing heat of his lips and tongue.

His hand slid to her breast and she arched against his palm, hating the layers of robe and the binding vest that separated her from his magical touch. Her breath frantic, she ground her body against his, on the verge of culminating but wanting more than anything on earth to share that fulfilment with him.

Then, shockingly, he was gone, leaving only the cool night against her fevered flesh. The loss was devastating.

Frightened and confused, her limbs shaking with frustration, Juliet opened her eyes to find Ross standing above her, his broad shoulders blocking the stars and his chest heaving with strain.

Yet in spite of his agitation, when he spoke it was in a voice whose irony had been refined to saber sharpness. "As you pointed out, now that our inconvenient attraction is out in the open, it is wonderfully easy to deal with. Aren't we *fortunate?*"

For a moment Juliet didn't understand. Then, with a flash of pure outrage, she realized that his lovemaking had been a deliberate tease, a vivid demonstration of just

how frustrating and difficult their situation was. If he had
been within her reach, she might have planted a fist right
on his perfectly shaped jaw; Ian had always said that she
hit well for a girl.

That impulse was immediately followed by the appalling realization that Ross was giving her exactly what she
had claimed to want: restraint. It was Juliet who had set
the limits in their curious relationship, just as it was she
who had made the first sexual advance. After which she
had blithely made that idiotic statement about how much
things would improve.

Helplessly she began to laugh. "Leave it to you to turn
gentlemanly behavior into a weapon, Ross. Very well,
you've made your point, though that was a beastly way
to do it."

She stood and began brushing loose sand from her
robe. "My saying that everything would be easy now was
one of my more foolish remarks." She bent over for her
mantle, then shook it out with a snap. "But I still think
it is an improvement that we can acknowledge the . . .
the pillar of fire between us."

"It is an improvement, though I can't agree that there
is anything very fortunate about our present situation,"
Ross said ruefully. "Now it's my turn to apologize. As
you said, that was a beastly way to make a point. If it's
any comfort, stopping was as harrowing for me as for
you."

"At least you managed to keep your head when I had
lost mine. For that I must thank you." Juliet pulled off
her veil and shook it out. "Now that we are through
harrowing each other, it's time to get back to the camp."

Before she could wind her tagelmoust around her face
again, Ross put an arm around her shoulders and pulled
her to him for a moment, brushing an affectionate kiss
on her cheek before releasing her. "Have I ever mentioned that you are the most admirable, maddening female I have ever known?"

"While you, O perfect gentleman, could drive a saint
to violence, and I am no saint."

"I suspect that a saint would be boring, and you are
never that," he said with amusement.

They began walking back to the camp in amiable silence. But as they wound their way through the silent dunes, Juliet's sense of well-being slowly evaporated, leaving her chilled and fearful of what the future would bring.

Bleakly she realized that it was not physical intimacy that she should have been worrying about. The sandstorm had brought about something far more dangerous: an emotional closeness more seductive than kisses.

15

❦

The last leg of the journey was rather public, for
Ross's identity had long since ceased to be a secret.
The tale of the *bozkashi* match and of his mission
to the amir had run ahead of the travelers, so after the
caravan crossed the broad Oxus river into more heavily
populated territory, people began coming to see the ferengi. The Uzbek and Turkoman callers were curious and
wanted to touch his blond hair, but most were friendly.

However, there were exceptions. The last night before
the caravan would reach the city of Bokhara was spent
in the caravansary of Karakul. As Ross and his companions ate their evening meal, a shabby rat-faced Uzbek
crossed the courtyard, then squatted down to watch
them.

Thinking the man might be hungry, Saleh said, "Will
you honor us by sharing our humble fare?"

The visitor spat on the ground. "I will not defile myself
by sharing bread and salt with a ferengi spy and his dogs.
I have come only because tonight will be the last opportunity to see what the infidel looks like."

"Look all you like," Ross said mildly.

The Uzbek's slit-eyed gaze went to Ross's face. "Tomorrow you will be met by the amir's horsemen. They
will be carrying baskets with bandages to blindfold you,
chains to bind you, and knives to butcher you," he said
with obvious relish. "You are a son of death, ferengi."

"Are not all sons of man also sons of death?" Ross
took another bite of his bread. Having long since learned
that piety was the best defense in this sort of conversa-

195

tion, he added, "Only in God does man find eternal life."

The Uzbek glowered at him. "Paradise is only for the Faithful, ferengi swine. Tomorrow night you will dine in hell." He rose to his feet and stalked away.

Ross swallowed the last of his bread, then said into the silence, "Anyone care to lay odds on whether that unpleasant fellow was telling the truth about what will happen tomorrow?"

Juliet, who had become more vocal since Murad discovered her identity, said acerbically, "No point in wagering with a man who may not be around to pay off his losses."

"British humor is very strange," Murad said, giving them a disapproving glance. "But no matter, for that son of a swine was lying. How could one such as he know the amir's plans?"

"Very likely he invented that story as a way of ruining a night's rest. However . . ." Ross brushed crumbs from his lap. "If any officers of the amir approach the caravan tomorrow carrying baskets, I want all three of you to move away from me. If I am to be butchered, I don't need company."

Ross glanced at Murad. Several days earlier, Ross had taken the youth aside and persuaded him that if something happened to Ross, serving and protecting his master's wife would be a deed of great honor. Remembering that conversation, Murad gave a nod of agreement.

Then Ross caught Juliet's eye and repeated, "If in doubt, you will keep your distance."

Even more reluctantly than Murad, she nodded, then looked away. Satisfied, Ross poured himself more tea. At least he could count on Saleh's good sense.

As he sipped his tea, he reflected on how the incident in the sandstorm had changed his relationship with Juliet. As she had predicted, admitting their mutual attraction had cleared the air and eased the situation—in some ways. Ross no longer attempted to completely conceal his feelings from his wife's perceptive eyes, and they were more relaxed with each other.

But as he had known at the time, in other ways the situation was far more difficult, for his simmering desire had risen to a level just short of full boil. He couldn't decide which of his actions had been more insane: kissing her in the first place or stopping even though she had been warm and willing.

Juliet had been more than willing; she had been eager, and that knowledge was a constant torment, especially at night when Ross was trying to sleep. He was haunted by precise tactile memories of her slim body moving under his, her ardent mouth, the feel of her hands on him. And, infuriatingly, his memory also supplied equally exact, though more distant, memories of what it was like to be inside her, for them to be joined together without doubt or inhibition.

He had wanted to teach her a lesson, and instead he had almost been swept away himself. He was still not quite sure why he had drawn back from what he had wanted fervently to do. The fact that a few minutes earlier Juliet had explicitly rejected the idea of becoming lovers was a factor, but he suspected that self-preservation was the major cause. The remote part of his brain still capable of logic had known that bedding the demented Amazon he had married would be a massive mistake; after her blood had cooled, Juliet would surely have despised him for taking advantage of her momentary weakness, and relations between them were already quite volatile enough.

Unfortunately, the knowledge that he had acted wisely could not quench the slow, frustrated burn of arousal that tormented him whenever he thought of Juliet. As he finished his tea, he uttered a silent prayer of thanks for loose, concealing Asiatic clothing. However, yearning for Juliet did have one benefit: it helped distract him from the question of whether he might be butchered like a feast-day lamb the next day.

Though none of his companions referred to his possible fate, an undercurrent of tension was present the rest of the evening. So far, nature had supplied the journey's worst hazards, but from now on the enemies would be human and far more dangerous.

After another restless night, Ross rose the next morning and put aside his Asiatic garments for English cloth-

ing. As he had told Juliet back at Serevan, whatever
influence he might hope for came from his status as Ian's
countryman and kin, and his well-tailored blue coat,
white shirt, and tan breeches instantly proclaimed that
he was European. He even donned his black English hat,
a folding style which he had brought because of its ability
to survive being packed.

The rat-faced Uzbek must have spread his story
around the caravan, for most of the other travelers kept
their distance from Ross. Some were unobtrusive in their
avoidance, while others shunned the ferengi as if he were
a plague carrier. Given the amir's reputation for quixotic
violence, Ross didn't blame them.

Nonetheless, the first part of the day's journey was
quiet. By noon they had left the trackless desert behind
and were traveling along a shady, poplar-lined road. The
land was dead flat, and lushly irrigated orchards and
fields ran as far as the eye could see. After the desolate
Kara Kum, the country seemed both prosperous and
crowded, for the road carried a steady flow of traffic in
both directions, heavily laden ponies competing with
bored donkeys and high-wheeled carts.

They had passed through the village of Shahr Islam
and were only five or six miles from Bokhara itself when
Ross saw a large dust cloud in the road far ahead of
them. Since it was unusual to travel at high speed during
the midday heat, he said to Murad, who had the keenest
vision among them, "Can you make out what kind of
party is coming toward us?"

The young Persian shaded his eyes and squinted
against the brilliant sunshine. "Three men. They are
dressed as royal chamberlains—and two are carrying
baskets."

Ross tensed as he remembered what the rat-faced
Uzbek had said the night before. His journey from Constantinople had had its risks, but they had been no worse
than on any journey through wild, unsettled lands. Bokhara, however, represented a very different kind of danger, for putting himself in the power of a xenophobic
madman was like a fly landing on a web and asking for
the spider's mercy.

Until now it had always been possible to turn back,

but the point of no return was at hand. If the men in the distance were indeed royal chamberlains and were coming for him, there was a small but very real chance that he might be killed within the next half-hour. He did not consider that likely; even if the chamberlains were hostile—and they might not be—they would probably take him prisoner rather than slaughter him out of hand.

What had the Uzbek said would be in the baskets—bandages, chains, and blades? If ever he needed his English sangfroid, it was now, for it took a special kind of courage to remain stoic while waiting to see if his doom had arrived. On the whole, Ross would prefer being attacked by marauding Turkomans, but his voice was calm when he said, "You all know what to do. Now do it."

His companions slowed their mounts and merged into the caravan. As the chamberlains thundered toward them, all of the travelers watched warily. Some cast sympathetic glances at Ross, but no one spoke, though the air twanged with tension.

Riding alone and wearing his European clothing, Ross was readily identifiable, and the riders galloped right up to him, then pulled up their horses with a flourish. The leader, who wore a lavishly patterned silk robe, announced, "I am the amir's grand chamberlain. You are the English Lord Khilburn?"

Ross reined in his camel and inclined his head respectfully. "I am, O servant of the great and powerful king, the successor of the Prophet."

The chamberlain gave a broad gap-toothed smile. "Nasrullah Bahadur, the King of Kings and Commander of the Faithful, bids you welcome. As a token of his desire that there be peace between our great lands, he invites you to be his guest during your stay in Bokhara." The man waved a hand at his minions, who opened the baskets and brought forth a lavish spread of food that included fresh fruit, roast horseflesh, and jugs of tea.

It was the most welcome anticlimax Ross had ever experienced. Reining in his giddy relief, he said formally, "The amir does this insignificant traveler great honor."

The chamberlain's speculative glance shifted from Ross to the caravan, which had ground to a stop, all its members watching the show. "Have you no slave, Lord Khilburn?"

Ross made an instant decision. Although the amir's invitation was no guarantee of limitless royal favor, for the moment Ross's head would stay attached to his shoulders. It was time for their party to split according to their plan, though he still hated the idea of Juliet staying with him and facing at least some of the same dangers. "I have one, but he preferred to stand aside until it was clear whether fortune would smile or frown on me."

The chamberlain's lip curled. "Like a dog running off with his tail between his legs."

For Juliet's own sake, it was important that she not be perceived as a loyal servant, so as Ross beckoned to her, he said matter-of-factly, "One's own life is sweet. Why should a son of the Prophet, on whom be peace, risk his life for a ferengi?"

Silently Juliet rode up beside him. She was leading the pack camel that carried Ross's baggage; the other beast had been placed in Murad's charge.

After a curious glance at Juliet, the chamberlain said, "We shall eat now. Then we shall escort you to the royal palace so you can make your obeisance to the amir."

Startled at the swiftness of events, Ross said, "You mean I will be able to present my petition today?"

"If it pleases his majesty, yes." The chamberlain turned and barked, "The rest of you, be off about your business!"

The members of the caravan set their beasts in motion and streamed by. Saleh and Murad deliberately avoided looking at their erstwhile companions, while others, including Muhammad and Hussayn Kasem, called friendly farewells and good wishes. The Kasems had already given Ross instructions on how to find their house in Bokhara, along with solemn assurances that they would help his mission in any way they could.

Within a few minutes Ross and Juliet were alone with the royal officers. As they settled down for a picnic under the poplars, Ross asked, "My lord chamberlain, surely you have heard what brings me to Bokhara. Is my brother, the British Major Cameron, still numbered among the living?"

The chamberlain's dark eyes became opaque. "That is a subject that you must discuss with the highest. I am but an ignorant servant." Opening a jug, he said, "Especially for you, we have brought tea with milk and sugar. That is the English fashion, is that not so?"

"Indeed it is. Once more I am flattered by your courtesy."

It was the best meal Ross had had in weeks, and having just received a stay of execution, he enjoyed it thoroughly. Juliet also ate well, though she said nothing. She was thoroughly into her role of dark, enigmatic desert marauder, her eyes darting around warily, as if expecting attack. After snatching her food, she hunkered down a little apart from the others to eat.

The Bokharans watched with interest as she raised food to her mouth behind her veil. One of the deputy chamberlains said to the other in Uzbek, "That slave is a wild one. The ferengi is lucky the fellow has not taken his gold and perhaps his life."

Ross ignored the comment; he had decided to use his fluent Persian so that he could communicate freely with Bokharan officials, but to conceal his knowledge of Uzbek on the chance that he might overhear useful comments by men who thought that he did not understand. Even if the comments weren't useful, they could be amusing, like the one he had just heard.

As they finished the meal, the grand chamberlain said, "Your slave is a Targui of the Sahara, is he not? Once or twice I have seen one of his tribe in Bokhara."

"Aye, but he is a servant, not a slave. Among his own people, he is of high rank. He serves me only as long as it pleases him." Ross bit into a ripe, juicy date. "The Tuareg are great thieves. In their own language, the words 'to plunder' and 'to be free' mean the same thing. But Jalal usually does what I ask, and he's good with camels."

"Does he speak or understand Persian?"

"A little, I think." Ross gave a bored shrug, clearly indicating how tedious he found the topic of his servant. "It is hard to tell just how much he understands."

"The lad has unusual gray eyes, like a Baluchi," the

chamberlain said reflectively, his gaze still on Juliet. "It is said that the Tuareg are a handsome race."

"The women, who go unveiled, are very handsome. Of Jalal himself, I cannot say, for I have never seen his face."

Curiosity finally satisfied, the chamberlain rose to his feet. "And now, Lord Khilburn, we will ride to Bokhara."

The Silk Road had turned Bokhara into the richest oasis in Central Asia, an arrogant citadel guarded by the perilous deserts that surrounded it. The city had not changed in the years since Ross's first visit; he doubted that its massive walls and lofty watchtowers had changed in centuries.

When they reached the giant gateway that was the western approach to the city, Ross halted his camel, preparatory to dismounting. The chamberlain frowned. "Why are you stopping?"

Ross raised his eyebrows. "Is it not forbidden for unbelievers to ride in the city?"

"Usually, but exceptions are made for those in the amir's favor," the chamberlain said. "Of course you will have to dismount when we reach the royal palace. Even I will, for only the amir and his grandees may ride within the palace walls."

Ross nodded and set Julietta in motion again. He and Alex Burnes had had not only to put aside their mounts inside the city but also to change to humbler garments, since they were infidels. Because they were traveling as private individuals rather than as representatives of the British government, they had quietly obeyed all local customs so that they would not attract unwelcome attention.

The city skyline was dominated by minarets and domes. Bokhara was one of the holy cities of Islam, and it was said that a good Muslim could pray in a different mosque every day of the year. Ross and Burnes had decided that that was an exaggeration, but certainly there were a couple of hundred mosques and dozens of religious colleges.

On this journey it was not possible to avoid attention. The wide street that led from the entry gate to the palace teemed with people who stopped to stare at Ross, with more emerging onto their flat rooftops to see him. A hum of comments about his clothing, coloring, and general foreignness arose from the watchers. As on the trip across the Kara Kum, the general tone was more curious than hostile. Once a young water carrier who had pressed against a wall to let the riders pass called out cheerfully, "Salaam Aleikum!"

Ross smiled and lifted his hand. "And peace be unto you."

The great public square in front of the royal palace was called the Registan. Ross remembered it from his previous trip, for the square was the heart of the city, and it churned and buzzed during all the daylight hours. In the center was a great market with canopies shading sellers of fruit, tea, and goods from all over Asia, but most of the throng were present to talk, to see and be seen.

The diversity of the crowd was incredible. The majority were either oriental-eyed Uzbeks from Bokhara's ruling class or people of Persian descent, who were called Tadjiks when they lived in Turkestan. However, virtually every other race of Asia was also represented, from Hindus to Uighars to Chinese. The few women present rode astride like men, their bodies invisible under black horsehair veils that covered them from head to foot.

Two sides of the Registan were flanked by *medressehs*, religious colleges, and another side was bounded by a great tree-shaded fountain. But it was the vast thousand-year-old bulk of the royal palace that dominated; called the Ark, it loomed threateningly over the rest of the square.

At the entrance to the palace precincts, the entire party dismounted and Juliet moved forward to take Ross's reins. For a moment their gazes met. Quietly, under the noise of the crowd, he said, "This is it."

She nodded. "Tomorrow at this time, we could be headed home."

He doubted that she believed that any more than he did, but he supposed it was theoretically possible. As they walked up the ramp that led to the turreted entry gate, Ross felt the hair at the back of his neck prickle. This was his first visit to the Ark, for he and Burnes had never sought an audience with the amir, but he had heard many stories about it. Some who entered were never known to leave again.

The design of the Ark was similar to a European castle; in fact, the greatest of the medieval fortresses were designed by builders who had studied Saracen architecture during the Crusades. The towering outer walls enclosed a small city of buildings and a broad courtyard where royal servants and slaves moved back and forth about their business.

The grand chamberlain gestured for a groom to come and take their mounts to the stables. "It is customary to take one's slave into the palace proper," he said with a dubious glance at Juliet, "but he must be silent and cause no trouble."

As Ross removed a leather case from his saddlebags, he asked Juliet in Tamahak, "Think you can behave yourself, slave? It might be better to stay with the camels."

"I wouldn't miss this for anything," she murmured as she took the leather case from him.

The grandest of the buildings was the palace, and a wide flight of steps led them to the main entrance. Inside the palace, high ceilings and marble floors provided a cool contrast to the shimmering heat outdoors. Silently the grand chamberlain led his guests through a series of passages to a large room where other petitioners waited for an audience with the amir. As the chamberlain had said, most men had slaves with them, so Juliet's presence was unremarkable.

An even more richly garbed man came up. He was about sixty years old and appeared to be Persian. To Ross's surprise, the man said in accented, almost unintelligible English, "Welcome to Bokhara." He bowed. "I am the Nayeb Abdul Samut Khan, commander of the amir's artillery. I have had the honor to serve with others of your splendid race in Afghanistan."

Ross bowed back. "The honor is mine." Switching languages, he said, "While you have a masterly command of my native tongue, I prefer to speak in Persian, so that all men may hear and understand that I have nothing to hide."

"Very wise, Lord Khilburn," the nayeb said with an approving nod, "for there are many men that do not value the British as I do." Switching to Persian, he said, "I have been sent to ask if you will submit to the mode of salaam when you are presented to the amir."

"Of what does the salaam consist?"

"A man who comes before his majesty must stroke his beard and bow three times, saying '*Allah Akbar, Salaamat Padishah.*'"

Guessing that there had been ferengis in the past who had balked at performing the ritual, Ross said peaceably, "I would willingly do it thirty times if necessary, for it is fitting to say that God is great and to wish peace to the king."

Abdul Samut Khan nodded, satisfied, then gestured to the case Juliet carried. "What is that?"

"A modest gift for the amir, as a token of the esteem in which I hold him."

Juliet opened the leather case. Ross lifted out a flat wooden box with a brass plate set in the lid. Flipping up the lid, he revealed two superbly made flintlock holster pistols nestling in velvet-lined niches.

The nayeb sucked in his breath at the sight of the pistols, for the weapons dazzled like jewels. Every square inch of metal and wood was chiseled and engraved in elaborate patterns, and the walnut stocks were inlaid with gold wire. Moreover, they had been made by one of Britain's finest gunsmiths, so they should be as accurate as they were beautiful. Ross had bought the pair on the assumption that they would prove useful, perhaps as a gift for some Arab chieftain in the Levant. His instincts had proved sound, for the pistols were truly a gift fit for a king.

Reverently Abdul Samut Khan lifted each of the pistols and checked to see that it was unloaded before replacing it. "Very good," he said, handing the box back to Juliet. "Now, give me your passport and any letters of introduction that you have."

Ross produced his travel papers and the letters he had been collecting since Constantinople. There were an even dozen, starting with the sultan and ending with the khalifa of the Turkomans. All the letter writers asked, in incredibly elaborate language, that the amir look favorably on Ross's petition.

The nayeb accepted the documents, then gestured toward a stone bench along the wall. "Wait here."

Ross sat and crossed his legs, a vaguely bored expression on his face for the benefit of the curious, while a couple of feet away Juliet squatted by the wall in a dark ball of flowing robes. The wait was surprisingly short—less than half an hour—before the nayeb returned for him.

Under the resentful gazes of those who had been waiting longer, Ross followed his guide from the room, Juliet behind him with the gift case. A short walk brought them to the crowded audience chamber. On the left, arches opened to a courtyard bright with flowers. Inside the chamber, courtiers whose richly patterned robes were precisely graded to reflect their status watched eagerly to see what the ferengi would do.

But Ross paid little attention to his surroundings, for finally, after four long months of travel, he was in the presence of the Amir Nasrullah, called the most brutal ruler in Asia. The man who had murdered his own father and brothers to secure his throne was about forty years old, and stout, with a long black beard. Though the audience chamber was lavishly decorated, he himself wore clothing as plain as any mullah.

Ross removed his hat and held it in his left hand as an English mark of respect, then performed the obeisance. Lacking a beard, he had to stroke his chin, but his bows were deep and he called out *"Allah Akbar, Salaamat Padishah"* in a resonant voice.

Straightening from his final bow, he looked the amir full in the face. Nasrullah's eyes were small and rather beady, and the muscles of his face twitched convulsively. Nonetheless, he had the aura of power that absolute authority bestows, plus a bright, unstable glitter that was all his own. It was said that his four Persian wives despised him.

Speaking in a high, rapid voice, the amir said, "You honor us by your presence, Lord Khilburn. Have you come on a mission from the English queen, our sister in royalty?"

Nasrullah knew perfectly well why his visitor had come, but Ross went along with the pretense. After bowing again, he said, "Nay, I do not come on official business, but to beseech your great mercy for my brother, the British Major Ian Cameron."

The amir raised his hand before Ross could say more. "I am told that you have brought a gift for me."

"The merest trifle." Juliet stepped forward and Ross took the pistol box from the case, then opened it for the amir. "I beg that you will condescend to accept this unworthy token."

Nasrullah's eyes widened with genuine pleasure and he gave a soft sigh, like a child receiving an especially longed-for sweet. "Exquisite." He lifted one of the pistols in his hands and caressed it, running his fingers over the softly gleaming surfaces in the same way a man might caress his lover. "Come. I wish to try them." Rising to his feet, he swept imperiously across the room and out to the courtyard.

Ross, Juliet, and the courtiers trailed after him. The courtyard was an enchanted garden with a pink marble fountain tinkling in the center and cooling palms waving high above formal beds of brilliant carnations and roses. As Ross inhaled, he noticed that the heavy scent of patchouli underlay the lighter floral fragrances, and guessed that the fountain was perfumed.

Above their heads, the palm fronds rustled dryly as Nasrullah came to a halt and demanded that his visitor load the pistols. Ross had come prepared, and the leather case contained tins of black powder and lead balls. After pouring a measured charge of powder down each barrel, he rammed balls down on top, sprinkled priming powder in the pans, then handed one of the weapons to the amir.

Without bothering to aim, the amir fired the pistol at the fountain. The heavy ball cracked the pink marble and ricocheted away as perfumed water began seeping out of the wide basin. "Splendid, splendid!"

While courtiers coughed at the acrid smoke, Nasrullah exchanged pistols and fired the second one, this time blasting a clump of scarlet carnations to shreds. "Magnificent!"

As Ross reloaded, the amir said mischievously, "Of

course, the real test of a weapon is how well it performs the task for which it was created." Lifting one of the reloaded pistols, he continued, "And the task of a gun is to kill."

Alerted by the note of unholy amusement in the ruler's voice, Ross expected trouble. But nothing could have prepared him for the soul-shattering fear he felt when the amir swung around and pointed the gun directly at Juliet's head.

16

For an endless terrifying moment, Juliet stared down the deadly black muzzle of the pistol. Under almost any other circumstances she would have dived for cover while reaching for her own concealed knife. But here, in the amir's palace, surrounded by his guards, she dared not do that, for escape was impossible and anything she did might endanger Ross.

Then her view of the pistol was blocked out by her husband's broad blue-clad shoulder as he stepped between her and the amir. In a voice that held just a faint hint of reproach, he said, "Among my people, it is considered a grave breach of etiquette to kill another man's slave without cause."

Juliet heard a burst of unnerving laughter, punctuated by the shattering crack of another gunshot. For an agonizing moment she thought that Nasrullah had fired at Ross, but an instant later fragments of palm frond spattered down on them.

"God forbid that I should offend the customs of a guest's people," the amir said genially. "You are right. It is far more courteous to kill one of my own slaves."

Her heart still pounding with reaction from her narrow escape, Juliet edged back toward the nervous crowd of courtiers, at the same time moving to the side so that she could better see what was happening. Those courtiers who were fortunate enough to be at the back of the group had already slipped away.

Nasrullah scanned the people in the courtyard consideringly. "Who among these jackals has the least value?" His gaze fell on a serving boy who had just entered the

209

garden carrying a brass tray mounded with fresh fruit.
Juliet guessed the child was using the courtyard as a
shortcut to another part of the palace.

"You, boy." The ruler gestured toward the far side of
the courtyard with the pistol. "Go stand over there."

The child was no more than ten years old and probably
of Persian blood. Immediately grasping the amir's intention, he gasped and dropped his tray. The brass hit the
ground with a hollow gonging sound and fruit bounced
in all directions as the boy tried to run, but two guards
immediately stopped his flight.

As one guard dragged the chosen victim to the other
side of the courtyard, the other removed the child's turban and ripped it into two long strips. Then the men
used the fabric to lash the boy's wrists to two palms so
that he could not run away. Their task accomplished,
both guards stepped hastily out of the way before Nasrullah could decide he preferred larger targets.

Hopelessly the child stared at his royal master. His
face was sheened with sweat and his small chest rose
and fell in short, harsh pants of fear. The courtyard was
absolutely silent except for the tinkling of fountain water
and the incongruous chirping of birds in the palms.

Calmly the amir pointed his weapon at his living target
and pulled the trigger. As the gun blast echoed painfully
from the marble walls and another cloud of smoke rolled
out, the boy screamed, a sound of desperate, bloodcur-
dling terror.

It took several seconds for the smoke to thin enough
to show that the boy still stood upright between the trees,
unharmed. Sobbing desperately, he twisted and tugged
at his bonds.

Nasrullah frowned. "I missed. Give me the other pistol. This may take some time, for I am not an expert
marksman."

The thought of standing here watching this maniac
blaze away at the child turned Juliet's stomach. How
many shots would it take? And would he be satisfied to
wound his target, or would he keep going until the boy
was dead? For a brief, murderous moment she considered going for her knife and plunging it into the amir's
throat, but common sense held her back. Barely.

Then Ross spoke in the cool tone which could be either maddening or comforting, depending on the circumstances. Now it was the voice of sanity in a mad world. "If it is proof of the weapons' deadliness that you desire, that is easily provided."

Raising the second pistol, Ross aimed it into a palm tree and fired. A moment later, the small mangled body of a sparrow fell to the ground. "It seems a pity to waste a slave," he said mildly. "And a sparrow is a more challenging test for a weapon."

Temporarily nonplussed, the amir looked from the dead bird to Ross and back again. Then he smiled with cold cruelty. "You are an excellent shot, Lord Khilburn. Since you are so concerned for my slave, you may display your marksmanship on his behalf."

He beckoned one of the guards over and gave an order Juliet could not hear. The guard stooped and picked up one of the pomegranates that had been dropped earlier, then went over to the child and placed it on top of his head, murmuring a sharp command for the boy to stand still.

Turning back to his visitor, Nasrullah continued, "Shoot the pomegranate from the boy's head and I will make you a gift of him. Miss and I will shoot him myself, however long it takes."

Only someone who knew Ross as well as Juliet would have noticed the nearly invisible tightening of his facial muscles. "Very well," he said emotionlessly, accepting the terms of this grisly game of William Tell.

As he reloaded his pistol, Juliet felt his inner turmoil as sharply as if it were her own. The boy was standing at the outer limit of the weapon's accuracy, and Ross faced the probability that he would either accidentally shoot the boy or miss and deliver him into the amir's lethal clutches. The child's only hope was that Ross make a flawless shot—and if he failed, she knew that he would never forgive himself.

None of his disquiet was visible as he raised the pistol and took careful aim at the small reddish sphere. For Juliet it was one of those moments that become engraved forever on the mind. Ross looked handsome and calm and utterly English, as relaxed as if he were target-shooting in a London gallery. A shaft of light spiked through the palm fronds and touched his hair to blazing gold. On the far side of the garden the child held rigidly still, his eyes so wide that white was visible all around the dark irises. The sound of his panicky breath filled the air.

Juliet uttered a fervent silent prayer for both the boy's sake and Ross's. Then the gun roared out.

Each time a shot was fired, it took longer for the smoke to dissipate. Impatiently the amir stepped forward to see the results, Ross following more slowly behind. Before they were halfway across the courtyard, the smoke cleared enough to reveal that the boy was unhurt and crimson fragments of ruptured pomegranate were smeared on the white wall behind him.

Nasrullah burst into laughter and clapped Ross on the back. "Splendid, splendid! You are a magnificent marksman." Stepping up to the tethered boy, he ran a languid hand down the downy cheek. "You have won yourself a slave, Lord Khilburn," the amir said. "He is a pretty child. Enjoy him."

Shaking with repressed fury, Juliet stepped forward and untied the bonds from the boy's wrists. The child looked up at her uncertainly, alarmed by her veiled countenance. Under her breath she said gruffly, "Do not fear. All will be well."

Then she took his hand and led him back toward the group of watchers. When they halted and turned to watch the rest of the scene, his fingers stayed curled in hers.

With the merest hint of irony, Ross was saying, "Your majesty is merciful and generous. I thank you for the gift."

In a lightning jump, the amir said, "You claim that Major Cameron is your brother, yet you do not resemble him except in height. Did your father have you by different wives?"

"No. Major Cameron is not my brother by blood, but by marriage," Ross replied. "His sister is my wife."

"Ah-h-h." Nasullah stroked his beard. "Have you only one wife? While that is said to be the ferengi practice, surely men of rank such as yourself need not abide by such a paltry custom."

"Some men have concubines," Ross admitted, "but our law binds all men, of all ranks, to one wife at a time."

The amir snorted. "How tedious. A man needs variety."

"Variety is not without charm, but it comes at the cost of deeper love," Ross replied. "A man who has a dozen horses will cherish none of them as much as the man who has only one. In the same way, a man with but one wife will know her better and value her more than a man with a harem full of wives and concubines."

Though he did not so much as flick an eyelash in her direction, Juliet felt as if his comment was aimed at her, and she felt a curious blend of pride and guilt. Ross was much too good for her, but she had always known that.

Nasrullah was less impressed. "That sounds to me like what a man tries to make himself believe when he has no choice."

Ross smiled. "As you will, your majesty. There are many truths, and this is one of mine."

With another abrupt shift the amir said, "It is extraordinary. I have two hundred thousand Persian slaves in Bokhara—no one cares for them. Yet I take a single British captive and a person comes all the way from England to demand his release."

Juliet tensed and could feel matching tension in Ross. They had reached the heart of their mission.

With a complete lack of pride, Ross dropped to his knees before the amir. "I do not demand, I beseech. If you are holding my brother captive, I beg that you release him. Knowing how the laws of hospitality are honored in your great land, I cannot believe the reports that he has been brutally murdered."

"Your plea is most moving, Lord Khilburn, and perhaps if you had come several months ago, I would have granted your petition. But, alas, you come too late." Nasrullah's voice dripped with spurious regret, but his dark eyes gleamed with malice. "It grieves me to inform you that Major Cameron has been executed."

Juliet closed her eyes and took a shuddering breath as she surrendered the last faint hope. Her brother was dead.

The Persian boy squeezed her hand hesitantly and she

realized that her hand had tightened on his. It was to his credit that, after all he had just endured, he was sensitive to her distress. Forcing her eyes open, she saw that her husband had become as still as she. After a long, long pause Ross said, "Might I ask what he did to deserve such punishment?"

There was a dangerous silence, for the amir was seldom questioned, but after a moment he shrugged. "His credentials were not in order, so there was some question of whether he was truly representing the British government. Then Cameron was caught spying. When confronted with the evidence, he converted to Islam and swore loyalty to me, only to recant a few days later." Nasrullah's eyes were cold as death. "According to our law, if a man says he will turn Muslim, he must do so or die."

"I see." Ross got heavily to his feet. "Those are indeed grave transgressions. Yet since he has paid for his crime, I beg that you allow me to take his body home for burial."

"I have wasted enough time on this matter for today," Nasrullah said brusquely. "I will consider your request and speak with you another time." He glanced around until his eye caught that of one of his guards. "The foreign minister has questions for Lord Khilburn. Take the ferengi there." Then the amir strode back into the audience chamber.

As Ross watched the ruler move away, his right hand curled into a fist. He forced his fingers to relax. Nasrullah was as cruel and mad as his reputation, and Ross and Juliet would need the devil's own luck to get out of Bokhara with their necks intact. Schooling his expression to impassivity, he followed the guard from the courtyard, Juliet and the boy following.

Abdul Samut Khan led them to a small office where the Bokharan minister of foreign affairs was dictating to a Persian scribe. The minister was an Uzbek with bushy brows and a permanent scowl, and for the next hour he subjected Ross to a sharp interrogation while Juliet and the boy squatted silently in a corner of the office.

The minister began by asking whether the British people would be angry at news of Major Cameron's death.

When Ross affirmed that they were already upset by the major's captivity and would surely be furious at news of his death, the minister frowned and asked how far it was from England to Bokhara. He relaxed when he learned how great the distance was, then embarked on a series of questions on the internal politics of Britain and Russia. He was well-informed on the latter, not surprising when the Russian empire loomed over Central Asia like a thundercloud.

However, there was a brief, dangerous flurry when the minister asked the names of the four British "grand viziers," then accused Ross of lying because the names were different from what Ian Cameron had given the year before. Wearily Ross explained that there had been a recent change of government, which led to the complex process of explaining how the British constitutional monarchy worked.

The Bokharan was mollified when his visitor was able to name the previous government's chief ministers, though Ross doubted that his interrogater really believed that an administration could change peacefully. To install a new government without bloodshed was contrary to the tenets of Asiatic rulership.

The questions went on and on, and Ross was so tired that he was having trouble concentrating. The caravan had set out long before dawn, and he had endured a full and stressful day since. Now dusk was falling, but the foreign minister seemed indefatigable. Finally Ross asked, "May my servant take my new slave to collect his personal belongings?"

The minister agreed, and sent a guard to escort Juliet and the boy to the slave quarters. They returned half an hour later, Juliet carrying a small bundle of possessions tied in a square of cotton fabric. When they appeared, the foreign minister became suddenly affable. "My apologies, Lord Khilburn, for keeping you so long. I will wish to speak with you again, but that is enough for today. You must be fatigued from your journey." With a clap of his hands he summoned armed guards to take the visitors to the quarters that had been assigned to them.

After retrieving their camels, they left the royal palace and were escorted to a massive walled compound about half a mile from the citadel. When they entered the main house, the nayeb bustled up to them. "Greetings, my friends." He bowed. "Welcome to my humble abode."

"This is your home?" Ross asked with surprise.

"Indeed. The amir often allows me to act as a host for distinguished visitors. Let me show you to your apartment."

The two rooms assigned were on the upper level and shared a balcony that overlooked an enormous garden behind the house. The apartment was simply but comfortably furnished, with white walls, cushioned divans, and handsome Bokharan rugs. One chamber had a rope bed, while the other was equipped with a table suitable for eating and writing. Servants were already bringing in their baggage and placing it in the bedroom. As the nayeb lit several oil lamps, he said, "I shall give orders for a meal to be served to you here in a few minutes. Do you wish your servants to stay with you, or shall I send them to my own slave quarters?"

"Jalal can sleep here on the floor. The boy . . ." Ross studied the child for a moment. "I would like him to dine with me tonight so I can speak with him, but he can sleep in your selamlik. I imagine that you have other boys around his age."

The nayeb nodded. "Is there anything else I can provide for your comfort?"

"A bath," Ross said promptly.

"You are welcome to use the hammam."

Ross would have given six months of his life to do that, but unfortunately Juliet would not be able to do the same, and she surely felt as grubby as he did. Summoning all that remained of his nobility, he said gravely, "It is against the custom of my people to use hammams. Do you have a large tub that could be brought here, and a screen to place in front of it?"

"A tub?" Abdul Samut Khan said, perplexed. "Major Cameron was also my guest, and he did not object to the hammam."

"But he was Scottish and I am English." Ross injected a martyred note into his voice. "I realize that this is a great inconvenience, for water must be carried in and out for a bath. If it is not possible . . ."

"No, no, it shall be done," the nayeb said, though his expression made it clear that he thought his guest's request was eccentric in the extreme. "I believe that there are large tubs in the laundry. I shall give orders that a bath be prepared for you after you have dined."

Abdul Samut Khan was turning to go when Ross said, "You mentioned that Major Cameron was your guest. I should like to discuss him with you."

The nayeb's eyes flicked around, as if he was looking for unwelcome ears. His voice dropping, he said, "And I wish equally to talk with you. Tomorrow morning." Then he left.

There were a ewer of water and a basin in the room and the three of them had just enough time to wash their hands before the meal was served. The little boy dug into the rice and lamb greedily; from his thinness, it appeared that he had been on short rations in the palace.

When they had all eaten, Ross began questioning his new possession. Juliet had already introduced the boy as Reza, so Ross asked, "Were you born here in Bokhara, Reza, or were you brought here as a slave?"

The child's bright gaze fixed on him. Now that he was not terrified, it was clear that he had a quick understanding. "I am Persian-born, my lord. My father is a grain merchant in Meshed."

"Tell me how you came to be taken captive."

"I was visiting my uncle's farm in the country. My uncle warned me not to wander far in the fields, but I was only small and did not heed him. Then Turkoman bandits came and stole me." As gravely as a little old man he added, "As a ferengi, you may not know this, but it is forbidden for a good Muslim to enslave another Muslim. However, Shiites are considered heretics, so we are sheep to the Turkoman wolves." Reza's expression turned hard and adult. "Someday I shall return to my home, though it takes twenty years, and there I will learn the use of weapons. Never again will I be caught by such as they."

"How long have you been a slave?"

"Two winters."

"It is against the law of my people to hold slaves, so you are now free again," Ross said, glad that the problem of the boy could be solved so easily. "Before winter comes again, you will be with your family in Meshed."

Reza gasped; apparently it had never occurred to him that his new master would set him free. He scrambled around the table, fell on his knees, and seized Ross's hand. Pressing kisses on it, he said, "All blessings upon you, my lord. This is twice you have saved me today—first my life, and now my soul. Never will I forget what you have done. Never will I allow any man to curse the ferengi in front of me. Never—"

"Peace," Ross said, laughing. He pulled his hand free, letting it rest for a moment on the boy's silky black head. He had always liked children; if he had had a son, he would have liked one as bright and resilient as this boy. Looking over the small dark head at Juliet, he added, "Jalal, take him to Saleh tomorrow. When Abdul Wahab next leads a caravan westward, he can be trusted to deliver Reza to his family in Meshed."

Reza stood. Now that he was no longer a slave, he exercised his newfound freedom to throw his arms around Ross for a heartfelt hug. Then he did the same with Juliet.

After a few more minutes of talk, Ross dismissed the boy to find a bed in the nayeb's slave quarters. When he left, Ross noted that the only door to the main house was solid wood and had a heavy bar on the inside. It was comforting to know that they could ensure privacy when they wanted it.

He turned to speak to Juliet, only to be interrupted by a knock on the door. It proved to be two of the nayeb's slaves carrying a giant laundry tub that was even larger than an English hip bath. Immediately behind was another pair of slaves carrying a folding screen of Chinese origin, then a whole line of women bearing towels, soap, and canisters of steaming water. Bemused, Ross watched the procession go by. The tub was set in a corner of the bedroom and the screen placed in front of it. After hot scented water was poured in, the servants bowed their way out.

Finally Ross was alone with Juliet. Too alone; the communal nature of caravan travel had offered protection from his more unruly impulses. He dropped the wooden bar across the door and turned to face her. More than anything on earth, he would have liked to take her in his arms and hold her for a few minutes—simply hold her, nothing more.

But of course once she was in his arms, what he wanted would change, so he said only, "You can take the first bath." He kept his voice low, since it was possible that spies might be listening. Fortunately the nayeb was probably the only person in the household who understood English, and surely he had better things to do than listen at doors.

Juliet was sitting cross-legged on the divan, and as he spoke, she pulled off her tagelmoust. For a moment she buried her head in her hands wearily. Then she looked up and said with equal softness, "That is three good deeds you have performed today: saving a life, freeing a slave, and arranging a European-style bath so that I could have one too. And of those three deeds, I think you deserve the most credit for the last."

Ross grinned. "Why do you say that?"

"Saving Reza's life is something you could not *not* have tried to do, and freeing a slave you didn't want cost you nothing, but passing up the delights of the hammam was a real sacrifice," she said feelingly as she got to her feet. Her voice self-mocking, she added, "If called on to lay down my life for yours, I would do so, but I do not have the nobility to decline your offer of the first hot bath."

Ross laughed, then went into the bedroom and rummaged in his baggage until he found a plain lightweight cotton robe. "I don't imagine you'll want to put your present clothing on again until you've washed it, so you can wear this."

"A saint," she murmured as she took the garment from him, her fingers not touching his. "I married a saint."

"Just don't stay in so long that the water cools," he warned, "or you may find out how wrong you are in your judgment."

"My judgment is excellent," she said loftily. "In fact, women almost always have better judgment than men."

The devil took Ross's tongue and he murmured, "The proof of that is that you married me, and I married you."

Juliet's gray eyes widened; then she went off into peals of laughter. "True, true, it's all true," she gasped. "My judgment was excellent and yours was dreadful."

Why did she have to laugh like that? Perhaps Ross had hoped she would take offense at his remark and erect more barriers between them; instead, her ability to poke fun at herself was enchanting. With a lopsided smile he said, "I don't know what the problem with me was, but I don't think it was my judgment."

Suddenly sober, Juliet said softly, "Oh, Ross, I do like you so. If only . . ."

When she didn't continue, he asked tightly, "If only what?"

She stared at him hopelessly for a moment, then turned and slipped into the bedroom. Ross spun about on his heel and walked through the arch that led to the balcony. When he was outside, he clamped his hands on the railing while he took slow, measured breaths. She liked him. Wonderful. She admired his judgment. How flattering. During the sandstorm, she had also admitted that she desired him.

What a pity that love was not on the list, for the breach that divided them was so deep that only love might have a chance of bridging it. And even that, perhaps, would not be enough; it had not been enough a dozen years ago. As always, the truly maddening thing was that he still did not understand why she had left. The reasons she had given made sense, yet he could not escape the feeling that they were a smoke screen, designed to obscure a deeper truth.

Slowly he exhaled, knowing that his thoughts were running in an all-too-familiar circle. Turning his attention outward, he noted that the temperature had dropped pleasantly. Though city sounds were faintly audible, Abdul Samut Khan's compound had a countrylike sense of peace. It was so quiet that it was impossible to ignore the faint sloshing sounds in the bedroom. Impossible not to imagine her stepping into the water, first one long shapely leg, then the other. Sitting so that the water came up to her breasts. Would she wash her hair first, or after she had scrubbed the rest of her? Soap sliding over that lovely, moon-pale redhead's skin . . .

He found himself breathing faster, his hands white-knuckled on the balcony railing. If he didn't get a grip on himself, he would spontaneously combust, leaving a pile of smoldering ashes on the mud-brick floor.

Reluctantly he smiled. That would be one simple way to leave Bokhara, but it would be more to the point to study the nayeb's residence. It was a small palace in its own right, with a high wall that would keep people in as well as out. Perhaps in the morning, when he met with Abdul Samut Khan, he could get a tour of the grounds. His mind went back to the meeting with the amir, analyzing every nuance and impression for future use. He was still doing so when Juliet said quietly, "Your turn now."

"That was quick," he remarked as he left the balcony and joined her inside. She was keeping well back from the archway so that no one could see her from outside.

"Your implied threat of what you might do if I hogged all the hot water terrified me," she explained with a straight face. "I'll wash my robes later. By the time they are clean, the water will not be fit for human use."

She was running her fingers through her hair to comb the worst of the tangles out. Thick red tresses fell halfway to her waist, and even wet, they glowed like dark fire. It had been a mistake, he realized distantly, to give her a cotton robe of such light fabric. The material clung to her damp skin, making it clear that she wore nothing underneath—certainly not whatever she had been using to flatten her breasts. She had grown in that area over the last dozen years. As she crossed the room to perch on the divan, several inches of robe trailed on the floor, giving the highly inaccurate impression that she was frail and delicate. Slender, yes; frail, definitely not. Not a woman who could defeat a burly camel driver in a knife fight.

Before his staring could become too obvious, he went into the bedroom, stripped off his clothing with sharp, tense movements, and climbed into the tub. The warm water felt wonderful and helped loosen his tight muscles. As he started washing his hair, he thought wryly that he would be better off if the water were cold—though even chunks of ice floating in the tub would not be enough to cool the fire in his veins.

After Ross had finished bathing, Juliet washed her clothing, wrung out the garments, then hung them up. In the bone-dry desert air they would be wearable by morning. Then she joined Ross in the sitting room. He was sprawled full-length on the cushioned divan, hands folded under his head. He had also changed to a loose Asiatic robe, a striped dark blue that emphasized the tousled gold of his hair.

When she entered the room, he gave her a brief smile before returning his idle gaze to the ceiling. He looked drained, which wasn't surprising; she was exhausted herself, and she hadn't had to converse with the amir or endure that grueling interview with the foreign minister.

There was an irresistibly domestic air about the evening that made it seem as if sharing that wide rope bed would be the most natural thing in the world. Thank God Ross had iron willpower; as Juliet studied the long, lean length of him, she would not have given a ha'penny damn for her own.

She settled down on the floor several feet away from her husband, modestly tucking her cotton robe around her feet and ankles. The deep, crimson-patterned carpet under her was a beauty; after a brief scrutiny, she decided that it had been made by the Tekke Turkoman tribe. They might be marauders, but they made wonderful rugs.

Absently she began combing out her damp hair in the feeble hope that doing so would straighten some of the wild curling. "What do you think of what the amir said this afternoon?"

Ross frowned. "Nasullah's reasons for executing Ian seem trumped up. He was certainly an official British representative, and God only knows what the amir considered spying."

"I can't imagine Ian converting to Islam, either," Juliet said sadly. "I suppose they just invented random excuses to justify murdering him."

"Perhaps the nayeb can tell me more in the morning, but my guess is that the recent British defeats in Afghanistan are the real reason he was executed," Ross said slowly. "With the British forces in retreat, the amir probably decided that it wasn't necessary to curry favor with the ferengis, so he put Ian to death." He sighed. "It's ironic—if the British had won, your brother might be alive now."

"So Ian paid the price of empire," Juliet said bitterly. "The damned bloody British empire."

"It's a great waste," Ross said quietly, "but Ian knew what he was doing. Did I tell you that I saw him several years ago when I was in India? He took a month's leave and we spent it roaming the hill country together. He loved the army, you know, and he accepted the risks of the life he had chosen."

"He should have stayed an officer rather than letting himself be sent on a diplomatic mission." Her mouth twisted. "You had seen him much more recently than I. Even though I had buried myself at Serevan, it never occurred to me that I would never see Ian again. I always thought that someday we would surely get together and tell each other all of the mischief we had gotten into, just like we used to do . . ."

For a moment her voice broke. Then Juliet shook her head, hard. It was her own fault that years that passed since she had seen her brother, and she had no right to allow her grief to further burden Ross. With an effort, she asked in an even voice, "What happens now?"

Ross shrugged, his unfocused gaze never straying from the plaster ceiling. "The amir will summon me for another audience in a week or two. With luck, he will give permission to take Ian's body back to England and we will leave as quickly as possible."

"And if we aren't lucky?"

"He refuses to release Ian's body, which would be regrettable but not disastrous," he said in a flat voice. "Disaster will be if the amir refuses us permission to leave."

Juliet nodded silently; everything he said confirmed her own speculations. "Then what?"

"We'll worry about that when it happens." Ross sat up and swung his legs to the floor. "Do you want the bed? I don't mind sleeping on the floor."

"Neither do I." She smiled and gestured toward the

pallet she had made up against the wall. "As a faithful slave, my rightful place is lying by the door with dagger in hand to defend my master."

A dagger would be equally useful for defending her virtue, Ross thought dryly. He did his best to avoid looking directly at Juliet as he said good night and went into the bedroom. It was going to be difficult enough to sleep knowing she was in the next room; there was no point in adding more fuel to the fire.

17

❧

W hen the haunting call of the muezzin sounded at
dawn, Ross awoke feeling much refreshed. It
was rather nice to sleep in a bed again, and
knowledge of Juliet's closeness had given him pleasant
dreams rather than ruining his rest.

After dressing, he emerged, yawning, into the sitting
room to find that his wife was already up and clothed
once more in her anonymous Tuareg garb, though she
had not yet covered her face with her tagelmoust. As she
perched on the divan, the dark robes and veil framing
her pale face gave her a fleeting resemblance to a medieval nun. A sacrilegious image; no nun should ever radiate such restless energy or such sensuality.

Oblivious of his improper thoughts, she asked, "Do
we need a plan for the day?"

Ross thought about it; he was never at his best when
he awoke. There was only one thing he was good at first
thing in the morning, and without female cooperation it
was impossible to demonstrate. Wrenching his mind back
to Juliet's question, he said, "I hope to talk to Abdul
Samut Khan as early as possible. Besides finding out
more about Ian's captivity, I want to learn whether I am
an honored guest or a prisoner."

"A little of both, probably."

"That's what I suspect, but you should be able to go
out without hindrance." He paused, mentally reviewing
what needed to be done. "I'd like you to visit Saleh
and Murad and make sure they have met no unexpected
problems. Probably you should check with Saleh before

225

you take Reza to him, but I think the sooner the boy is away from my dangerous presence, the better."

"Shall I buy a couple of horses?" she suggested. "The camels aren't very convenient for riding in the city."

"That's a good idea. Then you can take the camels to Hussayn Kasem. He said he'd stable them for us, and if we don't need them again, he'll give Julietta a good home."

Juliet grinned. "You really are sentimental about that silly beast."

He considered pointing out that the camel appreciated affection more than its namesake did, but decided that it was too early in the morning for inflammatory statements. "This looks like a good time to show you the sundry gifts, bribes, and weapons I have hidden in my luggage."

"Very well." She swung lithely to her feet. "Every time you dug into your bags, I wondered what new treasure you would come up with."

"The art of successful exploring has much to do with having a good supply of gifts," he explained as he led the way into the bedroom. "I think I'll disarm Abdul Samut Khan by giving him one of my compasses and explaining how it works. That way, when he has my luggage searched, he won't think the compasses are dangerous spy devices."

Ross showed Juliet everything that might be useful to her if something happened to him, and had just concluded by giving her a small pouch of gold coins when a knock sounded from the other room. After pulling up her veil and tucking the pouch away, Juliet opened the door to find a boy who politely invited the honorable Lord Khilburn to break his fast with Abdul Samut Khan.

Glad that the nayeb was willing to have their discussion early, Ross followed the slave to the master of the house's private quarters, where his host greeted him jovially.

Ross returned the greeting, then folded down to a spot by the table and produced the two gifts he had decided on. The first was an Arabic translation of *Robinson Crusoe*, which had proved wildly popular everywhere in the Islamic world. Since the Koran was always studied in

its original Arabic, all educated Muslims could read the
language fluently, and Abdul Samut Khan accepted the
book with obvious pleasure.

Then Ross handed over the compass, a gleaming brass
instrument of beautiful workmanship. "You might find
this an interesting curiosity."

The nayeb examined the compass's glasses, reflectors,
and screws with bright-eyed interest while Ross explained
its use. "It always points the way north, you say?" He
twisted it back and forth, fascinated by the action of the
needle.

"Exactly," Ross said. "So it can be used to determine
the direction of Mecca."

"Ahhh . . ." Abdul Samut Khan nodded enthusiastically. "Truly an instrument of great holiness. Might I
purchase it from you?"

"No, for it is a gift, a small mark of gratitude for your
hospitality in receiving me into your own house."

After a cursory demurral, Abdul Samut Khan accepted
the compass with an air of satisfaction; Ross guessed that
the nayeb had a great fondness for gifts, the more valuable, the better. With goodwill abounding, they turned
their attention to an excellent breakfast of lamb kebabs,
rice, bread, tea, and the special luxury of coffee. When
they had finished eating, Ross said, "Can you tell me
more about Major Cameron's death?"

Abdul Samut Khan sighed. "A great pity. My royal
master was distressed that Major Cameron went first to
Kokand, the enemy of Bokhara. Perhaps that could have
been overlooked, but then it turned out that the major
did not carry authorization from the Queen of England.
The lack cast doubt on his credentials."

Ross's brows rose. "But surely he had papers from
Lord Auckland, the Governor General of India."

"Aye, but that is not the same. Not satisfied with
Major Cameron's documents, my royal master imprisoned him and requested a letter from your queen stating
that the major was what he claimed to be. But though a
message was sent to London, no such assurance was ever
received. The amir waited many months beyond the time
it took a message to go to England and return. He even
built posting houses in the desert to hasten a reply, but

in vain. If Cameron was a genuine English envoy, your government should have vouched for him."

Ross felt a deep burn of fury; it sounded as if Ian's life might have been spared if an acceptable response had been sent to Bokhara, only some damned official in Whitehall had decided that such a reply was "inappropriate." Still, Ross felt obligated to defend his country's position. "Since Major Cameron was sent from India, the governor general was the correct person to consult if the major's bona fides were questioned. The queen herself would not respond, particularly not when Bokhara was holding her officer captive."

Uneasily the nayeb repeated his earlier point. "But Cameron claimed to serve the queen, and she did not acknowledge him. What was my master to think?"

Ross wondered if the amir really understood the size and complexity of the British empire; probably not, in which case he might have genuinely expected a personal reply from the British sovereign. But it was equally likely that the lack was just a pretext for committing murder. Abandoning the point, Ross said, "You say that Major Cameron was caught spying. What did he do? To behave dishonorably seems very unlike him."

"He tried to smuggle letters out of prison."

"Did the letters contain treason? Information that might harm Bokhara?"

His host glanced away. "Undoubtedly they did."

"Since Major Cameron was in prison," Ross said patiently, "no doubt he was simply trying to let his family and his army superiors know his condition, as is only natural."

Not meeting his guest's gaze, Abdul Samut Khan replied, "Perhaps that was natural, but it was not wise. The writings of a ferengi are always viewed with great suspicion."

Probably because no one read English well enough to recognize treason when he saw it, Ross thought bitterly. This discussion would achieve nothing, for Abdul Samut Khan was duty-bound to support his ruler. Deciding to go to the question most important to the family, he asked, "How did Major Cameron die?"

His host's eyes brightened. "With great courage. For

months he had been in the Black Well, and when they brought him forth his skin was white as snow and covered with sores and his eyes twisted against the sun. But he stood tall, making the sign of a cross over his heart and declaring that he died as a Christian. Then the executioner severed his head with one great blow. He died quickly, without pain. A most inspiring sight."

Ross nodded, his expression grim. The account matched what Abdul Wahab had told him in the caravansary of Sarakhs.

The nayeb spread his hands. "What is there to be done? Perhaps a mistake was made and the amir's letter or your queen's reply was lost, for the road to England is long and dangerous. A great pity, but now Major Cameron is dead. Do you think your countrymen will punish Bokhara for an honest mistake?"

If the amir believed that there was no chance of reconciliation between the two nations, there would be no reason to spare Ross's life, and several good reasons to imprison or kill him. "As you say, it is a great pity, but nations should not go to war over a misunderstanding," he said carefully. "When I return to England, perhaps the amir can send an ambassador with me to express regret for the error. This can become an occasion of strengthening the ties between our lands."

The nayeb beamed. "A splendid notion. I shall suggest that to my master." He got to his feet. "Come and see my garden. It is at its best in the morning."

Ross followed obediently. When they stepped from the house, they were met by an enormous Uzbek of military bearing. Abdul Samut Khan said, "Lord Khilburn, I would like you to meet Yawer Shahid Mahmud. He is the captain of my household guard and will be responsible for your safety."

In other words, this was Ross's chief jailer. Yawer was a military rank comparable to a British major, and Shahid had a tough air of command. He was tall for an Uzbek, only a couple of inches shorter than Ross, and massively muscled. Judging by his malevolent expression, he had no use for ferengis, though he managed a curt greeting when they were introduced.

As Ross walked away with his host, he felt the yawer's

gaze burning into his back. It didn't take any special
perception to guess that the man was a source of potential trouble; he looked like the sort who would accept a
bribe, then accuse the briber of treason.

As they strolled down a walkway into the garden,
Abdul Samut Khan waved gracefully at the flowers.
"There is an old Persian proverb, perhaps you know it?
'If you have two loaves of bread, sell one and buy a
hyacinth.' "

"I have heard the saying, and there is great wisdom in
it," Ross replied, wondering what his host really had in
mind; somehow, he doubted that it was philosophy.

The garden was a large one, and when they were well
away from the possibility of listening ears, the nayeb's
detached manner suddenly vanished. Turning to Ross,
he said vehemently, "I could not talk freely in the house,
for Bokhara is a nation of spies. Slaves watch their masters, street boys sell information to anyone who will pay
their price, husbands cannot speak to their wives in bed
without being overheard. I am Persian, you know, I have
enemies, for many are jealous of my influence with the
amir. For that reason I must be doubly cautious, but I
had to tell you that executing your brother was a dreadful
deed. He was put to death without sin or crime on his
part."

As the nayeb turned earnest dark eyes to his guest,
Ross felt immediately distrustful. His host might genuinely feel that executing Ian had been wrong, but he
served the amir and it would be a mistake to forget that.
Temperately Ross said, "Ian's death grieves me greatly,
but from what you said, the execution was more a result
of misunderstandings than evil intent."

"I tried to change the amir's mind. Indeed, I offered
him fifty thousand ducats if he would release Cameron,
but Nasrullah said only that he was a spy, and as a spy
he must die." Abdul Samut Khan gave Ross a shrewd
look. "I am not a rich man, and paying such a great sum
would have beggared me, but I was sure that the queen
would reimburse me if my gold saved her officer's life.
Do you not think his life worth fifty thousand ducats?"

"It is impossible to put a price on a life, but I know
that my government would never pay such a sum," Ross

said firmly. "It would be seen as a ransom, and paying it would endanger the life and freedom of every British traveler everywhere."

For a moment the nayeb looked perplexed about the reasoning. Then he ventured, "If the queen would not pay that much, would Cameron's family have done so?"

Ross shook his head; the talk of money was sounding alarm bells in his head. "The Camerons are a family of ancient blood and great warrior skills, but they are not wealthy. Even if they wished to, they could not have paid such a vast sum."

Abdul Samut Khan looked regretful. "But you are a lord and he was your kin; surely your family could have ransomed him home, as they would you if you were held captive."

Ross guessed that they had come to the crux of the matter; the nayeb wanted to know what Ross's life was worth, so it was time to start lying. "If I were imprisoned, my family would mourn but they would not attempt to buy my freedom, for they would see my fate as the will of God. I am but one of many sons and my father would consider it unjust to beggar his other children to save my unworthy life."

His manner must have been convincing, for the nayeb sighed with disappointment. "A pity." Then his expression turned crafty. "They say that when Nasrullah became amir, for a time he loved justice and religion but soon he reverted to cruelty and dancing boys. He is a wart on the arse of Turkestan. Let the British government send officers to Khiva and Kokand to persuade their khans to march on Bokhara. Then let the queen give me a small sum, perhaps twenty or thirty thousand ducats, and I, Bokhara's master of artillery, will support the invasion."

The speech made Ross even warier. The nayeb might be trying to lure Ross into indiscretion, or he might be quite willing to sell himself to the highest bidder; in either case, he was not to be trusted. "I am not a representative of my government, nor did I come to foment rebellion against the ruler of Bokhara. I wanted only the truth of my brother's fate, and now I have that."

Abdul Samut Khan said shrewdly, "You do not trust

me, do you? That is good, a wise man is cautious. But I was a friend to Major Cameron. Look, in his own hand he wrote a testimonial to all I did for him." Reaching inside his coat, he drew out a sheet of paper and handed it over.

Ross felt an eerie prickle along his spine when he unfolded the paper. There, in writing that was shaky but recognizably Ian's, were the words *"I write this document to attest the good offices rendered to me by the Nayeb Abdul Samut Khan."* After listing several instances of kindness, he ended, *"I sign this Ian Torquil Cameron at Bokhara, the fourteenth of September in the year of our Lord 1840."*

A letter from a dead man. His hands not quite steady, Ross refolded the paper and handed it back. "On behalf of the major's family and myself, I offer my most profound gratitude for what you did for him."

Abdul Samut Khan nodded gravely. "As I was his friend, I will also be your friend."

Perhaps he would be. But in spite of the nayeb's words, Ross did not trust him.

After Ross had gone off to meet with the nayeb, Juliet went in search of food for herself. Eventually she found the kitchen and an adjacent servants' dining area. Reza was there and he greeted her enthusiastically. Apart from acknowledging Reza, Juliet did not speak with any of the other servants, simply ate her bread, drank her tea, and left. As usual, she was watched with considerable curiosity, but after she ignored one or two attempts at conversation, no one disturbed her.

The real challenge came when Juliet went outside to the compound's main gate and started to walk through the archway. Immediately a watchman armed with a sword and a lance stepped in front of her and barked, "Halt!"

She stopped but did not back off. Letting her hand drop to the hilt of her knife, she stared down at the guard, who was several inches shorter than she, and said in her most guttural Persian, "I am prisoner?"

He hesitated, clearly unsure what the Targui's status was. Then, deciding that the ferengi's wild servant was unimportant, he stepped aside.

Without looking back, Juliet swaggered down the street as if she knew where she was going. Saleh had drawn her a map of the city, marking the major streets and buildings, and now she wanted to orient herself as quickly as possible. Fortunately the brilliant turquoise-colored dome of the Grand Mosque was a landmark visible throughout much of the city, and she used that to guide herself to the Registan.

It was interesting to see the life of the square from street level rather than camelback. Sobriety of dress was not considered a virtue here; everyone who could afford them wore robes of brilliantly patterned ikat silks. They were the most famous product of Bokhara, for the city was a great producer of silk as well as an essential oasis on the ancient Silk Road.

Saleh had once told Juliet that many families raised silkworms at home, incubating the eggs, feeding tender mulberry leaves to the voracious hatchlings, then patiently harvesting the valuable cocoons. With a faint smile he had added that silkworms were one thing he did not miss when he left his childhood home.

In the center of the Registan, Juliet bought a delicious concoction of crushed ice and grape syrup called *rahat i jan,* the delight of life. Cleverly designed icehouses made it possible for all Bokharans to enjoy iced drinks all summer. It was a luxury she had never experienced in Britain, but of course in Britain one didn't need ice; rather the contrary.

After she worked her way around the giant square, she set off through the narrow, twisting streets to find the Djuibar quarter, where Saleh's brother lived. Aided by the map and her own excellent sense of direction, Juliet managed to reach her destination without getting seriously lost.

Saleh's brother Tura was a master weaver and his house was a testimony to the prosperity of the silk trade. The servant who opened the door for Juliet had been told to expect her, so she was immediately escorted to a well-furnished room where Saleh and Murad were enjoying a late-morning cup of cardamom-flavored tea.

The three exchanged greetings as effusively as if it had been months since they parted rather than twenty-four hours. Saleh was in high spirits from being reunited with his brother after a separation of almost thirty years, but he frowned sympathetically when he heard of the interview with the amir and the confirmation of Ian Cameron's death. Then he relayed what his brother had told him about the amir's dangerous unpredictability and the poisonous atmosphere of suspicion and intolerance that the ruler deliberately fostered. It was fortunate that Juliet and Ross had been circumspect the night before, for Abdul Samut Khan's household certainly contained spies, possibly serving several different masters.

It was a sobering discussion, and when Juliet finally left to return to the nayeb's house, she had lost much of her earlier enthusiasm for exploring an exotic new city. The more she learned of Bokhara, the more she realized how dangerous the situation was. Ross had known from the beginning and had had the courage to come in spite of that knowledge. He had always had a patience and a steadiness of temper that Juliet lacked; she resolved to do her best to match him.

18

The stressful days that followed tested Juliet's resolution to the limit. She was free to come and go as she pleased, but Ross's status, as they had suspected, was somewhere between guest of honor and prisoner. Though he was allowed to travel about the city, three armed chamberlains accompanied him everywhere, allegedly for his own protection.

Ross was permitted visitors, and a steady stream flowed through the nayeb's house. Some callers were men he had met eight years earlier, who came to renew the acquaintance. Included were Muslim mullahs, Jewish dyers, and Hindu bankers, all of whom delighted in talking with the ferengi. Once or twice Islamic zealots came and tried to bait Ross into indiscretion, but he was adept at avoiding their traps.

Other visitors were emissaries from the amir, who asked endless questions about European technology and agriculture ("There are no camels in England?" one asked in disbelief), medicine and arts, trade and history, and whether Queen Victoria could execute anyone she wanted to. Once Ross even demonstrated how to silver a mirror and sent the result to Nasrullah; the nayeb said that the amir accepted the gift with great pleasure.

Though Juliet spent much of her time exploring Bokhara, occasionally she sat silently in the corner of the nayeb's main reception room during one of what Ross ironically called his salons. She was fascinated by the breadth of his knowledge, for he was never at a loss for explanations. One day, when they had been in Bokhara about three weeks, she returned in the early evening to find a delegate from the amir asking about witchcraft in England.

Without even blinking, Ross mentioned the Witchcraft Act, then went off on tangents about druids and medieval trials by ordeal, before moving into the evolution of Anglo-Saxon common law. He was still going strong when Abdul Samut Khan appeared and genially bore his guest off to dinner.

Since Ross was much in demand, Juliet took most of her meals with the household slaves, who treated her like a piece of furniture, to be walked around but not otherwise noticed. Reluctant to return to the empty rooms, on this particular night Juliet stayed with the other servants after she finished eating. One of the grooms was telling stories, a traditional and highly satisfying form of Asiatic entertainment.

However, when the stories were replaced by general conversation, she went back to their apartment and settled down on the divan to do some mending. She found it ironic that in the guise of a man she was being more domestic than she had ever been as a woman, but boredom was a powerful motivator. Besides, she took secret satisfaction in lavishing care on her husband's possessions, since she could not do the same with the man himself.

To her regret, the easy camaraderie that had been briefly between them had vanished, seared away by the pillar of fire. Her husband had retreated behind an impenetrable barrier that hurt Juliet even though she knew it was necessary. Ross had said the night of the sandstorm that staying together might drive them both mad, and as usual, he had been right. Though Juliet kept herself busy in the hopes that activity would tire her to the point where desire would ebb, that never happened.

Through hot days and restless nights the tension grew like a thunderhead. Partly that was because of uncertainty about the amir's intentions, but the deeper cause was the suffocating frustration that came from being physically close but emotionally separated. It was a time of taut silences and deliberate distance, and Juliet knew that something must change soon, for it was impossible to continue like this much longer.

Tonight Ross returned from his dinner with the nayeb relatively early. As he came in and barred the door, Juliet put down her sewing and stretched her arms over her head. "The amount that you know never ceases to astonish me," she said in the low voice that had become standard for them as a defense against listening ears. "Are you never at a loss for an answer, no matter what they ask you?"

"My Cambridge education is proving invaluable, but even so, sometimes I have to make things up," Ross said with a wry smile. "I've found it dangerous to admit ignorance, because the amir's questioners will assume that I am deliberately concealing information. It's safer to be wrong than silent."

"You may be faking, but you do it well. You certainly had me convinced." She looked down to set the last stitches in the shirt she was mending, then knotted the thread and bit it off. "Your shirt is done. I'm running out of things to do. Perhaps I should have let my mother teach me knitting, as she was always trying to do."

Juliet started to stand, intending to return the garment to Ross's room, only to find that he had stepped up to take it from her. There was a moment of mild collision that knocked her off balance, and Ross automatically reached out and caught her arm to steady her.

It should have meant nothing, except that everything that happened between them was charged with meaning. As Juliet recovered her footing, Ross's face was only a few inches from hers, close enough to see the texture of his tanned jaw, the precise shape of his mouth. She was acutely conscious of his hand on her elbow, and more than anything else on earth, she wanted to lean forward and press her lips to his. Only knowledge of the consequences of intimacy held her in check.

Juliet raised her head, and for a moment their gazes struck and held. And when they did, she caught her breath at the pain she saw in his eyes. Over the last weeks Ross had been a master of restraint, yet now she saw what his restraint was costing him. The iron control she so admired was drawn to the snapping point, and it terrified her to realize how close they stood to the abyss.

It would take so little, scarcely anything at all, for them to surrender to passion and fulfillment. And disaster.

She wrenched her gaze away, hating herself for her cowardice. Ross's hand dropped and he stepped away. "I have trouble imagining you doing something as placid as knitting," he said in a voice that was almost normal. "Perhaps you should take up wood carving. A knife is more your style than a needle." Then he said good night and retreated to the bedroom.

The whole encounter was over in seconds, acute longing buried as if it had never reared its menacing head. Juliet put out the oil lamps and curled up on her pallet. Except for the first night in Bokhara, when she had used Ross's cotton robe, she slept in her Tuareg garments, her tagelmoust ready to cover her face at a moment's notice. At least with a barred door to protect her, she didn't have to sleep with her face veiled as she had when crossing the Kara Kum.

A lamp stayed lit in the bedroom, and she could hear the faint scratching of a pen. Ever the scholar and observer, Ross continued to make notes of what he was learning in Bokhara; Juliet suspected that was his way of coping with tension. For her part, she merely lay still and bit on her veil until she finally began to relax.

She had just drifted into a light doze when someone began pounding on the door. Instantly awake, she rolled to her feet, pulled the veil over her face, and opened the door. Half a dozen soldiers shoved their way past, pushing her to one side. At their head was Yawer Shahid Mahmud, the captain of the nayeb's guard.

As Ross emerged from the bedroom in his shirtsleeves, Shahid barked, "Come with me, ferengi swine. His royal majesty wishes to see you immediately." The yawer's broad face wore a triumphant expression that chilled Juliet's blood. From the beginning he had hated Ross, and now he openly rejoiced in his enemy's downfall.

Ross went very still with the knowledge of what this summons must mean. "Very well," he said calmly as he unrolled the sleeves that had been pushed up his forearms. "A moment while I put on my coat." As relaxed as if he had just been invited to tea, he turned and went into the bedroom.

For a wild moment Juliet wondered if he would emerge with his pistol and try to fight his way out, and her hand tightened on the hilt of her knife so that she could join in. However, Ross had more sense than to take on half a dozen armed men, and when he reentered the sitting room, his hands were empty. For a moment his gaze sought Juliet. His face was as impassive as carved marble, but when their eyes met, his held a message.

Then the yawer snapped that enough time had been wasted and the moment was over. The soldiers surrounded Ross and escorted him out. As the door closed behind them, Juliet knew that Ross had not just been reminding her of her promise not to do anything foolish; he had also been telling her good-bye.

For the first time in her life, Juliet was literally paralyzed by fear. She sank to her knees on the floor and folded over, shaking violently at the realization that she might never see Ross again. He might be put in prison. He might be executed this very night.

It wasn't possible. *It wasn't possible!*

But it was. The amir could, and possibly would, order Ross's death in an instant, for no reason at all. His viciousness was so notorious that Bokharans merely shrugged and said, "This is a royal act," when they heard stories of men who were murdered for protesting when Nasrullah took their wives. And the amir was guilty of worse crimes than that.

Savagely she bit her lip, using pain to combat her panic. She must think of what could be done to help Ross, not wallow in fear. She struggled to her feet and barred the door, then went into the bedroom, where the lamp still burned and a sheet of paper was half-covered with Ross's neat writing. She felt that if she turned her head, she would catch sight of him. But he was gone, possibly forever.

During the weeks they had shared these rooms, she had never so much as touched the rope bed because it was Ross's, but now she needed the sense of his presence. She lay down on the mattress and clutched one of the pillows to her stomach, curling around it in a despairing need for comfort.

What could be done? Nothing tonight, for good citizens did not go out in the streets after the king's drums beat out their curfew. Abdul Samut Khan would be of no use; the fact that Shahid had taken Ross away meant that the nayeb was either helpless or actively working against Ross.

The Kasems were her best hope, for they had great influence in Bokhara. She would go to them first thing in the morning and ask if they would exercise that influence on Ross's behalf. There was also a Persian ambassador in the city; if Juliet revealed herself as Gul-i Sarahi, the ambassador might intervene, for her fortress at Serevan had helped the shah maintain his eastern border.

She had used the last three weeks well and learned a great deal about the internal workings of Bokhara; as the dark hours passed, she sifted through every possibility she could think of to help Ross, from straightforward to desperate. She refused to consider that all her plans would go for naught if Nasrullah had already impulsively ordered her husband's death.

It was well after midnight when another knock came on the door. At first she did not notice, for it was much quieter than the earlier one. When she finally heard, she got up and went grimly to find out who had come. If the soldiers had returned for her, they would have a fight on their hands; Ross might have gone quietly so that she would not be endangered, but she had no reason to exercise restraint.

More likely than soldiers was the nayeb, coming to shed crocodile tears for his guest while he commandeered the dear departed's possessions. Juliet secured the veil over her face and lifted the bar. Then she stepped back and dropped a hand to her knife as the door swung open and a man entered the room. The light from the bedroom was faint, and it took a moment for her to realize that the intruder's head glowed like burnished gold.

It was Ross. At first she just stared, not quite believing that it was really he. Then, without even checking to be sure that he was alone, she swept her arms around him, her heart pounding with relief.

He welcomed her embrace, one arm going around her while the other efficiently closed the door. Near weeping,

Juliet said, "I was sure they had taken you away to prison, or worse."

For a moment more his cheek rested against her temple. Then he gave an uneven laugh and released her so that he could bar the entrance. "That's the impression Shahid wanted to give, and it could well have turned out that way." He peeled off his coat and walked into the bedroom, dropping the garment onto the divan.

Following on his heels, Juliet asked, "What happened?"

"I was taken to a small audience chamber, where Nasrullah was pacing back and forth like a tiger in a cage. If he had a tail, he would have been switching it," Ross said wearily as he sat down and pulled off his boots. "After I performed the salaam, he snarled that he had considered my request to take Ian's body back to England and decided against it because 'Major Cameron was a traitor and an apostate and death was not enough to cleanse the stain of his dishonor.' "

"That's a great pity." With a sigh, Juliet settled on the divan several feet away from Ross and pulled the veil from her face. "But it's less important than whether we can leave."

Ross unwound his cravat and tossed it toward his coat. As he did, his white shirt gaped open at the throat, exposing curling sandy hair. Catching an unexpected glimpse of what was usually covered was disquietingly erotic, and Juliet had trouble wrenching her gaze away. The tumult she had experienced when her husband was taken had left her emotions raw, and she knew it would take very little to fracture what was left of her control.

Unaware of her reaction, Ross subsided into the cushions, his expression fine-drawn as a medieval painting of a suffering saint. "The amir did say rather jovially that while he would not release Ian's bones, he was willing to send my bones instead."

She shuddered. "His sense of humor is as revolting as the rest of him."

"I can't say that I found his jest very amusing myself. He is a most exhausting gentleman to visit," Ross remarked. "Since my mission to discover Ian's fate has now been accomplished, I asked permission to leave Bokhara. That set Nasrullah off on another tirade, the gist of which was his wanting to know why I disdained his hospitality after all he had done for me. Three ambassadors had come from Herat saying he should execute me, yet he had not listened to them. How could I demand to leave when he had treated me like a brother?"

"As I recall," Juliet said tartly, "he slaughtered four of his own brothers. Or was it five?"

"The number varies depending on whom you ask." Ross rested his head against the whitewashed wall. "In my most tactful manner—Mother would have been proud of me—I said that I was deeply grateful for his generosity but that my father is old and frail and if I am absent too long, I might not see him on this earth again."

"That at least is true."

Ross cocked an amused eyebrow at her. "I am not averse to using the truth if it will serve. At any rate, my statement mollified the amir a little, which is surprising in light of the general belief that he poisoned his own father. After allowing that aged parents should be respected, he asked in a hurt voice if I would rather leave Bokhara without honor and in disgrace, or with honor and filled with favor.

"Naturally, I expressed a preference for leaving with his majesty's favor—it seemed the politic thing to do. Nasrullah said that if I was patient, I would soon be free to go with his blessing. Then he spun on his heel and disappeared through the curtains and my audience was over. Shahid was most disappointed to have to escort me back here."

Juliet buried her face in her hands, her body shaking with chill even though the night was warm. Ross had been lucky tonight, but it sounded as though Nasrullah might just as easily have ordered his execution. Luck never lasted forever. "Do you think the amir will grant you permission to leave?"

There was a long pause before Ross said in a neutral voice, "He has nothing to gain by keeping me prisoner."

That was true. But since the British had suffered setbacks in Afghanistan, Nasrullah might equally decide that he also had nothing to lose by executing his "guest"—and it was well known that he despised Europeans.

Raising her head, she said in a choked voice, "Tell me the truth, Ross. You think we're going to die here, don't you?"

He met her gaze without flinching, and in his stark eyes she saw that he had accepted the likelihood of his own death. "I almost certainly will," he said quietly, "but you and the rest of our party won't be stopped if you try to leave. I think you should all go with the next westbound caravan."

Perhaps Saleh and Murad should, but Juliet could not imagine abandoning her husband while he was alive. She looked at him hopelessly, her throat tight. Ever since they had met in Persia, she had held herself away because she could not bear to become intimate while knowing that he would inevitably leave her. There could be no future for them, for if by some chance Ross did want her back as a wife, she would be forced to make an impossible choice between living a lie or revealing an appalling truth that Ross would never forgive her for.

But now they truly had no future. The shadow of death had narrowed time down to this instant, this infinitely precious shower of moments. What did consequences matter when life could be measured in hours or days? "Time is running out, Ross," she said, her voice laced with anguish. "Let's not waste what little we have left."

The atmosphere changed, becoming as charged as the wind before a storm. Ross became utterly still, his brown eyes shocked and wary.

For a moment Juliet thought he did not understand her oblique words, or, infinitely worse, that he was rejecting what she offered. Burying all her pride, she said, "You have every right to despise me. But if for tonight you can pretend to forget the past . . . if you still want me, for passion or solace or even anger . . ." knowing that she was doing this as much for herself as for him, she stretched out a pleading hand. ". . . I am yours to do with as you will."

She did not know whether she could bear it if he refused her—but he did not. Instead, face taut, he wordlessly reached out and caught her hand in his.

As soon as their fingers touched, all the passion that simmered between them flared to stunning life. They came together with fierce inevitability, mouth to mouth and body to body, with none of the hesitation of new lovers.

It had been mad to speak of forgetting the past, for recognition of Ross's touch was imprinted on every fiber of Juliet's being. She would know his kiss anywhere, in the darkest night, the most distant land. Dizzy with reunion, she felt as though they had stepped off a precipice and were falling out of control into some strange new land.

An instant later she realized that they were literally falling, tumbling the short distance from the divan to the Turkoman carpet, with Ross absorbing most of the impact when they hit. They stayed locked together as they rolled across the floor in a flurry of fabric and tangled limbs, coming to a halt at the foot of the bed. Neither would interrupt the embrace, for bruises were unimportant compared to the overwhelming need to meld into one space, one flesh. Violent emotions demanded violent expression, and they kissed feverishly, their bodies grinding together in a frenzied attempt to unite.

They were tearing at each other's clothing when Ross abruptly went still, then pressed his face against Juliet's neck while he inhaled in ragged gulps. When his breathing had slowed a little, he pulled away and stood. "I've waited a dozen years for this. We're going to do it right." Bending over, he grasped her hands and effortlessly lifted her to her feet.

All that mattered to Juliet was that finally they were together again, and details of technique seemed irrelevant, but as she opened her mouth to protest, he drew her into his embrace. "Slow down, my lovely vixen." Holding her motionless against him with one arm, he stroked a gentling hand down her head and back. "You're like an armful of lightning—exciting, but moving too fast for full appreciation. Though we may not have much time, at least we will have tonight. As you said, let's not waste it."

For an instant she resisted, for her body ached to join with his. But Ross was right: their reunion demanded something more caring and more memorable than a frantic coupling that would be over in minutes. She had always loved the fact that he had the strength of wisdom and patience, so different from her own reckless temperament.

Forcing herself to relax, Juliet melted into his embrace. "If I am lightning, you are the rod that brings me back to earth and saves me from self-destruction." She pressed her lips to his throat, taking the time to savor the salt flavor of his skin, the intimate pressure of his beating pulse. With her tongue she felt the rate increase; it was gratifying to know that his control was neither effortless nor unlimited.

He gave a long sigh of pleasure before reluctantly stepping away. "The first thing to do is remove all these clothes." Deftly he unwound her tagelmoust and dropped it on the floor, then pulled the sheathed dagger from her sash. "You won't be needing this." Knife and sash joined the pile on the carpet.

Lifting her braid, he untied the ribbon at the end and ran his fingers through the bright tresses until they spilled freely across her shoulders. "This is how I thought of you most often," he said softly. "With your hair blazing across the pillow like fire. Gul-i Sarahi, the flower of the desert." He buried his face in the heavy silken mass, his warm breath caressing her throat.

"I hated my hair until I met you," she whispered. And because Ross had loved the outrageous color and uncontrollable curls, she had never cut it since they met.

He submerged his hands in her thick locks and began massaging her scalp with his fingertips. Juliet let her head fall forward onto his shoulder while sensual pleasure rippled through her. There wasn't a single part of her body that didn't love Ross's touch, and he knew it.

After a delicious interval, she decided it was time for another kiss and raised her face, but he said, "Not yet."

Since Juliet was not wearing her mantle, the next item of apparel to go was her long robe. She raised her arms as Ross lifted it over her head, leaving her standing in her loose trousers and the vest she wore to flatten her breasts.

Then he halted, his arrested gaze fixed on her chest. At first she didn't realize what the object of his attention was. Then she remembered. Her cheeks flamed and she put a protective hand over the ring suspended around her neck on a gold chain.

Undeterred, he extricated the ring from her nerveless fingers. There was no need to ask what it was, for it was Ross who had placed that golden band on her hand on their wedding day. Inside were engraved their names and the date of their marriage. Juliet had taken the ring off several weeks after she had left him, but she had worn it on the chain ever since, except for brief occasions like the night they had dined at Serevan and she had worn a low-necked dress.

He studied the simple band, turning it in his fingers as if expecting it to vanish from his grasp. Then he raised his sardonic gaze to hers. She knew instinctively that he would not say anything; equally clearly, she knew that she must, even though the meaning of the ring was blatantly obvious. Quietly she said, "There was much that I didn't want to forget either."

"Good." His expression both wry and tender, Ross released the ring and transferred his attention to the quilted cotton binder that covered her torso. It was fastened by four small string bows down the front. He undid the first and peeled back the fabric panels, then bent over and pressed his lips to the cleft revealed.

Juliet gasped, and her knees began feeling buttery. Without haste, Ross undid one bow after another, kissing the expanding curves as they were released. When the last fastening was untied, he slid the vest off her shoulders so that it could be set aside. Her pale skin was marked with red lines from the unnatural constriction.

He cupped her breasts and moved his hands in slow circles, murmuring, "A crime to suppress such beauty."

His expert touch stimulated the flow of blood, bringing her breasts to tingling life. Juliet caught her breath as her nipples stiffened against his palms. "It is almost worth having them bound for the pleasure of having you set them free."

Her trousers were also fastened with a bow, and his next step was to untie it. The shapeless garment immediately collapsed around her ankles. For the first time Juliet felt shyness, because of the number of years that had passed since she had been naked before him and concern that her body might have changed for the worse.

Ross, however, appeared to have no complaints. "Were you always this lovely and I forgot?" His admiring gaze was as seductive as a caress. "Or have you continued to grow more beautiful with every year?"

Juliet blushed, glad that it was not the sort of question that required an answer, but his approval was enormously gratifying. She had never felt really attractive except with Ross, and once more he was making her feel like the most desirable woman since Helen of Troy. Deciding that action was the best cure for embarrassment, she said, "It's my turn now," and reached for the buttons of his shirt.

"Soon." Smiling, he touched his forefinger to her lips. "But I'm curious about what has changed, and since the light is dim, I'll have to supplement sight with touch. For example, this appears much the same." He bent his head to her left breast and took the nipple into his mouth. Under the pressure of lips and tongue, it hardened still further. As heat blazed deep inside her, he murmured, "Mmm, exactly as I remember. And your reaction hasn't changed either."

After he had given her other nipple equal attention, he shaped her breasts with thoughtful hands. "There seems to be more fullness here."

"Is that a complaint?" she asked, shifting her weight so that the softer parts of her undulated provocatively.

He caught his breath and for a moment his fingers tightened. "Not in the least."

Then his hands opened and glided down her ribs and waist in a purely tactile exploration of her contours. "So many lovely curves." He circled behind her without breaking contact, then lifted her hair and pressed his lips to the nape of her neck. "All of them elegant."

With leisurely skill he feathered kisses down her spine before turning her to face him. Then he knelt, drawing his palms over her hips and thighs. "A little rounder here as well, in a thoroughly alluring way."

He pressed his face against the curve of her belly, the faint prickle of whiskers a counterpoint to the damp heat of his mouth. As his lips moved lower, he slipped his right hand between her knees and began drawing teasing patterns on the inside of her thighs, his touch drifting gradually upward. Her legs loosened in response, opening in instinctive invitation.

His left hand cradled her right buttock, steadying her, as his fingers brushed through auburn curls, between silky folds, to the searingly sensitive flesh below. Juliet gave a small choked whimper and caught his shoulders for support. She had forgotten, oh, God, she had forgotten, that it was possible to feel like this. . . .

Waves of heat throbbed through her and she was on the verge of falling when he stood and caught her against him with his left arm. The fabric of his shirt and trousers tickled along the bare length of her body when she wilted against his chest, trusting him to support her. As her fingers curled weakly at his waist, his right hand probed deep into her intimate flesh, feeding a fire that threatened to consume her.

She had wanted to please him. Instead he was pleasing her and she was helpless to reciprocate, too dazed, too bewitched, to do anything but stifle her cry against his shoulder as her body closed around his hand with long, voluptuous contractions. His strength was the only constant in a dissolving world.

It took time for her trembling limbs to steady, but when they did, she raised one hand and twined her fingers through his hair, hoping her touch could convey what was beyond the scope of mere words. Ross had always been the most generous of lovers, and that had not changed. She would have fallen in love with him all over again for that generosity, except that she had never fallen out of love, not for a single instant of the last dozen years.

He murmured into her ear, "Sorry, I seem to have gotten rather carried away."

He wasn't sorry at all; he sounded thoroughly pleased with himself. She felt an absurd desire to giggle. "I'm not sorry, and I'm the one who needs to be carried away."

He grinned and made a move to bend over and lift her. "An excellent idea. It's time to adjourn to the bed."

"No! Now it's my turn." Her strength was returning; not enough to wrestle a lion, perhaps, but enough. She straightened up and went to work on the buttons of his shirt. When they were undone, she tugged his shirttails loose, then pulled the garment off. "The real reason I behaved so badly at Serevan," she said with a hint of laughter, "was that I wanted to see more of you."

His hand curved up around her neck so that he could stroke the responsive nape. "Shameless woman."

"Absolutely." She skimmed her hands over his bare upper body, enjoying the feel of smooth skin over hard muscle. "I paid for my sins, though, because seeing made me want to touch, but I didn't dare. For example, I wanted to do this." Tenderly she pressed her lips to the scar the bullet wound had made below his shoulder. "I was horrified to think how close you had come to being killed."

Briefly that thought jarred her from the moment, reminding her that once more Ross was on the brink of death. Determinedly she shook the knowledge away. Tonight the shadows of the past had no power; only the present was real.

She laid her open hand on the center of his chest. The steady rhythm of his heart was overlaid by warm skin and softly textured hair that tickled her palm, denser than she remembered. "You've changed too. When we first married, I thought you were the most splendid creature I had ever seen, and I could not imagine improvement."

"Have I altered for better or worse?"

She was surprised to hear the question in his voice; he was so patently glorious that it was hard to realize that he might not know it himself. When they met, he had had the grace and supple proportions of youth. Now maturity had added weight and power to his chest and shoulders. Remarkable how much stronger, how much more masculine, a man looked in his thirties than at twenty-one. "Definitely for the better," she assured him. "It hardly seems fair the way time will often improve a man's appearance but seldom a woman's."

She traced the edge of his ear with her tongue, then nibbled down the length of his throat to the hollow at the base. Now that the urgent edge had been taken off her desire, she was free to luxuriate in the subtle signs of his response, his skin going taut wherever she touched, and his breathing irregular. The musky scent of sex surrounded them as she bent over, taking his nipple between her teeth and teasing it with delicate care. The nub of flesh instantly went rigid and Ross gave a long, shuddering sigh.

Juliet's patience began eroding and she unfastened the buttons of his trousers, revealing more of the line of tawny hair that arrowed down his muscular midriff. Beguiled, she slid her hand down his abdomen, slipping under the loosened fabric in search of firm masculine flesh.

Unlike their encounter in the sandstorm, this time she did not catch him by surprise and he welcomed the caress, pressing hard into her hand. "I was speaking metaphorically when I referred to the pillar of fire, but it's literally true as well," she said with deep satisfaction as she caressed the heated silk-velvet length.

His fingers dug into her shoulder with bruising force and he began shaking all over. "Wait," he gasped.

She paused a moment and looked up, seeing that his head was thrown back and his torso sheened with perspiration.

"As wonderful as this feels," he managed to say, "I would rather be inside you."

Once more he was right. Sexual release was not enough; for emotional fulfillment they needed to be as intimately joined as man and woman could be. She dropped to her knees and peeled off his close-fitting trousers. Because of the desert heat, he was not wearing drawers, so she did not have to remove another layer of fabric to bare his long, powerfully muscled legs. She sat back on her heels and drew admiring hands from his hips to his calves, feeling the flex of tendon and muscle beneath her palms, distracted by the sight of so much lovely male anatomy.

"I've always been good at patience, but I believe that I've just run out." Ross leaned over and swept Juliet into his arms, then carried her the three steps to the bed. Deftly he pulled back the upper sheet and deposited her in the middle of the cotton-filled mattress.

Laughing, Juliet reached up and caught his hand. "Remind me of what happens next."

For a moment his eyes darkened and she knew as

clearly as if words had been spoken aloud that he was thinking of the lost years, when rumors of her profligate behavior had drifted back to England. They no longer belonged to each other and no one else; that was one thing that had changed, and for the worse. Over the last dozen years there had been other women, other beds, in his life, and it was her fault. Though she was sure Ross had not been a virgin when they married, she had never doubted that he would be faithful to their wedding vows, for fidelity was the bedrock of his nature. It was also her nature, but, tragically, she had not realized that until too late.

The moment was like a tear in the fabric of their love play; underneath, the dark waters of past and future anguish lent poignance to everything they said and did. Only passion might heal the perilous breach that threatened to open between them. Wanting to remove that darkness from his eyes, with sudden desperation she pulled him down onto the bed. "Now, Ross," she whispered huskily. "Please."

Her words shattered the dam of control he had managed to maintain until now. His primal need was a flood that engulfed her, his open mouth meeting hers as his hard thigh spread her legs. As he moved above her, she reached down to guide him. Their bodies came together with absolute sureness, hers rising impatiently to meet him, his moving slowly until he located the right place, the precise angle.

He groaned as he sheathed himself in her slick, heated flesh with one powerful thrust. "It's been so long, Juliet," he murmured against her mouth. "A lifetime too long."

She opened herself gladly, her breath mingling with his, her hips lifting to receive him more deeply. The empty years had lasted forever, yet the exact feel of him was burned into her body and her soul. She reveled in the ancient rhythm of thrust and response, loving the way he filled her, the feel of his weight crushing her into the mattress, the splendid rightness of their joining. How could she have thought another man could be his equal, even for a moment, even when she had been drowning in hell's own despair?

She had known she would find emotional satisfaction

and physical pleasure in their mating, but she did not expect to find uncontrollable desire rising inside her, not again, not so soon. But her hunger was as undeniable as it was improbable, and passion spiraled higher and higher, a potent vortex that tightened around their joining until she cried out, a long formless sound of need as her muscles convulsed around him. His fiercely driving body paused, suspended at its deepest penetration. Then he surged against her in endless uncontrollable pulsations.

In the exhausted aftermath, she held him close, caressing the long line of his back and buttocks with a languid hand. Neither of them spoke, for words could add nothing to their contentment. When his muscles tautened in prelude to shifting his weight away, she clasped her arms around his waist so that he could not leave her. He settled back with a pleased sigh, then rubbed his cheek against hers and brushed hair from her damp brow, the exhalation of his tranquil breath a caress against her temple.

Now that Juliet had time for stillness, she knew with deep humility that she had given him a different, and more valuable, gift than simple pleasure. For a man's wife to leave must be a massive blow to his masculinity, no matter how strong his confidence and no matter what the woman's reasons. And she had given Ross precious few reasons; certainly not the most compelling one. But if he had ever doubted his ability to satisfy her, he could not do so now.

Experimentally she contracted her internal muscles where they were still joined, and was delighted to feel him begin to firm inside her. God willing, this would not be the only night they would have, but come what may, they would not waste a moment of what time they had left.

As she pressed her lips against his cheek, she uttered a small prayer of thanks. By taking the time to rediscover each other, they had lighted not a small candle that would be quickly extinguished and forgotten, but a bonfire that blazed bright enough to challenge inevitable night.

19

❧

Ross woke slowly, drifting in the most profound peace he had ever felt in his life. When he married Juliet, he had not properly appreciated peace, for at twenty-one he had never known spiritual devastation; that he had discovered after she had left him. The pain of the intervening years made him value this present tranquillity all the more.

The lamp had burned out but a faint lessening of darkness hinted of coming dawn. He and Juliet lay on their sides, her back curving along his stomach, his arm around her waist and his leg entwined with hers. He was glad the night was cool enough to make this closeness comfortable; in fact, he had pulled a sheet over their damp bodies before they finally went to sleep.

Last night's astonishing passion had been profoundly satisfying, everything he had remembered and more. Yet if he could stop time and live in one instant forever, he would choose a moment like this, when they were relaxing together in a state of absolute harmony.

He wondered how many more such moments they might have. Though he had described the interview with the amir lightly, at the time he had not believed he would leave the palace alive, except, perhaps, for a short journey to the Black Well, where Ian Cameron had endured a living death before being put out of his misery. Ross was not sure why his captor had let him return to the nayeb's house, but suspected that Nasrullah enjoyed playing with him, offering hope only so that it could be jerked away.

He supposed that in one sense, after last night he could

die happy, for he and Juliet had finally found their way
back to each other. But he didn't want to die; he wanted
to live, to return to England with his wife so they could
raise children and start an institute where scholars and
adventurers from many lands could meet and learn from
each other. But most of all, where he and Juliet could
simply *be,* enjoying every precious day together.

Soon they must apply themselves to the prospects of
escape, but for the moment he was content to savor the
fact that Juliet was once more in his arms, his wife in
fact as well as in law. It would take more than one night
to slake his desire for her; he doubted that a lifetime
would be enough. If the dozen years of separation had
taught him anything worth knowing, it was to appreciate
the rare passion between them.

She exhaled, more asleep than awake, and nestled
closer against him. His body reacted with immediate interest. He had always enjoyed the languid lovemaking of
the morning; it was the only activity he had any enthusiasm for before breakfast.

No nightgown could ever be as seductive as Juliet's
bare, satin-smooth skin. He cupped her breast in his
hand and stroked the nipple with his thumb, enjoying
the way the texture changed from suede-soft to pebble-
hard under the gentle friction.

Almost purring, Juliet mischievously rubbed her shapely
backside against his groin. Taking that as encouragement, he nuzzled through her thick hair and kissed the
tender skin below her ear while he caressed all the lovely
curves and hollows he could reach, moving ever lower.
When his fingers slid through the soft curling hair to the
sensitive hidden flesh below, she inhaled sharply, her
hot, liquid response making it clear that she was now
quite awake enough.

Since he was feeling lazy, he decided the position they
were in was just fine. Guessing his intentions, Juliet
raised her upper leg and he slid into her welcoming body.
The night before, she had been surprisingly tight, almost
virginal, but she had adjusted quickly. Now she gave a
delighted sigh and rotated her hips, pivoting around him
in a thoroughly inflammatory way.

An advantage of lying folded together in this particular

fashion was that he could continue to touch her intimately, ensuring that her response kept pace with his own. And when, as soon happened, she began twisting convulsively, he held her tightly to prevent them from separating as he culminated himself.

All of her tautness vanished and she melted back against him, as boneless as a pillow, but far more pleasant to hold. He whispered in her ear, "That was the finest way imaginable of preparing to meet the day."

Her gray eyes fluttered open and she asked with mock innocence, "Did something happen and I missed it?"

They were still joined together, so he arched his pelvis against her. "Does this refresh your memory?"

Her eyes widened. "So it does." Chuckling, she rolled onto her back and drew his head down to rest on her breast. "In some ways this reminds me of our wedding night."

"More like the morning after," he interjected as he relaxed. She made a superlative pillow.

"That's true, the morning after was much like this. I hadn't known it was possible to make love in such a position. Of course," she added with a smile, "at the time I was quite vague even on the basics."

"You were a quick learner."

"The resemblance to our wedding night comes from the sense of wonder and discovery, but this was even better because there was no uncertainty," she said shyly. "Then I wasn't at all sure what to expect, because it was the first time. Thank heaven you knew what to do."

Ross gave a wry smile and twined a lock of her curling hair around his forefinger. "I was probably more nervous than you. It was my first time too."

"Really?" she said, suddenly intent. "I always assumed that you had . . . had experience."

"Experience, as you so delicately put it, is always available to a young man of fortune, but I found the thought of buying a woman's favors distasteful," he replied. "Nor was seducing a maid an acceptable alternative—I had no desire to father a bastard or ruin a girl's life. It was simpler to put my energies into things like learning Arabic."

"No wonder you became so proficient with languages," she said with a gurgle of laughter. "But how did you know what . . . ?" Embarrassed, she broke off her question.

"There are times when a scholarly mind is useful," he explained. "A fortnight before our marriage, I hired the services of a very expensive courtesan and asked her to show me what women liked. She was amused by the idea and demonstrated everything very thoroughly, though she kept saying it would be better if I participated."

Juliet grinned. "How marvelous. You were actually able to resist her blandishments?"

"Yes," he said simply. "After I met you, I didn't want any other woman."

Tenderly she brushed his cheek with the back of her hand. "Your research project worked. I never suspected that you were as much a novice as I."

"I'm glad I managed to convince you. From the perspective of my advanced years, it isn't significant, but at the time it seemed desperately important that I not betray my ignorance."

A brittle note came into her voice. "You certainly have experience now. It shows."

He felt a twinge of annoyance. "Reproaches, Juliet? Surely you didn't expect me to become celibate after you left."

"No," she said sadly, "of course not. I just find myself feeling a few unworthy twinges of jealousy."

If the subject had been less emotionally charged, he might have found her honesty endearing or flattering. Instead, her words fueled his irritation.

Rationally he had accepted that there was no reason to remain faithful to a marriage that was essentially over, but Ross had never been comfortable with the fact that technically he was committing adultery whenever he sought the solace of a female body. The uneasy balance he had struck between conscience and need had been less than satisfactory both physically and emotionally. He rolled onto his back so that they were no longer touching. "I don't think you have any right to jealousy, though if it's any comfort, I'm sure that over the years my failures of fidelity were considerably fewer than yours."

"Reports of my debauchery were greatly exaggerated," Juliet said in a choked voice.

"Exaggerated, perhaps, but not invented out of whole cloth," he said tightly. Something dark and dangerous was stirring in the black depths of his mind, a scene he had buried, though he had never been able to forget. And as the memory forced its way to the surface, with it came fury. "I don't know how many of the stories were true, but I had to believe the evidence of my eyes."

She sat up and drew away from him, to the edge of the bed. In the predawn light her face was pale and unreadable. "What . . . what do you mean?"

His hands clenched as he fought to bring his anger under control, but it would no longer be denied. "Do you remember when you stayed at the Hotel Bianca in Malta? I do."

Juliet gasped and drew her legs up, wrapping her arms around them. "What were you doing in Malta?"

He pushed himself up on one elbow and stared at her, his eyes narrowed. "What the hell do you think I was doing? I had come after you. You were my wife—did you think that you could end our marriage with one cryptic note?"

His pulse began pounding as the past unrolled before his inner eye in all its gut-wrenching agony. It had been late when he had disembarked at the port of Valletta. He had gone direct to the Hotel Bianca, said to be the best hostelry on Malta. He had learned that Juliet had taken ship to the island, but expected that finding her would require a search. Nonetheless, when he registered he asked, without much hope, if his wife, Lady Ross Carlisle, had arrived yet, for she would be meeting him soon.

When he described her, the concierge's face had lit up. Ah, yes, the beautiful fire-haired English lady, indeed she was here. Ross's bags had already been taken up to his room, but the romantic concierge gave him a knowing smile and another key, along with directions to Juliet's room "in case the English milord did not want to delay his reunion until morning."

It was very late and Ross knew he should wait, but he had been unable to stop himself from taking advantage of the concierge's indiscreet helpfulness. The room was easy to find, at the south end of the second-floor corridor.

His heart had beat faster at the knowledge that Juliet was just a few feet away from him, but he paused before knocking. Though emotionally he was convinced that if they saw each other everything would be all right, logically he knew that she might be ambivalent about the unexpected arrival of her husband. But he did not seriously doubt that they could solve the problem, whatever it was; there was too much love between them for their marriage to be over.

While he stood indecisively, the door had unexpectedly swung open and a man emerged. As the door was pulled shut and locked from inside, Ross froze, feeling as if he had been kicked in the belly. The man's clothing was disheveled, as if pulled on in haste, and he had a sleek smile of tomcat satisfaction on his handsome face. Letters of flame on the wall could not have said more clearly that he had just had a sexual encounter with the woman on the other side of the door.

And Ross had recognized him, which somehow made the whole nightmare worse. It was the Comte d'Auxerre, a French diplomat who had once been pointed out to Ross at a ball in London. A tall fair man in his late thirties, he had been popular with society hostesses.

The count did not know who Ross was, for they had never been introduced, and Ross was not important enough to have been noticed by a distinguished foreign visitor. After a moment of surprise, the Frenchman saw the heavy old key in the newcomer's hand and gave a tolerant chuckle. "Ah, so the young lady is as hot as her hair. Enjoy yourself, my friend. She is worth the loss of a night's sleep." Then the count had politely circled the younger man, unaware of how close he had just come to death.

Alone again, Ross had stood paralyzed, his body chilled yet drenched with sweat, his hands clenching and unclenching as he realized that his world had just irrevocably shattered.

The pain of his nails digging into his palms brought him back to the present; a present that was almost as painful as the past. Harshly he said, "When I arrived at the Hotel Bianca, I was told you were a guest, so I went up to your room. I was about to knock when one of your lovers walked out, looking very pleased with himself. The Comte d'Auxerre. Do you remember him, or was he just a passing fancy, forgotten by morning?"

A spasm crossed Juliet's face and she bent her head, retreating into a tight little ball, but she said nothing. A stray beam of early sunlight glinted mockingly from the gold chain around her neck.

Her very silence increased Ross's anger. He had never spoken of what he had seen in Malta, but now the anguish could no longer be denied. "It never occurred to me that I would find you in bed with another man," he said bitterly. "It had been only three weeks, Juliet. Three bloody weeks. Was he the first, or had you found a different man in every hotel between Chapelgate and Malta?"

She shook her bent head, her long hair veiling her face, but she made no attempt to defend herself.

Ross rolled out of the bed and stalked to the window, which was covered with slatted blinds that admitted air and light. Staring through the thin slats at the empty courtyard, he snapped, "Have you nothing to say for yourself? Surely you can find a confession or a denial or a boast. Say *something,* dammit. With a little effort, perhaps you can convince me that I went to the wrong room."

"I can't deny it. What you think happened that night . . . happened," Juliet said, her voice almost inaudible. "You are right to despise me. But having come all the way from England, why didn't you try to see me, if only to tell me what you thought of me?"

Ross swung away from the window and flattened his trembling body against the roughly textured wall, his nails digging into the plaster as he struggled vainly to master himself. The answer to her question was the blackest piece of self-knowledge he had ever faced, and it shamed him. Nonetheless he answered, for in his rage he wanted Juliet to know what she had done. "I left because I was afraid that if I saw you, there was a very real chance that I might kill you."

For an endless time, only the rasp of Juliet's shallow breathing disturbed the stillness. At length she said bleakly, "This is why I have tried to keep my distance from you since Serevan. I feared that if we became intimate again, all the barriers and denials that made it possible to live would be destroyed. And that is what has happened."

She slid from the bed and knelt on the floor, lifting her crumpled robe and holding it in front of her while she blindly gathered her clothing with her other hand. In the distance, muezzins could be heard calling the faithful to prayer from a dozen different minarets. It was light enough now to see detail, though objects were still flat and colorless.

Bleakly Ross wondered how it was possible to go from joy to disaster in a handful of moments. Juliet was right that intimacy had destroyed the barriers; for years he had successfully suppressed his anger, even through the last difficult weeks when he had been constantly with his errant wife. But in some mysterious way, becoming lovers again had weakened his control, and once it began to unravel, his anger was unstoppable.

As he tried to understand why, he suddenly realized that Juliet was crying, huge soundless tears running down her face as she fumbled for her scattered garments. Her grief was all the more devastating for being expressed in total silence.

The pain inside him did not diminish, but the nature of it changed, as did his anger. He swore a wordless oath at himself. He could feel her drawing away from him emotionally and knew that soon she would be gone past recalling. The thought was unbearable. For a brief ugly moment he had wanted to wound his wife, to make her suffer as he had suffered. Yet by doing so he had hurt not just her but himself, for he could not endure the sight of her pain, no matter how much she deserved his fury. His voice raw, he said, "Juliet, I'm sorry I lashed out at you. I shouldn't have done it."

"I'm sorry too—for everything. I was mad to think the past could be overcome. Remember the poetry of Omar Khayyam?" She looked up at him, her eyes wide and bleak, the long lashes clumped by tears. *"The moving finger writes and having writ, moves on. And all your piety and wit, won't call it back to cancel half a line. Nor will your tears wash out a word of it."* She closed her eyes, her face twisted with misery. "Last night I wanted to give you the only gift in my power. Instead I hurt you unforgivably, and not for the first time."

Swiftly he crossed the room and knelt beside her. The knife wound which he had seared with red-hot steel was now a sullen, almost healed line curving around her upper arm. It was a reminder that there was no one like Juliet anywhere and that her uniqueness was what he had loved about her. Choosing his words with care, he said, "I can't say that the past doesn't matter, because it does, enormously. But that was then. This is now."

"The past *is* now, for we are what our deeds have made us. Last night was a mistake. We opened Pandora's box, and I don't think it is possible to have the pleasure without the pain." Ravaged by her guilt, Juliet was unable to meet Ross's gaze. There was unbearable irony in the knowledge that he had actually followed her halfway across the Mediterranean and reached Malta on that fateful night. If he had arrived a few hours sooner, she would have greeted him with open arms; their marriage would have survived and perhaps become stronger. But by the time he had reached the Hotel Bianca, it had already been too late.

Ross caught her chin with his hand and turned her to face him. "No! Last night was not a mistake. You were right: it would be a sin to waste what time we have left." With a faint wry smile he softly quoted another of the Persian poet's verses. *" 'Make the most of what we yet may spend, Before we too into the dust descend.'* Don't pull away from me again, Juliet. I need you too much."

It was impossible to deny his plea, especially when her own need was so desperate. She leaned forward to kiss him, her mouth fierce and compelling. In one powerful move he pulled her hard against him. They were both kneeling and the robe she still held became caught between them, but his hands feasted on her bare back and buttocks, kneading and arousing wherever he touched.

The robe fell away as he bore her down to the carpet and their naked bodies intertwined, each of them seeking wholeness. Pain and anger were transmuted to passion, and they came together as if their earlier gentle lovemaking had never happened, using desire as a drug in a vain attempt to deny what had proved undeniable.

Ross made love to Juliet with the same dangerous wildness that she had seen in him after the *bozkashi* match. It was a purely masculine act of possesion, yet it was also lovemaking, rooted in aching emotion. Her response came straight from the heart as she tried to say with her body what would have sounded false in words: that she loved him, had always loved him, though he had reason not to believe her.

Perhaps it had been a mistake to become lovers again, for pain lurked perilously near the surface. But now that they had come together, it was impossible to draw apart. For better and for worse, they were joined under the shadow of death.

20

❦

After their fierce mating, they lay spent and silent for fear of what words might bring. Juliet's head rested on Ross's shoulder, her bright hair a mantle over his chest, her fingers laced with his. With his other hand he slowly stroked the back of her neck and wondered where they would go from here. In the last six hours they had experienced passion driven by rediscovery, sweetness, and finally desperation; if he weren't so tired, he would be impressed by his stamina.

Now it seemed that a fragile truce had been established, but nothing had been settled, not really. Instead, he guessed, they would go on like this, together but guarded, neither of them willing to deal with the painful issues that had briefly flared out of control and very nearly divided them again.

A peremptory knock sounded on the door and they both tensed as a servant announced that Abdul Samut Khan wished Lord Khilburn's company for breakfast. Both of them jumped to their feet and began scrambling into their clothing while Ross called out that he would be honored to join the nayeb.

Ross envied Juliet the simplicity of her enveloping Tuareg garments; she was fully dressed, looking exactly as Jalal always looked, while he was still wrestling with his cravat. Before she went to admit the servant, Ross said in a low voice, "I'll probably be out all day. Will you be here tonight?"

Her brows arched. "Of course."

He was glad to hear that; he had not been entirely sure. After pulling on his coat, Ross ran a comb through his hair, arranged a calm expression on his face, and went off to his host.

The nayeb greeted him volubly. "My dear Lord Khilburn! Was the interview with the amir a difficult one? If only I had known you would be summoned last night, I would have accompanied you." He took Ross's hand and guided him to a spot by the table, his cold eyes a disquieting contrast with his effusive manner. "Unfortunately, important matters concerning the artillery demanded my attention and I did not learn what had happened until this morning. What did his majesty say?"

"It was no great matter," Ross said easily as he settled onto a cushion. He suspected that the nayeb already knew what had happened the night before in the audience chamber, word for word and inflection for inflection. "The amir merely said that he had decided not to allow me to take Major Cameron's body home for burial. Naturally I regret that, but it is his majesty's right to refuse. When I asked permission to depart, he said that it would be granted soon."

Abdul Samut Khan glanced about warily. A guard stood by the door at the far end of the room, his expression bored; no one else was present. "If only that were true," the nayeb said in a low voice. "But the amir is notoriously volatile. He will grant you permission, only to withdraw it again and again, as he did with your brother. So it will go until he takes offense at something you do—or perhaps for no reason at all."

Ross gave his host a level stare. "Then what—the Black Well, or will he execute me out of hand?"

"I cannot say." The nayeb frowned. "The situation is difficult, and about to become more so. You must have heard that there has been trouble between Bokhara and Kokand. Yesterday the amir decided to personally lead an army against his enemies. As chief of artillery, I will go with him. That is why I was busy last night—I was making preparations to go to war, for Nasrullah wishes to leave in ten days and there is much to be done."

"I see." Ross considered the implications as he ate pieces of melon; the Bokharans claimed their melons were the world's best, and they were probably right. "How will this affect me?"

"Since the amir did not have you executed last night, I think you will be safe until he leaves, for he will be too busy to think of you again." The nayeb paused to sip his tea. "If the campaign against Kokand is successful, Nasrullah will return in great spirits, willing to grant favors to all. But if the campaign goes badly, as I fear it will, his mood will be . . . dangerous. Very dangerous indeed."

"What do you suggest I do?"

Abdul Samut Khan glanced around again, then leaned close. "You should fly from Bokhara while the amir is away. Go to Khiva—the amir there is a friend to Europeans."

This was all very interesting, but Ross guessed that something more was coming. "The way to Khiva is long and perilous. It will be difficult for a lone ferengi to escape.

"Naturally I will do anything in my power to aid you, honored friend, even at the risk of my own life." The nayeb stroked his beard reflectively. "While escape is not impossible, it will be expensive, very expensive. If you have enough gold, I can arrange everything before I go. The amir will not learn of your flight until he returns, and by then you will be safe in Khiva." He spread his hands apologetically. "If I were a rich man, I would take care of all of the expenses myself, but, alas, I have not the resources."

In other words, the ferengi was to place all his money in his host's unreliable hands and hope for the best. Ross was not impressed with the nayeb's stated willingness to risk his life, for it was unlikely that the Persian would be blamed for what his ungrateful guest did in his absence. Perhaps if Abdul Samut Khan was well-paid, he really would help Ross escape; perhaps not. The only way to find out would be for Ross to place his life in the nayeb's hands, and that he was reluctant to do.

Concealing his cynical thoughts, Ross said, "You are very brave to make such an offer, but it would be dishonorable to flee when the amir has shown me such generosity."

His host gave him an exasperated look. "Honor is all very well, Lord Khilburn, but this is a matter of your life. Nothing can save you from the amir's wrath save flight."

"I will think on it."

Abdul Samut Khan's expression changed. "There is another alternative. Become one of us. If you convert to Islam, the amir will welcome you as a trusted adviser and grant you beautiful wives and great riches. Stay, Lord Khilburn."

Ross had the odd feeling that for once the nayeb was sincere; however, becoming one of Nasrullah's advisers was not an alluring prospect and would probably be as hazardous as Ross's present situation. "You honor me, Abdul Samut Khan," he said austerely, "but that is not possible. I have a wife, a family, and responsibilities in my own country."

The nayeb sighed. "I do not think you fully realize the seriousness of your situation. Dead you will be of no use to yourself or your family; alive and living in Bokhara, at least you will be of use to yourself."

Once again Ross promised, "I shall think on all you have said. But now I ask that you excuse me. The imam of the Tekkie of Khalfa Husein graciously invited me to visit the Tekkie monastary this morning, and I do not wish to keep him waiting."

Before he could rise, Abdul Samut Khan began shaking his head sadly. "That is not possible, honored Khilburn. The amir has given orders that you cannot go about the city anymore."

"I see." Ross masked his face to conceal what a blow the news was. "Can I send messages and receive visitors, or will I be held in close confinement?"

"You may write letters and have visitors, and you have the freedom of the compound, but except when you are in your own rooms, you will be guarded at all times," the nayeb said apologetically. His voice dropped again. "As you see, your situation is grave. Again I say that you must flee. Only give me gold and I shall make the arrangements."

"How much gold would be needed?"

A calculating gleam showed in his host's eyes. "Perhaps . . . ten thousand ducats?"

Ross shook his head. "I have no such fortune. It appears that my fate must stay in God's hands."

The nayeb said quickly, "Give me what you have and also your note of hand saying that the British ambassador in Teheran will pay the difference. You see how I trust you."

"But the British ambassador will not honor such a note, for I am here privately, not as a representative of my country. I cannot permit you to risk ruin on my behalf." Deciding that it was time to leave, Ross stood. "I thank you for your concern, Abdul Samut Khan. You have given me much to ponder."

"Ponder well, ferengi," the nayeb said with exasperation. Raising his voice, he said to the guard at the door, "Zadeh, you must stay with Lord Khilburn at all times except when he is in his rooms. Do not let him out of your sight."

The guard opened the door for Ross, then followed him out.

Since leaving the compound was forbidden, Ross decided to go back to his rooms and write a note to the Tekkie imam to explain his absence. He must also write to his other acquaintances; with luck, some would be willing to visit him in the nayeb's house.

As they made their way through the sprawling house, a soft whisper came from behind him. "Do not trust Abdul Samut Khan, Lord Khilburn. He pretended to be the friend of Yawer Cameron, then betrayed him, and he will do the same to you."

Startled, Ross realized that the warning must have come from his guard, Zadeh, who was one of the younger soldiers assigned to the nayeb. Without turning his head, and keeping his own voice low, he said, "What do you think of his offer to help me escape?"

"He would use it as an excuse to take your gold, then see you charged with spying and executed," was the prompt reply.

"I suspected as much," Ross murmured. "Tell me, if I tried to escape from the compound some night, are there any among the guards who might . . . look the other way?"

"There are many who would wish to help you," Zadeh

said cautiously, "though since there is risk involved, a small gift would be appropriate."

Ross nodded, then went into his rooms. He suspected that it would be both cheaper and safer to bribe the guard directly rather than rely on the nayeb's uncertain aid. But escaping from the compound would be only the first step, and the easiest.

Juliet spent the morning with Saleh and Murad, discussing possible courses of action, for instinct told her that time was running out. Practical conversation was a relief, for it kept her from thinking about the soul-searing night with Ross.

Later she visited several caravansaries to learn when caravans were expected to leave and what the destinations were. Toward the end of the afternoon, when the heat was at its worst and the city baked under the brazen yellow light of Central Asia, she returned to the nayeb's house.

She had entered and was walking along a dimly lit corridor when she encountered Yawer Shahid Mahmud. He had never deigned to notice her existence before, but today a speculative glint came into the burly officer's eyes when he saw her.

There was no one else about, and Juliet felt a prickly sense of warning. Her gaze straight ahead, she tried to walk past the Uzbek, but he reached out and caught her arm before she could slide away. "Not so fast, Targui. I have not been hospitable enough to you. Your name is Jalal, is it not?"

She did not answer, just glanced at him with narrowed eyes. He was an inch or two taller than she, and much heavier, and she did not like the way he was looking at her.

Shahid continued, "I have wondered why your master would tolerate such a surly slave, but now I know that you have hidden charms." He gave a slow, unpleasant smile. "You should have been quieter last night."

Juliet swore to herself. In spite of their efforts to keep their voices down, they had been overheard, and it was undoubtedly her fault. When Ross returned from seeing the amir, she had been in his arms even as the door closed. The yawer, balked of his prey, must have decided to linger outside to see what he could learn. Now he knew Juliet was female, and she had a horrible suspicion of what he intended to do about it.

She tried to pull away, but the Uzbek twisted her arm, forcing her toward the wall. "There is a famous Pushtu love song called 'Zakmi Dil,' which means 'Wounded Heart,' " he said softly. "Perhaps you have heard it? It goes *'There's a boy across the river with a bottom like a peach, But alas! I cannot swim.' "*

He smiled again and touched his tongue to his lips. "In Bokhara we are fortunate, for the great river Amu is many miles away and there is no need to swim." With sudden violence he spun her around and slammed her face first against the wall, jerking her right arm up behind her back. "You move like a youth, as slim and graceful as a woman."

He grabbed her buttock with his free hand and squeezed hard, his fingers digging deeply into her flesh. "Ah, yes, boy," he said hoarsely. "Your bottom is very like a peach. You should not waste it on an unbeliever."

Later there would be time to be grateful that he had not guessed the deeper secret of her identity; at the moment, Juliet was more concerned with escaping unravished. Rather than strike out immediately, she forced herself to hold still while Shahid fondled her, his hot breath quickening.

"You like that, don't you, boy?" He gave a coarse chuckle. "Now I'll show you what a real man is like. You'll never let that whey-faced ferengi touch you again." For a moment he pinned her against the wall with his massive body, his pelvis grinding her into the plaster. Grimly Juliet endured it, knowing that she would have only one chance to overcome his advantage of weight and position, so she must choose her time well.

Her moment came when he reached down for the hem of her robe, his growing excitement and her lack of resistance making him incautious. As soon as his hold slackened, Juliet raised her leg and smashed the heel of her boot back into his kneecap with the force of a kicking mule.

Shahid shrieked in pained surprise and lurched sideways as his knee gave way. His grasp on her arm tightened as he fell, but Juliet was prepared. She wrenched away at an angle that would have broken his elbow joint if he had tried to maintain his grip, at the same time pulling her dagger from its sheath.

By the time the yawer realized that this would be no easy conquest, she was behind him and her knife was at his throat. Using her most guttural tone and the ugliest Persian obscenities she knew, she snarled, "Filthy swine! If you wish to fornicate, find a sow like the mother who bore you."

When he began struggling to break away, she pressed her razor-edged blade into his windpipe with enough pressure to draw blood. "If you raise your puny rod near me again, I will cut it off and shove it down your throat." Then she stepped back and gave him a kick in the kidneys to ensure that he would not be able to pursue her any time soon.

As he collapsed, groaning, she turned and resumed walking down the hall, forcing herself to maintain a normal pace, as if she was totally unafraid of what he might do to retaliate. Nonetheless, she kept the dagger ready in her hand and listened hard for the sound of footfalls in case he should recover more quickly than she expected. The force of his furious gaze burned between her shoulder blades until she turned the corner.

When Juliet was out of his sight, she drew a trembling wrist across her forehead before she cleaned and sheathed her dagger. She had been lucky; if Shahid had not underestimated her, she would have been in serious trouble. As long as she was in this house, she would have to be careful, for he was the sort who would take being bested as a mortal challenge.

A pity that killing the head of the household guard would not go unremarked. Then she smiled shakily and continued on her way. In truth she was not so coldblooded that she could slit a man's throat in anything short of a life-or-death situation, and this had not been that. Not quite. But she did not like to think of what would have happened if Shahid had discovered she was a woman. After raping her, he would undoubtedly have claimed her disguise was *prima facie* evidence that she and Ross were both spies, and then nothing could have saved them.

When Juliet reached their rooms, she found a servant just leaving, so she brushed silently past and closed the door behind her. After dropping the bar in place, she pulled off her tagelmoust and buried her sweaty face in the fabric.

Ross was sitting on the divan with a notebook, but he looked up with quick concern. "Is something wrong?"

"Not really." She managed an uneven smile as she emerged from the folds of her veil. "Shahid Mahmud made an improper advance but misjudged my ability and willingness to defend myself. Fortunately I was wearing boots rather than sandals."

"Damnation!" Ross swore furiously as he swung to his feet and pulled her into a protective embrace. "How did the bastard discover that you're a woman?"

"He didn't." In spite of the late-afternoon warmth, Juliet found herself shaking with relief as Ross's arms went around her. There was nothing like a bit of crisis to reduce a relationship to essentials; for them, that meant mutual comfort and protection. "He heard enough last night to guess that our relationship is not strictly master and servant, but it must not have occurred to him that I could be female."

Ross's embrace tightened. "I see. A pity we can't kill him. At least he can hardly complain to the nayeb that my servant would not allow himself to be raped. I suppose that all you can do is exercise caution and not let him find you alone again, but just in case, it might be wise to carry your pistol."

"Avoidance is better. Killing or wounding Shahid would bring about an investigation that we can't afford." Wearily Juliet stepped away from Ross and sank onto the divan. On the low table was a dew-covered pitcher of the ice and grape-syrup mixture that had just been delivered by the servant. She poured goblets for both of them. "It is time to talk about how we are going to leave Bokhara."

"The situation has just gotten worse." Ross sat down and gave her a summary of his interview with Abdul Samut Khan.

Juliet frowned as he finished. "So now you are under house arrest. I hope the nayeb is right that the amir will be too busy to think of you between now and the time they go to war. I think we should make our escape as soon as Nasrullah leaves the city."

They had both finished their *rahat i jan,* so Ross lifted the pitcher and refilled their glasses. "You have been exploring possibilities ever since we got here—what do you propose we do?"

Juliet gave him a fond smile; she had always loved the fact that Ross was open to suggestions as only a truly strong man could be. "First, I think we should send Saleh and Reza back to Persia. There is a large caravan leaving for Teheran in a few days. That will leave just you and Murad and me."

Ross nodded, following the direction of her thoughts. "And the three of us are the strongest. You're thinking we should get some good Turkoman horses and ride west as fast as we can? I've thought about that and agree that it may be our best chance, but it will be dangerous. Crossing the Kara Kum was bad enough in the spring— at this season, the heat is killing and we'll probably be pursued at least part of the way."

"Yes, but Turkoman raiders have been marauding through that desert since long before Genghis Khan. We can survive it too, as long as we travel fast and light." She leaned forward, her hands moving emphatically. "We came here along the main caravan track, but there is a secondary route that goes south of Merv and Rafitak. If we go that way, we are less likely to be pursued, and less likely to run into Turkoman raiders as well."

"It is a minor track because the water supply is less reliable," Ross pointed out, "and without a knowledge-able guide, we'll have trouble finding what water is there. Horses can travel much faster than camels, but they need water more often, and we won't be able to carry enough to get us and our mounts across hundreds of miles of burning desert."

"Murad has not traveled this particular route, but over the last several weeks he has talked with men who have, gathering detailed information on where the water holes are."

Ross made a face and leaned back against the wall. "Murad is well-intentioned but he got lost even in Persia, which he claimed to know. Are you willing to put your life in his hands?"

"Yes, because I think this is our best chance," Juliet replied. "There is desert in all directions, but it would be dangerous to go east or south because of the fighting around Kokand and Herat. North to Khiva would be better, but eventually we would have to go back across the Kara Kum anyhow. If we head west, all we have to do is reach Serevan, and with luck we can do that in five or six days of hard riding."

"We may be that lucky, though I wouldn't bet serious money on it." Ross ran his hand through his gold hair, his face troubled. "I'm willing to take the chance, but I hate the idea that you and Murad will be risking your lives unnecessarily. Perhaps Murad should draw me a map and I can go alone."

"Three people will have a better chance than one." Juliet leaned forward, her expression fierce. "We've been over this before. Murad knows the risks and is willing to accept them. And make no mistake, Ross, there is no way in hell that I will let you go across that desert without me."

He looked startled for a moment, then gave a slow smile and reached out and gently brushed her cheek with his knuckles. "What a terrifying female you are. It sounds as if I have no alternative but to agree to your plans."

Juliet gave him a mock scowl. "Right you are, ferengi."

His momentary amusement fading, Ross reached inside his coat and drew out a small folded piece of paper, then handed it to Juliet. "I wrote this today. It will probably never be needed, but I thought you should have it."

She examined the note distrustfully. It had been sealed with wax and marked with Ross's signet ring. "What is this, your last will and testament?"

"No, that is in England—I always put my affairs in order before I leave the country. Though since we are on the subject, your income is guaranteed for the rest of your life," he said in an expressionless voice. "What I just gave you is an affidavit verifying that if you have a baby next year and say that I fathered it, you're telling the truth."

Juliet stared at the affidavit as if it were a viper. She was quite aware of the possible consequences of the previous night's passion, but the issue was so profoundly complicated and upsetting that she had refused to think about it. "This will only be relevant if you are killed but I survive and bear a child," she said tightly. "That isn't very likely."

"True," Ross agreed, "but it would be remiss of me not to make provisions for the possibility. There is a great deal of property involved—if we were to have a son, he would be the next Duke of Windermere, and a daughter would be a considerable heiress. Since we have been separated for years, if you just sent a letter to England saying that I had left a legitimate heir, you would certainly face doubts and perhaps legal challenges from whichever cousin inherits after me. I wouldn't want you to have to face that."

Juliet's trembling fingers curled over the statement spasmodically. *Our son. Our daughter.* "You think of everything," she said, her tone brittle. "But what if I have a baby and don't want to give it up?"

"I'm not suggesting that you give it up—I just want to ensure that any heir of mine will receive what it is entitled to." His voice roughened. "This is probably the only hope of a child I'll ever have. If the amir decides to remove my head in the next few days, I'd like to die with the knowledge that perhaps I've left something meaningful behind me."

Juliet had not known that he cared that much about having a child. She had not dared let herself know. Her voice low, she said, "Don't worry. If . . . what we are talking about comes to pass, you can trust me to do everything in my power to give your child the future you would want for it."

"I do trust you." He took her hand, his fingers lacing with hers. "I'm just trying to make matters as simple as possible."

If Ross died, nothing would ever be simple again. Juliet closed her eyes to block incipient tears; she had already cried once today, and that was one time too often.

She was grateful that a knock sounded on the door before she had to speak.

This time the servant on the other side proffered an invitation for Lord Khilburn to dine with Abdul Samut Khan. Ross muttered something unflattering under his breath. "I'm a little tired of his company, but I suppose there is no help for it." Raising his voice, he ascertained that there was time for a bath and ordered that water be brought up.

After Ross had bathed and gone to join his host, Juliet took advantage of the water, soaking a long time as an antidote for the stresses of the last twenty-four hours. Then, clean and dry, she settled down and worked through her escape ideas step by step, making notes of questions that must be addressed.

Finally Ross returned from his dinner. Juliet had not been quite sure how the evening would end, for over the last day there had been both joy and conflict between them. But Ross made it very simple by yawning and offering her his hand. "It's late, Juliet. Let's go to bed."

Taking his hand and going with him was the most natural thing in the world.

21

Five days after Ross's fateful interview with the amir, Juliet had a private meeting with Muhammad and Hussayn Kasem. Knowing that if she went to their home her Tuareg garb would make her conspicuous to the ubiquitous Bokharan spies, she had sent a message saying that she would come to their busy fabric shop, where she would blend into the steady stream of people.

When she entered the shop's shadowed interior, Hussayn approached as if she were just another customer, but it did not take long for him to guide her into the back of the building on the pretext of searching for new stock. The shop was a labyrinth of rooms, all piled with rolls of lush fabric that glowed with color like Aladdin's cave. Drawing aside one last embroidered curtain, Hussayn gestured Juliet into a small thickly carpeted room where his father sat cross-legged by a samovar.

Unhurriedly the Kasems served their guest with tea and spiced cakes as inquiries were made into everyone's health. After etiquette was satisfied, Muhammad said, "I have heard that Khilburn is now confined to Abdul Samut Khan's house. I find that disturbing, for the British officer Cameron was treated the same way shortly before he was sent to the Black Well."

"What you have heard is true." Carefully Juliet set down her delicate porcelain teacup. "Khilburn has decided that the amir is not going to grant him permission to leave, so he must escape in secret. He has sent me to beg for your aid."

"There is no need to beg, for it will be our privilege

to assist him," Muhammad said graciously. "What might we do?"

"Escaping the nayeb's house should be easy, but it will be harder to leave the city because the gates are always guarded. Also, we will need desert-bred Turkoman horses, the kind of mounts that it might not be possible to purchase in the city." Juliet drew out a small leather purse that clinked with gold coins and laid it beside the samovar. "We will need three horses. Of course Khilburn will pay for them, for such animals come very dear."

"It would be dishonor to accept money from the man who saved my father's life," Hussayn said as he waved away the money. He stroked his dark beard absently as he thought. "It should not be difficult to pass through a city gate if you leave with a caravan, for in such a crowd the guards are more concerned with checking goods than people. If you make your escape from the nayeb's house on a night when we have a shipment leaving, you can join our group until you are safely outside. It would be best if you choose a caravan leaving by an eastern gate, for that will bring you out near our country estate, where we will have horses and supplies waiting."

Juliet had hoped that he would suggest exactly that. Bowing her head, she said, "Excellent. Do you know when, in the next few weeks, you will be shipping goods from the city?"

After conferring, the Kasems offered several possible dates. Then the discussion moved to other aspects of the escape plan. When the three of them had covered everything that Juliet could think of, she rose to take her leave.

His eyes shrewd, Hussayn remarked, "Your Persian is far more fluent than you showed on the journey across the Kara Kum, Jalal. Are you in truth a Targui?"

She hesitated a moment to choose an explanation that would contain the essence of truth. "No, my lord, this is but a disguise. I am also a ferengi. For many years, I have been . . . sworn to Khilburn's service. I could not allow him to undertake such a dangerous mission without me."

"I see," Hussayn murmured. "Khilburn is fortunate in

his servant. But then, he is a man who inspires loyalty. May God protect you both on your journey home."

As she bowed and left, Juliet fervently seconded the Bokharan's wishes.

Waiting was hard. Ross chafed at his inactivity and the fact that he could do nothing except behave in a manner that would not excite suspicion. Juliet was much busier, for no attempt was made to keep her in the compound. After securing the help of the Kasems, she took advantage of her voluminous robes to bring in items they would need and smuggle out what they wanted to take on their journey. Apart from gold, weapons, and the *bozkashi* cap Dil Assa had given him, Ross wanted to save only his journals, which recorded his observations on Turkestan and its inhabitants. They were, however, discreetly silent on the much more interesting subject of his personal life.

Two things made Ross's confinement bearable. The most important was the nights with Juliet, which were passionate and fulfilling beyond anything he had dreamed possible, and were equally rich in the subtler, more enduring rewards of companionship. Though death was an ever-present threat, in a way Ross had never been happier in his life. He supposed that death itself was what made each moment with his wife infinitely precious; it was as if a lifetime of possible happiness was being compressed into a handful of enchanted hours.

But their oasis of joy was surrounded by invisible barriers more impassable than the mud-brick walls of the nayeb's compound. The subjects which must not be mentioned included much of the past, all of the future—and neither of them ever spoke of love.

Ross's other diversion was the friends who continued to visit him at the nayeb's house. He was grateful, for in a city saturated with spies, it took some courage to call on a man under the amir's displeasure. Two or three guards were always in the reception room where Ross received guests, which tended to inhibit discourse, and all conversations had to be carried on in Persian so the guards could understand what was being said.

Ross found that his ability to understand Uzbeki made

for interesting eavesdropping. The guards had put together some sort of betting pool on the subject of whether Lord Khilburn would be executed outright or put in the Black Well, and if the latter, how long he would survive.

No one offered to bet on the proposition that the ferengi might leave Bokhara in good health.

Three days had passed since Juliet's meeting with the Kasems. As usual, she was out. Ross had spent the afternoon playing chess with an Armenian merchant whose stately demeanor masked a killer instinct for "the game of kings." The Armenian's first visit had been a courtesy call on a fellow Christian, and since he and Ross had enjoyed each other's company, the merchant had come often since. Ross was just saying good-bye to him when three more friends arrived.

The newcomers were prominent in the local Jewish community and included Ephraim ben Abraham, whom Ross had met on his earlier visit to Bokhara. At that time Ephraim had asked Ross to take a letter to England and give it to Moses Montefiore, a financier and philanthropist whose fame reached even to Turkestan. Montefiore had sent a reply to the Bokharans, and eight years later the parties were still in occasional communication with each other.

When Ross arrived in Bokhara for the second time, he had been invited to Ephraim ben Abraham's home. After thanking Ross for his part in establishing the correspondence with London, Ephraim had asked for the latest news of the British philanthropist, so Ross had offered the story of how Montefiore had been knighted by Queen Victoria in spite of opposition from some of her ministers. The young queen had declared that a Briton was a Briton, no matter what his religion, a sentiment that was received with great approval in Bokhara.

Even more popular was the story of how the newly dubbed Sir Moses, wearing his ceremonial robes as Sheriff of London and Middlesex, had personally carried a kosher chicken into the Guildhall so that he could dine with the other dignitaries without breaking the dietary laws of his faith. The listeners had roared with laughter and Ross had since been asked to tell the story several

times at other people's homes. Now that he was confined, his friends called on him instead.

After the usual elaborate greetings and ceremonial
cups of rosewater-flavored tea, Ephraim ben Abraham
said, "Honored Khilburn, pray do us the honor of singing
a Hebrew song, for your voice is sonorous and sweet."

Ross gave Ephraim a puzzled glance, for it seemed an
odd request. As a boy, he had coaxed the local vicar into
teaching him Hebrew, which was the only Middle Eastern language available in the wilds of Norfolk, but while
his knowledge had endeared him to the Bokharan Jews,
he had never sung for them. Still, he had been in the
school choir when he was a boy, and he enjoyed singing,
so he began one of his favorite psalms.

As senior officer in the household, Yawer Shahid Mahmud was above menial tasks like guard duty, but every
day he stopped by for an hour or two so he could glower
at the ferengi. He was present now, talking with his sub-
ordinates on the other side of the reception room. After
hearing a few bars of the psalm, he broke off his conversation and raised a hand to stop Ross. Suspiciously he
asked, "What are you saying?"

Ross obligingly translated the words, starting with,
*"By the rivers of Babylon we sat down and wept, for we
remembered Zion."* By the time he reached, *"How can
we sing the Lord's song in a strange land?,"* Shahid had
lost interest. With a snort, he turned his back and resumed his conversation.

Ross started the song again. By the time he was halfway through, his throat was tight, for the sense of exile
that the ancient words conveyed struck close to his heart.
Perhaps a different psalm would have been better.

When he was done, there was a deeply respectful silence. Then Ephraim said, "Many thanks, honored
Khilburn. Now I shall teach you a hymn of the Jews of
Turkestan. I will sing a line, then my friends will sing
the refrain. It is simple and you will be able to learn it
easily."

After the first few phrases, Ross was able to join in
with the others. As Ephraim had said, the song was simple, a prayer of rejoicing. After a bored glance, none of
the Uzbek guards paid attention.

When the hymn was done, Ephraim beamed at Ross. "Excellent. Now we will do another, more complicated song. If you do not understand the words, just ask me to repeat them." His expression became intent. "You understand?"

Beginning to be intrigued, Ross nodded.

Plaintively Ephraim chanted in Hebrew, *"I have just learned that not one but two Europeans were condemned to the Black Well, though they had committed no crime."*

His two friends intoned, *"The Mighty of the Mighty is He."*

"One was thy brother," Ephraim sang, *"the other an officer of great Russia."*

Arrested, Ross stared at his visitors, too startled even to join in the following refrain.

Catching Ross's gaze with his own, Ephraim continued, *"One prisoner was taken to the place of execution, where he died proclaiming his faith, may peace be upon him."*

The other men chorused, *"The Blessed of the Blessed is He."*

Ross's heart began pounding as he realized that this was no song, but a bold attempt to pass information under the very noses of his guards, in the guise of liturgy. And the message was a stunning one.

"The other man still endures the living death of the Black Well," Ephraim sang, *"but no one knows his name."*

Unable to listen in silence any longer, Ross interrupted tensely, "Excuse me, I did not catch the words of the last line. Does it go like this?" A slight tremor in his voice, he asked, *"You do not know which man lived and which man died?"*

His visitor answered sadly, *"Alas, I do not. Witnesses who knew both men were there at the fatal hour, but they cannot agree which one was killed."*

The others chimed in, *"The Great One of the Great is He."*

Once more Ross put a question. *"And the survivor still dwells in the Black Well?"*

"Aye, he lives, more than that we cannot say."

Ross swallowed hard. When the refrain was over, he said, *"So my brother may yet be among the living."*

"Aye, but he may also be dead. I know only that a European still languishes in the Black Well," Ephraim answered.

His friends added, *"The King of Kings is He."*

Eyes compassionate, Ephraim finished, *"Surely this knowledge is as bitter fruit to thy tongue, but a brother has a right to know his brother's fate."*

Ross burned with questions, even though they would be futile, since Ephraim had said he knew no more. Before Ross could decide what to say, Abdul Samut Khan entered the reception room.

Immediately Ephraim gave a bland smile. "Please, honored Khilburn, tell us the story of Sir Moses Montefiore's chicken."

Before Ross could begin, the nayeb said, "Lord Khilburn, I would like you to join me for an early dinner." Turning to the Jewish visitors, he said, "Of course, you would also be welcome."

It was an invitation for form's sake, and everyone present knew it. Rising to his feet, Ephraim ben Abraham said, "You do us great honor, Abdul Samut Khan, but alas, the dietary laws of our faith forbid our acceptance. It is time we took our leave."

Ross stood and bade his guests farewell. As he shook Ephraim's hand, he said quietly, "I thank you for your songs. I shall carry them in my heart always."

"As your songs will be in our hearts," Ephraim replied. *"Shalom,* my brother Khilburn."

As they left, Ross knew that he was unlikely to see the three again, for in a few days he would be gone or dead. Then the nayeb made an impatient gesture and Ross pulled his chaotic thoughts back to the present. It would take time to think through the implications of what he had just learned, but for the moment it was necessary to play the amiable guest.

In spite of his host's initial hurry, the meal was a leisurely one. When they had finished eating, Abdul Samut Khan called for a *nargileh,* a water pipe. Smoking in public was a criminal offense, but the custom was common indoors and the nayeb often indulged. This particular *nargileh* was a beautiful specimen with an elaborately cut crystal bowl.

The water burbled softly as the nayeb drew on the flexible tube. He gave a sigh of satisfaction, then withrew his mouthpiece and offered the tube to Ross, along with a fresh ivory mouthpiece for his guest's use. "Please, join me."

Ross had never developed a taste for smoking, but at least the water pipe cooled the smoke and made it less objectionable. As he fixed the mouthpiece and inhaled, his host said, "Have you had time to consider the matter we discussed several days ago?"

So Abdul Samut Khan was still hoping to make some profit from his guest. "I have thought it over, and my answer is the same," Ross replied as he returned the smoking tube. "I have not the gold required, nor the desire to thwart the amir's will. What shall be, shall be."

The nayeb's expression hardened and he inserted his mouthpiece in the tube with a snap. "Yawer Shahid Mahmud will stay here to supervise your confinement. Naturally he is disappointed that he will not go to war with us, but your dignity requires that you be guarded by an officer of rank." Abdul Samut Khan's voice dropped. "Though he is in my household, his loyalty is to the amir, and I cannot predict what he might do if the battle reports are not good."

In other words, Shahid might decide to slaughter his prisoner if the war went badly. Ross accepted the *nargileh* tube and drew a mouthful of mellow smoke, then exhaled it slowly. It sounded like a none-too-subtle attempt to frighten Ross into bolting. And it was a good threat; if Ross's only choice was between Shahid and Abdul Samut Khan, he would choose the nayeb, who might possibly do what he was bribed to do. But luckily there was another choice. "I appreciate your concern for my welfare, but with your artillery skills, surely the Bokharan army cannot help but triumph."

"You have a smooth tongue, Lord Khilburn." The nayeb gave a reluctant smile. "I cannot decide whether you have great innocence or great guile. But enough of gloomy topics. On a more pleasant note, I intend to give a small feast for a few friends the night before the army leaves. It will take place in my gardens and there will be music and dancers—Persian dancers, who are much more skilled than those of Turkestan. You shall find it most enjoyable. To go to war is to risk death, so one should celebrate life. As the great Persian poet Omar Khayyam said, *'Make the most of what we have to spend, Before we into dust descend.'* Is that not so?"

Ross smiled to hear the same verse he had quoted to Juliet. On this he and his host were in complete agreement.

When Ross returned from dining with Abdul Samut Khan, Juliet waited until he had barred the door, then pulled off her veil and came over to give him a hug. "It has been a successful day," she murmured as she wrapped her arms around his broad chest. She never tired of touching him. "I had no trouble leaving the city, and our rifles and ammunition were right where we left them. Now everything is hidden on the Kasem estate, just waiting for us. In two days, Saleh and Reza will be leaving for Persia, and three days after that, we'll be on our way home."

Ross didn't respond to the remark, just held her tightly and buried his face in her hair. Juliet's brows drew together. "Has something happened?"

"I'm afraid so." He released her and took off his coat. "And I don't honestly know if it is good news or bad."

Intrigued but unalarmed, Juliet followed Ross as he went into the bedroom. Picking up her comb, she plumped down on a silk cushion. "So it can't be that bad. Tell me about it."

Ross pulled off his cravat, then wearily rubbed the back of his neck with one hand. "I was visited by Ephraim ben Abraham and two of his friends today. They told me that not one but two Europeans were imprisoned in the Black Well. One was Ian, the other a Russian officer, and one of the two was executed while the other was spared." He took a deep breath. "The hell of it is, they don't know which was which."

Juliet stopped combing her hair as the blood drained from her face. "So Ian may be alive, but we don't know for sure."

She had been mourning her brother for weeks; to learn that he might be alive was as great a shock as hearing that he was dead. In fact, this was worse, because of the uncertainty. She wanted to swear or weep but didn't know which. Trying to convince herself that Ian was the man who lived, she said, "I always thought that report of the ferengi crossing himself didn't sound like Ian. Surely it would be more likely if the man executed was of the Orthodox Church."

Ross's gaze was sympathetic, but he would not encourage false hope. "Perhaps, but lately the amir has had better relations with Russia than Britain. It is more likely that he would have executed a Briton."

Juliet skipped to the underlying question. "Why would the amir claim he executed Ian if he didn't?"

Ross shook his head. "I have no idea. It could be policy or it could be sheer bloodymindedness. Nasrullah may have decided that saying he had executed a spy would intimidate other potential spies, but that it was wasteful to kill a Briton who might someday be useful as a hostage. Or there could be other reasons. We'll probably never know."

Juliet raised her fist to her mouth and bit her knuckles, hard. Then she closed her eyes for a long moment. When she opened them again, her gaze was hard. "Now that we know Ian might be alive, what are we going to do about it?"

Ross's mouth twisted and he began to pace. With his golden hair and his long, lithe strides, he was like a caged lion. "I doubt that we can do anything."

"We must try to rescue him," Juliet said, knowing that she could not possibly abandon her brother if he was alive, any more than she could have deserted her husband.

Ross's glance was sardonic. "In other words, after we escape from the nayeb's compound, we break into a heavily guarded prison, remove a man who is probably in dreadful physical condition from a twenty-foot-deep hole, smuggle him out of the city, then get him safely across the Kara Kum desert in the most hazardous season of the year. And he may not be Ian."

"We came here to try to save him," she said stubbornly. "Knowing that he may be alive, we can't just walk away."

Ross sighed. "Once more, for what seems like the hundredth time, we are back to the question of whether there is any value in a person committing suicide in a good cause. You know how I feel about that."

Juliet's temper flared. "In other words, you're too much of a coward to try to save him."

"Of course I'm a coward," he said promptly. "I've been in a flat panic ever since I left Constantinople, and the last few weeks have left me quivering like a bowl of aspic. But the issue isn't fear: it's whether it is *possible* to do anything."

Ross's words disarmed Juliet to the point where she would have smiled if she had not been so upset. She had seen enough of her husband in action to know that an accusation of cowardice was patently absurd. "I'm sorry," she said contritely. "I should not have said that. But I can't bear the idea that Ian might be within a mile of us and suffering terribly. We *must* do something." She ran her fingers distractedly through her hair. "Do you think Abdul Samut Khan knows whether it is Ian in the Black Well? If so, perhaps you can bribe the truth out of him."

"If he knows, I don't think he'll tell us, or he would already have hinted that he had valuable knowledge." Ross frowned. "In one sense, knowing whether the prisoner is Ian or the Russian is not the crucial issue. It will probably be impossible to find out which man is in the Black Well, and in any case, I don't like the idea of leaving any European to the amir's tender mercies." He stopped pacing and swung around to face Juliet. "I want to propose a bargain to you."

She eyed him warily. "What kind of bargain?"

"We must determine whether we have a chance of rescuing the prisoner. If it is possible—not guaranteed, but possible—I promise that I will participate wholeheartedly in a rescue scheme." Steel entered his voice and he caught her gaze with his. "In return, I want you to agree that if the prison is so well-guarded that there is no realistic hope of success, we will *not* make a suicidal attempt. Instead, we will leave Bokhara as we planned. When and if we reach Teheran, we will contact the British and Russian authorities. Diplomatic pressure might be more effective than heroics on our part."

Unless the man in the Black Well died in the meantime. But Ross was right; trust him to cut through the emotional tangle to the underlying truth. There was a difference between taking a risk with some hope of success and going to certain death; they must decide which category a rescue attempt fell into. Still . . . "Who decides what is possible?"

"I was afraid you'd ask that," he said ruefully. "Since we are going to be working with sketchy information, we'll just have to talk it out, with me hoping that you'll be reasonable. Otherwise it's a stalemate—I doubt if you can successfully invade the prison without my help, while I won't leave Bokhara without you."

Juliet arched her brows. "You should know better than to expect me to be reasonable."

"I said hope, not expect." He gave her a fleeting smile. "Just remember that the longer we stay, the greater the chance of trouble. Tonight Abdul Samut Khan hinted rather broadly that Shahid Mahmud might decide to deal with us on his own if the army is away very long, and he is one man who will want to destroy you as well as me."

Juliet winced. She would take her chances with Shahid if she was armed, but she didn't want him to corner her in a corridor again. "Then there is no time to waste. We need to find a man who is familiar with the prison— Saleh's brother or Hussayn Kasem may know someone who can answer our questions. And it might be worth talking to Ephraim ben Abraham in more depth."

"If you visit him, take Saleh," Ross suggested. "He has an honest face and Ephraim might talk to him."

"Are you saying that I don't have an honest face?"

"As Jalal, you don't have any face at all." He began unbuttoning his shirt. "You realize that the odds of our reaching Persia alive have just gotten considerably worse? Until today, I thought the worst danger would be crossing the Kara Kum. If we go after the ferengi prisoner, we'll be lucky to get out of the city at all."

Juliet shrugged fatalistically. "Perhaps our Muslim

friends are right and what will happen is already written. Or maybe they are wrong and it isn't written, but in either case there isn't much point in worrying." She rose and went to stand in front of him so that she could take over the work of unbuttoning. "Your faithful servant is the one who should remove your clothing, O master," she murmured as her fingers strayed to the warm flesh below the fabric.

He gave a slow smile and caught her hand for a moment, holding it against his heart. "You may not be an obedient servant very often, but I like the times when you pretend."

Juliet felt a rush of tenderness so profound that it defied speech, so she leaned forward and kissed his bare throat, feeling the pulse of life beneath her lips. There could not be another man anywhere who would understand and accept her as Ross did. Soon she would lose him, either to death or to England, but she made a promise to herself that before that happened, she would somehow find the courage to tell him how much she loved him.

Information about the prison came with unexpected ease. The next day Juliet visited Saleh and Murad early. The boy Reza was off playing with Saleh's nephews, so she was able to speak freely. Without mentioning the source, she described what Ross had been told and their hope that they might be able to rescue the prisoner in the Black Well.

When she was done, Saleh frowned. "It will be difficult, but it is to your advantage that the army is just leaving the city. With so many soldiers departing, there will be confusion in the palace and the prison, perhaps a shortage of guards. You might accomplish something that would be impossible at another time, but it is essential to learn more about the prison."

"I was hoping that your brother might know a man who works there, or that he knows a man who will know another man."

Before Saleh could reply, Murad said, "You need seek no further, for I know exactly the right person."

When the other two stared at him, Murad grinned.

"His name is Hafiz and his father keeps a silk shop in the next street. We met in a teahouse and have become friends. Hafiz works for his father in the day and in the prison at night, though he does not much like being there. He wants to earn enough money to open a teahouse of his own."

Saleh stroked his beard. "Truly it is God's mercy that brought the two of you together."

Juliet leaned forward in excitement. "If Hafiz will help us, he might have his teahouse much sooner. Can he be trusted not to betray us to the amir?"

Murad considered carefully. The last weeks had matured him. While he still had an engaging boyish grin, he was more thoughtful now, more likely to think before he spoke. Juliet guessed that he was attempting to be more like Ross.

Finally Murad said, "Yes, I believe he is an honest man, and I know that he wishes to earn money."

Saleh nodded approvingly. "An auspicious combination."

"Can I meet Hafiz now?" Juliet asked.

"He should be at his father's shop." Murad glanced at Juliet. "Would you like to buy some silk from Hafiz's father, Lady Khilburn? I think that will be a good place to begin."

So together they went to buy silk.

It was almost curfew when Juliet returned that evening, and Ross was becoming worried over her prolonged absence. However, when she breezed into their rooms and removed her veil, her face was glowing. "You know the Arab term *baraka*? It means the grace or power of God."

"I'm familiar with the concept." Ross gave her a welcoming kiss, his arms going around her hard in his relief. "That was how I felt toward the end of the *bozkashi* match, as if I was filled with transcendent power and could not fail."

Juliet dropped a floppy package wrapped in cheap cotton onto the divan. "Well, the *baraka* is with us."

"Does that mean you discovered something useful?" He glanced at the package she had brought in. "Or just that you had a successful day of shopping in the bazaars?"

She grinned, unfazed by his teasing. "I did buy rather a lot of very expensive silk. Not the local kind, but some that was imported from China. Exquisitely light, almost transparent. A complete waste of money, but buying it was a vital step in the information-gathering process. It turns out that a friend of Murad's works at the prison, and from what he told me, the procedures are surprisingly casual. I think we might be able to talk our way in through pure audacity. I also called on the Kasems and Ephraim ben Abraham."

Ross sat her down on the divan, then pulled her boots off and began rubbing her feet. They were long and slender and shapely, like the rest of her. "You've had a full day."

"That feels wonderful." As he massaged her feet, Juliet gave an ecstatic sigh and wiggled her toes with pleasure. "After you hear what I've learned, even you will admit that we have a decent chance of getting Ian out of the prison."

"It might not be Ian who is there," he said softly.

Her face clouded for a moment. Then she shook her head, refusing to think about it. "Every marriage needs one person in charge of worrying, and in this marriage, you're it."

Slightly taken aback, Ross stopped massaging her feet. "I always thought of it as having common sense."

Juliet leaned forward and gave him a sweet, hot kiss. "You're in charge of that too." Then she settled back and began recounting all that she had been told.

By the time she was done, Ross was willing to admit that there was a possibility that they could get into the prison, and more important, get out again—if none of a thousand different things went wrong. Lavish bribes would have to be paid, which was not a problem. The danger was that many people would be involved, and each additional person increased the likelihood of error or betrayal.

Still, they had a chance, and he had made a bargain. They would not leave Bokhara without trying to rescue the mysterious man who languished in the Black Well.

Perhaps the *baraka* was indeed with them, but as his massage progressed from Juliet's slim feet to higher and more interesting places, the phrase that came to mind was not Arabic but the ironic motto of the Roman gladiator: *Nos morituri, te salutamus.*

We who are about to die salute you.

22

As a climactic shower of silver and amber light blazed across the sky, Abdul Samut Khan clapped a jovial hand on his guest's shoulder. "Splendid fireworks, do you not agree? The Chinese engineer who does them for me is a master of his craft."

"Indeed he is," Ross said. "Your festival will be long remembered."

When the last rockets had faded away, slaves relit torches and lamps. The nayeb's description of a small feast for a few friends had been an understatement of massive proportions, for several hundred guests, many of them officers, were enjoying the nayeb's hospitality. Tomorrow the army would march for Kokand to the sound of drums and the firing of cannon, but now an air of fevered pleasure-seeking filled the gardens.

Mountains of food had been served and Ross had caught a couple of whiffs of burning hashish, but the absence of alcohol meant that the crowd was orderly compared to a European one. In one corner a storyteller resumed spinning tales of the famous Nasreddin Hoja to a rapt audience, while mimes performed on an impromptu stage at the far end of the compound.

Of course there were no women, except for Juliet, who skulked around in the shadows, unobtrusively observing. Ross guessed that the ladies of the nayeb's harem were all wistfully watching the festivities from behind their latticed windows.

"Now it is time for the dancing," Abdul Samut Khan said with great anticipation. "You will sit with me in front." He had kept Ross close all night. It was an honor, of course, but also an effective way of ensuring that the ferengi did not take advantage of the confusion to try to escape. To underline the point, Yawer Shahid Mahmud was never far away.

As the nayeb guided Ross through the amiable crowd, he murmured, "Even though I leave in the morning, it is not too late for you to change your mind about escape. I implore you, Lord Khilburn, heed my advice, for I cannot guarantee your safety while I am away. Tonight, when all is confusion, would be a perfect time to slip away."

His host was nothing if not persistent. Ross smiled gently. "It is good of you to be concerned for me, but you are the one going into war. Surely I will be in less peril than you."

Abdul Samut Khan scowled. "When I saw the amir today, he said you will no longer be allowed to have visitors. He does not wish you to become involved in treason while he is away."

"I see." Ross almost tripped over a tortoise with a small oil lamp on its back. A number of them were crawling about the quieter parts of the garden, illuminating the flowerbeds. He bent over and carefully shifted the creature to a safer spot. "Will I be confined to my rooms?"

There was a brief pause while the nayeb calculated whether there was any advantage in keeping the prisoner in closer confinement. "The amir wished that, but I spoke on your behalf and persuaded him to allow you to retain the freedom of the compound. Of course you will be guarded at all times."

"Of course."

They reached the roped-off square where the dancing would take place. A tent at one end housed the dancers, and soprano giggles could be heard coming from inside. Musicians were already playing and the night air throbbed with flutes and drums and stringed instruments that Ross could not identify. The music was passionate, with plaintive minor-key melodies weaving through deeper, earthier strains.

Abdul Samut Khan escorted his guest to the side of the dance floor where carpets and cushions had been laid on a dais for the most important guests. The other three sides of the square were filling with onlookers. Ross saw

Juliet choose a spot directly opposite him. In her silence and dark veil, she seemed a specter at the feast, a reminder that this gaiety would soon be over.

He hoped that under her tagelmoust she was having a good time. It really was a very decent party, if one could forget the fact that tonight might be their last night together. Just over twenty-four hours from now, they would make their hazardous attempt at escape; if anything went wrong, they might not live to see the next dawn. Ross wrenched his gaze away from Juliet, suddenly impatient to be alone with her. He would watch enough of the dancing to satisfy his host, then excuse himself.

A shout went up from the onlookers as half a dozen dancers suddenly came whirling onto the floor with snapping fingers and tinkling finger bells. Dancing boys were common, but these performers were women—lithe, voluptuous women, whose bodies moved in ways designed to rivet the attention of any normal man. Vast expanses of golden skin were revealed by their colorful costumes, but their faces were covered with translucent veils through which soft features were dimly visible. To an Eastern audience, the display was as provocative as thinly veiled breasts would be to a European audience.

The first dance was slow, with each succeeding one a little faster. The swirling skirts and rolling hips of the dancers were an invitation as old as time, and soon the crowd was clapping with the music, the noise adding a harsh urgency to the night. With the fourth dance, the music changed and the lead dancer dropped to her knees. Pelvis grinding suggestively, she bent her shimmying body backward until her head brushed the floor.

Sight and sound had a primitive power that bypassed the mind and went directly to the blood. His breath quickening, Ross glanced across the floor and his gaze met Juliet's for a moment before two dancers came between them. He wanted to fulfill the pagan promise of the dance, but only Juliet could quench the fire in his veins.

When the lead dancer sprang to her feet again, Abdul Samut Khan beckoned her to come to him. She wove her way through the troupe, then dropped to the ground in front of the nayeb in a posture of deep submission. She was only a yard from Ross, so close he could have touched her sweat-sheened, lushly curved body. "Yes, master?" she said in a husky voice.

The nayeb gestured to Ross. "Here is the man of whom I spoke earlier."

Lithely the dancer realigned herself so that she was coiled in front of Ross. She was still breathing hard from her exertions and her ripe breasts threatened to burst from her minimal bodice. Golden bracelets jingling, she purred, "Tell me what you desire, O lord of the ferengi."

A wave of heat coursed through Ross's body, for the dancer was the embodiment of sensuality and she was acting out a man's deepest fantasy. It was impossible not to be affected, and he had to swallow hard before he managed to say, "You dance very well."

"Zahra is my gift to you for the night, Lord Khilburn." Abdul Samut Khan accompanied the comment with a knowing elbow in Ross's ribs. "I realized that you have been deprived of what a man needs for health and happiness, so take her to your room and dance with her to your heart's content."

Zahra slithered forward and lifted her veil so Ross could see her face. Though the movement was coy, the invitation was as blatant as if a Western woman had ripped open her bodice. Her black lashes fluttered over dark velvet eyes as she raised a languid hand to run her fingers through Ross's hair, whispering, "Like fine-spun gold."

She was a gift few men would—or could—refuse. If Ross had been the man he claimed to be, with a staid wife back in England, it would have been almost impossible to resist temptation, at least a temptation that was half-naked and in his lap. But he wasn't that man, and his wife was thirty feet away.

Glancing up, he found that Juliet's gaze was on him and even across the width of the dance floor her outrage was palpable. Ross almost laughed out loud. Deciding that it was time for the night's real entertainment to begin, he removed the warm hand that was creeping up his leg. "A thousand thanks for your consideration, Abdul Samut Khan. Zahra is magnificent, a gift fit for

an emperor, but since I am a married man, I must decline
your generosity."

The nayeb gave him an astonished glance. "Your wife
is on the other side of the world and Zahra is right here."

"True, but the laws of my religion forbid adultery, and
there is no exemption for being far from home."

His host's heavy brows drew together. "There will be
a troupe of dancing boys next. Would you prefer one of
those? That would not be adultery."

After detaching the plump fingers that had resettled
on his knee, Ross got to his feet. He saw that the spot
on the other side of the floor where Juliet had been was
now empty, and hoped she wasn't circling around so that
she could knife him in the ribs. "But it would be equally
a sin in the eyes of my people."

The nayeb looked at him with disbelief and some respect. "Truly you are a devout man."

"Perhaps, but I am still a man, and subject to temptation, so I think it best that I retire to my chamber before
I succumb." Ross patted Zahra on the head. "Sin was
never so sweet."

Unmollified, she pulled her veil over her face again
and flounced up to join the other dancers, her eyes snapping with anger. The way Abdul Samut Khan's gaze followed her gave Ross a reasonably good idea of where
Zahra would be spending the night.

After taking leave of his host, Ross worked his way
through the sweaty enthusiatic crowd, Yawer Shahid
Mahmud and another soldier behind him. The air was
fresher inside the house, but scarcely quieter, for the
pulsing beat of the dance music permeated the mud-brick
walls. When they reached the door of his rooms, Ross
turned to bid his escorts good night.

The young soldier bobbed his head amiably, but
Shahid responded with a scowl. "Because of you, ferengi, I have been deprived of the pleasure of going to
war."

"I regret that," Ross said, a statement that was true
for a number of reasons. "It is a crime to waste a warrior's skill, but the decision to keep you in Bokhara was
not mine."

The yawer jerked his head at the guard, who prudently

withdrew out of earshot. Then, eyes narrowed, Shahid said, "Nonetheless, you are responsible, and you shall pay for it."

Ross suppressed a sigh. "I'm sure you have a suggestion for how I can make it up to you."

"In gold or in blood. The choice is yours." Shahid's face twisted threateningly. "Give me two thousand gold ducats and I shall guard you as tenderly as a mother with her firstborn babe. If you refuse . . ." He shrugged his massive shoulders eloquently.

"No one in Bokhara seems to believe this, but Englishmen are not made of gold," Ross said mildly. "Good night, Yawer Mahmud."

As he started to open the door, Shahid snapped, "So the devout infidel retires to his bed, there to hump his Tuareg boy."

Ross's hand tightened on the knob and he half-turned to the Uzbek. "I do not hump boys, Tuareg or otherwise." His eyes narrowed. "I believe that is a military habit."

"Lying swine." Shahid spat on the floor. "Once Abdul Samut Khan is gone, you will be my prey." He beckoned the young soldier closer. "Don't think you will escape tonight, for your door will be guarded."

Impassively Ross went into his apartment, then closed and barred the door, thinking that he was getting a little tired of extortion and melodramatic threats.

A single lamp burned in the reception room, and the door to the balcony was open, admitting the full volume of festival merrymaking. He glanced around for Juliet, surprised not to see her, for he had assumed that she had preceded him into the house. Then he realized that she must have returned or the lamps would not be lit. Hungry to have her in his arms, he crossed into the bedroom.

Another flickering lamp revealed Juliet as a dark form curled at one end of the divan. As he entered the bedroom, her caustic voice said, "What, no chubby charmer?"

Ross grinned and began removing his coat and boots. "I was tempted, naturally, but knowing that you would cut out my liver had a dampening effect."

"Wise man." Juliet's gaze followed him but she did not rise.

Ross had thought that mock jealousy was just another of their teasing games, but her aloofness made him wonder if she might be genuinely upset; with most of her face covered by the tagelmoust, it was hard to judge her mood. Softly he said, "Surely you don't believe that I was interested in that dancer."

She gave a snort of disbelief. "Of course you were interested. What man wouldn't be?"

"Not seriously interested," he amended. "Even wrapped in a black blanket and scowling, you are more alluring than she."

"I'm glad you have such good judgment." With one dramatic gesture, Juliet swept to her feet and cast aside her mantle and tagelmoust to reveal a dancer's costume of black silk so sheer that every detail of her body was visible. Outlined in dark surma, her eyes shone like silver as she gave a slow, provocative smile. "I improvised this out of the silk I bought from Hafiz's father. Now I'm going to prove that there is nothing that plump hussy does that I can't do better."

Ross's breath caught in his throat and for a moment he couldn't breathe. A cord around Juliet's hips secured a number of ethereal veils, and more floated from her shoulders to cover, but not conceal, her torso. Though she was completely covered, even her cascading hair dimmed by a veil, the transparency of the fabric gave the effect of total, seductive nakedness.

She spun gracefully into the center of the room, veils swirling about her like smoke. Irresistible as Delilah, she said huskily, "Shall I dance for you?"

"Oh, yes . . ." Ross whispered as he sank down on the divan, unable to take his gaze off her. "Please do."

For a moment Juliet closed her eyes, immersing herself in the potent currents of sound that eddied through the night. Then she began to sway sinuously. First just her twining arms, then her lithe torso, then her hips and legs, until her whole body was a physical expression of the music.

Juliet was a born dancer. Ross knew that she had learned Highland reels as a child in Scotland and later effortlessly mastered formal European ballroom figures. Heaven only knew what exotic performances she had seen or participated in over the years. Now she drew on everything she had ever learned to create a sensual dance that was all her own.

He watched, entranced, as she went beyond skill to the level of true art, where spirit and movement and music were so much in harmony that it was impossible to separate the dancer from the dance. Juliet was fire and grace and freedom, everything he had ever loved and despaired of in his wife.

But most of all she was the embodiment of desire, and without a single touch she raised Ross to fever pitch. Drifting layers of silk first revealed, then concealed her exquisite body. A brief flash of her long slim legs might be followed by a tantalizing glimpse of dusky nipples, then the dark triangle between her thighs. Red hair, white limbs, smoky silk; no more was needed to fuel a fire.

But watching was not enough. The next time she swirled within reach, borne on the passionate beat of the music, Ross caught an edge of the veil that covered her head. It came away in his hand, revealing the light-struck brilliance of her hair.

She laughed and grasped the other end of the veil that he held. "Dance with me, O my master."

Ross understood her invitation; in many Middle Eastern societies men and women could not touch in public even if they were allowed to dance together, so they used a scarf to connect them without physical contact. Rising to his feet, Ross began moving to the music, joined to Juliet only by the silk veil that ran taut from his right hand to hers.

Gazes locked, they circled each other slowly, so intent that it seemed as if they held still while the world revolved around them. He had met Juliet in a waltz, a formal dance with conversation above and yearning below, and even then they had had an instinctive understanding of each other's rhythms. Now they had come full circle, and in the dark heat of a Central Asian night they shadowed each other in a *pas de deux* of desire.

As Ross yielded to the music, he found himself execut-

ing steps he had never consciously learned. Soon they
were improvising patterns of increasing complexity, their
motions so perfectly attuned that they might have been
controlled by one mind, not two. Steps quickened and
gestures became more dramatic as they separated to the
full length of the silken tie that bound them, then spun
together again, close enough to feel their mutual heat
but never quite touching.

Borne by a whirlwind of passion, they soared higher
and higher, knowing that soon they would take flight,
for they were linked by an intricate web of passion, conflict, and caring as tangible as the fabric stretched between them. Ross's gaze caught Juliet's in a wordless
invitation to come closer, but she swung away again. He
pulled on the veil to draw her back. "Not so far, my
houri."

He raised his arm and she pirouetted beneath, her flying hair a molten shower of red and gold and amber. "A
houri is not so easily captured, O master," she said in a
throaty voice.

The tempo of the music increased, throbbing and
pounding around and through them in an utterly pagan
rite of fertility that could have only one possible conclusion. Suddenly impatient, Ross gave a sharp tug on the
silk to bring her into his arms. "But capture you I will."

Juliet pivoted in a tight circle, her hair whipping across
his face before her back came to rest snugly against the
front of his body, heating him from chest to thighs. She
smelled of roses and spice and woman.

His breath harsh with urgency, Ross dropped the
twisted fabric that had joined them. Then he slid his
hands under the whisper-light silk that floated over her
torso so he could savor the sleek, yielding female flesh
beneath. Once he touched her, it was impossible to stop,
and his questing hands glided from tapering waist to taut
stomach, hungry for the irresistible eroticism of her supple skin.

After tracing around her navel with his middle finger,
he stroked the underside of her breasts with his thumbs,
then kissed her ear through the fine-spun strands of her
hair. When she quivered in response, he raised his hands
and captured the soft, fluid curves of her breasts. The

nipples hardened beneath his palms and she gave a long, breathless moan. Then she leaned back into his embrace and rolled her buttocks against his groin, deliberately finding and inflaming his arousal.

He gasped and lowered one hand to her hip, slipping under the silken veils, skimming the surface of her abdomen, through softly textured hair, until his fingers found the moist, swollen folds below. She shivered and made a small delicious sound deep in her throat as her head fell back against his cheek. For a long suspended moment they stayed locked in sensual abandon.

Then suddenly Juliet spun away, the eternal temptress. As she slid from his embrace, Ross caught a handful of veils. They came away in his grasp and drifted to the floor as silent as eiderdown, baring most of her long, lovely body.

She laughed and seized the edges of his cotton shirt. "Two can play at that game." She tore down, rending the garment to the hem, then tugged it off, nipping his upper arm with her teeth as the shirt came away.

The bite was the final spark that kindled the passion that had been building between them. Ross swept Juliet into his arms and onto the bed, following her down and trapping her writhing body with his. As his open mouth found her breast, she fought him like a feral creature that could be possessed only through conquest.

They mated like panthers, with teeth and nails and thrashing limbs. It was the last and fiercest phase of their primal dance, possible only because underneath their wildness was absolute trust in each other. When Juliet worked her arms free and began clawing at his chest, Ross captured her wrists and pinned them to the bed with his left hand while he spread her legs with his thighs and opened his strained trousers with his right hand.

For Juliet, the game ended when Ross entered her with one powerful thrust, sliding hot and hard into her eager body. This was not simple play but the most profound reality she had ever known, the physical expression of all the tormenting emotions that bound them. She bit his shoulder, tasting salt against her tongue, wanting to merge with him so completely that they would truly be one flesh.

Explosion might have been almost instantaneous, but Ross would not allow that. Instead, with diabolical skill he raised her to a pitch of unbearable need until her whole body burned with white heat. The words she had feared came without her volition as she cried out, "Ah, God, Ross, I love you so."

More than anything on earth, she wanted him to reciprocate, to tell her that he loved her even if it was a lie, or only a small part of a complicated truth.

But he did not. Instead he silenced her with his mouth, filling her so completely that there was no room for anything but passion and fulfillment. She dissolved into shuddering contractions that seemed as if they would go on forever.

He broke the kiss, making a hoarse wordless sound as his control finally splintered. She felt his rhythmic convulsions deep inside her, resonating until she could no longer tell his urgent flesh from her own. She had wanted them to be one, and for a few brief instants they were.

But as their throbbing limbs slowed and softened, silent tears were running down Juliet's face. Together they had touched the farthest limits of passion, a place of devastating joy that surpassed every amorous fantasy she had experienced during the long, lonely years.

She would have traded it all for love.

Ross had barely had the strength to finish removing his trousers and Juliet's veils so they could sleep in comfort. As he lay down and drew her into his arms, he murmured that if Zahra had walked into the room, he would have been unable to lift his head, much less anything else. Juliet had given a low, satisfied chuckle and doused the lamp. Then they settled against each other and slept the sleep of exhaustion.

As dawn traced rosy streamers across the sky, they made love once more. This time desire was soft and sweet, with Juliet lying sprawled on top of Ross, her tangled hair tickling his cheek and throat as they moved in gentle tandem. Hard to believe that this tender, accommodating lady was the same wildcat who had left her marks all over his back and chest. But that was part of the mystery and wonder of her.

Looking back, it seemed to Ross that their marriage was a play with distinct acts, starting with the magic of discovery and progressing through fulfillment, estrangement, loss, and anguish. The latest, and possibly last, act was their fragile reconciliation in the face of danger, and now it too was drawing to a close. Of all the stages, this had been the shortest and most intense.

It was a melancholy thought.

Juliet had said that she loved him. Ross knew better than to take seriously a declaration made in the throes of passion, for passion was a notorious liar. He was not even sure that he wanted to believe her, for that would open the door to fears and confusion too deep and painful to confront.

Thank God that in a few hours the time for action would finally be at hand. Life and death were so much simpler, so much more clear-cut, than love.

23

Finally the time had come to depart. It was late and most of the household should be asleep, tired by the festivities of the night before and the turmoil that had surrounded Abdul Samut Khan's departure today. After looping the rope around the leg of the bed, Ross paused to study Juliet's face for a moment. "I really can't say that a mustache suits you."

She grinned. "But you look rather good in a black beard."

"Let me know if it starts coming off." His levity dropped away and he gave her a quick, intense kiss that said more than words ever could. They both knew that when they left this room, they were putting themselves in the hands of fate, but to dwell on that fact might weaken them.

Ross wrapped the doubled rope around himself, climbed over the windowsill, and disappeared from view. Juliet adjusted the veil of her tagelmoust over her face, thinking that if she had met her husband on the street, she might not recognize him. He was abandoning his European clothing and he was dressed in the robes and turban of a royal chamberlain, but that was just the simplest aspect of his disguise.

After an early dinner they had spent several rather giddy hours creating disguises, using materials that Saleh and Juliet had procured in the bazaar. First they had both applied a weak-solution blend of walnut juice and caustic to darken their faces and hands. Then Ross dyed his brows and lashes a dark brown. But a false beard and mustache, bought from a shifty-eyed merchant who asked

304

no questions, were what changed his appearance most. Besides concealing his features, they were necessary because facial hair was almost univeral among Central Asian men. Most of the dark beard was shaped to fit around Ross's chin and jaws and was attached with a resinous adhesive.

Then, to complete his disguise, Juliet had painstakingly applied individual hairs all around the edges of his beard and mustache to create a natural-looking hairline, for his disguise must be effective at very close quarters. The results would not hold up to a determined tug, but Ross now looked like a Bokharan of Afghan or Persian origin.

Juliet herself was less convincing, for her mustache did not conceal the fact that her features were more feminine than masculine. However, since she was wearing Bokharan dress, she could pass as a young male servant at a distance or in subdued light, and that was good enough for what she would be doing.

Leaning out the window, she watched Ross's descent down the side of the building with concentrated interest. Earlier he had explained how mountain climbers used a rope to lower themselves quickly down a cliff face, but this was the first time she had seen the technique in actual use.

After he reached the ground, it was Juliet's turn. She took one last look around to check that nothing had been forgotten, smiling a little as she thought of her one concession to sentiment. Without telling Ross, she had decided to take her dance costume of the night before. Feather-light, it had been easy to fold the veils and conceal them in a pocket under her robes; God willing, perhaps she could dance again at Serevan.

Then Juliet put sentiment aside and went out the window. After reaching the ground, she tugged one end of the line so that the length slithered around the bed leg upstairs, then dropped down beside her. Swiftly Ross coiled the rope and slung it over his shoulder so that there would be no telltale evidence of their departure. Since their apartment upstairs was barred from the inside, with luck it would take until midday tomorrow for the nayeb's servants to realize that the prisoners had escaped.

With Juliet leading the way and Ross a dozen paces behind, they began quietly circling the edge of the gardens, staying in the shadows even though there was only a sliver of moon. Since it was summer, most of the household slept on the flat rooftops for coolness, and unexpected noises might alert a restive sleeper.

For a very reasonable bribe, Zadeh, the helpful guard, had promised to unlock a seldom-used postern door at the far end of the compound, so leaving the nayeb's property should be the easiest part of the night's work. Even if Zadeh reneged or had been unable to obtain the key, they had the rope, so it would not be too difficult to scale the wall.

Unfortunately, the plan went awry when Juliet slipped cautiously around the corner of the stables, only to run straight into the unsteady form of Yawer Shahid Mahmud. He smelled of horse and alcohol; apparently he had been out drinking in an illicit tavern and by sheer bad luck had just arrived home.

As Juliet backed hastily away, Shahid growled, "Watch where you're going, *daous*," using a mildly insulting ephithet.

Juliet muttered a hoarse apology and tried to circle around him, but it was too late, for the dark tagelmoust she had worn to blend into the shadows was now a dead giveaway.

Suddenly realizing whom he had within his grasp, Shahid grabbed her wrists. "Well, if it isn't the ferengi's fancy boy." His voice turned ugly and he twisted her arms back. "Quite a stroke of luck, for I'm in the mood to finish what I started before, and you won't catch me unaware this time."

Juliet stood still, making no attempt to escape. With Ross right behind her, she wasn't worried about what Shahid might do, but the officer's voice was so loud that she feared he might wake the grooms sleeping above the stables.

"It's time I saw your face." With surprising swiftness he managed to secure both of her wrists with one beefy fist, then lifted his other hand toward her veil.

No longer content to passively await rescue, Juliet

jerked back and kicked at her captor's ankle. Where the devil was Ross?

She got her answer an instant later when she saw a flicker of movement behind the Uzbek, but before Ross could strike, Shahid sensed his presence. With a bellow, the yawer released Juliet and started to spin around. His shout was cut off by the sickening thud of a heavy pistol butt smashing into a human skull. Then Shahid pitched sideways, hitting the hard ground like a falling oak.

Juliet stared down at the massive sprawling figure, then asked in a soft undertone, "Do you think he's dead?"

"Unfortunately not, but he'll have the devil's own headache when he wakes up." Ross tucked his pistol inside his coat. "So much for our well-laid plans. Let's get out of here and hope that no one will wake up and come out to investigate."

As they sprinted the last hundred yards to the postern, Juliet knew that they had been lucky that Shahid had not had a chance to see Ross's disguise. And the postern door, praise God, was unlocked as it was supposed to be. But that was as far as their luck went. Even as Ross pulled the door closed behind them, they heard excited voices rising in the gardens. The unconscious officer had been found.

Juliet swore under her breath. When Shahid awoke, it wouldn't take him long to realize that the ferengi had escaped and the hunt would be on. Still, the alarm would probably not be raised until morning, so it should not affect tonight's attempt to extricate the prisoner from the Black Well.

The streets outside the compound were silent, for the king's drums had already beat out the curfew. Anyone abroad at this hour was required to carry a lantern. Since patrols enforced the law, Juliet and Ross kept to the shadows, hoping no one would see and remember their passing. She led, unerringly finding her way through the twisting maze of streets she had studied for weeks.

A quarter-hour of swift walking brought them to the arches of a small covered bazaar that was now deserted for the night. Murad waited there with four horses. He jumped when Juliet materialized out of the shadows near him, then scanned the newcomers with approval. "Very good, Lord Khilburn. You look exactly like a Bokharan court official."

"Let's hope the prison guards think so." Ross rested a hand on the young Persian's shoulder. "Are you ready to enter the lion's den? It might be very dangerous."

Murad managed a quick smile, though tension was obvious in his voice. "More dangerous for you than for me."

"But I do it for love of my brother. It takes greater courage to risk one's life for a stranger." Ross squeezed the younger man's shoulder, then said in a different tone, "Now it is time for the king's chamberlain to ride."

It took only a few moments to make the final preparations. While Murad uncovered one lamp and lit a second, Ross removed the dark scarf he had worn over his white turban on their surreptitious journey through the city and Juliet took off her tagelmoust. Underneath she also wore a white turban.

After packing the extra garments and the rope in saddlebags, they all mounted and rode the final half mile to the prison, which was a massive high-walled structure behind the royal palace. For the moment they were done with stealth; only bluster could make their present mad mission a success.

The entrance to the prison was barred by a heavy gate with a smaller door set in the middle. When their party reached it, Ross pulled out his pistol and, without dismounting, banged the hilt on the small door.

A voice sounded from the guardhouse above his head. "Who goes there?"

Ross took a deep breath. The point of no return had been reached. Speaking in Uzbek, he said, "Saadi Khan, bearing orders from the amir."

"Saadi Khan?" the guard said doubtfully.

"I am a *makhram*, a royal chamberlain, fool. Now, let me in!"

Responding to the note of command, the guard signaled one of his fellows to open the door. It was just large enough to admit a man on horseback. Ross trotted through into the courtyard, followed by Murad and Juliet, who led the fourth horse.

As soon as they were inside, Ross ordered, "Take me to the officer in charge."

"Yes, sir," said the highest-ranking of the soldiers, the equivalent of a corporal. He escorted the newcomers to the front steps of the main building.

There Ross and Murad dismounted, leaving Juliet with their horses. Her turban and mustache were adequate to allow her to pass as a young man in the dark courtyard.

With an arrogance modeled on Shahid Mahmud's, Ross swaggered up the steps, Murad right behind him. The corporal turned them over to a different guard, who escorted the visitors to the chamber occupied by the officer in charge of the night watch.

The lieutenant on duty looked up with a supercilious expression. If Murad's friend Hafiz was right, the man was new to this posting and unlikely to recognize that Ross was not a genuine palace official. He was also the sort who bullied his underlings and fawned on his superiors, which made him an ideal candidate for intimidation.

The lieutenant stroked his beard, eyeing Ross with disfavor. "Since the amir is out of the city, what royal business could you possibly have that cannot wait until morning?"

"*This* business." Ross pulled a document from inside his coat, then tried to look nonchalant as the officer examined it. The order was a forgery, written in official style and marked with a royal seal that had been carefully removed from a legitimate document. The forgery had come from the household of Ephraim ben Abraham; Ross and Juliet had speculated how and why such skills had been learned, but had known better than to ask.

Ross stopped breathing when the lieutenant frowned over the order. Then the officer said, "I do not understand."

Relieved that the problem was content, not form, Ross said with studied exasperation, "You aren't supposed to understand. Your job is to produce the ferengi prisoner, not waste my time with foolish questions."

"But why now, when his majesty is away?"

"It is precisely *because* he is away, imbecile! A foreign spy is a diplomatic embarrassment, dangerous to keep and dangerous to kill. Problems of this sort are best

solved when the amir is known to be occupied with more
important matters. Now, are you going to obey your orders, or are you going to become part of the problem?"

"My superior has not given me authority to release a
prisoner," the lieutenant said doggedly, but his confidence was starting to wane in the face of his visitor's
imperious manner.

"The document in your hand is all the authority you
need." Not for nothing was Ross the son of a duke; when
he chose to, he could bluster with the best. He shifted
his weight forward to the balls of his feet, emphasizing
his superior height. His voice dropped, becoming deep
and threatening. "I've had quite enough of your foolishness. Saadi Khan is not accustomed to being kept waiting. Take me to the prisoner *now*."

By the time Ross finished speaking, the lieutenant's
expression had changed to servile obedience. Scrambling
to his feet, he said, "A thousand apologies, sir. I did not
mean to offend. It is just that such a procedure is most
unusual."

"So is having a ferengi captive," Ross said tersely.

"If you will come along with me, sir." The lieutenant
lifted a lamp, then led the way down a narrow, winding
staircase that descended to the lowest level of the ancient
building.

At the bottom of the stairs they began walking along
a corridor lined with heavy doors, their progress haunted
by the sounds of misery. In one cell a voice droned prayers in classical Arabic, while ragged, hopeless sobs
emerged from another. The very walls were saturated
with suffering and decay.

His face rigid, Ross looked neither right nor left. Two
jailers from the dungeon-level guard room fell in behind,
torches in their hands, but the flares were a feeble
counter to the rank, suffocating blackness. He could not
help thinking that the slightest suspicion that he and
Murad were frauds would mean that they would never
see the light of day again.

Finally they reached a rough-hewn room at the end of
the passage. The hole in the floor was covered with a
wooden hatch, and a rope and pulley were suspended
from the ceiling above. Ross stared at the hatch. Finally

he had reached the Siah Cha, the Black Well, the Central Asian version of the oubliette.

One of the jailers leaned over and lifted the hatch away, releasing a stench that caused everyone to step back. Ross's stomach clenched, but this was no time to show weakness. "By the Prophet's beard!" he snarled. "Is the prisoner even alive?"

One of the jailers, a squat man with a broad, unintelligent face, said helpfully, "I think he eats the food we drop down."

The other jailer, who had a sharp, ferretlike face, shrugged. "That don't mean nothing. Could be eaten by rats or sheep ticks. The ticks are specially bred for the Well."

Ross was grateful for the false beard; it helped conceal his expression. Tightly he said, "Get the prisoner up here."

The squat jailer undogged the end of the rope that ran through the pulley, then lowered the line into the hole. When it reached the bottom, he yelled down in Persian, "Put the loop around you and we'll pull you up. A gentleman here to see you." He smiled nastily. "He says the amir is going to set you free."

It must have been an old taunt, for the only response was a guttural, weakly uttered phrase from the bottom of the hole.

The lieutenant cocked his head, then said regretfully, "I don't understand Russian so I don't know what he's saying, but at least he's alive."

Ross's mouth twisted; he also recognized the language, though Russian was not a tongue he spoke. So it was the other officer, not Ian. Later he would allow himself to be disappointed, but now he must concentrate on getting the poor devil below away from this evil place. With bitter humor he said, "I imagine that he is saying the Russian version of 'Go fornicate with yourself.'"

The lieutenant smiled appreciatively, but the ferret frowned. "He's probably refusing to take the rope so we can pull him up."

"Then go down after him," Ross ordered.

The two guards looked at each other with obvious reluctance. "He's a mean bastard," the squat one said. "Might attack anyone who comes after him."

"And you're afraid of a prisoner who has been starving down there for months?" Ross said incredulously.

Anxious to assert his authority, the lieutenant said to the ferret, "Pull the rope up so we can use it to lower you down."

The ferret shook his head stubbornly and edged toward the door. "Time I was getting back to my post. I'm in charge of the cells in the other wing."

The lieutenant swelled with rage while the squat guard tried to look unobtrusive so he wouldn't be called on. Seeing that a time-wasting confrontation was imminent, Ross let his fury boil over. "Imbeciles. Must I do everything myself?"

He took the rope and leaned over to secure the upper end. Then he impatiently snatched the torch carried by the ferret, wrapped the rope around himself, and went down into the dungeon in a controlled slide. The walls were damp, and the stench, which had been foul above, was indescribable.

Twenty-one feet was a long way, and it seemed much longer, but finally he reached bottom, almost falling when his feet skidded on the slimy stone. The chamber was roughly ten feet square, hardly large enough to lose a man in, but it was littered with so much nameless offal that it took time to identify as human the long, ragged shape lying by one wall.

Ross brought the torch nearer and saw that the man had wildly tangled dark hair and beard and had thrown an arm over his head, apparently to protect his eyes from the unaccustomed light. His only garment was a pair of ragged European trousers. Under the filth, his skin was dead white and his body was so thin that every rib was visible. There were also open sores visible, perhaps the work of the specially bred sheep ticks. Had it not been for the oath that had emerged from the dungeon earlier, Ross would have thought he had found a corpse.

He knelt beside the prisoner, speaking quietly in French, which an educated Russian should understand, while the men above would not. "I'm a friend, here to take you away. Do you think you can walk? That will make it easier to help you."

Suddenly the man rolled over and lashed out at his visitor with surprising strength. Startled, Ross sprang to his feet and backed across the cell to avoid the attack. Then he sucked his breath in with shock.

The prisoner's face was gaunt and filthy, and he had lost one eye, for the right lid hung nervelessly over a slight depression, but his appearance was not what chilled Ross's blood. Far more stunning was the fact that as the man crashed to the floor, he said in English with a faint, familiar Scots accent, "You'll not fool me again, you bloody-minded son of a bitch."

The prisoner sprawled on the dungeon floor was Ian Cameron.

Yawer Shahid Mahmud had been told more than once that he had a head like rock, and he proved it by recovering consciousness less than an hour after being assaulted. The grooms had taken him into the house, so he woke in his own quarters. After his eyes blinked open, Shahid lay still and tried to sort out his memories. The tavern, a Tadjik dancing boy with a great ass, the ride home. He raised a confused hand to his head, thinking that the ache was worse than just the effect of too much wine.

The stables . . . what had happened by the stables?

Then he remembered and sat up with a bellow, ignoring the pain that lanced through his skull. "Damnation, the bastards have gotten away!"

A flurry of activity followed as two soldiers were sent up to the ferengi's rooms. They had to break down the door to confirm what Shahid had already guessed: Lord Khilburn and his Tuareg slave had fled.

It was unthinkable that the ferengi be allowed to get away with his insolence; Shahid's honor was at stake. Rage cleared his mind as nothing else could have. If Khilburn had gone to ground in the city, sooner or later he would be found; the network of informants would guarantee that, for the ferengi's appearance was too distinctive for him to hide for long.

Khilburn would know that, for the man wasn't stupid;

he would probably try to leave the city as soon as possible. In fact, he might have already done so, because summer caravans always set out at night, when it was cooler.

Pursuit would be hampered by the fact that most of the army had left the city with the amir. Where could Shahid get more troops? Probably at the royal palace, he decided, and perhaps at the prison as well, since it was so secure that guards were scarcely needed.

Determinedly he got to his feet. He would go to the palace right now; the captain of the royal guard was a friend of Shahid's and could be trusted to supervise the search for the ferengi within the city. The captain would also know which gates were being used tonight by caravans. Shahid would borrow some men at the palace and perhaps go to the prison for a few more. Then he would check the city gates and, if necessary, follow the departed caravans into the countryside.

As Shahid wound a turban around his throbbing head, he smiled with vicious anticipation. When he had run Khilburn to earth, he would exact punishment for the humiliations the ferengi had inflicted. It was common knowledge that criminals were often killed while resisting capture. That fate would surely befall Khilburn. But the Tuareg boy . . . Shahid was becoming powerfully curious about just what charms were hidden under those black robes. He intended to find out before Jalal also met his fate.

Before Ian could gather himself for another assault, Ross whispered urgently, "Ian, it's Ross Carlisle. Don't waste time wondering how it can be true, just accept that I'm here."

His brother-in-law pushed himself to a sitting position, his breathing harsh, and stared at the intruder. "It's . . . it's not possible. You're another goddamned dream. A nightmare. You don't even look like Ross."

"Wrong. Under this fake beard, I'm as real as you are." Ross paused to think of something that would prove his claim. "Remember the time you took me hunting in India—how furious you were when I had a clear shot at a tiger, but I wouldn't take it, so the beast got away?"

"Jesus Christ." The other man's remaining eye closed for a moment, then opened again. It was a bluer gray than Juliet's, a color that was unmistakably Ian. Hoarsely he said, "Ross?"

The hope and despair in that unsteady voice nearly broke Ross's heart. Grimly he suppressed the reaction, for there was no time for emotion. Nor was this the time to mention Juliet, whose presence might strain Ian's belief to the breaking point. Lightly he said, "None other. Credit goes to your mother, who wouldn't accept that you were dead. But now we must both get out of here before they start wondering what's taking so long."

He slipped his free arm under Ian's shoulders and helped him to his feet. "I'm pretending to be a royal chamberlain—all you have to do is keep quiet and pretend you don't know me."

Ian said, "Wait. Must take this." He bent over and lifted a rectangular object wrapped in a dirty rag, then peeled off the fabric to reveal a small leather-bound book with Cyrillic lettering on the cover. As he slid it into the pocket of his ragged trousers, he explained, "Pyotr Andreyovich's Bible. Promised I'd send it to his family if . . . if I ever got out." His face suddenly twisted and he began shaking.

Ignoring Ian's filthy state, Ross wrapped an arm around him, hoping that the primitive comfort of touch would pull the other man back from his shattering despair. "You'll get out, I swear it," he said softly. "Just come with me and in a few minutes you'll be free. Not out of danger yet, but free."

When Ian's trembling had eased, Ross looped the rope under his arms, then shouted up in Uzbek, "Pull him up! And don't be afraid, you sons of dogs. He won't hurt you now."

The rope tightened across Ian's chest, then lifted him into the air. A minute later he was pulled over to solid ground.

Ross was alone in the Black Well. Though he knew it was illusion, the dank stone walls seemed to be moving inward. Fiercely he told himself not to be a fool, but when a faint rustling sounded behind him, he whirled

instinctively, his torch causing grotesque shadows to flare
in wild, threatening patterns.

What if the lieutenant discovered the deception and
left him here? How long would it be until the torch
burned out, leaving him to the demons of the dark? His
heart began beating faster. If Murad and Juliet were also
captured, who in the distant world would ever learn or
care what had become of Ross Carlisle?

Savagely he bit his lip, using the immediacy of pain to
stem the rising flood of fear. In the space of another
heartbeat he was himself again, but the brief moments
of panic were enough to give him a sense of what it was
like to be a prisoner here. It was a tribute to Ian's
strength that he had had enough spirit left to attack what
he thought was another tormentor.

The rope suddenly dropped down on the floor beside
Ross; it was one of the most welcome sights he had ever
seen. Rather than put it around his chest, he stepped
into the loop and grasped the line higher up so he could
be lifted in a standing position and get out of this abomi-
nable cell a few seconds sooner.

It took the combined strength of both jailers and
Murad to raise Ross's weight. After swinging to the floor
of the chamber and stepping off the rope, he turned and
threw the torch into the noisome depths of the Well,
hoping it would incinerate some sheep ticks.

Murad was staring at Ian, who leaned against the wall,
eye closed and wrists tied with cruel tightness as a parting
present from the amir's men. In the stronger light, he
looked worse than he had below. When Ross turned
away from the dungeon, Murad gave him a worried
glance. Ross knew exactly what the young Persian was
thinking: how on earth were they going to get someone
in Ian's condition across the Kara Kum?

That was another thing Ross refused to worry about
just now. Brusquely he said, "Come. I've wasted enough
time here."

Obediently the lieutenant turned and led the way out,
Ross right behind him, while Murad and the squat jailer
took Ian's arms to help him up the narrow stairs. In the
duty officer's cubicle, the lieutenant asked for a receipt
for the prisoner. Ross wrote one impatiently, his skin

crawling with his desire to get away before something went wrong. It seemed that they had been inside forever, and much remained to be done before dawn.

But the courtyard was still dark and quiet when they went outside to where Juliet waited with their horses. Murad helped Ian to the fourth mount and boosted him into the saddle, then cut his wrists free so he could hold on to the horn.

Juliet began staring at the prisoner as soon as he came down the steps, but even after Ian was mounted she was unable to recognize her brother. Frowning, she glanced a question at Ross. He gave a slight nod and swung onto his horse.

They rode out, still unchallenged. Now they must cross the city to an empty house, where they would have an hour or so to prepare to join the caravan that was assembling now. But first they must reach the safe house without attracting dangerous notice. Silently they rode as far as the deserted bazaar where Murad had met them, then turned their mounts through the arches into the sheltered interior.

While Murad stationed himself by the entrance to watch the street, Juliet brought her horse up to Ross. "Is he really Ian?" she asked in a voice tight with tension.

"Definitely," Ross reassured her. "He doesn't know yet that you're here. I thought it was more than he could absorb at once."

Juliet didn't wait to hear more. She spurred her horse over to her brother, calling softly, "Ian, it's Juliet."

Though he had been slumped forward over his saddle horn, he lifted his head on hearing her words. The lamp cruelly lit his haggard face and ruined eye, but after a moment of shock, recognition lightened his expression. "My God, Juliet. I should have known that my incorrigible little sister was involved." Amazingly, a faint, familiar trace of humor could be heard in his rusty voice. "The mustache doesn't do a damned thing for you."

Laughing and crying, she hugged her brother, almost pulling him from his horse in the process. It seemed impossible that it was really Ian, after so many tears and dashed hopes. He hugged her back, but they were not allowed long for a reunion. Ross said quietly, "We must go now. Juliet, get the chapan for Ian."

Returned to awareness of their situation, she released her brother and pulled a dark coat from her saddlebag, then helped him put it on. After it had been loosely belted in place, Ross produced a length of white muslin and wound a hasty turban around Ian's head, then examined the results.

Dryly Ian said, "I imagine that I still look dreadful."

"True," Ross agreed, "but much less conspicuous than a shirtless man with hair and beard like a desert hermit. This will do until we get across the city."

Ross went over to Murad and was about to speak when the young Persian suddenly waved in a frantic signal to keep quiet. After dismounting from his horse, Ross went quietly to the archway to see what the problem was.

Galloping toward them were half a dozen soldiers, and the leader's lantern showed the grim face of Yawer Shahid Mahmud.

For a moment Ross stood stock-still, for it seemed as if the riders were coming straight toward them. He was reaching into his chapan for his pistol when the group swept by in a thunder of hooves, heading toward the prison.

Damnation, how had Shahid gotten on their track so quickly? Ross swung into his saddle and motioned the others into the street. Turning away from the prison, they set off through the dark streets; the sooner they left the city, the better.

The lieutenant at the prison had already been bullied enough for one night and was not enthusiastic about lending men to Shahid Mahmud. However, he was outranked and outshouted, so grudgingly he allowed the yawer to take three soldiers.

Mission accomplished, Shahid turned to leave. As he did, he said more to himself than the other officer, "That ferengi will never get out of Bokhara alive."

The lieutenant said, "Saadi Khan has probably already executed the ferengi. At least, he seemed anxious to do so."

Shahid swung back, suddenly alert. "What do you mean?"

Several confused minutes passed before it was established that two different ferengis were under discussion. On hearing that a royal chamberlain had taken the foreigner from the Black Well, Shahid said suspiciously, "This chamberlain—describe him."

The lieutenant shrugged. "Saadi Khan was taller than you, but apart from his height, there was nothing special about him. Dark beard and eyes, perhaps thirty years old." He thought a moment. "Foreign-born, I think. He spoke Uzbek with a slight accent. Might have been Persian or Afghan."

"He spoke Uzbek?" Shahid frowned, thinking that the removal of the prisoner tonight must have been coincidence. Then a horrible thought struck him; what if Khilburn *did* know Uzbek? He could have been listening to everything said around him and laughing at his captors the whole time. Beards could be faked, certainly well enough to deceive an imbecile like this lieutenant. And Shahid did not know of any royal chamberlains named Saadi Khan. "Did the fellow have a youth with him, perhaps wearing a dark veil across his face?"

"There was a young man with him, but he wasn't veiled."

Shahid began swearing under his breath, producing a steady monotone of curses. Even without proof, he was sure that Khilburn and his damned Targui had come here and removed the ferengi spy from the very shadow of the royal palace.

Spinning on his heel, he barked at his new recruits, "Come. We must go to the city gates. I'll get those bastards if it's the last thing I ever do."

24

🍎

R oss was not sure who owned the empty house, but they owed the use of it to Hussayn Kasem; dragging Muhammad out of the flooded wadi had certainly proved to be one of the best day's work Ross had ever done. Even when the news about Ian forced him and Juliet to alter their plans, Hussayn had responded with grace and efficiency, offering them extra mounts and the use of this house so that they could clean up the prisoner, if they were successful in their rescue mission.

When they reached the safe house, the horses barely paused long enough to allow Ross and Ian to dismount before Juliet and Murad rode off to a nearby stable owned by the Kasem family. As part of the revised plan, they would now trade the horses for a camel and two donkeys, which they would ride when they joined the caravan and rode through the city gate.

Ross had chosen to act as valet and nursemaid to Ian, guessing that his brother-in-law would prefer his help to that of Murad or Juliet. Ian seemed barely conscious as he was guided across the courtyard and into the small building, but once they were inside, he said with some vigor, "I'd trade my immortal soul to be clean. Is that possible?"

"It should be. We tried to supply everything that a newly liberated prisoner might need." Ross unshielded the lamp and checked the two back rooms of the house. Over his shoulder he said, "There's a laundry tub here, with buckets of water, soap, and towels. Sorry it isn't possible to heat the water."

"Too much luxury might be fatal in my present condition," Ian said as he made his way into the back room. "I think that the very worst aspect of that hellhole was the filth."

The tub was large enough for Ian to sit down in the water, though space was tight. After stripping off his own chapan, Ross wordlessly helped his friend scrub away the accumulated grime. Ian's hair had to be soaped and rinsed three times before the distinctive auburn color, several shades darker than Juliet's, was recognizable.

As Ian clambered out of the laundry tub, Ross observed, "You look remarkably better than you did an hour ago."

Ian gave a faint ghostlike smile. "I feel remarkably better, though there is considerable room for improvement." He swallowed, his Adam's apple prominent in his thin neck. "I keep thinking that this is a dream and I'm going to wake up soon."

Guessing that Ian's mental state was as fragile as his physical one, Ross once more opted for lightness. "I can't imagine that your dreams would be so disrespectful to my exalted rank that you would choose a marquess for a bath attendant."

Ian's gaze sharpened. "Your brother died without an heir?"

"Unfortunately, yes." Ross lifted a towel and started drying the other man. "Do you think you can stay in a saddle? Once we get outside the city, we're going to switch to some Turkoman horses, then ride for Persia as fast as we can."

"Nice of you to ask if I can manage, but it sounds as if sitting around and waiting for me to recuperate would not be a wise choice. Don't worry, I'm stronger than I look. If worse comes to worst, tie me on the horse. And if it looks like we might be captured . . ." Ian's breath roughened and his muscles tensed. "Promise that you'll kill me if that happens."

Appalled, Ross opened his mouth to protest, but Ian grabbed his arm, the bony fingers like a vise. *"Promise me!"*

Like a dank wind from the grave, Ross remembered those moments when he had been alone in the Black Well; he couldn't blame Ian for preferring death. With effort, he kept his voice steady as he said, "I promise, but I don't think it will come to that." As he finished the drying, he continued, "Sit down. You need food and some treatment for those sores."

Ian sank down on the uncushioned divan. "You thought of everything."

"If we didn't, it wasn't for lack of trying." Knowing that a man who had been on sparse rations for months would have trouble digesting meat, Ross had asked that a rice dish be left in the house. Across the room, a straw basket held two pottery crocks, one of which contained a pilaf of rice mixed with bits of chicken, vegetables, and yogurt. There was also a jug of tea, packed in straw to keep it warm. Ross handed the tea and crock of rice to Ian. "Don't make yourself ill, but try to get some of this down. You're going to need your strength."

"It's been months since I felt hungry. I think my stomach gave up from sheer lack of use." Ian rolled a bite-size ball of rice, then popped it into his mouth and washed it down with a swig of tea. "How the devil did you and Juliet find me?"

While Ian ate, Ross began spreading salve on his brother-in-law's sores. They were ugly, and some might scar, but all were superficial. As he worked, he gave a brief summary of what Juliet had been doing for the last dozen years, then went on to describe how the two of them had come to Bokhara.

When Abdul Samut Khan was mentioned, Ian grimaced. "So you've had dealings with that treacherous bastard too. He can be charming when he wants to, but he's so greedy he'd sell his own grandmother for dog meat if the price was right."

Ross glanced up. "He showed me a letter you had written, saying how helpful he had been."

"That was before he asked me to give him a note of hand for ten thousand ducats, to be paid by the British ambassador in Teheran," Ian said dryly. "When I refused to do it, he denounced me as a spy. The amir was already suspicious, and when the nayeb spoke against me, it was the last straw. The next day I was arrested and taken to the Black Well."

"He tried to extort money from me too. I'm lucky he

was called off to war before he got around to charging me with espionage. We're getting away just in time." Finished with the salve, Ross stood and began to give Ian a rough haircut and beard trim so he would look like a Bokharan rather than a desert hermit. "Once we learned that you might still be alive in the Black Well, we couldn't leave without trying to rescue you. But why do you think the amir claimed you had been executed?"

"Because he thought I had been. Instead, Pyotr Andreyovich was the one beheaded." Ian gave a ragged sigh and leaned his head against the wall. "Colonel Pyotr Andreyovich Kushutkin of the Russian army. He was caught spying several months before I arrived in Bokhara."

"A trumped-up charge, like the one against you?"

"No, it was quite genuine in his case. He was an enthusiastic player in the Great Game—his only regret was that he had been caught. Pyotr Andreyovich was some years older than I and had been in the Well longer. He had developed the most horrible cough—sometimes he went on for hours, and there was blood." Briefly Ian closed his eye, a spasm crossing his face at the memory. "When they came to execute me, he said that since he was dying anyhow, they might as well take him instead of me."

"No one noticed the difference?" Ross asked, startled.

Ian gave him a sardonic glance. "Pyotr Andreyovich and I were about the same height and had hair about the same shade, though his was more brown than red. But as skinny and filthy as we both were, and hairier than baboons, it would have taken someone who knew us very well to tell the difference." He swallowed hard. "So he died in my place. I was feverish at the time or I would have protested more. Still, it didn't seem to matter much, except that he was released from his misery. But now . . ." His voice trailed off.

"Wherever Colonel Kushutkin is now, he must be pleased with his decision," Ross said quietly. "From what you say, he probably would not have survived until now, but you have. Now you can send his Bible to his family, as he wished."

Ian's expression eased a little at the words. "He kept

a journal in the blank pages at the front and back of the testament, using a pencil he had on him when he was imprisoned. He taught me Russian and I helped him with his English. Spy or not, one couldn't have asked for a better cellmate. Present company excepted, of course." Ian began putting on the Turkestani clothing that Ross handed him. "Since my jailers thought I was him, I swore at them in Russian whenever they spoke to me. No one ever guessed that I wasn't Pyotr Andreyovich."

After dressing, Ian wound a turban, wrapping one of the turns of fabric over his blind eye. When he was done, he said, "You and Juliet—you've reconciled?"

Ross hesitated, thinking that that was a complicated question, one that he did not have a clear answer for. Finally he said, "Yes. For the moment."

"Good." Ian sat down and pulled on Ross's best pair of leather boots, which he had donated to the unknown prisoner. "Then perhaps something worthwhile has come out of this mess."

Hearing a sound in the outer room, Ross turned swiftly, but it was just Juliet, returned from exchanging their mounts. Her eyes widened when she saw her brother. "Amazing. It's hard to believe that you're the same man who came out of the Black Well less than two hours ago."

Ian said with dry humor, "Eton College and the British army were wonderful preparation for a year or two in a dungeon."

Juliet's face lit up and she went to give her brother a longer, more leisurely hug than had been possible earlier. But while she accepted the words at face value, Ross saw how much effort it took Ian to create that illusion of jauntiness. A stiff upper lip did not come cheap.

Stepping back from the hug, Juliet said to Ross, "Have you told Ian how he and I are leaving Bokhara?"

"Not yet." Ross lifted two folded garments and handed one each to Juliet and Ian. "Riding in camel panniers and wearing these women's mantles, you'll make a nice pair of wives."

"Ingenious. We'll be totally covered and the panniers will disguise height." Ian lifted the horsehair mantle and dropped it over his head. Called a chador, it was a huge, shapeless black sack with a small woven screen over the eyes so that the unfortunate occupant could see out.

After rubbing off her mustache, Juliet also donned her chador. The longest garments available were too short for her and Ian, but once they climbed into the panniers, the deficiency would be unnoticeable. "Time to go. The sooner we're outside the city, the sooner we can take these wretched things off."

She and Ian left the room, her hand on his elbow giving him unobtrusive support. Ross took a quick scan to make sure that nothing had been forgotten. Ian had the Bible; his ragged trousers were being left behind. Tomorrow a Kasem servant would come and clean up all traces of the late-night occupants.

When Ross stepped out into the courtyard, he could hear camel honks and driver curses, the unmistakable sounds of the caravan that was assembling only a few hundred yards away. To his delight, the camel turned out to be Julietta, thoughtfully sent by Hussayn. While Juliet and Ian squeezed their tall bodies into the panniers, Ross greeted Julietta and fed her an apple, which she gobbled happily. Then he mounted one of the placid donkeys as Murad got on the other. A few minutes' ride brought them to the square where the caravan was preparing to leave, and it was easy to merge into the unruly mass of animals and men. If their luck held, in another hour they would be outside the city.

Shahid Mahmud found that two caravans had departed from Bokhara that night, a small one south through the gate of Namazgah and a larger one east toward Samarkand. After sending a patrol after the southbound group, he personally went to investigate at the Samarkand gate.

Main gates were not opened at night, so traffic was channeled through a small side door that would allow only one beast to exit at a time. For that reason Shahid had hoped that some of the large caravan would still be within the city walls, but he was too late; by the time he reached the gate, the last of the eastbound caravan had already departed. However, the customs officials who had checked loads and passports were still on duty, and furious questioning elicited the information that several men who fitted Khilburn's description were in the caravan.

Shahid had been a hunter ever since he learned to ride as a child, and his finely honed predator's instinct told him that Khilburn had left this way. Picking the dozen best-trained and best-armed soldiers to accompany him, he set off into the night. It was unlikely that the ferengi bastard would stay with the caravan long, but he couldn't be more than an hour ahead. And no matter how far and fast he ran, Shahid would be right behind him.

The last piece of advance planning clicked flawlessly into place; four superbly fit Turkoman desert horses were waiting at the remote barn that had been previously agreed upon. Also there were the rifles and ammunition that Juliet had retrieved from their hiding place the previous week.

What was unexpected was the presence of Hussayn Kasem himself. As Juliet supervised the changeover to the horses, Ross thankfully peeled off his itchy, uncomfortable beard and said farewell to Julietta, who bawled sadly, as if guessing that she would not see him again. After a last affectionate rumpling of her long ears, Ross turned and almost fell over Hussayn, who had been waiting with an amused smile.

After greeting his friend, Ross said, "I'm grateful for the chance to say thank you and good-bye, Hussayn. What you have done for us is beyond price."

The other man made a deprecatory gesture. "You gave me back my father—it is only right that I help you regain your brother."

"You helped me far more than that." To offer payment would have been an insult, but on impulse Ross pulled out the ancient Greek coin he had received for being the victor in the *bozkashi* match. He had carried it with him ever since. "Will you accept this as a token of a journey I will never forget?"

Hussayn smiled, his teeth white and even. "I will accept it as the token of a man I will never forget."

"If and when I return to England, I intend to found an institute where men of goodwill can gather from all over the world and learn to better understand and respect each other," Ross said hesitantly. "Perhaps someday you might visit me there."

Hussayn shook his head. "It is not a journey I will ever make, but who knows? Perhaps when my son is grown, he will."

They shook hands for what both men knew would be the last time. Then Ross swung onto his spirited bay mount. Dawn was beginning to show in the east. By the time the sun had fully risen, they would have circled Bokhara and would be on the road west to Persia. By noon they should be crossing the Oxus.

For the first time, Ross allowed himself to believe that perhaps this mad escape attempt really would succeed.

Bellowing and firing their long-barreled rifles, Shahid Mahmud and his men stopped the Samarkand-bound caravan, then proceeded to search all five hundred beasts and hundred-plus humans. A tall bearded Pathan had a terrifying few minutes at the hands of a Bokharan soldier before the yawer himself verified that the suspect was not Khilburn.

As the sun rose over the horizon, Shahid gathered the travelers and threatened to treat them all as accomplices unless someone could give him information on the ferengi spy and his party. Doubtfully a young Kazakh said he had seen a camel and two donkeys turning away from the main group.

It was enough to confirm Shahid's instincts. Like a dove to its cote, the ferengi was going to circle Bokhara and head west toward his own home rather than penetrate deeper into Turkestan.

Gathering his soldiers, Shahid set off at a gallop. He should be able to seize his prey before reaching the Oxus, but even if he did not, no matter. If necessary, he and his handpicked patrol would follow their quarry into the Kara Kum.

Like a hound on the scent, nothing save death could stop Shahid now.

25

🍏

Even a dozen strenuous years in Persia had not prepared Juliet for the rigors of their flight across the Kara Kum. The scorching sands were an anvil for the sun, the merciless rays a hammer that pounded their frail human bodies. Without the cooling effect of the "wind of a hundred days," it would have been impossible to cross the Kara Kum at all.

But the wind could also be an enemy, for summer was the season of sandstorms. Half a dozen times a day, flurries of biting sand slowed their progress and clogged their lungs, though they were never struck by another storm as virulent as the one that had trapped Ross and Juliet in the dunes.

After they had been ferried across the Oxus, they rode for twenty-four hours straight until exhaustion forced them to rest under improvised tents made of stretched blankets. But even then, the baking heat made real sleep impossible.

When the sun neared the horizon, they remounted and pushed on, riding through the night and the next morning to reach a feeble well around noon. The small amount of water available was not enough to refill their waterskins, so they halted for several hours while more water oozed into the well from the deep sands. Then they were off again.

The choice of the secondary route across the desert had been a good one, for after crossing the Oxus they saw no other travelers. Guided by compass and stars and Murad's carefully researched knowledge, they made their way across the trackless wastes. Though they avoided the softest sand, which would slow their mounts, soon both humans and horses were tinged the dusty yellow-brown that was the color of Central Asia in summer.

By the third day Juliet was sure they were safe from pursuit. Nonetheless, when they stopped for their midday rest, Ross climbed to the top of a nearby hill with his small spyglass to see if there was anyone else in the vicinity. Too exhausted to sleep, Juliet decided to join him, knowing that it would be restful to spend a few minutes alone with her husband.

Ross sat in the shade of a rocky outcropping, gazing at the shimmering heat-drenched hills with the spyglass idle in his lap. Juliet knew that he had slept less than any of them, for even during halts he stayed alert for danger, but he managed a tired smile when she sat down beside him. "How are you faring?"

"Well enough." She sighed and loosened her tagelmoust so that she could feel the wind on her face. "But when I get home, I'm going to spend the first week alternating between my bed and the hammam."

There was no water for shaving, and several days' worth of gold stubble glinted on Ross's jaw, but he was still the handsomest man she had ever seen. Needing to touch him, Juliet laid her hand over his where it rested on his thigh. Immediately he turned his hand over and interlaced his fingers with hers. Peace and comfort seemed to radiate from their joined hands; her tired mind was intrigued to learn that such simple contact could be so soul-satisfying, as refreshing as water in the desert.

"It won't be much longer now," Ross said. "We're at the halfway point."

They sat in silence, enjoying the moments of closeness, until Juliet said, "It's interesting that, alone among us, Ian is getting stronger rather than weaker. The first night, when you had to lash him to his saddle and lead his horse, I was afraid he might not survive the trip."

"Instead he ate as much as he could, slept like the dead when we stopped, and woke up capable of managing his own mount. He's incredibly strong, or he would never have survived the Black Well." Ross's eyes twinkled. "No doubt Ian would say that a dungeon is good preparation for an arduous journey."

Juliet tightened her fingers around Ross's. "I'm almost afraid to say it out loud, but it looks like we might have accomplished the impossible." Suddenly she grinned. "And much as I hate to admit it, my mother's intuition was correct."

"What happens when we reach Serevan?" Ross asked softly.

Juliet's brief sense of well-being ebbed away. "I don't know," she said, her words no more than a whisper.

"No more do I." Ross released her hand and lifted the spyglass to scan the horizon. Then he stopped and frowned.

"Do you see something?" Juliet asked.

"A dust cloud that looks more like riders than a sandstorm." He handed the spyglass to her. "What do you think?"

She took her time, trying to distinguish detail against the bleached sky. "It's definitely a group of riders, perhaps ten or twelve men," she said at length, "and they're coming from the direction of Bokhara. Do you think we're being followed?"

"It's possible. If someone tracked us far enough to learn that we are going to Persia, but not on the main caravan route, this is the only other possibility."

Juliet scrambled to her feet. "Perhaps we should leave."

Still seated, Ross shook his head. "Not just yet—even Turkoman horses need rest in this heat, and while Ian is doing amazingly well, he's not made of iron. I'll stay here and watch the riders. When they're closer, we can decide if they look threatening. Go get some rest—you're not made of iron, either."

"Could I lie down here beside you?" she asked rather shyly, knowing that being near Ross would strengthen her more than anything else could. "I promise I'll try to sleep."

For answer, he caught her hand and tugged her down until her head was in his lap. His hard thigh made quite a decent pillow, and to her surprise, she drifted into a doze.

The shadows had lengthened when Ross shook her shoulder. "It's time to get moving again. The riders behind us are dressed like Bokharan soldiers, and I can't think of any reason for them to be here except for pursuing us."

"Damnation." Juliet stared in dismay at the dust cloud, which was now close enough to see without the spyglass. "I didn't really believe that anyone would be so persistent."

"Shahid Mahmud would be." Ross got wearily to his feet. "He took a very personal dislike to both of us and he's the bulldog sort who never quits."

They hastened down the hill to wake the others, and were on their way within five minutes. Through the night they pushed on steadily, but the next morning, when Ross stopped at a high point to check the trail behind them, they had made only a little headway on their pursuers.

Frowning, Ross put away his spyglass. The men behind must be aware of their presence, for both groups were moving as fast as possible under these conditions, and the interval between them was fairly constant. If Ross and his companions could keep up their present speed, they would be safe, but almost any kind of trouble would slow them, with disastrous consequences.

As Ross rejoined the others and gave the signal to continue, he offered a silent prayer of thanks that Ian was equal to the pace they were setting. Having survived the Black Well, Ian was not about to die now that he was free, and the forge of the desert had refined him down to raw willpower and tenacity. He would not allow his condition to become a souce of problems.

But trouble did come later that day, when the next water hole turned out to be dry. It had been two days since the last well, and they had only a little water left in the waterskins. Carefully rationed, it would last the humans for perhaps two more days, but the horses would need water long before then.

Grim-faced, they set their course for the next water hole.

Mercilessly Shahid drove his troops through the tawny, shifting dunes. At the outer limits of vision was another party moving away at high speed, and he knew beyond the possibility of doubt that it was his prey.

Instinct had led Shahid this far, an almost uncanny ability to think like his quarry. It had worked with gazelles and lions, and now it was proving no less effective with the ferengi. At the Oxus, a ferryman gave a description confirming that Khilburn was traveling west with three men, including the Targui, but it was instinct that told Shahid they would take the seldom-used southern route, with its unreliable water supply.

When they reached the dead well, Shahid knew that he would win, for unlike the ferengi, he and his men had two packhorses carrying extra waterskins that were still full. Soon Khilburn and his friends would slow, and then they would be ripe for the plucking. A fierce light in his eyes, Shahid forced his grumbling troops to push on faster.

Another endless, exhausting day passed. Juliet found it eerie to know that the pursuit was growing ever closer. When she glanced over her shoulder, she saw that their enemies were still beyond gunshot range, but that would not be true much longer. Allowing her weary horse to drop back by Ross's, she said, "I think it's time to find an ambush site and wait for them."

Ross grimaced. "It may come to that soon. Our rifles are our one great advantage, especially since most Uzbeks aren't the marksmen that Pathans and Afghans are. But there are still a dozen of them to only two guns for us."

Juliet gave a worried glance at the sky. "If we're going to make a stand, we should do it soon, before the sun sets."

He studied their surroundings, which consisted of low, rolling sand hills. "I would cheerfully trade all of this sand for a nice rocky defile, with us holding the high ground."

Juliet smiled faintly. "I would trade all of this sand for just about anything you could mention."

Their conversation was interrupted by a shout from Murad, who had just rounded the next sandy hill. Alarmed by the note in his voice, Juliet and Ross spurred their horses forward until they caught up with the other two men.

Less than a quarter of a mile ahead was a party of black-hatted Turkomans. There were at least twenty young men and no women or children, so it was a raiding party—and the Turkomans had seen the newcomers and were cantering forward to investigate.

Juliet muttered an oath. "Talk about being caught between the devil and the deep blue sea."

"Frankly, those are two choices I would prefer to these," Ian said acerbically.

Juliet tried to decide what would be the best course, but her weary mind was blank. They might have been able to outshoot the men following them, but there were too many Turkomans to fight, and trying to outrun both hostile groups would be hopeless, given the debilitated state of their horses.

Ross exhaled with a soft, rueful sigh. "There's only one solution. Throw ourselves on the Turkomans' mercy and hope that the laws of hospitality protect us." Then, to Juliet's horror, her husband spurred his horse directly at the Turkoman war party, his right hand raised in a sign of peace.

"He's right," Ian said tersely. Putting his heels to his mount, he followed Ross.

Juliet and Murad exchanged an appalled glance. "They are mad to trust themselves to Turkoman marauders!" Murad exclaimed.

Juliet couldn't have agreed more, but she didn't have a better suggestion. "Are not madmen holy in Islam?" she said wryly as she adjusted her tagelmoust. "And is hospitality not sacred? Let us pray that these Turkomans believe both of those things."

With a kind of light-headed bravado, she raced after Ross and Ian, who were now face-to-face with the Turkomans. Behind her hooves sounded as Murad did the same. They joined the group just as Ross said, "We beg your hospitality, for the last well was dead and our horses are sore pressed."

"You ask hospitality?" The elaborately dressed young man who seemed to be the leader was incredulous;

doubtless he was more accustomed to travelers fleeing in
the opposite direction.

For a moment their fate wavered in the balance between social obligation and bandit greed. Then another
Turkoman said excitedly, "It is Khilburn, the ferengi
who defeated Dil Assa and won the *bozkashi* match!"
He edged his mount forward for a better view. "With
my own eyes, I saw him do it. Never would I have believed an infidel could play *bozkashi* so well."

Two other men who had been at the *bozkashi* match
chimed in. One was a cousin of Dil Assa's, and he described how Dil Assa had given his opponent the wolf-
edged cap after the match.

Suddenly the suspicious mass of Turkomans dissolved
into a laughing, boisterous group. The youth who had
made the first identification said curiously, "I heard that
you were traveling to Bokhara to ask for your brother's
release, Khilburn. Did the amir grant your request?"

"No, he refused." Ross paused with deliberate showmanship. "Hence, because Nasrullah gave us no choice,
I and my friends Murad and Jalal"—he nodded at both
in turn—"were forced to steal my brother from the Black
Well."

As the listeners gasped with amazement, Ross gestured
at Ian. "And here my brother is, reclaimed from the
amir's dungeon." With his bandaged eye, full red beard,
and gaunt height, Ian was a figure to impress even Turkoman marauders.

When asked how the rescue had been accomplished,
Ross briefly described his disguise, forged documents,
and bluster, a story his audience found uproariously
funny. When the laughter died down, Ross said, "Some
of the amir's soldiers are pursuing us and are scarcely
more than a gunshot behind, with a dozen rifles to our
two. This is another reason we beg your aid."

The leader, who had introduced himself as Subhan,
grinned. "It will be a pleasure to assist the legendary
Khilburn." Turning to his companions, he said, "We
come from an oasis and are well-supplied with water.
Will four of you exchange waterskins with our friends?"

Within two minutes the exchange had been made.
Then Subhan said, "Our way lies opposite yours. When

we meet your pursuers, we will chastise them for their effrontery at following you into the Kara Kum. The desert is *ours*, and none may pass safely but at our pleasure." A chorus of agreement rose around him.

"A thousand thanks." Ross inclined his head gravely. "Courage such as yours comes from the heart and is beyond price, but nonetheless I would like to offer a small token of our gratitude." He had delved into his saddlebags when the water was being transferred, and now he tossed a heavy leather pouch to the Turkoman leader. "Though I cannot host a feast in person, I beg that you use this to celebrate and honor your generous courage."

Subhan tucked the bag inside his chapan, to the sound of cheers. "We will sing songs and dance the night through in your honor," he promised, "and someday I will tell my sons, when I have some, of the day that I met the legendary Khilburn."

After a final exchange of courtesies, the groups separated, the ferengi party westbound and the Turkomans eastbound. Less than a quarter-hour later, when Juliet and the others had stopped to water their horses, the crack of rifle shots began rolling over the sandy wasteland. They all stopped to listen.

Murad grinned. "I never thought the day would come when I would be grateful for the fact that Turkomans are bloodthirsty barbarians."

"As long as they're on our side, they can be as bloodthirsty as they want." Juliet finished watering her horse, then took a small mouthful herself, moistening her cracked lips and rolling the precious fluid around her mouth before swallowing. As she remounted, she thought that it was typical of Ross to have found a way to harness that bloodthirstiness on their behalf. He was a man in a million. What a pity that she wasn't the woman in a million who deserved him.

As he bandaged his grazed wrist, Shahid cursed with vicious fluency. The damned Turkomans had almost ruined everything with their unexpected attack. After getting off to a noisy start, the skirmish had subsided to occasional shots and colorful shouted insults, continuing in desultory fashion until darkness fell. Shahid's force had scattered and eight of his soldiers were gone beyond recall, lost not to death but cowardice, for they used the fighting as an excuse to retreat. By now the swine would be halfway back to Bokhara.

But Shahid had managed to rally three of his men, and they were the toughest, the most dangerous, and the most willing of his patrol. They would be enough to finish the job. The Uzbek calculated that it would take about two more days to regain the hours that had been lost to the Turkomans; they should overtake Khilburn about where the desert joined the hills.

Shahid remounted and ordered his three men to do the same. Then they set off into the night after the ferengi. The next two days were difficult, for they had to push themselves to the limit to gain on their prey, but four men raised less dust than a dozen, and Khilburn seemed to have no notion that he was still pursued.

The infidel was finally overtaken in the rugged hills that marked the edge of the plateau of Persia. The rough terrain favored the pursuers and, without being seen himself, Shahid was able to lead his men along the stony track until he had his enemy in view. As a clear sign that fortune was on his side, the trail ahead dipped into a broad ravine before rising once more. Khilburn and his men were on the far side of the ravine and below the Bokharans as they picked their way up the steep track. It was a perfect site for an ambush.

Shahid ordered his men to dismount and take cover. When all of their weapons were loaded, the rifles aimed, and more ammunition ready to hand, he gave the signal to shoot.

The target he chose for himself was the swine Khilburn.

In spite of the constant blazing heat, Juliet thought that the last two days of travel had seemed easier, for they knew that the worst was behind them. The next well they reached after meeting the Turkomans had been bountiful, and they had obtained enough water to last them all the way home.

When the rugged hills came into view, Juliet had recognized their position and led the group to the most direct route to Serevan. Now, as they climbed the side of a ravine, the brisk wind brought the scents and cooler air of the highlands, and the travelers were in blithe spirits. "We're within five miles of the fortress," Juliet announced with deep satisfaction. "There will be time for a leisurely visit to the hammam before dinner."

Ross chuckled. "You're like a horse with the scent of its own stables in its nostrils."

Juliet smiled, unabashed at the simile. They were riding in a close group, Ian just below her, and Ross and Murad ahead.

"You did it, Murad," Ross said cheerfully. They reached a wider section of the track and he brought his horse up alongside the Persian youth's. "You led us safely across the Kara Kum on a route that you had never traveled yourself. I think that qualifies you as a master guide."

Murad laughed. "Words are all very well, Khilburn"—he leaned forward to emphasize his point—"as long as you don't forget the bonus you promised if I did my job well!"

Then the playful atmosphere vanished as a ragged volley of rifle shots rang out. One of the men ahead of Juliet cried out, but she didn't waste time looking to see which one. As bullets ricocheted from bleak stone, she dived from her horse and scrambled behind a tumble of boulders, then forced her mount down so that it would also be protected.

A dozen feet up the hillside, Ross had already taken cover, pulled out his rifle, and begun firing across the ravine, his face calm and his hands steady. Ian was just a few feet away from Juliet, behind the same pile of boulders. As she whipped her rifle from its saddle holster, he said dryly, "Thank God they're bad shots, whoever they are."

Juliet suspected that it was probably the stiff wind blowing through the ravine that had saved them, for it was strong enough to affect the trajectory of a ball at this range. Even so, their assailants had not been entirely ineffectual, for one of them had hit Murad. It was he who had screamed before tumbling from his horse and rolling several feet down the slope. Now he lay unconscious, his left sleeve drenched with blood, in a position too exposed to permit his companions to go to his aid.

Swearing, Juliet peered cautiously between two boulders and scanned the opposite hillside. Heat shimmered from the barren, sun-blasted sides of the gorge, distorting the air and making it hard to judge distances. One of their assailants fired again, the puff of dark smoke revealing his position before the sharp crack of the gun echoed through the ravine. Ross and Juliet both returned fire, then had to drop swiftly when their bullets attracted more in reply. The acrid scent of black powder stinging her nostrils, Juliet thought back to the initial volley and decided that there were probably between three and five attackers.

She reloaded and looked for other targets, but none were visible. "One is by that twisted pine. Have you spotted the others, Ross?"

"Two behind that pile of dark scree and one lower, to the left." He punctuated his words with a shot, then ducked again. "I think Shahid Mahmud and his merry men have caught up with us."

Juliet did not dispute the remark; she suspected that Ross was right, for only someone who hated them and had the instincts of a bulldog would come so far, undeterred even by marauding Turkomans. Seeing a sliver of white rise above the dark scree, she fired and reloaded, then fired again, angling the shot in the hope that a ricochet might damage someone behind the stone ridge.

In the lull that followed, she pulled out her pistol and gave it to Ian, along with ammunition from her saddlebags. "A pity we haven't another rifle, but this might be helpful if someone tries to sneak up on us."

"A rifle would be wasted on me, for losing an eye has probably wrecked my aim." He checked the loading, then cocked the hammer. "But given that this is perfect sneaking country, I'll feel better with a pistol in my hand."

He was right about the terrain, for the ravine was such a jumble of broken rock that a careful person could move almost anywhere without being exposed to fire for more than an instant. Ruefully Juliet said, "For the moment, it's a stalemate."

"If we don't change the odds, Murad might bleed to death," Ross said, his voice hard. He fired again, reloading without haste. "And I don't want to leave the initiative in their hands. I'm going to work my way up to that ledge, which should give me a good range of fire over the whole ravine."

Juliet scanned the hillside behind, which rose in a series of rough steps. "I'll make sure they're too busy to shoot at you."

Ross gave her a faint, sweet smile, as if they were in their bedroom in Bokhara rather than fighting for their lives in a sunstruck mountain ravine. "Your skills are so much more useful than the more typical music and embroidery."

She almost laughed. "Just remember to keep your head and other valuable parts of your anatomy down." She watched for a moment as he started up the slope, rifle in hand. His green-and-gray-striped chapan and white turban were so imprinted with yellow dust that he blended into the rugged terrain, and he knew how to move swiftly and silently, taking advantage of every scrap of concealment. Hardly the usual skills of an English marquess; in this, at least, they were well-matched.

Then Juliet turned and gave full attention to the opposite side of the gorge, grateful that her breechloader could be reloaded and fired so swiftly; their enemies would not realize that only one person was shooting at them. But as she pumped off rounds at every sign of movement, she hoped that Ross was successful, for she didn't like their situation one damned bit.

Shahid Mahmud's cursing became a steady stream of obscenities, for his perfect ambush spot was flawed by wind and a rocky terrain that offered the enemy too many places to hide. By misjudging the wind's force, the Bokharans had lost their initial advantage of surprise; now that both parties had gone to ground, they might spend the rest of the day blasting away at each other without damaging anything but their ammunition supplies. Damn the wind, damn his men for not being better shots, and most of all damn himself for hitting the guide rather than the ferengi.

Then his eyes narrowed as he saw a wisp of dusty green move on the far side of the ravine. Khilburn was the only one in his party wearing that color. The Uzbek kept a sharp watch and was soon rewarded by another glimpse of green farther up the slope.

Shahid swore even more as he realized that the infidel was climbing to a better position. Because the other side of the gorge rose toward the plateau, the bastard could go higher than the Bokharans; if he wasn't stopped, he would secure an impregnable position. Hence Shahid must stop him, but he would have to cross to the far side of the ravine for the best shot.

Shahid crouched and dashed to another boulder, to the right and below him. Immediately a ball whizzed by, so close that it buzzed like a lethal hornet. Bare seconds later another bullet chipped stone by one of the other Bokharans. Damnation, the ferengi's men were good shots. But they'd have to see a target before they could hit it, and as Shahid began gliding from boulder to boulder, he made very sure that no one saw him.

Climbing the blistering hillside had been slow work, but Juliet did a superb job of covering him, and Ross managed to reach his objective without attracting lethal attention. The ledge turned out to be a tilted shelf of stone that angled downward more steeply than he had realized from below. Flattening himself on his stomach, he crawled down the slanting surface, the coarse stone gritty under his fingers.

When he reached the edge, he raised his head cautiously and looked across the ravine. As he had hoped, he had a clear shot at three unsuspecting Bokharans. His mouth tightened when he saw that none of the men in sight had the distinctive burly build of Shahid Mahmud. A pity; if Ross could have shot the officer, it might have stopped the fight without anyone else dying.

Very well, so be it. Ross did not enjoy killing, but if forced to choose between the lives of his friends and those of nameless strangers, he would do what was necessary. He spent a moment planning his shots, forcing himself to think of the Bokharans as targets rather than men. Then he set the rifle to his shoulder, took careful aim, allowed for the effect of the wind, and squeezed the trigger.

The first ball sped deadly and true into the target's chest. Without pausing to watch the man crash to the ground, Ross reloaded and fired again. The second target was moving, trying to flee this unexpected new peril, and Ross hit only his shoulder, but it was enough to make the man shriek and drop his weapon as he spun about and clutched the wound. He wouldn't be doing any more serious shooting today.

By this time the third Bokharan had ducked out of Ross's view, but putting two of the enemy out of action greatly improved the odds for the ferengis. After reloading again, Ross inched his way a little farther down the slab, taking comfort in the fact that another ledge jutted out about twenty feet below him; even if he fell, he probably wouldn't break his neck. Lifting his head, he tried to locate Shahid Mahmud, who must be somewhere on the far side of the gorge.

Ross never felt the bullet that hit him.

Juliet wanted to applaud when Ross's shots rang out over the ravine. When the second bullet provoked a yell, Ian gave an approving nod. "Sounds like Ross got one."

Fiercely Juliet said, "Two. With his marksmanship, his first shot would have killed someone outright."

She glanced up and saw a puff of black smoke drifting from his ledge, dissipating rapidly in the stiff wind. Catching a brief glimpse of his white-turbaned head, she winced at the precariousness of his position; a good thing he had a better head for heights than she did.

Another shot blasted out, rebounding harshly from the barren walls of the gorge. Juliet knew immediately that something was wrong, for the gun had the sound of a Bokharan weapon but had been fired from the ferengi side of the ravine.

In the next instant, right in front of her horrified eyes, her husband pitched over the edge of his ledge. At the same time, a hoarse victory shout echoed obscenely through the gorge.

Ross fell with eerie slowness, his descent broken by the tenacious shrubs that clung to the rocky cliff. One of the branches caught his turban and ripped it loose to wave in the wind like a banner, exposing the burnished gold of his hair. His rifle fell separately, spinning in the sun before hitting somewhere below with a hard metallic clatter.

Then he vanished from sight as he landed on a ledge below the one he had been shooting from.

"Ross!" Juliet screamed. Sheer blind, mindless terror possessed her so thoroughly that she did not even know that she had started running toward him until Ian grabbed her and dragged her to the ground.

"Jesus Christ, Juliet!" Ian swore. "If you're going after Ross, keep down—you can't help him if you get killed too. Give me the rifle—I'll try to cover you." He wrenched the weapon out of her nerveless fingers, then uncocked the pistol and pressed it into her hand. "Take this. You might need it."

Numbly she accepted the weapon, anything so that Ian would release her to go to her husband. When he did, she raced frantically up the slope, keeping down, but only barely.

Ian watched his sister for a moment, then turned and pointed the rifle across the ravine, letting off a shot just to let the enemy know that the ferengis were still in business. To his surprise, the bullet went exactly where he had intended. With grim humor he started shooting in earnest. He was pleased to learn that losing an eye didn't seem to have hurt his marksmanship at all.

His blood singing with triumph, Shahid began moving toward his victim. There was a chance Khilburn was still alive, for Shahid had been shooting from an awkward angle and the fall from the ledge, while dramatic, was not in itself sufficient to kill unless he landed badly. First Shahid would make sure that the ferengi was dead; then he would climb to the higher ledge and use the vantage point to shoot the others at his leisure. Though perhaps, if he was careful, the Targui would survive long enough to suffer further indignities. His rifle ready in his hand, the Uzbek snaked his way across the broken ground.

When Juliet scrambled onto the ledge where Ross had fallen, she found that it was an unexpected pocket of sand and gravel held together by tough grasses. She prayed that the relative softness had mitigated the effect of the fall.

Ross lay on his side, his face handsome and relaxed, as if he were sleeping, but the blood staining his blond hair told a more frightening story. Her breathing jagged with fear and exertion, Juliet knelt and checked his throat for a pulse. When at first she could not find one, suffocating despair flooded through her. Then, miraculously, she felt a strong beat under her fingertips, a pulse that represented not just his life but her own, for if Ross were dead, the best part of Juliet would die too.

Her heart a jumble of prayers, gratitude, and threats of what she would do if God didn't spare her husband, she laid the pistol on the ground and made a quick examination. Apparently the bullet had grazed his skull, but there seemed to be no other major injuries.

Needing a bandage, Juliet jerked off her tagelmoust. Her hair broke out of its crude braid and spilled over her shoulders, but she brushed it back impatiently, then tore off strips of cloth. She had just finished tying a pad over Ross's wound when she heard the rattling of pebbles as someone approached.

She whipped her head up just in time to see Shahid heave himself onto the ledge, his rifle at the ready. He was less than ten feet away and there was a paralyzed moment of mutual shock as they stared at each other.

"A woman!" the Uzbek gasped, his eyes widening with astonishment as he saw Juliet's face and the thick waves of bright hair that tossed in the wind. "So Khilburn's Targui boy is really a skinny ferengi whore."

The Koran commands mercy toward women and children, but that was a directive Shahid had never obeyed. An expression of evil delight on his face, he raised his rifle to shoot. "Now you will join your lover in death."

But he was too slow. During the stunned moment when Shahid was absorbing the fact that she was female, Juliet raised the pistol and cocked it.

Then, holding the gun with both hands so there would be no mistake, she shot Shahid Mahmud through the heart at point-blank range.

26

The ear-piercing crack of Juliet's pistol pulled Ross back to hazy awareness. Though his body refused to move, he managed to open his eyes a slit, just enough to see the impact of the ball spin Shahid around, then knock him from the ledge. As the Uzbek's body crashed noisily down the cliff, Juliet lowered her pistol with shaking hands.

Turning to the ravine, she shouted, a faint tremor in her voice, "Men of Bokhara! Your mission is over, for your officer, Yawer Shahid Mahmud, is dead and the ferengi is mortally wounded. If you withdraw now, we will permit you to take your weapons and depart in peace and honor. But if you continue fighting, you will be hunted down and killed like dogs."

As she paused for breath, Ross felt an obscure satisfaction at hearing that he was mortally wounded, for it explained why he felt so strange, not quite connected to his body. There was no pain, merely numbness, an endless, drifting lassitude, as if he were a piece of flotsam drifting out on the tide of death.

Juliet continued, her words echoing from the stony ravine, "I am Gul-i Sarahi and my fortress, Serevan, is less than a farsakh away. Already my men will be on their way here, drawn by the sound of gunfire. You will have no chance against them."

At first there was no reply. Then a voice bellowed from the other side of the gorge, "What of our dead?"

"Shahid was a brute and a bully, but he had the virtue of courage and he died while doing his duty," Juliet called back. "If you leave peacefully, I swear that he and

344

any other man who has fallen will be buried with honor and in accordance with Sunni custom."

There was another pause, as if the survivors were conferring. Then the spokesman yelled, "How can we trust you? If you will show yourself, we will do likewise."

Ross wanted to call out to her, "For God's sake, Juliet, don't trust them!" But he could neither speak nor move, just watch helplessly as she rose and stepped to the lip of the ledge.

Tall and proud, Juliet Cameron Carlisle, the Flower of the Desert and the Marchioness of Kilburn, raised her open hands above her head to show that she was weaponless. For a long, suspended moment, it seemed that the ravine held its breath. With her blazing hair and black robes whipping in the wind, she was like an ancient warrior goddess, offering peace but equally capable of dealing death to any who betrayed her trust.

Ross saw her in profile, and the image struck him with knife-edge clarity. She was a sight he would never forget for as long as he lived—which apparently would not be very long. The thought mobilized him, for if he was dying, he must tell her that he loved her. Strange how at the end of life so few things mattered; certainly not possessions or knowledge or pride. Only love.

In a voice that could not conceal shock at the identity of his opponent, the Bokharan spokesman shouted, "We accept your terms. One other man died, Meshedee Rajib by name. We shall leave his body on the track so that you may find and bury him."

"It shall be done." Juliet dropped one hand, leaving the other lifted as if in benediction. "You are brave warriors, and I wish you well on your journey to Bokhara. Go in peace."

"And peace be upon you, lady." Within moments, the clatter of horses' hooves sounded from the far side of the ravine.

Ross wanted to seize the moment to tell Juliet all that he wished to say: that he could not regret loving her, in spite of all the pain their marriage had brought them both: even though it had led to this bleak hillside. With immense effort he stretched out his hand, trying to catch

Juliet's attention, but movement sent jagged pain shafting through his head and once more he fell into darkness.

He came around again when deft hands probed his aching body. Recognizing her touch, he opened his eyes and whispered, "Juliet," not sure that he had made a sound until she turned to him, vivid joy on her face.

He tried to speak again, but she laid a finger over his lips. "Hush, love, save your strength."

He would have laughed if he had not been so dizzy. "For what . . . should a dying man save his strength?"

"Oh, Lord, you heard what I told the Bokharan soldiers," she said ruefully. "I only said that you were fatally wounded to persuade them to leave." She leaned forward and brushed his forehead with a feather-light kiss. "You're not dying, love. In fact, you were amazingly lucky. Shahid's bullet grazed your skull and knocked you from your perch, but the bushes on the cliff slowed your fall and you landed on a fairly soft ledge. You'll have a handsome collection of bruises, but nothing seems to be broken."

It took a moment to reorient his jumbled thoughts toward continued existence. When he had, Ross asked, "Murad?"

"Ian says the bullet went right through his arm and the wound is clean. He banged his head when he fell from his horse, but he should be fine."

Ross exhaled with relief. "We were fortunate."

"Very, but now it's time to get the wounded back to Serevan. Do you think that if I help, you can get down to the horses?"

"We'll see." With Juliet's considerable aid, Ross managed to sit upright. After that, everything became a chaotic blur of pain, confusion, and wavering consciousness. His clearest awareness was of being jogged along on a horse, which gave him a strong sense of *déjà vu*. Yes, this had happened before, when he was wounded while riding with Mikahl. He was getting bloody tired of being shot, then hauled around like a sack of potatoes.

He decided that it really would be easier to surrender to the blackness. So he did.

*   *   *

The next time Ross became conscious, his mind was very clear and he felt deeply rested. Apart from an ache in the side of his head, he felt fine. Experimentally he contracted, then relaxed muscles in various parts of his body, discovering that most were sore from his fall, but there was nothing seriously wrong. Opening his eyes, he found that the room was tinted with the soft, pure light of early morning. He guessed that he was at Serevan, and from the look of the superbly patterned antique rugs hanging on the whitewashed walls, it must be Juliet's own bedroom.

That being the case, he was not surprised when he came to the belated realization that he was not alone in the bed. He turned his head and found that Juliet slept next to him, one hand tucked under his arm. She was an admirable sight to start the day, for she wore nothing but the gold chain that supported her wedding ring. In the pale dawn light her fair skin glowed with pearly luminescence and her hair looked dark, with only hints of auburn. Carefully he drew the sheet down to her waist so he could see more of her graceful curves. He definitely was not dying, not the way his body reacted to her nearness.

But what had been so clear when he thought he was on the brink of death was clear no longer. He did not doubt that he loved Juliet; that was a truth so immense that it was inarguable.

The problem was not love, but life. Danger had drawn them together again; without that bond, did they have a marriage? In Bokhara they had ignored their differences by tacit consent because they had needed each other so much. But against all the odds, they had survived, and now they must face the explosive unanswered questions of the past.

With a desire so great it was pain, Ross wanted Juliet to come back to England with him, to be his wife in truth as well as law. With any other woman he would have thought that joy and passion and affection would be enough to make a marriage worth keeping, but he feared, with deep, angry despair, that those would not be enough to keep Juliet by his side.

His hand unsteady, he stroked her hair. She must have

visited the hammam, as she had planned, for the bright
tresses fell across her shoulder in a shining silken torrent.

At his touch, Juliet's eyes fluttered open and she gave
him a smile of uncomplicated sweetness. Then she raised
her hand to his face, her fingertips gliding over his lips
and cheekbone, as if memorizing. She opened her mouth
to speak, but he could not allow that, for talking would
bring them face-to-face with the abyss of the future. Desperate to delay that moment, Ross covered her mouth
with his, kissing her with all the power of his fears and
yearning.

She made a small choked sound deep in her throat and
responded with swift intensity, as if she too feared the
end that was drawing near. Their tongues met and
danced, their breath mingled, their arms twined. There
was such vivid immediacy in her presence, such rightness
in the flare of desire between them, that it was impossible
to believe this might be the last time.

He might never again know the soft warm pressure of
skin on skin, like this. Or feel the pebbled velvet texture
of her nipples with his tongue, like this. Or hear the
rough eagerness of her breath when he caressed her
moist, intimate flesh, probing and teasing, like *this*, until
she pulsed with anticipation. He could not bear it if he
was never again to hear her sharp, eager inhalation when
he entered her heated body, like *this*.

He tried to lose himself and his fears inside of her,
wanting passion so blazing it would bind her to him
forever. He tasted the anguish in her kiss, watching
the vulnerability that shimmered across her face as she
shuddered helplessly against him. He might never again
know such union, the terrifying exultation of losing control, like this, oh, God, like *this*. . . .

After passion there had been stillness and fragile
peace, the folding together of satisfied bodies as they
drifted into sleep, but when they woke again there was
a faint, uneasy distance between them. Wanting to fill
the silence, Juliet murmured, "If the *hakim*, the doctor,
knew I have allowed a wounded man to exert himself so,
he would never forgive me."

"I couldn't have been too badly wounded or such exertions wouldn't have been possible." Gingerly Ross explored the bandage on his head, wincing a little. "This will be sore for a while, and I seem to have used up most of the day's ration of energy, but even so, I'll be happy to tell the *hakim* that your treatment was miraculously effective."

His expression sobered and he reached out to touch the ring suspended around her neck. Sure that he was on the verge of saying something about the future, Juliet pretended not to see the gesture. With a cowardly desire to postpone the inevitable, she slipped out of the bed and said with forced brightness, "You must be hungry. Shall I have breakfast sent in? The melons are wonderful now, particularly after a week of dry desert food. Or there is just about anything else you might want. Except kippers, of course. Or oatmeal, but who would want oatmeal?"

"Juliet," he said gently. "You're babbling."

"I know." She ran a distracted hand through her hair and forced herself to slow down. "Having been away so long, there is much to be done today, particularly since Saleh has also been gone and won't be back for another ten days or so. I have to speak with the farm overseer, and the chief servants, and dozens of other things." All of which was true, but hardly the reason she was so nervous.

He gave her an ironic smile that said he knew exactly what was bothering her. "Then perhaps you had better get to work. For the time being, I'm inclined to take advantage of my invalid status to spend the day as lazily as possible. A few more hours of sleep should give me the energy to go to the hammam, after which I can sleep some more."

"That sounds like an excellent program." She bent over and gave him a swift kiss, then made her escape. But she knew that the hour of reckoning had only been delayed.

Ross spent the day almost as lazily as he had threatened; apart from the visit to the bathhouse, the most active thing he did was seek out his two travel companions. Ian still slept as his ravaged body tried to compensate for all of the punishment it had suffered in the past year.

Murad, however, was in high good spirits. Ross found him sitting in the shade of an arbor in the garden, sipping iced melon sherbet and trying to flirt with a giggling young female servant. On seeing his employer, Murad looked up with a grin. "And so our great adventure ends. Perhaps I will give up the work of a guide and become a storyteller instead, earning my living by spinning tales of the legendary Khilburn."

Ross had to smile. "At least it will be safer work than daring the Turkomans." He sat down and accepted a goblet of the melon sherbet. "I will be leaving for Teheran very soon, I think, perhaps as early as tomorrow. I would be happy to have your guidance there, but it might be better if you stay until your arm has healed."

"I shall return with you," Murad decided. "My arm is not so bad, and I will be glad to see my own home again. But will Lady Khilburn be ready to leave so quickly? Surely she will have much packing to do. At least, my mother would if she were setting off for another land."

Ross sipped his sherbet and watched the garden with unfocused eyes. "I doubt that she'll be going with me. We must . . . discuss the issue, but I think she will choose to stay in Serevan, which has been her home for so many years."

After a confused silence Murad said, "But you seem so . . . together. I thought you would want her to stay with you."

"I do, but I don't think the feeling is mutual."

"But she is your wife!" Murad said, scandalized. "A wife's place is with her husband. You must order her to accompany you."

"Orders won't work, for Lady Khilburn has a mind of her own," Ross said dryly. "Surely you noticed. And our customs grant women a fair amount of choice."

After another, even longer silence, the young Persian said flatly, "I do not understand."

"Neither do I, Murad. Neither do I." Perhaps, Ross thought tiredly, if he did understand Juliet, it would make a difference. But probably not.

*   *   *

The hour of reckoning came that night, after dinner. Juliet had managed to keep busy and out of sight all day. Several times she checked on Ian, but he still slept and she didn't have the heart to wake him.

That evening, she and Ross had dined with Saleh's lively family, which meant there was no private talk between them, but far too soon it was time to retire to bed. She could hardly exile her husband to another bedroom when she wanted his company above all things. No, more than that she wanted the simplicity they had known in Bokhara, when there was only the present, with no past or future.

Without looking at Ross, Juliet changed into an embroidered green silk caftan. Then she perched on the divan and began brushing her hair while she tried to think of a safe, neutral topic. Perhaps, like Scheherazade, she could postpone disaster indefinitely by talking of other subjects that would fend off the discussion she wanted to avoid.

Unfortunately, Ross had too much Western directness. Instead of changing out of the plain brown chapan he was wearing, he sat down next to her and said simply, "Juliet, come back to England with me. We're a dozen years older and wiser now, and you don't seem to dislike my company. Surely we can solve whatever problems you found in our marriage."

She stiffened, the hand holding the brush dropping to her lap. She had mentally rehearsed what she would say to convince Ross that staying together was impossible, hoping that if she were persuasive enough with superficial truths, he would not probe for the deeper truth that she could never admit. "I'm afraid that geographical compatibility is one problem that *is* insoluble," she said with brittle humor. "If you were not your father's heir, you could stay here in Persia. But I know your sense of responsibility too well to believe that you will turn your back on your obligations in England."

Ross leaned back against the cushions and regarded her with eyes that were cool and dangerous. This was not a battle he would yield easily. "You're quite right. My future lies in Britain now. But why is it so unthinkable that you could live there again? You seemed content there once.''

Her hands started to clench, and she forced them to relax. "I'm afraid I would suffocate in England. There were so many social rules, so many ways to make mistakes.''

"You adjusted to that by mastering the rules that interested you and blithely ignoring the ones that didn't," he observed. "More than that, you are a marchioness and in time will become a duchess. To put it baldly, you will be able to do pretty well any damned thing you please. Did I try to censor your behavior that much? You said that my criticisms hurt you, and I was undoubtedly less sensitive than I should have been, but I really don't think I was a tyrant.''

No, he had not been. It was time for another, more painful layer of truth. "The problem was not what you did to me, but what I did to myself." She looked at the hairbrush without seeing it, turning the handle restlessly in her hands. "I loved you so much that I was crippling myself by trying to please you. My sense of who I was, my independence, all of the things you liked about me— I could feel them eroding away. I didn't want to live that way, and I didn't want to become one of those boring, pliable women whom you said you could never love.''

He crossed his arms on his chest and simply looked at her. At length he said, "It's wonderfully flattering to think that you were that madly in love with me. But even if you were concerned about your independence then, I can't believe that will be a problem now. You're a forceful woman, not an unsure girl. Your character isn't going to crumble because some overbred dowager looks down her nose at you.''

She stood and paced across the room, the green silk swishing around her. "You're trying to reduce what I say to simple issues that can be refuted, but it's more complicated than that." She turned to face him. "The question is not whether I can tolerate England—I can— but I like Serevan better. I've built something of value here, helped people who lived in poverty and fear achieve prosperous, happy lives. How can I abandon them?''

He sighed. "I feel the shade of Lady Hester Stanhope hovering over us. I can't fault you for being concerned for your dependents, but you have built a strong, healthy community here—it won't collapse if you leave. Give Serevan to Saleh when he returns from Bokhara. He's as capable of guiding it as you are."

The fact that Ross was right didn't make Juliet's position any easier. Defensively she said, "But I don't *want* to leave Serevan. I have so much freedom here."

"It's the illusory freedom that comes from being a permanent outsider, insulated from the realities of Persian society by money and foreignness," he said, exasperated. "Is that how you want to spend the rest of your life, as a woman who can do what you choose because you're so eccentric that you're dismissed as if you were a force of nature, not a real person?"

She shrugged. "Lady Hester seems to have managed well."

"It is time to destroy some of your romantic illusions." He uncoiled from the divan and stalked over to her. "Yes, Lady Hester Stanhope was a remarkable woman, but she was also a monster of vanity and self-obsession. She settled in Syria not for freedom, but because she loved power and it satisfied her sense of self-importance to become a petty tyrant. You've collected stories about her; did you hear about the time your heroine decided it was her duty to avenge the death of a reckless French explorer? She bullied the local pasha into razing dozens of villages, and for the rest of her life she boasted about what a strong, forceful leader she was. She was *proud* to be responsible for slaughtering hundreds of innocent people!"

Shocked, Juliet stared at him with widened eyes. "Lady Hester wasn't like that! She was a woman of compassion who sheltered refugees from injustice."

Ross's mouth twisted. "I'll grant that sometimes she had compassion for the persecuted, but she was totally without consideration for those who were closest and most loyal to her. The greater the loyalty, the more cruelly she rewarded it. She preferred the admiration of ignorant villagers to the respect and friendship of her equals. She was incapable of living on an income several times the size of yours, so she borrowed huge sums that she didn't repay, then complained bitterly that no one would support her in the style she thought she deserved. At the end, having alienated everyone who ever cared for her, she died alone, dunned by her creditors and robbed by her servants."

Juliet wished she could believe that Ross was lying, but his revelations had a horrible ring of truth. She turned her head, not wanting to hear more, but she could not shut out his hard voice. "Is that what you want for yourself, Juliet? To die alone and loveless, an alien in a foreign land, surrounded by the tattered trappings of power? If so, I wish you joy of it."

"If Lady Hester was as you say, I am not much like her, nor will I end like her." Juliet made a confused gesture with her hand. "Why are we fighting about a woman I never even met?"

Ross's chest expanded as he took a deep breath. Then he said in a quieter voice, "Quite right, I wandered rather far afield. It's time to go back to basics, such as the fact that I love you, and in Bokhara you said that you loved me. Was that true, or were you just being effusive in a moment of passion?"

Juliet felt a rush of dizziness as the emotional ground began disintegrating beneath her feet. She had wanted him to love her; now that she knew he did, everything was infinitely more difficult. "I was speaking the truth," she whispered. "I love you. I never stopped, not for a moment."

He closed his eyes and a tremor crossed his face. Then he opened his eyes again, grim determination carved on every feature. Too late she realized that she had put a dangerous weapon in his hands: now that she had admitted how much she loved him, he would fight even more ruthlessly to change her mind, and she did not know if she could withstand him.

His first volley was as simple as it was unanswerable. "If you loved me, then why did you leave me?"

"I've told you why!" She began pacing again. "Several times, in several ways. Love is beyond price, but it isn't the only thing that matters. If you believed that love was the most important thing on earth, you would stay with me in Serevan rather than go back to England."

"Actually, I do believe that love is the most important thing on earth, though love comes in many forms besides the romantic kind." His eyes narrowed. "I find myself suspicious of your invitation to stay here. Making the offer gives you the chance to seem reasonable and willing to compromise, but at the same time, it's safe because you know I won't accept. I can't help feeling that there are other, deeper reasons why you left."

Juliet regarded her husband with horror. She should have known she could not fool him; not Ross, who understood her better than anyone else ever had. Unsteadily she said, "You're looking for mysteries that aren't there. I've told you the truth."

"Ah, but is it the whole truth? Somehow, I think not." His voice roughened. "God knows I've tried to be fair. I've never threatened you physically or financially. In return, don't you owe me the truth, if nothing else?"

His assault splintered her resolution, and before she could stop herself, she cried, "If I told you the whole truth, you would hate me, and I couldn't bear that!"

He became very still, his face like marble except for the vivid pain in his eyes. "So there is more. Tell me what it is, Juliet, because I can't think of a single damned thing you could reveal that would make me feel worse than I feel right now."

Folding down on the divan, she buried her face in her hands. "Why can't you just accept that our marriage is over?" she said, her voice raw with anguish. "I've said it before and now I'll say it again: divorce me. Then marry a woman who will love you as you deserve. Forget that you ever knew me."

"Do you really think it's that simple?" he said bitterly. "No court can dissolve the bonds that hold us together— years and miles didn't do it before, and they won't do it now."

"You may believe that today," she said wearily, "but when you are back in England, this whole strange interlude will seem like a bad dream. Now that you won't be haunted by questions about how and where I'm living, you can finally be free of me."

He stalked across the room and caught her chin with his hand, forcing her to look at him. "Very well, we can end this right now. I understand that divorce is easy under Islamic law—a man merely tells his wife 'I divorce thee' three times. Of course, it won't be legally binding, but here is your chance. Go ahead, divorce me if you think it is so easy."

When she stared at him in confusion, Ross said savagely, "Say it, Juliet! Repeat 'I divorce thee' three times and I'll go back to England and find some way to make it legal."

When she realized that he was serious, she swallowed hard, then faltered, "I . . . I divorce thee." Then her throat closed.

"Again, Juliet," he prompted, his eyes dark with anger. "Say it two more times and I will accept that our marriage is over."

After licking her dry lips, she tried for the second time. Six more words and she would have done the right thing: set Ross free. "I d-divorce . . ." Her voice broke and she began shaking violently. "I can't," she gasped. "I . . . just can't say it."

"I didn't think you could." He released her chin and spun away, saying with barely suppressed violence, "If you can't bring yourself to end our marriage, don't expect me to do it for you."

She had always thought his inner strength limitless, but her weaknesses had pushed him to his limits, and with agonizing clarity she saw just how much she was hurting him. "Very well, you've demonstrated how wrong I was to think that divorce was a realistic solution," she said unevenly. "But if we can't end our marriage, then let us at least separate peacefully."

"I find myself feeling curiously unpeaceful." He swung back to face her again. "You talk as if our marriage concerns only us, but have you considered the chance that you might be pregnant? It's certainly possible, considering that we've been going at each other like hares in heat. The subject was briefly touched on in Bokhara, when I thought it highly likely I would die, but now that I have survived, I find myself with a more personal interest in the outcome. If we have a child, will you raise it here, thousands of miles from its heritage? Will I have any say in its future?"

She had not expected this, and she began shaking her head, not in answer to his questions, but as an involuntary sign of her inability to deal with them.

There was a taut silence. Then Ross exploded, more angry than she had ever seen him. "I see. I suppose that you're saying that you know this won't be an issue. How naive of me—even if you have been unlucky enough to fall victim to biology, there are ways of taking care of that, and I'm sure you know what they are." He spun away and stalked toward the door. "If you find yourself inconveniently pregnant and decide to end it, don't tell me. I don't want to know."

Finally Juliet broke, for it seemed as if this whole agonizing struggle had been leading to this moment, when she knew beyond any shadow of doubt that she had been right to believe that their marriage was beyond redemption. "Don't act like this, Ross," she begged, the words wrenched from her heart. "You're making everything a thousand times worse." Then she broke down entirely. Beyond speech, she sank onto her knees and buried her head between her arms on the divan, weeping uncontrollably.

"Damnation!" Ross swore, his voice fractured and helpless. Then he was beside her, crushing her in his arms and rocking her back and forth as if she were a child. "I'm sorry, Juliet," he said in an anguished whisper. "So sorry. I don't want to hurt you, but I find this whole bloody situation incomprehensible and it makes me want to take the world apart with my bare hands. Since I love you and you love me, I just don't understand why we can't be together."

In a cold part of her mind that was distant from the shattered woman sobbing in Ross's arms, Juliet saw that there was an advantage in this, for she could use his guilt to stop his search for the elusive, disastrous truth. She was not proud of herself for using the knowledge, but as soon as she was able to speak coherently, she did so. "We must stop tearing each other apart, Ross."

She sat back on her heels so she could see his face. "Accept that this is the way it must be so that we can separate in peace rather than bitterness." Tentatively she reached out and took his hand. "Come to bed, where we can heal some of the wounds we've made on each other tonight. Stay here a little longer at Serevan, until the intensity of the last two months has had a chance to fade. Then you can go without hurting so."

"You don't ask much, do you?" Tiredly he touched the bandage on his head, as if it was paining him. "I don't expect being in love with you to fade—it hasn't in a dozen years, in spite of everything. And while I agree that it would be wiser to negotiate a settlement rather than clawing each other to shreds, I am quite incapable of making love to you knowing that it is the last time. It was hard enough this morning, when I still had a little hope, but now it would be impossible." He smiled without humor. "Apparently my sense of self-preservation is still working. While I've done my share of difficult and dangerous things, I'm not fool enough to let you cut my heart to shreds, then stamp on the pieces."

A chill wave swept through Juliet and she began shivering. So finally the end had come.

Ross stood, then tugged her to her feet with the hand he still held. Raising her fingers to his lips, he kissed them once, very tenderly, then released them. "I'll sleep in the room I stayed in on my first visit. Tomorrow, if you'll give me an escort, I'll leave for Teheran. The sooner this is over, the better for both of us."

She bit her lip to keep from crying out, but nodded assent.

Ross turned and walked across the room, his footsteps inaudible on the thick carpet. She watched his retreating back, memorizing every detail. His height and smooth, controlled stride; the way the brown chapan swung from his wide shoulders; the crisp gold waves of his hair, which needed cutting and almost brushed the top of his shoulders.

He opened the door, stepped through without looking back, then pulled it shut behind him.

It was over.

27

🍎

Juliet was not sure how long she sat on the divan staring sightlessly across the room. Knowing that she deserved everything he had said and more didn't make the agony any easier to endure. Strange how many kinds of misery could exist side by side, each separate and distinct. Stranger yet was that in the midst of so many deeper pains, there was still room to feel a very personal kind of humiliation over his refusal to spend the night with her.

The very walls seemed to radiate the anguish of what had happened in the last hour, and suddenly Juliet felt that she would suffocate if she stayed in the room an instant longer. After slipping on a pair of sandals, she went outside and crossed the wide courtyard, then climbed to the top of the massive wall that surrounded the fortress. Like a medieval European castle, the wall was wide enough for several people to walk abreast, and there was a parapet to protect defenders.

It was late, and most of Serevan slept, except for the handful of guards in the watchtowers. Juliet began walking along the wall, distantly grateful for the cooling breeze and the sense of openness. It was a beautiful scene, the light of a waxing moon silvering the rugged hills, but dramatic scenery was no antidote for a dark night of the soul.

From the western side of the fortress she could see the hills drop down toward the Kara Kum, whose sands then rolled off to Bokhara. Dully she turned away, not wanting to think of all that had happened since the last time she had paced these walls.

As she began walking again, she saw that someone else was out prowling the night. When she first saw the tall bareheaded figure leaning against the parapet, her heart gave a lurch of fear that it might be Ross. Then the man heard her footsteps and glanced in her direction, and she saw that it was Ian.

In the week since his rescue from the Black Well, they had scarcely talked at all, and not just because the arduous desert journey had not been conducive to casual conversation. Her brother's imprisonment seemed to have changed him in some fundamental way; he had turned inward so much that it was difficult to remember the exuberance that had once been his most notable characteristic. Considering what he had endured, such change was not surprising, but now he was almost a stranger and she was unsure how to talk to him.

The last thing she wanted was company, but since he had seen her, she couldn't turn away. With some reluctance she went to join him, hoping that the darkness would conceal the marks of distress on her face. However, the moonlight was bright enough to show that her brother looked much better: relaxed, shaved, and with his hair trimmed to European length. "Quite an improvement," she remarked.

"Amazing what solid sleep, a good meal, and a visit to the bathhouse will do for one's mind and body," he said as he turned to face her.

She gestured at his right eye, which was now covered by a neat black patch. "Very dashing."

"I don't know about that, but at least I won't frighten any small children." Absently he fingered the eyepatch. "This happened when the amir's men tried to beat a confession of espionage out of me. The other eye was injured at the same time, but it healed without permanent damage."

"Thank God for that," she said fervently. "You were lucky."

"So I was. Losing the sight in one eye is a nuisance, but losing both would be a disaster." He turned back to the wall and gazed out toward the desert. "In a fortnight or so, I should be ready to go down to the Persian Gulf and take ship back to India."

Juliet frowned, not wanting him to go before they had a chance to make up for some of the lost years. "There's no need to rush—you can stay as long as you like." She poked his ribs with a gentle forefinger. "I'd like to fatten you up. Also, Mother is waiting in Constantinople for Ross to return—she swore that she wouldn't go home until he came back safely. At this season, it would take only a few weeks for you to go there, and she would be ecstatic to see you. Your survival will confirm her maternal intuition that you hadn't died."

"For once, her instincts were right." Ian smiled a little, the pale moonlight illuminating his thin face. "I'd like to see her, but I can't take that much time. Remember, I'm an army officer and must return to duty and report on what happened. Besides, I have . . . other obligations in India."

"I'm sorry, I forgot that Ross said you were engaged. Tell me what your fiancée is like."

"Georgina?" He hesitated. "Beautiful and charming. Blond hair and blue eyes. Her father's a colonel, so she'll make a wonderful army wife. She always knows exactly what to say and do." After another pause he added, "She was the most sought-after girl in northern India."

Depressingly, her future sister-in-law sounded like the sort of female who would disapprove of Juliet. "Will Georgina and I like each other?"

"Well, I don't think you will *dis*like each other." Ian shook his head, then braced taut hands on the top of the stone wall as he said with sudden frustration, "Every day in that damned hellhole I thought of Georgina. She became a symbol of everything clean and sane and whole—of everything I was afraid that I would never feel again. Yet in my mind, her face is a blur—I can't even remember what she looks like."

"That's hardly surprising, considering that almost two years have passed since you saw her," Juliet said soothingly. "India must seem distant and dreamlike now, but when you return to your old life, everything will fall into place."

"I don't know if I can return to my old life," he said, his voice low and bleak. "Everything I believed in has been broken, and I don't know if the pieces will go back together again."

Her brother's despairing words made Juliet feel closer to him than at any time since they had met in Bokhara, for in their sorrow they were truly kin. She laid her hand on top of his where it rested on the cool stone. "Give it time, Ian," she said softly. "You've been free for only a week. And after all you've been through, it won't be surprising if the emotional damage takes longer to heal than the physical."

She had wanted to comfort him, but to her horror, her words undermined her own frail self-control. As grief surged through her, she bent her head in a vain attempt to hide her tears.

Distracted from his own misery, Ian said with concern, "What's wrong, Juliet? Something to do with Ross?"

"He's leaving for England tomorrow. I don't suppose we'll ever see each other again." She wiped her eyes with the sleeve of her silk caftan, then said helplessly, "Oh, Ian, I've made such a mess of things. A dozen years ago I left Ross in a fit of temporary insanity, then compounded my mistakes until they were unforgivable. Now it's too late."

"Ross won't take you back?" Ian said, surprised. "I've always thought he was one of the most understanding men I've ever known, and he certainly seems to love you still."

She shook her head. "He wants me to go with him, but I can't. He doesn't know what really happened, and I can't bear to tell him." Her voice broke. "I'm hurting him terribly, but telling him the truth would hurt him even more." For a moment, her husband's words repeated themselves in her mind: *I can't think of a single damned thing you could reveal that would make me feel worse that I feel right now.*

The problem was, Juliet knew better than that.

"What happened?" Ian asked gently. "Is it something that you could tell a brother, if not a husband?"

Juliet considered pouring out the whole sordid tale, but her stomach curdled at the thought. "No," she whispered. "I can't tell anyone. I just can't."

"Try," Ian said crisply. "If you have a secret that affects Ross, it's selfish to keep it to yourself. Let him make up his own mind." His voice softened. "More than that, happiness is a fragile commodity, easily lost and not easily regained. Don't throw it away because you did something stupid a dozen years ago." His arm went around her shoulders. "When you wrote and told me you were getting married so young, I thought you were insane," he said reminiscently. "Then I came for the wedding and met Ross, and decided *he* was insane for wanting to marry a hellcat like my little sister."

Hurt, Juliet tried to pull away, but her brother's arm tightened around her. "Show the head of your family some respect, vixen," he ordered, a trace of humor in his voice. "The fact is, you two are uniquely suited to each other. It was true when you married and it's even more true now. Don't let something so precious be destroyed without trying your damnedest to save it."

No longer able to control herself, Juliet began to cry, deep, painful sobs that racked her entire body. Her brother's other arm came around her, warm and reassuring. In spite of his thinness, he had the tenacious strength of steel wire.

Ian held her until her tears had abated. Then he murmured, "When we were childen, I thought you were the bravest person in the world, and it pushed me to the limits of my courage to keep up with you. Use that bravery now. Don't let fear prevent you from telling Ross the truth. He may well surprise you."

Juliet made a noise that was somewhere between a laugh and a hiccup. "You thought I was brave? When I followed you on your escapades, I was usually terrified but didn't dare admit it for fear you'd be disgusted and never let me go with you again."

"Really? Then it's a miracle we didn't get killed while trying to prove our fearlessness to each other." He brushed a tear from her cheek with the back of his knuckles. "Go and be brave, Juliet. Cowardice costs more and hurts worse."

She closed her eyes and laid her head against Ian's shoulder, hoping that some of his tempered strength would flow into her. Telling Ross what had happened was not what would take the most courage, though God knew that confession would be excruciatingly difficult.

Yet tell him she must. Because the subject was so painful that she was incapable of reason, she had never, until Ian had pointed it out, seen how selfish her secretiveness was. She had not wanted to have Ross hate her, yet hatred was the one thing that might persuade him to end their marriage.

As he had said, she owed him the truth, and in a very real sense the truth would set him free. Not her; she was imprisoned in a cage of her own forging, but for Ross's sake she must find the strength to reveal all that had happened in Malta. Not only would it free him, but it would also reduce his anguish, for he would no longer grieve so much for what might have been.

It would be a strange gift of love, but it was the greatest one within Juliet's power, and it would be the ultimate test of her courage. Opening her eyes, she said unevenly, "Very well, Ian, once more you've shamed me into pretending that I'm braver than I really am. I'll do what I should have done long since."

"Good girl. I always knew you could do anything."

"Fooled you again," she said with a watery chuckle. Then, with a surge of tenderness, she exclaimed, "I'm so glad you're alive, Ian."

"So am I." He hugged her shoulders. "Amidst all the high drama of escaping from Bokhara, I never said a proper thank-you, but believe me, I am intensely grateful for what you and Ross did, and Mother too. I'm lucky to have such a family."

More words were not needed, for the silence was warm with the closeness Juliet had feared was gone forever. For that, if for nothing else on this dreadful night, she was profoundly glad.

Knowing that her resolution would not last long, Juliet went to her bedroom only long enough to comb her hair, splash cold water on her face, and fortify herself with several handkerchiefs—large businesslike ones, not the frilly decorative kind. Then she took an oil lamp and made her way through the dark passages to Ross's room.

The door was unlocked, so she entered and hung the lamp on a hook, then went to the bed and looked down on her husband. Even in sleep, his face looked strained.

When she touched his shoulder, his eyes opened instantly and his whole body went rigid, but he did not move. After a long moment of mutual study he said, "I sincerely hope that this is not a misguided attempt to seduce me into temporary compliance."

Ross wasn't going to make this easy for her. "No such thing. I'm here because I decided that you were right, I do owe you the truth, no matter how painful it is." Her voice wavered. "Just don't say later that I didn't warn you."

"Then what happens?" He pushed himself up in the bed, the rumpled sheet falling about his bare waist. The honey-toned lamplight delineated him with heart-stopping clarity: the broad shoulders, the hard muscles, the gilded hair where a narrow bandage covered the wound he had received the day before. That and the ugly blue-black bruises he had suffered in his fall were all that kept him from appearing inhumanly perfect.

Wrenching her gaze away, she said, "That's up to you." She began to pace fretfully across the room, keeping to the shadowed end. "I'd better say this quickly, before I lose my courage."

"Go ahead." His voice was very low, as if he feared that a hard word would make her take flight.

Hands clenching and unclenching, she said, "What I said about being afraid of losing myself if I stayed in England was true. Sometimes I feared that I would be engulfed by you, would vanish entirely—not because of anything you did but because of my own weakness. Growing up, I had to struggle constantly against my father to be myself. I managed, but nothing prepared me for marrying you—for being so much in love that, if you'd asked for my soul, I would have given it to you in an instant. Still, in time I think I would have gotten strong enough to be both your wife and myself.

"Then something happened that made my fear so overwhelming that I felt I had to run away. I discovered . . ." She stopped walking and swallowed hard, finding it almost impossible to say what she had never before spoken aloud. "I discovered that I was pregnant."

She risked a glance at Ross and saw that he was staring at her as if she was a stranger, his face like stone. In a spurt of words she continued, "I didn't really feel old enough to be a wife, but I married you because I was too much in love not to. The knowledge that I was soon to become a mother terrified me. Much later, I came to understand that part of the problem was fear that I would become like my own mother. I think she had spirit once, but having four children and being utterly dependent on her husband crushed it. Her life revolved around placating a difficult bully. I swore I would never be like her."

"Did you think I was a bully like your father?" he asked, his voice dangerously controlled.

She made a sharp gesture of negation with one hand. "No, of course not, but you would have gone in the other direction and become too considerate, too protective. If you'd known I was pregnant, you would have wrapped me in cotton wool. Would you have taken me on the adventurous trip to the Middle East we had been planning?"

"I don't know. Certainly I would have been concerned for your welfare." The hand resting on his knee clenched. "You were right. I would not have wanted you to take unnecessary risks."

She felt distant satisfaction when he confirmed what she had suspected, but hastened to add, "That was only part of the problem—most of my fear was blindly irrational."

She began pacing again, searching for words that could explain the inexplicable. "I had a . . . a sense of doom, a conviction that staying with you would destroy both of us; I would become a woman that I despised and you could not love, and only duty would keep you with me. Yet I couldn't talk about my fears, because pregnancy is supposed to be an occasion for joy—I was sure that no one would understand, that there was something horribly wrong with me for feeling as I did.

"I felt trapped in an impossible situation. When you left for a few days to visit your ailing godfather, I found myself taking wild risks when I went riding, secretly hoping for an accident that might solve the problem. That's when I knew that I had to get away, before something terrible happened, and before my pregnancy was so advanced that you would notice. I bolted on sheer impulse and took ship for Malta, which my family had visited once and I remembered fondly."

Her head was throbbing and she raised one hand to her temple, knowing that the dull pain was because she was coming to the worst part. "By the time I reached Malta, I knew I had made a terrible mistake, but I was also sure that I had burned my bridges too thoroughly to ever go back. In my logical madness I knew that you might want the baby for dynastic reasons, or at least because you would feel responsible for it, but you certainly would never forgive a wife who had subjected you to such public humiliation."

Briefly she closed her eyes, remembering. "If I had known you were coming after me—if you had arrived even a few hours earlier, everything would have been different," she said despairingly. "But 'ifs' aren't worth the powder it would take to blow them to hell."

She drew a shuddering breath. "I still don't understand why I did what I did. Certainly there was no point where I made a deliberate choice to betray you. But I was eighteen and a fool, desperately lonely and sure that I was already ruined. The Comte d'Auxerre was amusing and flattering and looked a little like you." She swallowed hard. "I thought that just for one night, he might keep the loneliness at bay, so when he asked to come to my room, I . . . I let him."

His voice edged like broken glass, Ross said, "For God's sake, Juliet, don't tell me any more about this."

"Please, bear with me," she begged. "You need to know to understand what happened later." Her face twisted with bitter regret. "It's hard to believe how naive I was. Girls are warned never to be alone with men because a male touch will rouse us to helplessly wanton behavior, and I more or less believed that, because when *you* touched me I definitely lost all sense and control. Oh, I knew better than to think lying with another man would be the same, but I did think that for a few hours I might forget my misery."

Her restless pacing had brought her to the wall, and she stopped, staring blindly at the rough plaster. "I was so wrong," she said wretchedly. "I soon realized that I had made another horrible mistake, but . . . I felt that I couldn't draw back, not after I had agreed. I loathed every moment of it, not because of anything he did—it was just that he wasn't you. I felt like a whore—I despised him, and even more I despised myself. I was too ashamed to admit how I felt, so I pretended that nothing was wrong, but I made him leave as soon as I could."

Juliet turned to look at Ross, her gray eyes as dark and frantic as twisting smoke. "That was the only time I ever broke my marriage vows, Ross. I hated what I had done so much that I could never bear to let another man touch me. The rumors that trickled back to England were just that—rumors. I suppose they were inspired by the fact that I was young and wild and heedless, but I swear there were never any other men after that night."

Ross could no longer endure lying still, so he rose from the bed and jerked on his chapan, as if the garment could protect him from the dark emotions swirling through the room. He did not approach Juliet; he did not dare. It was bitterly ironic to learn that if he had reached the Hotel Bianca earlier, his wife would have welcomed him with open arms.

Instead, they had come within the width of a single door of each other, but because he was too late, they had both been utterly desolate, and utterly incapable of comforting each other. It was a bleak picture, but he steeled himself for worse to come. Tightly he said, "What happened then?"

Juliet spun away, her movements brittle and graceless. "I felt filthy, defiled . . . as violated as if I had been raped, but in a way this was worse because I was responsible. No one made me do what I did—it was my mistake from beginning to end. More than anything on earth, I wanted to die." Her voice dropped to a hoarse whisper. "So at dawn the next day I rode outside Valletta to a lonely cove, stripped down to my shift, and I . . . walked into the water."

Ross watched her with rising horror, the image of the desperate girl she had been as sharp as the reality of her now. Never, even at his most anguished, had he thought of taking his own life, and he could only dimly imagine what kind of distress had driven Juliet to want to kill herself. Reminding himself that she hadn't succeeded, he asked, "Who or what saved you?"

"The fact that I was too much of a coward," she said with sharp self-disgust. "I swam until I was too tired to lift my arms, then just relaxed and prayed for oblivion so I would feel nothing more. But I found out that it isn't true that drowning is a gentle death. My mouth filled with water, my lungs burned, and I panicked, so terrified that I had the strength to start swimming again.

"Even so, I should have died because I was so far from the shore, but a squall blew up. The way the storm pounded, I thought I really was drowning—I remember it in horrible detail, right up until the moment I lost consciousness. By then, I must have been very close to the shore, because I learned later that the waves washed me up safely near a fisherman's cottage. He and his wife took me in, naked and bleeding."

Juliet turned toward him, her face stark as death. "There, at their cottage, I miscarried. I killed our child, Ross." Silent tears ran down her cheeks. "You wanted to know the worst, and there it is. *I tried to kill myself, and instead I murdered our child.*"

She had warned him, but even so, the savage, visceral shock of her story was greater than anything he could have imagined. He felt as if an iron band was tightening around his chest, crushing his heart and soul. Blindly he turned to the window and threw open the shutters as his tortured lungs struggled for air. Then he stared into the empty night, so saturated with pain that he could not separate his own from Juliet's.

So they had once made a baby together. The child would be almost twelve now, but would it have been a son or a daughter? Red-haired or blond or some unexpected variation? He tried to bring an image into focus, but he couldn't. Instead, his mind unexpectedly dredged up a half-forgotten memory.

Ross was the only child his mother had ever carried to term, and when he was grown, she told him that she had miscarried three times after his own birth. Because of her vivacity, his mother had been called "the laughing duchess," while her quieter twin sister, Sara's mother, was termed "the smiling duchess." But once, when Ross was about four years old, he had found his mother curled in the corner of the great hall of the Norfolk mansion, weeping hysterically, her beautiful face slashed by her clawing nails. Terrified, he had run to find help for her.

It had been hours before his father had been able to leave his wife long enough to look for his son, who was hiding in a corner of the attic too small for an adult to enter. The duke had coaxed Ross out onto his lap. Then, his own face marked with grief, he had explained that Ross's parents had wanted another child to love as much as him, but it was not to be, and his mother was mourning the baby that would never be born.

It was a long time before the duchess was her normal self again, and there were no more pregnancies; Ross suspected that his father took steps to ensure that his wife would not endure such emotional and physical punishment again. But Ross had not forgotten his parents' pain, and now, a dozen years late and in a far country, he mourned his own lost child.

Yet that sorrow was only one among many, a distant ache, not quite real. There was far more immediacy in Juliet's wrenching account of all that had happened in Malta. Like a kaleidoscope that had been twisted, the past had just taken on an entirely different pattern.

Now that he knew the whole, he could believe her claim that she had never stopped loving him, for it was clear that what had kept them apart was not lack of love but her soul-destroying guilt. If the circumstances had been reversed, he might have felt as unworthy and self-destructive as she had; understanding that made it impossible to condemn her.

The wind caressed his face like a cool hand, and he realized that his cheeks were moist. There was a fitting symmetry to the tears, for he had not cried since that night in Malta, when he had wept for the loss of his beloved wife. Then his tears had been for himself, but this time most of his grief was for Juliet, and for the knowledge of how different things might have been.

It was a mark of Juliet's fierce sense of honor that she

took full responsibility for what had happened, rather than trying to blame anyone else. Yet she had been scarcely more than a child herself, so confused and tormented that she had tried to take her own life. Then, too vital to seek death again, but convinced that she had sinned past redemption, she had turned her back on all she had ever known and run to the edge of the world, where she had turned all her personal and financial resources to helping others.

Ross raised his hand to his head, where the bullet wound was throbbing under the bandage, beating like the king's drums of Bokhara. Inside he felt hollow, not like a drum, but with a strange blankness that he could not define.

Slowly he realized that it was the emptiness of deliverance, not loss. For years the legacy of his marriage had been pain and guilt and anger. The pain was a bone-deep part of what had shaped him, but now that he knew Juliet had not left because of some dreadful failing on his part, his guilt dissolved. And, infinitely more important, he realized that his anger was gone as well.

In Malta, when he had learned that his wife had betrayed their love and her marriage vows, his fury had equaled his anguish. Though with time his agony ebbed until it was a chronic ache rather than a raging insanity, for over a dozen years he had lived with anger, even when he and Juliet had been at their closest in Bokhara.

But now that he knew the truth, anger was replaced by compassion for a desperate, terrified girl.

He turned back to the room. Juliet was curled up in a shadowed corner of the divan, her head bowed forward and her copper-bright hair rippling over her drawn-up knees like a mourning veil. His wife, whose warmth and courage and quixotic gallantry made her unlike any other woman he had ever known. If she had had a simpler nature or less unflinching Scots integrity, their marriage would have been easy—yet if she had been anything other than what she was, he would not love her as much as he did.

As he gazed at Juliet, his emotional turbulence began ebbing away, leaving grief-scoured clarity in its wake. It was another irony that he had thought she had chosen

to become a wanton, yet she had lived more chastely
than he, and God knew that he hadn't lived a very rakish
life. Apparently nature had intended them both for monogamy. Passionate monogamy with each other.

A jury of moralists would judge Ross more sinned
against than sinning, but he had no interest in assigning
blame. Nothing could be done about past mistakes except to try to learn from them; what mattered now was
the future, and he saw quite clearly that if anything positive was to be salvaged from the wreck of the past, the
initiative must come from him. Since Juliet condemned
herself too severely to think she was worthy of happiness,
he must find a way to bridge the distance between them.

He took a deep breath, then crossed the room and sat
down next to her. "I know the worst now, Juliet. You
were right that the truth hurts, but wrong that I would
hate you. I still love you, and I still want to spend the
rest of my life with you."

She raised her head to reveal a face ravaged by tears.
"Ross, I betrayed you unforgivably, in every way a
woman can betray a man. How can you possibly want to
live with me again?"

"The most unforgivable thing you did was to leave me,
and that can be corrected." He literally pried her fingers
free from where they were clenched around her knees,
then took one cold hand between both of his. "It isn't
my forgiveness that you need, Juliet. It's your own."

Her mouth twisted. "You said that I was like Lady
Hester Stanhope, and it's true, for the people who most
deserved my love and loyalty are the ones I hurt most.
You, my family, the child I might have had if not for my
own wicked mistakes."

He shook his head. "I was wrong, for you are not like
Lady Hester in the ways that count most. You have her
courage, but where she was arrogant, you are loving.
You judge yourself far too harshly, for your errors were
those of youth and confusion, not malice or pettiness."

Her expression showed that she was unconvinced, so
he said in a conversational tone, "My outspoken mother
always did her best to educate me about women, for she
believed men and women should understand each other
better. Once she told me that the early months of preg-

nancy can bring wild, unpredictable mood swings; surely that had something to do with the irrational panic you felt when you discovered you were with child."

He began chafing Juliet's hand between his, trying to restore warmth to her chilled fingers. "Perhaps you would have had the miscarriage even if you had stayed home—many pregnancies end in the first two or three months. In fact, if the pregnancy was going badly, it might have affected how you were feeling. That happened to the wife of a friend of mine. She ran away too, but being much less adventurous than you, she only made it as far as her mother's house, where she miscarried in more comfort than you did. She's had two children since, without problems."

There was a long silence before Juliet said wearily, "If that was also true of me, it would explain a great deal, but nothing can really absolve me of responsibility for my actions. I showed every variety of bad judgment."

"If one can't show bad judgment at eighteen, when can one do it?" He opened her hand and began tracing the lines of the palm. "Being right is all very well, but it is through our errors that we grow. You made mistakes, but you have also punished yourself greatly for them. Don't you think you've suffered enough?"

"But you suffered as much or more for my mistakes," Juliet said sorrowfully. "How can I ever make that up to you?"

He smiled a little. "That's easy—the way to make amends is by being my wife, not by condemning me to a lifetime of loneliness."

Her fingers curled around his. A little desperately, she said, "I don't understand how you can still want me."

For a baffled moment he wondered what more he could do, for he had already said as clearly as possible that he loved and wanted her. Then he thought of the storytellers he had heard through the East, who knew how to multiply the power of words. It was worth a try. "Let me tell you a fairy tale."

She gave him a puzzled glance, so he tugged on her hand. After momentary resistance she allowed herself to be extricated from her corner. When she was seated on the cushions beside him, he began, "Long ago, in a far green country, there was a young man called Ross. Although he was reliable, serious, intelligent, and honorable, he was not very interesting." Ross thought a moment. "Probably all of those boring virtues are the reasons he was dull."

Juliet opened her mouth to protest, but he said firmly, "Silence. This is my fairy tale and I get to tell it my way."

In a lilting voice he continued, "The fellow had romantic dreams about visiting distant lands and having adventures, but being sober, more of an observer than a doer, and, as I said, more than a little dull, he might never have tried to make his dreams come true.

"He wasn't a prince, not even a lord except by courtesy title, but one day he did meet a princess named Juliet. Not only was she the most beautiful girl in the world, but she actually had lived in foreign lands and had had adventures, not just dreamed about them. When he was with her, everything seemed possible, the sun shone more brightly, and she made him laugh. With her he was immersed in life, not just an observer, for she brought out a passionate side of his nature that he had not known he possessed. Not just passion of the body, but of the spirit."

Ross raised her hand and kissed the palm, pressing his lips against the heart line. "He hadn't known what he was missing until he met her. Being no fool and quite madly in love, our hero persuaded his very young princess to marry him before she had time to have second thoughts. At first he was sure that, as in all fairy tales, they would live happily ever after.

"But any story worth telling needs conflict, and this conflict began when a dragon of dubious nature carried off the princess. Or perhaps she ran away with the dragon voluntarily—that part of the story is a little unclear and not really important. What did matter is that when she left, she took the sunshine away, and all the laughter died."

Ross could feel Juliet shrinking away from him, so he put his arm around her shoulders to keep her near. "Don't worry, the story isn't over. For the next dozen years, our hero did proper heroic things. He visited exotic lands, had adventures, saw wonderful sights, and met fascinating people. Sometimes he went home and wrote books and gave a few lectures and was told what a fine, brave fellow he was. Sometimes—not very often— he met another lady he liked, but he never found one who could make him forget his lost princess, or who could touch his deepest emotions. It was quite a decent life, for he achieved many of his dreams, and somewhere along the way he became much more interesting. But he never achieved the deepest, most secret dream of all, which was to find his long-lost princess.

"Then, just before his traveling days were done, he went on one last quest. And when he did, he found Juliet again and learned that she was not just the most beautiful woman in the world, but also the bravest. Occasionally he wanted to turn her over his knee and paddle her lovely derriere. More often he wanted to make love to her. And when he finally did so, he realized that he loved her as much as he had when he was twenty-one."

Ross turned on the divan so that he was facing Juliet. Her body was less taut now, and when he pulled her closer, she slid her arm around his waist and let her head rest against his shoulder. Softly he continued, "His princess felt that she had betrayed him, but he knew that he could trust her with his life, and he did. Together they were able to achieve the impossible. She even saved his life by slaying a very ugly monster, which was not a very ladylike thing to do, but vastly useful."

He began stroking her hair, letting the bright spun-silk strands drift between his fingers. "By the time the quest had ended, our hero loved his princess more than ever, and he knew that if he couldn't persuade her to come home, he would never have sunshine, or laughter, or passion again."

No longer a storyteller, Ross whispered, "Believe that I love you, Juliet. Then let us begin a life together again."

She caught his hand and held it against her cheek, not looking in his eyes. "It's strange," she said, her voice haunted. "More than anything on earth, I want to please you. I used to have fantasies that I would sacrifice my life for yours, and just before I died, you would forgive me. But while it would be easy to suffer for your sake, it is hard, so hard, to do something that will make me happy when I don't deserve it."

"If you want to please me, you have no choice but to be happy yourself, for when you are miserable, so am I." Ross's fingers tightened around hers. "Separately, we are two restless, lonely people, but together we can make each other whole. There has been enough pain, my love. It's time for joy."

Juliet felt as if her heart was breaking. She did not deserve such love and loyalty, yet Ross was right. They were bound together for life; nothing in the past had severed that bond, and she knew intuitively that nothing in the future would either. Ross had also been right to say that it was not his forgiveness that she needed, but her own.

It was time to forgive herself, for both their sakes.

She inhaled deeply, than raised her head and looked into his dark eyes. "I often wondered why I didn't die in Malta. Perhaps . . . perhaps it was to give me a chance to make everything up to you." Forcing her tears to remain unshed, she gave her husband a tremulous smile. "If you're sure you need me to be happy, I love you too much to say no."

There was a still moment when nothing more was said because nothing needed to be. Then Ross reached out and opened Juliet's silk caftan to find the ring suspended around her throat. Taking the chain in his hands, he broke it with one quick movement, the links biting into his palms, then took the ring and dropped the chain on the divan.

Slipping the gold band onto the first knuckle of her third finger, left hand, he caught her gaze with his and said solemnly, "I, Ross, take thee, Juliet, to be my wedded wife, to have and to hold from this day forward, for better, for worse, for richer, for poorer, in sickness and in health, to love, honor, and cherish, forsaking all others, till death do us part." Sliding the ring all the way onto her finger, he finished, "With this ring I thee rewed." Then he raised her hand and pressed his lips to her taut fingers.

The tears she had tried to suppress began slipping

down Juliet's cheeks as she lifted his left hand and clasped it tightly against her heart. Phrase by phrase, she repeated the vows, then finished, "Whither thou goest, I shall go, beloved husband, for I am yours, body, mind, and soul." Leaning forward, she kissed him, her touch both thanks and promise.

As breath and heartbeats quickened, Ross swept Juliet into his arms and carried her to his bed, and there they reconsecrated their marriage. For the first time since they had met again, there were no shadows or unanswered questions between them; the worst had been revealed and it had not destroyed their marriage, but made it stronger. They made love with passion and tenderness and a depth of tempered emotion more profound than anything their youthful selves had been capable of.

Afterward they lay in each other's arms and talked of a future that was no longer forbidden ground. Finally their voices slowed, but before they drifted into sleep, Juliet dared to ask a question that would have been unthinkable before. "If I had learned that you were in Malta and gone to you instead of the sea," she said hesitantly, "would you ever have been able to forgive my unfaithfulness?"

His brows drew together as he gave her question serious thought. "I would have taken you back because I loved you, and because you were my wife," he said slowly. "And I think we could have been happy again, but I would never have forgotten, and what you had done would have always been between us, like an indelible stain. But I feel as if we have spent the last four months forged by fires that have burned away everything unessential. Malta seems so distant, so unimportant, that forgiveness is not even an issue, because what we have endured has melded us together so closely that there is no room for shadows. For me, the past truly does not matter. What does matter is now, and that we love each other."

Content, Juliet rested her head on his shoulder and prepared to sleep in his arms. In a voice meant more for herself than Ross she whispered, "Now and forever, amen."

Epilogue

❦

Southhampton Harbor
October 1841

As porters carried their luggage from the stateroom, Juliet lay back against the sofa pillows and watched dreamily. She had done quite a lot of that lately, as she and Ross had slipped seamlessly into a marriage that combined the comfort of long acquaintance with the passion and wonder of first love.

It had taken a month to wind up her affairs at Serevan, though they had sent an immediate message to Lady Cameron in Constantinople, to end her uncertainty. As Ross had suggested, Juliet transferred ownership of the fortress to Saleh. They left Serevan the same day as Ian, she and Ross heading west and her brother, still thin but now tanned and fit, going south to the Persian Gulf.

The journey to Constantinople had been a leisurely one. In Meshed they called on Reza to assure themselves that he was well. His grateful family's hospitality was so pressing that they could have spent the rest of their lives if they had wished to. In Teheran they said farewell to Murad, leaving him with such a large bonus that he was, very briefly, speechless.

In Constantinople Juliet had had an emotional reunion with her mother, who was more than a little smug over the accuracy of her maternal instinct; not only had she been right about Ian, but her long-held belief that Juliet and Ross belonged together had been spectacularly confirmed. Her vigil over, Lady Cameron traveled with her daughter and son-in-law the length of the Mediterranean, leaving them in Gibraltar when she decided to spend a sunny winter with friends.

And now, finally, they were back in England. Juliet's musings were interrupted when Ross returned to the stateroom and perched on the edge of the sofa. "Ready to go ashore?"

"Yes, but I'm going to miss making love on the water. There's something very nice about the way the ship rolls."

He chuckled. "Remember the little river at Chapelgate? If you miss the water, we can put blankets on the floor of a punt."

"Sounds worth trying." Juliet gazed at him in admiration. "You really are the handsomest man in the world, all cool English elegance." Then the curve of her mouth became wicked. "Who would believe what a splendid *bozkashi* barbarian you were?"

"I will remind you what a barbarian I can be tonight." He laid a gentle hand on her stomach, getting a kick in return. "Hmm, the heir is restless today."

Juliet laid her hand over his. "He knows he's coming home."

"If it is a he, think of how much he will impress the other schoolboys when he tells them he was conceived in Bokhara." Ross stood and took her hand to help her up. "Time to go. I'm looking forward to getting home to Chapelgate. Tomorrow we can call on Sara and Mikahl and meet my new goddaughter."

Juliet was glad to have his help in rising, since she was not as nimble as usual. She had been slow to realize that she was pregnant, because she had felt wonderful, entirely different from the first time. Perhaps Ross's speculation was correct and there had been a physical problem before, or perhaps the difference was that now she was ready to be a mother. Either way, being with child again had mysteriously healed much of her grief and guilt about what had happened before. Perhaps she was too full of happiness to have room for guilt.

At the top of the gangway Juliet closed her eyes for a moment and inhaled. "Mmm, smell that wonderful greenness."

"I'm glad Britannia is cooperating and sending a fine sunny day for your return home." Ross took her arm to steady her down the gangway.

"I wouldn't have minded rain," she said cheerfully "Without it, there wouldn't be so many lovely trees and flowers."

They were halfway down to the dock when Ross sud denly exclaimed, "Look! Sara and Mikahl have come to meet us."

Juliet grabbed his arm in sudden panic. "I'm not ready to meet Sara again! She'll push me off the dock for the fishes to eat because of what I put you through."

Ross was not usually demonstrative in public, but now he turned his wife toward him and gave her a firm kiss. "No, she won't. Sara must have received my letter weeks ago, so she's had time to get used to the idea." He smiled down at Juliet teasingly. "I told her that I had traded three camels for you, which was too large an investment to abandon." He gave her stomach a quick, unobtrusive pat. "And you are definitely getting to be quite a large investment."

"Wretch!" Juliet said feelingly, but Ross's nonsense helped her regain a grip on herself. Following his glance she saw Sara, who was waving to get her cousin's atten tion. Her old friend was lovelier than ever, with a glow that spoke of deep happiness. She was being escorted through the crowd by a tall, dark gentleman whose formi dable presence was sufficient to keep anyone from jos tling his wife.

When Ross and Juliet reached the bottom of the gang way and stepped onto the dock, Sara abandoned her hus band and darted forward to hurl herself into her cousin's arms. Juliet hung back. She was reasonably sure that Ross's parents would be willing to let bygones be by gones, since their daughter-in-law was doing such an effi cient job of producing an heir, but gentle Sara, who could easily forgive transgressions against herself, could be a tigress in defense of those she loved.

Before Juliet could succumb to nerves, Sara's husband turned and bowed to her. "It appears that our graceless spouses are too busy to provide introductions. I am Mi kahl, and you, of course, are the woman for whom Ross paid three camels." His lazy gaze surveyed her approvingly. "He got a bargain."

She laughed and offered him her hand. "It's a great

pleasure to meet you, Mikahl. Ross has told me so much about you."

He rolled his eyes, which were the greenest she had ever seen. "I demand equal time to state my defense."

Juliet was still chuckling when Lady Sara released her cousin and turned to her. For a very long moment the two women regarded each other, Sara thoughtful and Juliet tense. Then a slow, impish smile crossed Sara's face. "Someday, in a year or two, I'm going to give you a tongue-lashing that will make your curly hair go straight. But it will have to wait, because just now I'm too glad to see you."

Then they were in each other's arms, half-laughing and half-crying. Juliet should have known Sara would accept anything that made Ross happy. As she hugged her friend, any doubts Juliet had had about living in England dissolved like smoke in a high wind.

When she and Sara were done with their embrace, Juliet glanced over at Ross, who was just disentangling himself from Mikahl's exuberant greeting. As the two couples began making their way through the crowd to Mikahl's carriage, Ross took Juliet's arm and said in a low voice, "The prince and princess came home, and now, as in all good fairy tales, they will live happily ever after."

"Lucky prince," she murmured, her eyes warm with love and tenderness, "and lucky, lucky princess."

Save up to **$400** on ***TWA***® flights with
The Great Summer Getaway
⊘ from Signet and Onyx! ⊜
Look for these titles this summer!

JUNE

EVERLASTING
Nancy Thayer

EARLY GRAVES
Thomas H. Cook

THE GREAT SUMMER GETAWAY

AUGUST

AGAINST THE WIND
J.F. Freedman

CEREMONY OF INNOCENCE
Daranna Gidel

JULY

INTENSIVE CARE
Francis Roe

SILK AND SECRETS
Mary Jo Putney

SEPTEMBER

LA TOYA
La Toya Jackson

DOUBLE DOWN
Tom Kakonis

Save the coupons in the back of these books and redeem them
for TWA discount certificates
(Up to a maximum of four certicates per household).

- **Send in two 2 coupons** and receive: 1discount certificate
  for **$50, $75, or $100** savings on TWA flights
  (amount of savings based on airfare used)
  - • **4 coupons: 2 certificates**
  - • **6 coupons: 3 certificates**
  - • **8 coupons: 4 certificates**

OFFICIAL GREAT SUMMER GETAWAY COUPON

Send in coupons, proof of purchase (register receipt & xerox of UPC
code from books) plus $2.50 postage and handling for each certifi-
cate requested to: **TWA/Penguin USA offer, Box 4000, Dept P
Plymouth Meeting, PA 19462**

NAME_____

ADDRESS_____APT. #_____

CITY_____STATE____ZIP_____

See back of coupon for more details.

Employees and family members of Penguin USA are not eligible to participate in THE GREAT SUMMER GETAWAY. Offer subject to change or withdrawal without notice. Limit 4 per household. Certificate requests must be postmarked no later than
December 31, 1992.   SS

ONE COUPON

ONE COUPON

TWA®/SIGNET/ONYX BOOKS
"GREAT SUMMER GETAWAY"

TERMS AND CONDITIONS

This certificate is valid for $50 to $100 off the price of a qualifying TWA® published fare to any TWA destination excluding Las Vegas, Cairo and Tel Aviv. Travel is valid one-way or roundtrip provided the minimum fare is met. Ticket issued in conjunction with this certificate is valid for travel through October 31, 1993. See the chart below for amount of discount.

Purchase a one-way or roundtrip ticket for at least:	Receive the following discount:
$200	$50
$300	$75
$500	$100

Discount cannot be applied to V or T class fares anytime. Discount applies to fares BEFORE application of any departure taxes, customs and security charges, other governmental fees or surcharges not part of the published fare. Travel is valid one-way or roundtrip provided applicable rules and fare minimums are met before discount. Applicable discount will be applied only once to the total fare of the ticket. Only one certificate may be used per ticket issued.

Additional blackouts:

Domestic:	1992:	Nov 24-25	Nov 28-Dec 1	Dec 18-31
	1993:	Jan 1-5	Apr 2-4/8-9/16-19	
Additional:	Florida/Caribbean	Southbound:	Feb 11-13	
		Northbound:	Feb 20-22	
	Super Bowl	To Los Angeles/Ontario/Santa Ana:	Jan 28-31	
		From Los Angeles/Ontario/Santa Ana:	Jan 31-Feb 2	
	Mardi Gras	To New Orleans:	Feb 18-19	Mar 26-27
		From New Orleans:	Feb 24-28	
	Kentucky Derby	To Louisville: Apr 28-May 1	From Louisville: May 2-4	
	Indy 500	To Indianapolis: May 26-28	From Indianapolis: May 31-Jun 1	
International:	1992:	Jul 1-Aug 31		Dec 18-31
	1993:	Jan 1-5	Apr 2-4/8-9/16-19	Jul 1-Aug 31

1. When making reservations advise the TWA agent that you're holding a TWA/Signet $50-$100 discount certificate and provide the source code located on the front of this certificate.
2. Open jaw itineraries and/or additional stopovers may be taken only when permitted by the fare type purchased.
3. This certificate is valid for tickets issued on TWA stock for travel on TWA and/or Trans World Express flights 7000-7999. Travel is not permitted on TWA-designated flights operated by another carrier. Any travel on another airline must be ticketed and paid for separately.
4. Consumer is responsible for transportation to nearest airport served by TWA and/or TWE.
5. Tickets may be issued by TWA or your travel agent. All certificate travel must originate and be paid for in the U.S. Certificates must be presented when ticket is purchased and will not be honored retroactively.
6. Once redeemed for tickets, certificates may not be reissued. Certificates will not be replaced if lost or stolen. No copies or facsimiles will be accepted.
7. Certificate cannot be redeemed for cash or applied against a credit card balance. Certificates are void if sold, bartered or purchased in bulk.
8. Ticket refunds/itinerary changes are permitted only in accordance with the fare type paid. Ticket refunds will be issued only for the dollar amount actually paid TWA for the ticket, less any applicable penalties. When the ticket is wholly or partially refunded, the certificate will not be replaced, and further discounts or upgrades will not apply.
9. Issued against this certificate may not be combined with any other coupon, Certificate, Frequent Flight Bonus award ticket or other promotional offer or upgrade program. This certificate is not valid with travel industry employee discounts, or with special travel programs, such as the TWA Travel Club℠, Senior Travel Pak℠, or Business Flyer Award℠ Program.
10. Use of this certificate for international travel is subject at all times to the applicable laws and regulations of foreign governments and is invalid where prohibited by local law.

Agency Commission: Travel agents receive standard commission on funds actually collected.
The check or money order is to be made out to TWA/Signet Offer for $2.50 postage and handling fee for each certificate ordered (maximum four per household).

Certificate requests must be postmarked no later than December 31, 1992.

Mail to: TWA/Signet Offer
Box 4000, Dept. P
Plymouth Meeting, PA 19462